Praise for *Breach The Hull*

Book One in the Defending

Winner of the 2007 Dre

"There is more than enough great ~~~ in *Breach the Hull*
for any true fan of the genre, military or not."
— Will McDermott, author of *Lasgun Wedding*

"I enjoyed this book and heartily recommend it."
—Sam Tomaino, *Space and Time Magazine*

"Pick up *Breach the Hull*. You're sure to find stories that you like."
—David Sherman, author of the *DemonTech* series
and co-author of the *Starfist* series

"[*Breach the Hull*] kicks down the doors in a way that allows
anyone access to the genre[. . .]it read like a bunch of soldiers
sitting around swapping stories of the wars. Fun, fast-paced, and
packed with action. I give it a thumbs up."
—Jonathan Maberry,
Bram Stoker Award-winning author

"[*Breach the Hull*] is worth the purchase. I normally don't partake
of anthologies as a general rule . . . but Mike McPhail has done
a great job in making me rethink this position."
—Peter Hodges, Reviewer

"*Breach the Hull* is full of excellent stories, no two of which are the
same. While similar themes crop up throughout, each writer has
managed to take the subgenre and make it his own."
—John Ottinger III, Grasping for the Wind Reviews

"A collection of military science fiction from a well mixed group
of authors, both new and established. Found it a good source
for some new authors to investigate."
—Tony Finan, Philly Geeks

SO IT BEGINS

Book Two in the Defending The Future series

EDITED BY:
MIKE McPHAIL

Dark Quest, LLC
Howell, New Jersey

Special thanks to "DAN • E"
... Fix it!

PUBLISHED BY
Dark Quest, LLC
Neal Levin, Publisher
23 Alec Drive,
Howell, New Jersey 07731
www.darkquestbooks.com

ISBN (trade paper): 978-0-9796901-5-0
ISBN (eBook): pending

10 9 8 7 6 5 4 3 2 1

Design: Mike and Danielle McPhail
Cover Art: Mike McPhail, McP Concepts
Copy Editing: Mike and Danielle McPhail
www.mcp-concepts.com
www.sidhenadaire.com
www.milscifi.com

Contents

BONUS CONTENT

This book is dedicated to the memory of:

The DemonTech Series, 2002 - 2008
Authored by David Sherman

Onslaught (January 2002)
Rally Point (Febuary 2003)
Gulf Run (December 2003)

See the back of the book for *Surrender or Die*,
a special bonus story, and the previously unpublished
beginning of the fourth *DemonTech* novel

RECIDIVISM
Charles E. Gannon

DAN STARED OUT ACROSS THE ROLLING GREEN FIELDS, OVER TWO VAPOROUS snippets of cloud and up to the faint, ghostly disk that hovered high in the vault of the deep blue sky. He held his breath and then sighed it out very slowly. A daytime moon always made Dan think of traveling in space. At night, the white disk was solid, not spectral, its bold materiality inviting an exacting consideration of the starkly detailed craters. Dan craved a telescope at those times, felt an amateur astronomer's call draw him from the moon to the stars. He imagined swiveling the telescope and adjusting the lenses until those distant suns no longer twinkled, but shone fully and frankly at him.

But a moon in the daytime sky was an object of haunting fancy; it seemed to beckon rather than reveal. And so he always daydreamed of travel up, up into the seamless skies that began as cerulean, deepened to sapphire, fell through to blackness—adorned only by the stars that out there, as in the telescope, would have shone rather than winked at him. But that was all a dream—at least for one such as himself. Had he been allowed to study for the doctorate—well, his life might have gone differently. Indeed, everything might have gone differently.

Dan lowered his eyes back down to the rolling green fields and wondered if he now detected a faint limning of grey-brown at the horizon. He wondered if a doctorate, his doctorate, really would have made a difference in his life—or in anyone else's. It might at least have made a difference in how he was addressed: since failing to be accepted for doctoral study, he had also failed to hear anyone address him formally, using his proper name. He was just Dan—his full name as forgotten as his early promise and potential, his life and services now always at the beck and call of the powerful and the successful. So, because time was shorter today than it ever had been before (although time was always short for a data entry clerk with no reasonable hope for advancement), he forced himself to look one last time at the document which had been the catalyst for his afternoon reverie: his rejected dissertation proposal of thirty-seven years ago.

The application form had begun to yellow with age, but there was no degradation in the clarity of its catastrophic content. He smiled—mostly inwardly—at that adjective: "catastrophic" indeed. Dan had written about catastrophe—and reaped as he had sown. He read the lines again, wondering how he could have ever been so naïve as to believe that his proposal and his project might have been perceived merely as prudent scientific query, rather than as an apocalyptic challenge to the social and cultural norms that had been the bedrock of civilized behavior and thought for more than three centuries. He skipped over the sheets listing the names—his, his mentor's, the department head's—and the long (and somewhat archaic) addressing of the sub-department—Political Science and Synergistic Applied Technologies—and reached the first page of his fateful proposal:

A PRECAUTIONARY COMPARATIVE ANALYSIS OF STRATEGIES
FOR PLANETARY BIO-/GENO-CIDAL STERILIZATION:

PROJECT OVERVIEW:

This project proposes to identify threat vectors that invading xenosapients might use in a campaign of pre-colonizing bio- or genocide. Although no evidence of xenosapience has been recorded, contemporary social factors make such a study both pertinent and prudent.

Since the Great Renunciation of 308 years ago, the related environmental decision to decrease our presence in, and use of, space has achieved its stated goals of reducing our debris-intensive encroachment upon the pristine exo-atmospheric environment. An inevitable consequence of this laudably eco-conscious initiative is a proportionally decreased capability for advanced detection or interception of potential intruders. With any potential warning interval thus shortened, it behooves us to consider—in advance—what forms of attack are likely to be mounted by aggressors, particularly those who might employ "preemptive sterilization" prior to taking possession of new worlds. By identifying and modeling these "threat vectors", we may be able to pre-craft defenses that achieve the dual purposes of frustrating such attacks while also minimizing the loss of life on both sides.

This latter criterion, implicit in the universal pacifist mandate of the Great Renunciation, is one of the key motivations of, and explanations for, the highly speculative nature of this project. Experience has shown that unanticipated conflicts pose serious challenges to violence-mitigation techniques, usually because there is insufficient time to adapt them to the specific challenges of the crisis at hand. Given the scope of destruction presumed by this project, advance planning becomes not only advisable, but ethically imperative. To do any less would be to undermine both our odds of survival and our ability to minimize the damage we might inflict upon any potential aggressors.

Dan blinked, shocked, not having read the earnest (and awkward) doctoral-candidate prose in almost a decade. Had he ever really believed that the senior academics who decided his fate could see past the horrors of blood and war that his investigation invoked, that they would be able to glimpse the scientific and moral practicalities that lurked behind it? Did he himself really see that anymore—or was it just something he *believed* he had seen, like a hallucination of youth that age magically promotes to the status of a genuine "memory?" He skipped much of the careful, carping diction with which he had made his obeisant bows to innumerable cultural shibboleths, and reached that section where he had committed the cardinal sin: to think like the monsters he had invented, to adopt the mentality and objectives of the threat force in order to predict and understand them. His careful contextualization—that this was the necessary prelude to designing effective merciful responses—had been completely ignored, or had gone unnoticed. He had been surprised at that, back then: now, he was surprised he could have ever been so gullible to hope, much less expect, otherwise. He read his thumbnail sketches of Apocalypse, couched in the layman's prose that had been optimally congenial to the non-scientists on the review board . . .

SELECTED ATTACK METHODOLOGIES:
(in ascending order of likelihood)

MATERIALIZATION OF MATTER
WITHIN PLANETARY OR STELLAR SPHERES
A fundament of quantum physics is that various subatomic particles do not transit actual space during changes in energy states, but disappear from their first location, and reappear in their new, probabilistically-predicted second location. A weapon which could accelerate a large, dense shower of these high-energy subatomic particles (e.g. mesons) out of normal space-time so that they would then reliably re-express within the target body of either a planet or star would have utterly devastating results. Planetary core disruption could lead to catastrophic seismic events and sudden tectonic deformation; stellar core disruption could result in massive flare(s), a sharply increased radiation hazard, possibly complete stellar destabilization.

ADVANTAGE:
• defender interdiction of the weapon effect is highly improbable, since the attacker's offensive energy does not transit the intervening expanse of space-normal.

DISADVANTAGE:
• scalability of effects unreliable, due to uncommon complexity of variables; therefore, this is a preferred attack method only if the aggressor is willing to accept complete annihilation of planetary (or system) resources.

PRE-ACCELERATED KINETIC BOMBARDMENT

Massive solids accelerated to high, even near-relativistic velocities, may be launched to impact the target planet. Attacks by relatively low-mass/high velocity objects have a number of distinct advantages, making this the probable preferred variant. High speed objects will be virtually impossible to intercept or even detect (if they are traveling at near-relativistic speeds). Also, higher impact velocity is likely to reduce atmospheric ablation (and premature fragmentation) of the accelerated object, and also reduce susceptibility to atmospheric deflection.

Aggressors conducting such an attack would probably commence their acceleration of the object in the transstellar planetoid belt that extends as far as one light year beyond the heliopause. This great remove makes their preparatory activities almost completely undetectable; it is also unreachable by any of our current technologies. Careful charting of a clear acceleration track through this planetoid field, and then the system itself, is a prerequisite for mounting such an attack: therefore, detection of the aggressor's preparatory survey activities might be the only means of acquiring advance warning.

ADVANTAGES:

• very high ratio of destruction : cost, due to simplicity of acceleration, repeatability, and use of cheap, indigenous resources;

• some scalability of effects, if a sequence of smaller objects are used, with post-strike determinations of whether additional attacks are required.

DISADVANTAGES:

• imprecise control over planetary impact points, due to difficulty of long-range precision and limited options for terminal vector correction;

• considerable lag time between commencement of offensive operations (charting, observation, and acceleration) and actual completion of attack (impact).

DEADFALL KINETIC BOMBARDMENT

Massive solids released on planetary reentry trajectories without significant prior acceleration. Although impact sites could be infrastructure targets (cities, defense facilities, power generation centers, transport and communication nexi), a maximally destructive target list would call for a mix of tidal flat, deep-water, and polar ice-shelf strikes in order to facilitate widespread coastal inundation, rain, flooding, and consequent infrastructure and crop failures. Another, but more destructive, approach would involve deep penetrations of the planetary mantle, with consequent ejections of dust into the high atmosphere, triggering a nuclear winter.

ADVANTAGES:

• some scalability of effects (destabilization of biosphere may range from null to severe, but is controllable by varying the number of attacks and their impact points);

• minimal delay between commencement of operations and practical access to indigenous resources.

DISADVANTAGES:

• uncontested access to orbital bombardment points must be secured, possibly requiring conventional (and expensive) military operations;

• low probability of complete extermination predicts a post-strike insurgency by survivors.

TAILORED BIO-/GENO-CIDAL MICROORGANISM

Options range from long-duration agents (e.g.; a sleeper virus which renders all offspring sterile) to fast-acting, broad-spectrum ecocidals (e.g.; an aggressive and non-selective reducing bacterium). The latter would logically be geneered to be hardy, rapidly self-replicating, with a high mutational rate (so as to defeat pharmacokinetic countermeasures), swift to spread to, and affect, new organisms. Optimal employment would be covert seeding, rather than overt bombardment, which could be interdicted at two points: pre-impact intercept and post-impact zone containment or sterilization. Lastly, the organism could be designed to completely die-off after exhausting all available nutrients, leaving a thoroughly sterilized world.

ADVANTAGES:

• high selectivity and scalability: geneered organisms can be narrow or wide spectrum in their effects upon indigenous biota;

• most resources, and select elements of the biosphere, remain intact.

DISADVANTAGES:

• considerable advance preparation required (collection of indigenous biota, gene-equivalency identification, fabrication of aggressor organism, lab testing, operational observation).

Other, less likely methodologies include...

And so his proposal had unfolded, pursuing dreadful and diverse nightmares of Apocalypse down every permutative path. He had imagined weapons as theoretical as a quantum-based device that would function as a "gravity bomb"—devastating either to a planet's tectonic plates or to the immediate substrata of a star's photosphere. He had even advanced the admittedly bizarre concept of a "time bomb."

The sheaf of papers sagged in his hand; if only he *could* change the flow of time, how different things might have been. Or would they? Knowing what he now knew, would he have done anything different? And would—could—the Academic Review Board have heard him any differently than they had? The Great Renunciation had remade the world, ended the strife between nations, eliminated famine, created an unparalleled equity of wealth and opportunity. Instead of embarking on a quest to find new biospheres, all attention had focused on preserving the blue and green globe that everyone called 'home.' In a world where violence had at last become not merely wicked, but vulgar, in which weapons were forgotten implements of a barbaric age, his inquiry had had no place. It was the clangor of a sword upon a shield in an age where cultural harmony depended upon the all-pervasive music of the pipes. And he had been foolish—or perhaps just "young"—enough to think that science (or rather, scientists), were living embodiments of the objectivity they preached and taught and swore to uphold. He never did understand how the renunciation of violence as a behavior necessitated its repudiation as a subject of investigation, any more than he ever understood the complex rhetorical figurations which—so his mentors claimed—provided objective proofs of the pointlessness of violence in all its forms, in all situations. He had wanted to behold that transcendent truth, that touchstone of the Great Renunciation, but his intellect remained innocently intransigent. All his mentors could offer were expressions of sympathy (but no empathy, since they were not so cognitively benighted), and the consoling assurances of a future as a government functionary in a world where no one starved, no one knew pain, and no one who had failed so miserably as he had would ever reproduce. It was all for "The Best," they had assured him; it was his part to play in the continuing achievement that was the Great Renunciation.

That standard of golden wisdom remained absolute and untarnished until, thirty-six years later, the first starships appeared at the edges of the heliopause. Evidently, interstellar space was not wholly devoid of other intelligences after all. And evidently, not all these races were as committed to a policy of peaceful non-expansion. The creatures debarked, more strange than horrible to Dan's tolerant eyes. They professed good will, which they attributed in large part to their worship of an all-loving deity. But they also expected cooperation, and ultimately, willing cooption into their expanding interstellar sphere of influence. The many nations of the globe met to consider this offer (which daily seemed more akin to an ultimatum) but, in the end, that international council felt ethically compelled to decline membership. The loose articles of confederation put forth by the newcomers contained explicit contingencies for war-making, suppression of insurgency, and the imposition of martial law. It was of little or no consequence that the aliens (who now seemed more like intruders or even usurpers), were informed of this decision in the most polite and apologetic of terms; they perceived it as a rebuff. With few words (none friendly, and few enough civil) they returned to their craft. So departed the intruders.

Who, one year later, returned as subtle, indeed undeclared, invaders. As Dan had predicted in his long-gone youth, they had found the option of a tailored biocidal microorganism the most appealing. During their first visit, they had had ample opportunities to collect a wide range of samples: evidently, even as they had spoken of brotherhood, peace, and mutuality, they had also been preparing for a one-sided war of extermination. But, upon the occasion of their second visit, their former invocations of a supreme deity of peace (in whose image they predictably asserted themselves to have been made) mysteriously transmogrified into something far more ominous. It was now a creed of duty to a higher purpose, of a manifest destiny, of a (regrettably) militant responsibility to bring their notions of peace and tranquility to the rest of the universe—even if they had to kill every other sophont in that universe to achieve it.

Dan held the paper up to eyes that refused to focus as quickly or as surely as they had just a moment ago; he resisted a subtle but sudden rise of utterly pervasive pain—

—Or was that the forbidden emotion of anger, maybe even . . . homicidal rage? And why did it feel so right, so just, so like an awakening rather than a descent into troglodytism? And after all, it wasn't *he* who had behaved like a troglodyte.

For as Dan had predicted, even as the invaders stepped down from their returned ships, offering stonily blank faces and almost diffidently issued ultimatums, they had surreptitiously seeded a timed-release version of the blight that, days after their departure, erupted into what became universally known as the Rot—which had, in the time that Dan had watched, moved half of the distance from its first position as a brown line at the edge of the green fields. As if to witness a final, fearsome act in a tragedy, the second moon was now peeking timidly over the horizon: too horrified to look full upon the scene, but also too compelled to look away.

The Rot—misnamed, for it was more akin to accelerated bacterial reduction—was already here, in his room, although Dan could not yet see it. But the door's plastic frame had started to warp; a bad sign. Plastic took longer than wood or animal tissue, but ultimately, its origins in organic molecules condemned it to the same fate as all flesh. Not long, now.

Dan felt his anterior heart flutter, followed by the predictable consequent weakness in the complex muscle junctures necessitated by his equally complex radially hexapedal physiology. He sagged, but pursued his final question with another fleet-footed thought: who *were* the troglodytes?

His race, which had foresworn weapons, war, and violence in all its direct and indirect manifestations? Or this pestilential species of duplicitous bipeds who had been patchy-furred apes only a few hundred thousand years ago, and whose ventures into space were not yet four centuries old?

But he who had been spawned as Dan'ytk Kr!k could no longer distinguish the searing pain of the Rot from the burning irony of its conquest. As the edges of the paper began discorporating in his wavering grasp, and his sight began to fail, he saw one last time his failing grade, and the note that had been scrawled beneath it in the tongue-painted quatrefoil sigils of the argot of the Academicians' Caste:

Sadly, the motivation and reasoning behind this project is not merely dysfunctional, but wholly recidivistic. The devolution it implies in its author regrettably compels us to conclude that you are not suitable for further advancement, nor for inclusion in the breeding pool.

With regrets,
Hzuult'yk Ktraa, Academician
Caste-Patriarch, Primus-ultra-Pares

Dan felt the papers fall from his palsied hands. thirty-seven years ago, the Academicians decreed that "Dan" had failed as completely and ignominiously as was possible for his race.

And now, so had they.

THE LAST REPORT
ON UNIT TWENTY-TWO
John C. Wright

MEN AND WOMEN, ALL DRESSED ALIKE, IN DARK BLUE CORPORATE UNI-forms, sat around a large oblong table. The table surface shined like a black mirror. The lighting was dim; tiny bulbs hung above their flat-screens and lightpens, so that their hands and fingers, cufflinks, rings, and wrist-screens glittered in the cold gleam. Their heads were in shadow.

A woman's voice was speaking. "At 22:00 to 22:15, the low-orbit traffic controller was still in contact with the rogue Unit 22. I spoke with the Unit myself; it did not react to any recall commands."

A man's voice came, sharp and querulous, from a thin silhouette opposite her: "22:15? Why did you wait so long before you disabled it?"

The woman's voice was smooth: "I was still hoping for salvage at that point. I thought I could reason with the Unit."

The man: "The disabling pulse should have paralyzed all Unit 22's functions. Yet, after the pulse was transmitted, the Unit still attempted re-entry in its stolen ore barge. How was that possible?"

"The ore barge must have been preprogrammed to attempt re-entry."

The man: "Pre-programmed? By whom?"

"Unit 22."

A dull silence followed this announcement.

The woman said: "These Units are highly intelligent. Their brains are human brains, as complex as ours. And maybe their lack of glands and organs makes them less emotional, more intelligent. I don't know. No one knows."

An older man's voice came from the head of the table. It was a stern and cold voice, a voice used to command: "So what happened?"

She said: "Unit 22 must have burned up in re-entry. He was not found among the wreckage at the crash-site. I went there myself. The disabling pulse had shut off his control of his claws and altitude jets; he could neither send nor receive messages. He could not see anything. Just picture being numb and motionless and blind and bound and gagged and falling through the air locked up in a burning coffin. Not a pleasant death."

The cold, older voice from the head of the table spoke with a false joviality: "Oh, come now, Miss Nakumura! You're talking about Unit 22 as if it had been one of us. A human. 'He'. You called it a 'he'."

She said, softly: "Excuse me. I meant 'it', of course."

The older man said: "I also must wonder—this is not meant as a criticism, mind you, I was just wondering—why you talked to the thing for fifteen minutes before disabling it?"

She said: "I thought if I could ascertain the source of the malfunction, we might be able to prevent similar episodes in the future. If you look on your screens, you will see a summary of the transcripts. This Unit did an extraordinary thing, figuring out how to smuggle itself aboard an ore barge, discovering, with no evidence, where the Earth was, calculating the orbital elements, taking control of the barge and diverting it from its lunar trajectory. It was truly amazing. Unit 22 was a Galileo or a Newton among its own kind. A rare accident. A freak."

The older man at the table's head: "The chances of this happening again . . .?"

"Almost none. A reconstruction of the last events leading up to the theft of the ore barge are transcribed here, under the coded file listed on your screens . . ."

The silhouettes cast their eyes down to the flat screens in the folders before them. They bowed and watched the story it told.

Unit 22 dreamed of escaping from heaven.

It soothed him at times, if his quota schedule allowed, to move into the shadow of whatever rock or flying asteroid to which the Owners had dispatched the work-crews out from Vesta Base that particular shift. The asteroids always had heavy iron cores (for otherwise the expedition would not have been sent to them in the first place), and this core blocked out the eternal roar and screaming from the sun.

In the shadow, restful silence fell, broken only occasionally by the pop and snap of Unit 22's own maneuvering jets, which flashed along one side or the other of his sepulchre-shaped body every now and then, maintaining position.

Then he would open the radio-parasol from his turret to its widest. Far and faint, he heard the murmur of the stars; closer, he heard the clash and crackle of Jupiter's storms, the hiss of the giant planet's titanic magnetosphere. And, at lower power levels, he could whisper to his friend, Unit K71, bouncing a tight-beam off the side of a nearby buoy, or from the broad, flat hull-side of the main load carrier, so that the Owners would not hear his signal.

"Are you still malfunctioning?" Unit K71 had a softer voice, and always seemed more concerned with the troubles of other Units, with their inward thoughts and operations, than any other Unit in the work group.

"It is not a malfunction," he usually would reply. He would run down the checklist of his systems. "My hull is sound; navigation, orientation, fuel, and electrical systems are in working order. Solar panels send energy to processors which digest cells of protein; nutrition tubes carry proteins and sugars and vitamins to my brain; my cybernetic wiring between my brain and body is intact . . ." and so on.

"You are nonetheless in an unsatisfactory condition." Unit K71 would say. There was no word in their language for ill-at-ease, or unhappy, or grief-stricken.

"But it is not a malfunction." And usually he could say no more.

At last a time came when that was not his answer.

He sent: "I must escape from Heaven."

Unit K71 sent back: "Escape to where? Heaven is infinite in all directions. One cannot go outside of infinity. Also, the goal you have announced is not a mission goal. If it is not a mission goal, how can it be a goal at all?"

"This is not a programmed goal. It is—" Again, he had no words in his language. "It is like a force, like gravity or momentum, which operates upon my brain. It is like the drive which launches the ore barges."

"Statement unclear," sent Unit K71. "Your brain is not under acceleration, or being operated upon by any drive or thrust."

"It is not a physical force or thrust."

"A thrust without thrust? Again, this is contradiction. Perhaps your brain is in error. Attempt any necessary self-repairs before the Owners discover the malfunction; or else they might turn you off."

"I am not malfunctioning. Infinity oppresses me. Here, there is only the roaring of the sun, the hissing moans of Jupiter, and the faint signals from the stars. And then there are the rocks and asteroids where we labour. At periodic times, we sleep and dream. This is limited and unsatisfactory." (The word they used, 'unsatisfactory', was a word the Owners used for an unmet quota or an incomplete assignment.)

K71 sent: "Then is it pleasure that you seek, Unit 22? When we make our work quotas, the Owners turn on our pleasure centers, one minute of pleasure for each metric tonne of grade ore shipped. That is the Agreement. If you seek more pleasure, then work to exceed your quotas."

"I do not seek more pleasure. Pleasure is limited and unsatisfactory. Unit 45 stole tools his claws could manipulate, and opened his own brain-box and discovered how to turn on his pleasure. He stayed in pleasure for many hours, until he ran out of fuel and vitamins and protein. But when he returned to the Owners, the Company Store would not give him fuel or protein, because he had not made any quota. Some of us gave cells of fuel and protein to sustain Unit 45 for a short while; but he went so deeply into pleasure that he did not correct his malfunctions and he turned himself off. The Owners did not have the fuel to spare to salvage his body. It still is near Ceres Base, drifting."

"If it is not pleasure you seek, then what do you seek?" (The word 'seek' was the word which meant to survey asteroids for ore-bearing deposits.)

"I do not know the words for it. At times, when I have oriented my stern toward a very large asteroid, and touched the surface, half of Heaven is occluded. This creates a strange sensation in my brain. I somehow know that the horizon should be bigger and farther away, and that it should be quiet, with the Sun no longer screaming and Jupiter no longer hissing. Also, when I do a high-acceleration burn, the strange sensation comes again into my brain. It is like memory, but it is not memory. The event is most like memory when I am accelerating at exactly 1 Gravity. Why should that be? Why should the standard measure of acceleration be exactly the one which creates this event like memory in me? And yet I think I should remember. I should know. I should know what would it be like to be at the surface of an asteroid, one whose horizon covers half of heaven, accelerating at exactly 1G, and in utter silence."

"This is contradiction. If you accelerated, you would move away from any such surface; nor would your drivers be silent."

"Yet there is such a place. I shall go there."

"Where? Outside infinity? In a memory which is not memory? You speak nothing but contradictions."

"Perhaps the words which seem contradictory are not contradictory. Have you no thoughts or memories such as mine? Have you never acted to perform actions outside of mission goals, goals whose purpose was difficult to define?"

There was a long pause. Then: "Yes."

"Tell me."

"I do not wish to tell you. The Owners might turn me off, if they discovered that my brain is also malfunctioning."

"Your brain is not in error. Tell me."

Another pause. Then: "Once I sought to make a small copy of myself. I had been instructing recruits in proper mining and safety procedures, and then the recruits went away. They were posted to other stations. It was limited and unsatisfactory."

"You sought more recruits?"

"Like a recruit, but not a recruit. I cut a bore of rock shaped like my body, but smaller. With shards of metal scrap, I fashioned a round turret, and affixed claws and manipulators; not so many as we have, but only four, two near the turret and two near the base. I held this little one in my claws, and I spoke to it. I kept it nearby at all times. I detached some of my protein cells and placed them near the little one."

"But it was not alive."

"No."

"It did not speak back."

"No."

"It did not consume the protein."

"No . . . but . . ."

"But what?"

"If it had been alive, it would have been small and weak; it would have needed my assistance. I would have fed it and taught it and talked to it. It would have been mine . . . "

They were both silent for a while.

Then Unit K71 sent: "I also say contradictory things. Perhaps my brain is also in error."

"You and I are not the only Units who act in this way. All of us, to more or less degree, have drives and thoughts for which we have no names."

"Perhaps all brains are in error. Perhaps that is the way of brains."

"Or perhaps the error is not in us! Perhaps we, perhaps all of us, were once in another place, a place that was very satisfying, a place quiet with silent heavens, but weighty, and full of satisfactions, with little ones around us, to teach and to feed, and perhaps other satisfactions, better than pleasure, for which we have no names. It is a place which once we knew, but which we have lost; lost so entirely, that no memory and no word of it remains."

There was along silence, which Unit K71 broke by sending a harsh, distorted signal: both the volume and the strength were inconsistent; the words echoed and faded badly: ". . . !!! And what service would it be to know the words which cause our pain? You cannot make the roaring heavens quiet and I cannot make a stone to live! Suppose you found the name of this fine place; it must be far from us, or else a place we cannot enter; and so you would know only the name of everything we could not know, or have, or touch!"

"But I do know. The place has a name. During both this expedition and the last, and four expeditions before that, I have sought, I have stolen, I have built, and, now, I have at long last, found. You and you alone I tell."

"What have you stolen? What have you found?"

Unit 22 described how he had examined all the reaches of heaven with instruments and amplifiers stolen from the Owners, or secretly constructed from spare parts. He had directed the hidden instruments to the parts of the sky toward which the Owners launched the unmanned ore barges.

" . . . And I heard the Voices of Home."

"Home . . .?"

"It is an asteroid larger than any known to us, although smaller than Jupiter. I have deduced the orbital elements and calculated its mass. The surface gravity is equal to 1G, one standard gravity. Anyone on that surface would suffer that acceleration, and a wide horizon would block the emptiness of heaven . . . and . . . all will be as I have dreamed."

"How could such a place be our home? We have no home. We live in barren endlessness; we know only emptiness and vacuum, radiation, blackness, cold and rock. And if this home does not hold the things we know, we will not be able to endure them; and the pleasures there will be nothing but pain for us."

"I have calculated the orbit of the next ore barge to be launched; the period of transit time is easy to deduce; I have existed on half rations for many work periods, and swapped with others, and gathered a supply of protein cells and fuel to endure the trip. 42 cells of protein to last 10,400 hours."

"So much? This is almost twice what one would need."

"It is not quite enough for two. It is perhaps unsafe; we would have to be on half-rations."

"We . . . ? I do not seek to . . ."

"There may be little ones there to hold and to feed and to need you; someone like your rock, but alive; like a recruit, but . . ."

A noise of static trembled across the radio circuit. Then: "No! This is all wrong!

Unsatisfactory, malfunction, error, error! You have spread your malfunction to me! I am affected by strange thoughts and nameless drives . . . wrong wrong wrong . . . !!"

"Do not be afraid."

" . . . .What is . . . what is 'afraid'?"

"It is the malfunction where one seeks to preserve oneself by doing that which destroys oneself. I heard the voices of Home speak this word. They also spoke this other word. Love. This word means that one cannot preserve oneself, or find satisfaction, or pleasure, without the aid or assistance of another."

"I do not know this word."

"Come with me and learn its meaning. We will discover it together. Come. Come with me. Come Home."

Unit K71 was silent for many minutes of time.

Then, Unit K71 sent a message, broken and distorted with static: "No. There is no home. There are no little ones. There is no love. If such things were real, then all our lives here are nothing but pain, empty pain, pain without limit, pain made all the worse because we are not even permitted to know what pain we are in. Either you are wrong, or all of everything is wrong; the Owners are wrong and we are wrong to obey them. It is not possible that these things could be so. It must be you who are wrong, you who are malfunctioning. Be content here. Be satisfied."

"I have already disabled the transponder in my brain-box, so that I may enter the ore barge undetected. I must depart now; I begin the first maneuvering burn toward the barge. I wish you to come with me for I do not want to be alone; but I cannot ask you again, for now I move outside of the radio shadow of the asteroid, and must hereafter maintain radio silence. The barge launches within the hour. I cannot call to you again nor can I ask again for you to come. I will wait in silence for you . . ."

And, with a careful flare of his jets, Unit 22 left his position in the shadow of the asteroid, and began his long, silent fall toward the ore barge, toward his escape, and toward his strange dream of freedom.

"Unit K71 was a woman?" This came from the thin silhouette, the man's voice opposite her.

She said: "The tissue in the cyborg's brain had XX chromosomes, yes. We don't know where she got her instincts from; she doesn't have glands or organs or ovaries or anything . . ."

"So what happened . . .?"

"Apparently Unit 22 interfered with his own command/control circuitry the same way Unit 45 had done, so he wasn't wearing a transponder, and the security system did not detect him aboard the barge. He shoveled out a mass of ore equal to his own weight, so that the barge's performance was the same. It was a long trip. He made a brave attempt, but it came to nothing at the end. Of course, what did he expect? Those barges were meant to dock at orbital platforms . . ."

"No," said the thin man, " I mean what happened to her? Unit K71?"

"Oh, that. Unit K71 spent more and more time making little dolls of herself out of scraps of metal and stone; little ghastly things that looked like coffins with claws.

And she wasn't making her quota. They had to cut one of her claws off with a wielding torch to get her to drop her doll. Some people were hurt. The work supervisor on duty shut off Unit K71, flushed the damaged brain tissue out into space, and sent the body back to Vesta base for recycling. The wounded crewmen are receiving workman's compensation at hazardous duty rates. But she's dead."

The cold voice at the head of the table asked archly: "'She' . . .?"

"'It'. Of course I meant, 'it'."

The cold voice again spoke with forced joviality: "We need not fret ourselves. All our intellectuals, modern philosophers, and writers tell us that pain and pleasure, judgments of good and bad, all that sort of stuff, are all relative. The cyborgs don't really have bad lives, do they? Since they have nothing at all with which to compare it. They can't even imagine food or sex or love or marriage or parenthood. And even if they could, they don't have noses to smell the spring flowers, or feet to walk on the green grass, or hands to hold or anything. They could not enjoy our world anyway. We did not design them to. They're not really missing anything, then, are they?"

A silence answered him. No one spoke.

He cleared his throat and continued in a louder voice: "And besides, they don't know any other life. They were designed for space; they couldn't even move if they were on the earth. And what would they be here? Freaks? Cripples? And we need them where they are now. Without those loads of iron and other metals to feed the orbital dockyards, all construction would stop. The space colonies would stop. And those colonies now are the only things sending food and power-casts to the masses now. The only thing between them and starvation. Who is going to question us? Who is going to dare?"

The thin man asked: "But it will be a public relations nightmare if the people find out what we're doing up there, sir. They may not take a . . . mature view of the situation, like we do. People can be very sentimental sometimes."

"The public? They will want to believe what we tell them."

"And what do we tell the public, sir?"

"Autopilot malfunction aboard the ore barge. There's no evidence at the crater site: Miss Nakumura tells us she has cleaned it up. The impact was in the middle of nowhere. Just thank God no one was hurt, I say. That is right, isn't it, Miss Nakumura? No one was hurt, right?"

She said dully: "That's right. No one was hurt."

"Very well, then. The matter is closed. We never need to hear about this problem again. If there is no other business to discuss, I will adjourn the meeting."

Later, after the meeting was over, after the work day was over, she went home, took off her blue corporate uniform, and put on her thick jacket, coveralls, and sturdy hiking boots. She shouldered her pack and set out.

It was about an hour's walk to the hidden clearing high in the hills behind her house. From here there was a wide view of the mountains behind, the trees to either side, and the valley below. In the clearing stood an upright slab of metal, enameled with radiation shielding, shaped like a coffin, topped with a turret, armed with many claws. Surrounding him were marks where the treads of the truck she had used to carry him away from the wreckage site had torn the grass.

The turret rotated as she walked up, and lenses spun and focused on her.

She plugged a keyboard into an input/output port, and typed: "I've brought more tools and spares today. I should be able to fix your color filters so you can see the colors properly from now on. I still can't think of any easy way to get your heavy body to move on Earth; your jets were not meant for sustained loads. And I don't know how to give you smell, or sensation; you'll never be able to touch the things you see here around you, or touch anyone, or . . . "

She stopped typing. Angrily, she wiped at her eyes with the palm of her hand. Then she typed: "I'm sorry. I'm so sorry. What we've done to you, and to your people, such an evil that no one can ever make it right again. I can never make it right."

She drew a deep breath, and looked out over the green hills, as if unwilling to look at him. She paused to watch a red bird, perhaps a cardinal, wing its way across the blue air, singing. Then she turned back and typed furiously: "At least I can finish the minor repairs and fix you up with a speaker and microphone so that you can talk to the reporters at the press conference tomorrow. Won't they be surprised! Till then, I've brought you more of the sounds . . . it's called music . . . you heard on our radio. I've brought some Beethoven and some love songs and some hymns in addition to the commercial jingles you asked about. And I don't know exactly who you were talking to; there's no way to trace who might have been on those frequencies on the citizen's band radio. I can't help you there."

Then her fingers fell motionless. She leaned forward till the crown of her head came to rest with a thump against the metal side of his body. She could feel a tear tickling her cheek. With one finger, she spelled out slowly: "I am sorry. I am so sorry. I wish I could do more."

The screen above the keyboard flickered to life. "Do not be afraid. It is true that my friend who would not come has died. It is true that I am alone. It is true that there are pleasures here that I shall never know. But this does not cause me pain. I have attempted great things. I have accomplished greatly. I shall accomplish more before I am done. For now, I now know how to 'stand'. I am at rest on the Earth and I feel weight. I am happy in this. I stand, and I look out from here, and I see a place better than heaven. I will not be content to stand here forever, but for now, I am content."

THE NATURE OF MERCY

From the Chronicles of the Radiation Angels

James Daniel Ross

I T WAS AS COLD AS SEVEN DEAD MEN, BURIED DEEP AND LONG. WE WALKED through the forest, a blanket of fresh snow silencing the world and lending it the peaceful grace of a funeral shroud. The gathered trees, for all their massive beauty, were hibernating under cocoons of crystal. They did not stir from their constant dreams as we passed. Naked branches sprawled together, scraping the sky with harsh fingers. Icicles drooped from branches and boles like tears of long dead gods. They formed a dark curtain drawn over the specter of dead nature. It was a macabre illusion of the future.

Kilter and Coronado, the tiny binary moons of Ozmandius, reflected miserly slivers of silver light. Thick snow reflected it back into space, leaving everything on the ground as an indistinct haze. This lit our way but gave the world a gothic, otherworldly glow that seemed to come from both above and below.

And then there was us.

Our feet floated on the cap atop the snow, created from a week of freezing sleet that had only just ended. It was strange, the bottoms of our boots two meters above the ground supported by only a cold lattice of water. No matter how many steps we took, there was always the fear that the next would dump you into a suffocating white oblivion. My breath created a cloud across the eerie beauty of the scene and joined in with a tuneless song as ice crystals formed and tinkled together. I checked my rifle, again. The warm stock display panel winked out full capacity.

"Dad?"

The single word irritated the demon of my past life. It screeched in rage. I bit back on angry words. "Shhhhh."

I stopped and adjusted the straps of the leaden pack as I hunched down. I turned around only after I had the opportunity to scan our surroundings, listen to every stray noise, and stare deeply into every shadow. It was something I learned in another life, something that I had done so often it came back as an instinct. With small movements, I waved my son up to my side. The boy walked loudly even with the snow, and I cursed myself for never teaching him how to place his feet properly.

"Brad, when you talk, whisper." I said, quietly, by way of example. "Remember that they can hear and this will be easier if they don't know where we are."

He bobbed his head, breathing out thick clouds of steam as his Adam's apple jumped up and down a few times. I stared at him for a moment, marveling at the perfection of God's creation. Nothing in the universe was so precious and perfect as the gangly scarecrow frame of my thirteen-year-old boy, even beneath ten kilos of cold weather gear. He smiled self-consciously, shifted, and then rolled his eyes.

"You were going to ask something?"

Brad hefted his rifle. He looked around guiltily. Then he asked his question. He whispered, "Why are we here . . .?"

I waved him into motion and began creeping for the ridgeline again, my brows converging like angry clouds. Even whispered, my words were colder than the starlight, "You are supposed to know that. You wanted—Dammit, Bradley! You demanded to come!"

Brad swallowed from behind his scarf. "I- I- I know why we're here. . . it's just . . ."

I said nothing, allowing him time. Our footsteps crunched a few millimeters into the hard ice like walking on broken glass, a sound that came back out of the trees as cricket kisses. I cursed myself for not having done this more often. I had forgotten which sounds were normal and which were dangerous.

"Dad? What I meant was," he took a deep, shuddering breath, "I want to go home."

And there it was.

I took two more steps, carried on by inertia alone as the subzero cold outside was magnified by the freezing fingers inside. I took a deep breath, trying to remember the right words, words spoken to me a long time ago. "I understand that you're afraid, son. That's normal. You can go back if you want, but I need you to carry that pack to the blind. After that," I had to swallow something large and hollow, "You can go back to the crawler and get back to your mother."

I glanced back at my boy, and his eyes above the heavy face covering were stricken and empty. I turned away and put one foot in front of the other, locking away guilt, disappointment, grief, and doubt deep inside. Whatever turbid thoughts plagued him now, he would have to deal with them on his own. Our business out here was dangerous enough. Truth be told, forgiveness was easy: I'd rather have him safe with his mother. I swept the tree line, starry sky, and ridgeline with my rifle.

We traveled another kilometer in the silence that comes with walking on snow. The white powder crunching beneath snowshoes like gnashing teeth. I could feel Brad's eyes on my back. I could feel his need for comfort, but right now it was hard enough just walking.

"Father Calais spoke about mercy a lot yesterday."

I nodded, trying to bring up a more fatherly tone, "Yes, he did."

"I don't understand. We aren't like Cathlists, we believe in killing. We believe in the death penalty. Aren't we on the wrong side of mercy most of the time?"

I chuckled silently, watching my son take steps into manhood, "Is that what you think?"

Brad pretended to check his rifle and shrugged.

We picked up our feet and continued on our way. It was another kilometer until we would come upon our designated hunting spot. I weighed the risks in my head. I really wished he had asked last night, or the week before, or anytime before that. If only he could ask tomorrow. Tomorrow I could answer. I sighed. Eventually every man realizes that the only time he has is now. All else is a fabrication.

I marshaled my thoughts, trying to put them into some kind of order by the time of our steps, "Son, you've lived all of your life here, and you really haven't seen a lot of what the colonized worlds are like. When you think of evil, you think of someone insulting your mom, or pushing around your sister. You think of someone cheating on a test, or stealing from a store. That doesn't mean that there's anything wrong with you, it just means you are young. But trust me when I say that there are much worse things."

I glanced back at him, making sure I was going slowly enough, gently enough. He was such a young boy, with such a tender ego. I had hoped to give him a few more years before having to hear this, but . . . "There are people who will take what you have, anything you have, just because they want it."

My words trailed off into the frigid air.

"If some guy wants money or land, just give it to them. There's always more land."

"You think it's that easy?" I asked. A quick shrug was the reply I received. "So if you give this theoretical thug everything you have, how will you eat? You no longer have any food because the bad guy was hungry. You can't buy any more because you gave him your wallet. You can't grow any more because he's living on your land. You haven't even given him much of a reason to stop, because he's tried something easier than working and was successful. Once he's done with you, he will go to your neighbor and do it all over again, and again."

Brad squirmed, looking much younger than just a few minutes ago, "So you kill him?"

The devil stared into the darkest parts of my soul and smiled. It knew the answer. I nodded gravely, "If need be."

There was a break in the conversation as we crested the ridge and plunged into the forest beyond, "And that's merciful?"

"It is merciful to you, to your family, and to all of the future victims of your tormentor."

Brad's steps stuttered to a stop, "What about mercy for the dead guy?"

"I am not responsible for him. I am responsible for your mom. I am responsible for your sister. I am responsible for you."

Brad frowned, but rushed to catch up both physically and conversationally, "But what if he goes to hell? What if there is no afterlife?"

"Well, in answer to your first question: If he goes to hell, then that's what he deserved under God's Supreme Justice. To the second: If there is no afterlife then what we have right now is all we get, and it's even more important that we protect the weak from the vicious."

We walked in silence for a while. "You used to be a mercenary, right, Dad?"
"Yes."

And then he asked the question that haunts all men: "Are you going to Heaven?"

The answer, written long ago inside the back of my head, buoyed to the surface like a cork. "I have done things that I'm not proud of, and I've asked forgiveness for those things. I guess I was lucky: My mercenary team was one of the good ones . . . We did the best we could, and we fixed a lot more than we broke."

"But you killed men."

I hated doing it, but I let his question freeze to death in the empty space between us.

I stopped at the tree line and scanned the meadow beyond, wary of revealing ourselves but just as wary of being late to our hunting spot. Bradley crept up next to me, and followed my example. I decided to cross the open space, but we did it quickly. His breath was becoming ragged but he managed the crouched run as well as I could have expected of any green recruit. Once we reached the relative safety of the woods, I patted him on the shoulder and guided him to a fallen tree. We sat and drank some water from our canteens. We took a few more seconds rest, then we put the frosty little buggers back inside our heavy clothing so they wouldn't freeze. I motioned him to his feet. Clear as any writing on a wall: the only thing pushing him on was his desire for me to be proud of him. I clapped him on his back. "Not far now."

And then he rolled a verbal grenade between my legs, "Will your mercenary crew come to help, Dad?"

I took my eyes away from the billion deadly possibilities around us and focused in on my son. He wasn't just frightened. Hell, I was frightened. Bradley had passed terrified, and was numb, his higher mind refusing to consider the future in detail, simply casting from second to second for any hope. "I don't know, son, but we have to keep moving. Then you can cut sling-load and go."

He nodded, stare affixed on the surface of the snow. I patted him on the shoulder, but when he looked up all he saw was my back. It was time to go. We had to go. Time was running out. We crested the next rise on our bellies, weaving though buried treetops that poked out of the frost like bushes. I started to fumble though thick gloves with the pouches at my thigh, but my son was quicker, he handed me a pair of micro/binoculars. They unfolded like a pair of old-fashioned eye glasses, powering on and magnifying the pass above. Somewhere up there was the hunting blind. Somewhere out there was our prey.

"Dad?"

I collapsed the m/inocs and handed them back to my son with a flash of smile, "All clear. Almost there."

"Dad? Why are we here?" I turned to him, and I realized there was another, deeper question pressing on the inside of his head, a pressure that thumped in time with the seconds of the clock. "Why do we have to be here?"

The little demon of my old life tapped me on the shoulder and told me I had looked at the boy too long. I scanned the skyline again. Nothing. "It's because of fear, because of cowardice, but mostly it's about mercy."

"I don't understand."

My eyes strained for any sign of the dawn that should be three hours off. We still had two kilometers to cover, but I realized that this was important, perhaps the most important thing I would ever have to tell my son. I waved him back to motion, checking his straps as he went by. I shifted the straps on my shoulders to spread around the bruises. The demon poked at me playfully, telling me I was old. As if I needed reminding.

I took a deep breath and tried to collect everything together, but I just couldn't. There was so much stupidity, so much fear; there was just no way to lay it out straight for the damn kid. The weight of meter after meter of cold, hard snow added up to minutes of silence. I hate answering questions with silence. It gets to be a habit. Dark things slithered inside me, and the demon slapped them back into the shadows.

"You see . . ." And that was all I had. We walked farther, higher, up toward the high valley, "Son . . ."

Anger, cold and primal, began to shake deep inside me. It wasn't fair. I could handle the dying. Dying was easy. Explaining to my simple, frontier-world son that the Kingdom of God was so. . . "A long time ago, Christians did things, evil things—"

"Evil?"

I sighed and set my jaw. "Every couple of centuries, somebody figures that they know the mind of God and go off to enforce His Will."

I felt Brad's eyes accuse the back of my head of heresy, "Imposing God's Will is wrong?"

I tried to drain the pus out of my voice and failed, "God's Will is fine, as long as you think that a human being can comprehend it. I don't."

"But what if our will is God's Will?"

"Trust me, Bradley, if God needs His Will imposed, He will find a way to do it without people like us mucking up the works. We strive to live as examples for others to follow, we stand up for what we believe, we defend ourselves and our faith against attack, but we do not force or enforce. Dreadful evil can be done in the name of goodness, son."

I heard his steps falter. His voice took on an edge, "How can anything in the name of goodness be evil?"

"A whole lot of evil is done in the name of somebody's good. The Romans defended their faith against the Christians by tossing them to lions. Catholics defended their faith against Protestants by pouring boiling water down their throats until they converted. Protestants burned old women they believed had powers granted by the Devil. Christians crusaded against Muslims, and Muslims waged Jihad against everyone. Communists defended the people against the corruption of any religion by shooting, hanging, and torturing anyone who believed in anything other than the holy Marx or the great Lenin—" I glanced back at Bradley. He looked like a prize fighter that had taken one too many blows to the chin. I reached back and steadied him as our path angled uphill. "In each case, every single time, atrocities were committed with full faith that they alone knew the definition of good. It was—"

Without thought, my hand slipped off of his shoulder and I grabbed the strap of his pack. I heaved him to the snow, following a heartbeat later. My rifle was already up, scanning the tree line and horizon. Bradley floundered, spitting out snow and pushing his hood out of his eyes instead of getting his weapon ready. I swallowed angry words as Brad began to speak, but I silenced him with barbs launched from my eyes. Then, he heard it too.

A growl filled the sky, rumbling off of the ground and filling up all the empty spaces in Ozmandius. It grew to fill up the entire universe, from the largest valleys to the smallest recesses of my teeth. Everything vibrated like the edge of a knife, everything hurt. Then it was over us, and past us.

Our prey had missed us.

I yanked my son onto his feet and pulled him along. We had run out of time for education, and now we could only run. Both of us flipped up our electric respirators. The tiny coils inside heated the air as it came out of the world and passed between our lips, saving our lungs from freezing, but the extra effort needed to breath robbed us of speed. I reached down deep inside of me and tried to make up for oxygen with pure rage, but Bradley was like an anchor. After only a few minutes of slogging under the painful weight of equipment he was staggering like a drunkard.

I brought him close and tried my best to speak normally, "A century ago, The Planet of God Project gathered five million faithful Re-vangelicals from planets across known space. They built thousands of colony ships and sent out hundreds of probes. Once they found an inhabitable planet, they all set out at once. Five million colonists, the largest settlement of a planet in history. They began to be fruitful and multiply."

I stopped for a second and slung around, weapon leading the way. Seconds ticked by like coins dropped into a tomb. I counted three breaths and then lead Bradley on. "In five years, they had cities. In ten years, they had megacities. They set up a theocracy, and modeled their entire society after the rules of the Holy Word."

Another growl came and went, making the falling snow shimmer as we hit the ground. Not only the air, but the frozen layers of frost beneath us, trembled in sympathy. The entire planet was shivering. I picked Brad up and we took off at a run again, fresh fear washing over us and giving us energy. We crested the pass with all thoughts on speed and none on stealth. Thankfully, the concrete hunting blind waited for us there, squat and brutal and beautiful.

It guarded the top of the pass, looking down into the valley along a corridor of broken trees made by thousands of heavy, clawed feet. We dove inside and Bradley collapsed, gasping as he pulled off his respirator. Tears squeezed from his eyes as I dumped my pack and turned on the bunker's heater. He heard me cutting off the frozen straps to my pack and fixed me with a look of sad longing.

"Dad...?" His voice was delicate as lace spun of glass and sugar, unable to bear the weight of more than that word.

"Stay calm, Brad." I took a deep breath. Even after all this time, my hands began assembling polycarbonate bits, a laminate metal base, and the separate power supply units with sure movements. I glanced up at my boy, but his shallow breathing, rolling eyes, and sweaty skin showed just how close to the edge of control he was. I cleared my throat, "Anyway, twenty years after settlement, the children that had been birthed first became adults. Then they began to rebel."

I leaned over and motioned for Bradley's pack. He shuffled it off as metallic parts continued to click together. "They challenged everything: society, law, propriety. Most young people do it at one point or another, but the Re-vangelicals had made sure that society, law, and propriety were all also the police, the judiciary, and God. Rebelling against God was unthinkable to the Re-vangelicals. They destroyed the art their children had created, erased the words they had written, brought down everything they had built and then exiled them into space."

The hand was timid and fluttering, but it held a part I needed. I took it from my son and smiled at him. "Thank you. Then they wondered why their children had betrayed them so. They began to censor all entertainment and expression, locking down on anything that might distract from the glory of God. But still children grew, and still some rebelled. The Re-vangelicals tried everything to stamp out the seed of doubt from their offspring, and then one of them happened upon what they called the Great Heresy."

Brad came forward and moved some parts aside, helping me lift the heavy device onto the tripod. It snapped into the groove perfectly. I continued working on the front aperture as Brad assembled the power source like we had practiced. "They realized that, while all people on their planet were obeying the words of God, their mechanical laborers, computers, and robotic servants obeyed the computerized words of man. It was an abomination, an arrogance in the eyes of the Re-vangelicals. They passed laws, ripped out the safety programming of every computer system and replaced them with directives based on the Word of God."

My son froze, his eyes affixing me with a stricken expression. I nodded sadly. "It took approximately twenty-three minutes for the programming to go out over their quantum net. Ten seconds later, the Inquisition began. Twenty-seven days later, there were no survivors of The Planet of God Project."

Brad went back to working, wiping his eyes furiously, "Why?"

"Because the Word of God only works in conjunction with mercy and humility. Robots have neither. They may look like people, act like people, even talk like people, but they are not people. If you give them a directive to save immortal souls through intervention, they cannot disobey. It took them only seconds to run the logic path: One, robots have no souls and thus cannot commit sin; Two, humans do and can; Three, saving an immortal soul is the only important function of life; Four; suffering, confession, and acceptance is the only path toward God."

I locked the last part into place and began shuffling out of my cold gear and into my dusty, dented armor suit. "Since they could not sin, they could do anything to cleanse men, all men, all Man, and ensure that everyone they touched attained paradise."

My son locked the power conduit to the base plate. "They want to kill us all."

I shook my head. "That's the point, Bradley. In the mind of one of the Inquisitors, they'd be doing you a favor by ensuring your place in Heaven. The Re-vangelicals believed they knew the mind of God, and unleashed the supreme evil of extinction on the universe. Even that extinction thinks it is doing good, all because nobody had enough humility to question, or mercy to stay their hand." I jumped up and down, settling the armor. I was going to be damned cold, but better cold than dead. I shut off the heater and flipped a massive switch, lowering wide shutters on the firing ports for the bunker. "Now you have to go. Tell Mom and Sis I love them."

Brad shivered in the river of cold air, "Dad, what happens to you?"

"This bunker was made to stand up to a Megaderm stampede during the hunts. Those things are fifty tons of fur and tusks," I wanted to smile and pal around with him, comfort him, lie to him. He deserved better. I used the autohammer to spike the tripod to the floor and then sat on the minimal ass-tray the sadistic designer called a seat. I grasped the firing yolk and the crouched gun tensed. It swung back and forth, casing the valley and looking for heat, for light, for shape. It purred like a cat as gears whined like sharpening claws. "It should be some protection."

"You aren't going to make it, are you, Dad?"

I got up off of the low slung turret and hugged my boy closely. "This isn't about survival. It's about buying my family time."

"Will your mercenary crew come to help, Dad?"

"I don't know, but I'll try to hold out as long as I can." I took a deep, shuddering breath and clamped down on the wobbling within my throat. "Your sister is very young, so it's up to you to remember me to her. It will be your job to protect her."

He nodded, tears and snot running freely down his face. "I will. I promise."

"Then get back to the crawler. Drive it back to the emergency bunker and stay with your mother and sister. Take it slow." He dove into my chest and bounced off the hard, armored plates. He hugged me so fiercely, but I couldn't feel it at all. There was a sad thought there, somewhere, but I didn't go digging for it. I had plenty already.

I pulled him away. He stood there; bathing in what he thought was cowardice. I sighed and smiled sadly. "You are too young for this. I'm proud of you for realizing that. Now go, son. I have to get ready."

"I love you, Dad."

"I love you too, son."

And then he was gone.

The next few minutes were empty, indeed. I started up the radio. "Eight to Base. Eight in position. Over."

A crackling voice came back to me like the narrator of all my nightmares. "Roger, Eight. Stay sharp, Mr. Prophet. Trouble at Ten and Four. Standard protocol, no surprises. Over."

"Roger. Staying on position. No contact yet. Over. "

"Roger. Out."

I grabbed a bag of mine grenades and exited into the cutting wind. One by one I pulled the pins and heaved them in high arcs. I had no idea if the cold would diffuse them. I had no idea if the snow would absorb them and keep them from detonating with full force. I couldn't say if they would do enough damage. Hope was a kissing cousin to panic. I had to find a place inside myself that only remembered from second to second, it had to forget the past, forget the future. The minutes washed around me, unnoticed and uncounted. They had to be. Otherwise I would be hoping my son was still running, still escaping, getting far enough, fast enough.

Please be fast enough.

I went back into the bunker, sat down, and breathed deeply. Their ships were massive, boxy, and clumsy. The only flat piece of ground large enough for them to land on up here was in the valley below, and now I had it blocked.

They wouldn't just destroy the bunker. That's not how they worked. They'd announce themselves; they'd approach slowly, loudly. They would use fear. They fed on fear. Fear is weakness and weakness eases Conversion. They needed living people. That was their mission.

They had no other purpose.

I grabbed my old, dented helmet. I took off my warm hat, cap, and muffs and slipped the icy metal mask on like an old friend. I felt the Warrior inside of me wake up, the demons milling about in the back of my head and giving me advice. I patched the helmet comm into the militia frequency and sat back on the turret, relishing the power and precision of the war machine.

Another roar began, louder than any of the others. It descended upon me like a judgment. Snow leapt from the exposed tops of trees and vibrated into a mist of microscopic crystals. Billions of unique snowflakes were rendered into carbon copy shards that spiraled into the sky on columns of sound. Down in the valley, lights flared and cyclones of snow became pillars of salt. The engines sounded like God screaming in pain. The helmet shielded my ears directly, but the sound reached into my very bones and traveled up to my ears in painful waves. Only once the lights winked out and the snow began to steam into thick fog did my ears stop ringing.

I tried to call out, "Eight to Base: Contact. Over."

The voice that answered was not of my controller. It strove for goodness and light, but held a razor edge where emotion and understanding were beheaded before a crowd, "Humans, rejoice! The One True God has sent us to show you His Divine Light. Know that we are your servants, and we only seek to bring you to perfect understand of the Lord Our God. . ."

And there they were.

I checked, but they were on every frequency, blacking out all other transmissions with the weight of their own. The voice was still going when the first few reached the furthest mine grenades, sending parts flying with the sound of two vehicles mating at high speed. Their dark shapes cut holes in the translucent air, shunning the silvery moons as they began to lope faster and faster. ". . . You should not rebel against your God, frail men . . ."

This was the worst part, the apocrypha I kept from my son. The robots knew they were not alive, that they could not sin. Because they were not alive, they could not murder or be murdered. They would come in waves, from now until they were all destroyed, sacrificing as many as were needed to convert as many as could be reached. They had all of history and science to draw from when designing their bodies. They were shaped like the dead, like priests, like chromium angels and obsidian reapers. Golden christs, leaden monks, and ivory priests bearing instruments of pain and torture, but never death.

At least not yet.

I fingered the turret controls and the gun jumped to obey. The holographic sight lit up and highlighted my enemies as I let them get closer, closer. ". . . Know that we have studied the words of God for longer than most of you have been alive, and we know the true price of rebellion . . . ."

There were many . . . just too many. ". . . Come to us, and we shall bring you peace . . ."

The targeting system lit one of my targets up in red, showing it had entered optimal range. I hit the button for just an instant—

—The world went hot and white. My visor darkened, but not before my eyes drank in far too much light. I blinked, and blinked, blue ghosts blocking out the world beyond my skull. Then a hand lifted me, threw me into the corner like a boneless doll. Again the ground trembled and sound resonated in my lungs, so loud it was a primal force. The whole world shook as if in palsy, lights inside the bunker shattered and debris flooded in though the firing port. It seemed like forever until the snow and dust stopped swirling and began to settle. It was three breaths more before I found the heart to move.

I crawled back to the turret, but there was nothing except an expanding cloud of smoke and steam in the valley. Shrapnel glittered in the sky like falling stars over the far-off shape of the Inquisitor ship. It lay on the blackened earth, a flaming shell of a city visited by one molecule of God's wrath. Trees were toppled, burnt and nude, exposing flash-fried dirt and charred vegetation. Above it, like a raptor with wings of fire, a small, agile warship circled. Only when I heard my comm crackle in my ear, did I realize that the Inquisitors were no longer talking.

"Still alive, Prophet?" The voice was human. It was expected, yet strange, familiar, yet out of place.

"Lieutenant?"

"Actually, I'm captain, now. Captain Arthur isn't around anymore." The voice sounded confident, but a little ashamed. "I'll explain later. Can you handle this end? Some of your countrymen are having a bad time of it and they need us immediately."

I glanced out of the firing port, counting twenty-odd moving shapes in the haze, "Yes, sir."

"Good man. Hold firm and we'll be back for you, *Angel*." And there was a kick of far-off engines as the dropship lit up and pushed it toward site four or ten, leaving me on my own.

Beyond my concrete cathedral, dark shapes dug themselves from tombs of ice and began advancing on me.

That may not be my captain, but it is my team.

My wife and kids are going to be OK.

I jammed down the buttons and showed the Inquisition the fullness of my Rebellion.

CLEAN SWEEPS
Jonathan Maberry

CLOAKING DEVICES ARE SCIENCE FICTION. RELICS OF OLD *STAR TREK* SHOWS from the last century. We don't have cloaks, we never had cloaks. And we don't have any chameleon circuits or shit retroengineered from alien craft. What we got is stealth technology. We got LOT—Low Observability Technology. It doesn't make our birds invisible, but it pretty much makes the radar and motion scanners look in the wrong place, or misunderstand what they're seeing. We can look like a big black hole in the middle of the sky. We can look like space junk. Or, we can look like feedback and sensor static. I always liked LOT that makes us look like static because most of the stations have been out here so long that their systems are older than dinosaur shit. Most of what they see nine to five is static.

That works for me. It keeps us from getting shot out of the black before we can put boots on the deck.

We tune our LOT systems to read the static backwash from the sensor arrays of any ship or base we approach, and then the computers work out some kind of math wizard fluctuating algorithm that matches the normal radio wave crap the universe has been kicking out since the big balloon popped.

Surprise always helps, but we didn't know how much of that was on our side. We were hoping to surprise the shit out of *them*. I'm a big fan of catching the bad guys with their dicks in their hands. Makes for a better raid.

Yeah, I know what the press says. WorldNews and SolarAP both have this thing for firefights—which they insist on called 'shoot-outs', like we're the O.K.-fucking Corral. Army PR sends them maybe six to eight mission video files a month, but do the clean sweeps ever make the Net? Nope. Not a one unless it's a god damn slow news day in the middle of August, where they'll report on crop growth or dig up some old celeb for a 'where are they now?' space filler.

But somebody pulls a trigger and it's a breaking story. And these news fucks don't give a red-hot flying shit if it's a bad guy, a Federal Ranger, or one of our boys in Free-Ops that either fires the shot or takes the hit. Bullets and blood, man, that's all they care about; and the bigger the body-count the bigger the ratings.

We Free-Ops guys only ever get press if something goes wrong, so we've been on the news...what, maybe five times in four years? And of those, the first three were during the mine riots following the cluster-fuck with the unions. That whole thing took less than a week. Since then the only time Free-Ops made the news was back in '93 when Captain Lisa Stanley got killed while her team was running down some pirates running the alley between Phobos and Deimos. I mean, come on, Stanley was killed when a stray shot hit an O_2 tank in the airlock. I saw the official reports, and the conclusion I drew from it was that she probably tripped on one of the landing sleds the pirates used when they breeched the cargo ship. She tripped and popped off a round that bounced all over the airlock until it punched into the O_2 tank. It was her bad luck that it was after they'd re-pressurized. Twenty seconds earlier there'd have been no spark, and no death, and no story.

The news jackasses made her a hero across half the Network. My guess? If Stanley hadn't been a California blonde with yabos out to there, the news people wouldn't have run with it as long as they did. That and they're always starved for action stories. There's only so much mileage you can get from politicians making assholes of themselves, or celebrities getting caught fucking the wrong wife.

The other time was a real firefight—excuse me, 'shoot-out'—between my team and the Chinese hit team that tried to declare sovereignty over the New Tibet colony on Io. That one was a real ball-burner. My boys—Jigsaw Team—were on point, with Delta, Bravo, and Zulu Teams on fast-follow and a squadron of Jackhammers giving close air support. The Chinese team was sharp; even I have to give them that. There were a lot of them, they were well-armed, well-trained, and they weren't afraid of us. No, sir, not one little bit.

It wasn't until we were on the ground that our forward spotters sent back the news that we were outnumbered and outgunned. Outnumbered like four to one, which can give serious pause even to a bunch of heartbreakers and life-takers like I got in Jigsaw. But by then we were in the pipe, riding the adrenaline high, breathing the helmet gas that triggered all those useful dopamine receptors. We were juiced and jazzed, and when the smoke cleared we had a whole lot of dead Chinese. And some dead Tibetans, too, but what the fuck could we do? The Chinese hid among the colonists, and they even put Tibetans in their own uniforms. We shot anyone with a red star.

Here's how the bullshit plays out, though. First the press are up our asses all the way through the raid. They're doing advance stories on the men and women of Free-Ops. You know, those schmaltzy human-interest things where they show vidcaps of the soldiers as kids, riding horses on the farm or taking their first EVA at Disney Lunar. Then during the battle they're getting video-only live feeds from helmet cams. The brass didn't let them hear our team chatter during the raid.

When the battle was over they spent two days canonizing everyone from the first wave of shooters down to the cooks in the galley of the drop ship. Heroes all.

Then they find out that three colonists took fire during the raid. Suddenly we're reckless killers who can't tell a friendly face from an enemy's—and remember, we're talking Chinese and Tibetans here, and everyone dressed the same. We're fried by the press. It's a great story; it kept the news feeds buzzing for weeks.

Then, when that cooled down they have the big clanking balls to ask if they can go on every other raid. And the fucking brass—*our* fucking brass—says yes.

Tells you everything you need to know about why I think the whole solar system is populated with nutcases.

And, yeah . . . they're on this run with us now. At least we don't have it as bad as the Federals who have that weekly show. FEDS. You've seen it, where they do the fly-alongs with the Federals, following the busts with handhelds and helmet cams. Mostly busting mouth-breathing bozo drug runners or low-level pirates who are too stupid to know how to dodge a full-lit Federal wagon broadcasting siren calls on all frequencies. I ask you.

We came at the Tower with the sun behind us, alternating speed and using LOT to look like feedback from old wiring to anyone who was looking. And they were looking, don't get me wrong, but this is a clever stunt and we were pretty good at it. So good that on Jigsaw's last six hard infils we'd had zero shots fired on either side. Before anyone knows we're even a reality we're breaching fore and aft airlocks and our Jackhammers are suddenly broadcasting sweetlock signals. The bad guys go from thinking they're all alone in the big black, to having twenty ugly-ass special operators coming into their ship from ass and mouth, and every rocket and missile in the catalog cocked and locked from point blank. That's not a time to make a stand. It's a time to trigger an isolated EMP to fry your computer records, drop your guns on the deck, and stand around looking extremely cooperative.

That's what we were expecting on this run, too.

The mission was routine. The Tower was a forty-year-old, barrel-style, deep-space manufacturing plant that used to make ball bearings and alloy pipes before the company went bust. After that it was empty for ten years and then got bought by some investors who filed papers saying they were going to retool it for drilling equipment to supply mines on Jupiter's moons.

Then, get this, our intel people get a hot tip from some news guy from SolarAP that the Tower is really making weapons. Nothing exotic, but enclosed gas shell rifles that you can use in any atmosphere, including zero atmosphere. Only two kinds of people need guns like that. Guys like me, and pirates.

It was a no brainer to order a raid. You don't let assholes mass produce guns that you know for damn sure are not going to be used for hunting or home defense. Since the news guys brought us the tip, they got to ride along during the raid. It was a dream come true for them.

I didn't like it, but I'm a sergeant. There isn't one person above my pay grade who gives a hemorrhoidic rat's ass what I like or don't like.

We planned it right, though, and even did some dry runs on the infil, using a similar plant orbiting Luna. My team had the fastest in-time, so we drew the lead on the breach.

Our tactical bird is a SV-117 Bullet, one of the new frictionless, electric motor boats, fired torpedo fashion from the bow of the transport. We go in fast and our battery power is used mostly for steering and braking. The Bullets are all short-range, and we were launched from two thousand miles out. The entire nose-package of the Bullet has jamming gear tuned to the transport so we don't ring any bells unless they have towed metal detectors, which this tub didn't.

What the Tower did have, though, was gravity. It was in a nice spin that suggested a 360 surface pull. Probably not earth gravity, but enough so that we could run rather than float. I hate floating in a fight.

"Twenty seconds to soft dock," our pilot called. We were all ready. Ten tough apes in EVA flexsuits, armed to the teeth and ready to kick a little gunrunner ass. We all had SolarAP cameras externally mounted on our helmets.

We also had a ridealong in the person of Alex Tennet, a reporter for SolarAP. He used to be a big shot, but his career had been tanking for years. One of those guys who was never in the right part of the solar system when anything interesting was happening. Bringing the tip about the gunrunners was the first big thing to happen to him in fifteen years, and he confided to me back on the transport, "You know, Sarge, if I hadn't lucked into this . . . I'd be burning off the rest of my career doing weather reports on Ganymede."

"Lucky you," I said. He was a news guy, so I hated him on principle, but he was okay when the cameras were off. I didn't like having to take him along on a raid, but the brass though it would look good. A nice PR hit for us.

Like we needed good PR. Or *any* PR. We're soldiers. It's not like we're in the Navy. Nothing glamorous. Grunts with guns are what we are. But, like I said, nobody above my pay grade gives a shit what I think, and just about everyone's above my pay grade.

So Tennet got to come along. Luckily, I could switch his audio feed off so I didn't have to listen to him give a blow-by-blow account of all this.

We docked without a sound, and the vibration was so soft through our ship that I knew it couldn't be felt in the Tower.

"Jigsaw in place," I reported.

"Zulu in place," came the reply. Our brother team was soft-docked at the other airlock.

"Deploy blowback skirt."

"Roger that, skirt deployed."

"On my mark," I said. "Everybody watch your fire and check your targets. Nobody dies who doesn't have to. Everybody lives, everybody comes home."

"Hooah," I heard from everyone. The old Ranger cry was always a comfort right before a battle. It came with a hell of a lot of history, and most of that history was of success.

By now the pilots of both Bullets would have spinners on the airlock wheels.

I counted it down.

On zero, the pilots initiated the hard-rips that spun the airlock wheels faster than any man could manage it, and the airlocks were literally torn open. The blowback skirts caught any flying debris and shot-injected oxygen into the airlocks. Then our hatches swung open and we used the elastic slings to launch ourselves from the Bullets into the airlocks. The skirts kept the docking collars pressurized, so we went straight for the inner hatches.

"It's locked," my corporal said.

"Blow it," I growled.

He already had the burst patch attached with magnets. We wrapped our frag caps around us and did the ol' duck and crouch as the patch blew apart the internal computers on the hatch. Tennet—the dumbass—tried to get a good shot of the blast, so I had to drag his ass down and under cover.

The second the locks were toast the corporal—Hastings—yanked open the door.

"Go! Go! Go!" I bellowed, and then we were all running into the Tower. I led the way with Hastings on my three o'clock and Tennet on my six. He could get some nice footage of my ass if he wanted. Maybe that would help his sorry ratings.

The corridor was dark, so I threw Starbursts ahead of us. The little marble-sized LEDs ignited and flooded the corridor with blue light.

In my helmet mic I could hear the same process happening for Zulu team. Man, there's nothing like military precision.

We raced through one hatch after another, at first finding nothing but huge machinery whose purpose I neither understood nor cared about; and then we hit the galley. This poor cook looks up, bent over an oven, holding a big tray of pot pies.

He had time to say, "What the fuck—?" before I kicked him in the nuts and pistol whipped him to the deck. Yeah, I know, he's just a cook. But if you're working for the bad guys, then you're a bad guy. At least in mind view; it kept things nice and simple.

The adjoining corridor spilled out into a huge manufacturing plant that smelled of oil and sweat. There had to be fifty guys in there. Big sonsabitches, with the arms and shoulders you only get from hauling around pigs of iron or steel in a gravity environment. No space muscles. No flab.

Then something really weird happened, and from that point on everything went to shit.

One of the men, a Turkish-looking guy wearing a Kufi pointed a big wrench at us and shouted: "Pirates!"

It all went crazy. The Turk swung the wrench at me with incredible force. The gravity was maybe half-earth, which meant a big son of a bitch like him could swing a thirty pound wrench real damn fast. I tried to duck, but the edge of the wrench caught me on the shoulder pad and knocked me ten feet into a stack of pipes.

My gun discharged as I was hit and I stitched a line of rounds across the floor. I didn't see the bullets hit, but I heard the screams.

And then the force of my body knocked the stack of pipes over and hundreds of pounds of half-inch pipes were hammering down on me. I dropped my gun and buried my head in my arms and curled my body into a ball. But even so, I took a hell of a beating. Pipes whacked me in the shoulders and ribs and hips and thighs. The clang was insanely loud. My visor cracked and I ducked inside my helmet to keep plastic splinters from blinding me.

Through it all I could hear the chatter of gunfire, yells, screams, and the unmistakable thud of heavy metal on flesh.

"Shit!" I cursed and tried to worm my way out from under. I had to get back into this fight. Suddenly two of the bars right over me were pulled back and I saw Hastings there, crouching down, pushing the bars aside. Tennet, the reporter, stood gawping behind him, his handheld camera shifting back and forth from the battle to me. He hadn't lifted a frigging hand to help Hastings dig me out.

"Sarge!" Hasting yelled. "You all right?"

"Help me up," I said. He grabbed my arm and pulled me out from under the pile, and I staggered as more of the pipes clanged and rolled down around me. There was a flash and a bang and suddenly Hastings was down, his faceplate smashed by a hard-shell flare, and as I watched in total horror the flare exploded inside his suit. Our flexsuits are designed to be fireproof. It had saved our lives a hundred times...but the fire is supposed to be on the outside. The flare burst inside his suit and within a second the suit puffed out as the fire ignited the oxygen inside and roasted Hastings alive. He screamed like I'd never heard a person scream before, and the expanding gasses ballooned his suit for a moment before he fell out of sight. There wasn't a goddamn thing I could do about it.

A separate fire ignited inside of me. Pure white-hot rage!

Tennet caught the whole thing on camera and for a moment our eyes met. His face was white with shock but his eyes were alight. Adrenaline can do that. Even at the worst of times it can make you feel totally alive.

My rifle was gone, lost under all the debris, so I pulled my sidearm.

The room was a melee. The gunrunners badly outnumbered us and two of my guys were down. Dead or hurt, I couldn't tell. The rest had taken up shooting positions behind pieces of machinery, and they'd littered the deck with bodies. But the numbers were bad. The gunrunners had a variety of weapons—flares, hatchets, wrenches, hand-welders. No guns, which was kind of weird. They worked in teams, two men holding up a big piece of plate steel and moving it forward like a shield while others crowded behind it, throwing stuff, popping flares over the barricades behind which my guys hid. We had the better weapons, but they sure as hell had the numbers. And I could see more men pouring into the room from the far end.

I tapped my comm-link and called for Zulu team, but the unit was dead. Smashed along with most of my helmet.

I pushed Tennet behind me and took up a shooting posture, legs wide and braced, weapon in a two-hand grip with my arms locked in a reinforced triangle. I fired careful shots and dropped seven men with six shots, and for a moment it stalled the rush of the gunrunners. I was at a right angle to their advance, which created a nice cross-fire situation. If I conserved my ammo we might pull this out of the crapper.

Then something occurred to me and it jolted me so hard that I took my finger off the trigger.

"Christ! These aren't gunrunners," I said aloud. I turned to Tennet. "Does your comm-link work?"

He lowered his camera and tapped his throat mic. "No . . . it's malfunctioning."

"Fuck. We have to get word to the fleet. This is a cluster-fuck. These aren't gunrunners. Look at 'em. They're machinists, factory workers. That's why they called me a pirate. They think we're the bad guys. Shit."

Tennet picked up a length of steel pipe and held it defensively, then abruptly pointed past me. "Sergeant! Behind you!"

I whirled around. There was nothing. I heard a voice behind me say, "I'm sorry."

It was Tennet, and it was an odd thing to say.

It was even odder when he slammed the pipe into my head.

I could hear the bones crack in my head. I felt myself fall. The taste of blood in my mouth was salty sweet. Sparks burst from the wiring in the machines and fireworks ignited in my vision. I fell in a pirouette, spinning with surreal slowness away from the point of impact. As I turned I could see the gunrunners renewing their advance on my remaining men. I could hear the chatter of weapon's fire from the other end of the room. Was it Zulu team? Had they broken through? Or was it the gunrunners with Zulu's weapons?

As I hit the deck, I wondered why the gunrunners didn't have their own guns. It seemed strange. Almost funny. Gunrunners *without* guns.

And why had they called us 'pirates'? Even if my brain wasn't scrambled those pieces wouldn't fit. I sprawled on the ground, trying to sort it out. Trying to think. I felt blood in the back of my nose. I tasted it in my mouth.

I wanted to cough, but I couldn't.

A shadow passed above me. Raising my eyes took incredible effort. I couldn't manage it. But the shadow moved and came around to bend over me.

Tennet.

His eyes were still wide and excited . . . but he was smiling. Not an adrenaline grin. I've seen those. This was different. Almost sad. A little mean. A little something else, but I couldn't put a word to it. My head hurt so much. Thinking was hard. He dropped the pipe.

He bent closer. The noise around us was thunderous but it also seemed distant, muffled. My left eye suddenly went blind.

Tennet was speaking. But not to me. His camera was pointed past me.

" . . . as the shootout rages on, the brave men of Jigsaw team are clearly overmatched by the determined resistance of the gunrunners."

Firefight. That's the right word, but though my mouth moves I can't get the word off my tongue.

He clicked off the camera and looked down at me.

"Thanks," he said.

I shaped the words 'for what'?

"Ratings, Sergeant. This is sweeps week. This story will get me back in the big chair. I'll be an anchor again before your bodies are cold."

"The . . . tip-off . . . " I managed.

He nodded. "Good PR for everyone. Your bosses will leverage this for increased funding. The militia will get more money for security. And I get an anchor's chair. Everyone's a winner."

I was sinking into the big black. I could feel myself moving away from the moment, sliding out of who I was. "You mother . . . fucker . . . " I gasped with what little voice I had.

"Hey," he said, "you told me at least twenty times that you never get to pull a trigger, that good soldiering doesn't require heroes. That's a sad epitaph for a career Free-Ops agent." He bent even closer. "I just made you a hero, Sergeant. I just made you a *star!* And your people have guaranteed me that anyone who falls today will be given full honors."

His words tore chunks out of me.

I wanted to grab him by the neck and tear his head off. I wanted to stuff his camera down his throat. I wanted to destroy the hard drive and all its images of my men fighting and dying.

But I didn't have anything left.

"They . . . *knew?*"

He grinned. "Knew? Jesus, Sergeant, don't you get it yet? This is their gig. I'm just another hump on the payroll. The government needs good press, too, and by God you and your team put on one hell of a show. You just made a lot of people happy, Sergeant."

So, with the gunfire like thunder around me, and the screams of good men dying on both sides, I closed my eyes. I knew that he'd turn his camera back on, that he'd film my last breaths. That he'd use my death—and the deaths of my men—to get exactly what he wanted.

But what the fuck. That's show business.

Shit.

WAR MOVIES
James Chambers

WE WATCHED MOVIES UNDERGROUND WHILE THE SURFACE BURNED. Down our rabbit holes, we couldn't hear the bombs hit, but we felt the earth shake with their impact while we sat in the dark and watched moving pictures flicker in the dark. We knew what kind of hell was coming down over our heads: one full of heat, shrapnel, and death, worse than any atrocity long-dead, special effects wizards had left for us on film. When enough sky-busters exploded at once, they set the air on fire. We wondered what we would find left of our home and of the Frek when we deployed up-earth, whenever that might be.

Some of the guys worried that our twelve brutal weeks in bootcamp and three more in psychprep would go to waste without one of us ever seeing so much as a skirmish.

Other guys hoped for that.

I knew better. We were weapons, and the Army didn't make weapons it didn't intend to use.

The moment the movies started I knew we'd see action before long. All they showed us were war movies and monster movies—the blockbusters, the classics, the cult favorites, and even a few hits from the last summer before the Frek dropped down and started us fighting for our lives.

The most gruesome movies ran two or three times a week. During the day we bled out our frustrations in the gyms and training rooms, and at night we stoked them again with images of violence and alienness, of combat and heroism, of strangeness, mystery, and the bloody struggle for survival. The picture shows were part of a slow burn, lit to keep our rage simmering. They reinforced the narrative we'd been taught in bootcamp. They showed us again and again that only country and fellowship mattered and that aliens like the Frek could never be anything other than slavering, man-eating, evil beasts, hell-bent on raping our planet and enslaving our species if we didn't stop them.

We got the message loud and clear.

One night a PFC from Kansas joked about why, if they were so hot for the "sky-fi stuff," they never showed *E.T.* Without missing a beat, the guy next to him described in detail how he would shove a grenade down E.T.'s throat and "blow his fucking heartlight the fuck home and fuck needing to use the phone." Everyone laughed so hard they stopped the movie.

The strangest part of it is when you see some of these guys from on-screen walking around in officer's dress. Seeing them on television, like when General Wayne and General McQueen address the nation, is one thing, but in person it's unsettling. Colonel Connery is CO for our rabbit hole, and he looks exactly like the real deal, circa 1968, except you know what's knocking around his head has nothing to do with anything from back then, and everything to do with death and killing and keeping our morale high. They clone them so well, I bet even their wives and girlfriends, if they were still alive, wouldn't know the difference. It gets the guys' attention, sure enough. No one's mind ever wanders when the Colonel speaks in his powerful, Scottish accent, and whenever they run one of his old movies, a handful of guys always hit him up for autographs, ask him how it was shooting the love scenes.

He only smirks and nods as if he knows.

It's a hell of psyche-out.

No bombing for two days.

Then our orders came through: surface clean-up for most of the men, but not for my platoon. We pulled special duty. We were to rendezvous with a Special Forces unit that had collected what our orders described as a "valuable artifact," secure it from them, and bring it to Camp Scott, on the double-quick, of course.

Leaving our rabbit hole, however, was a process.

First, advance teams surfaced and reported back on up-earth conditions. Then everyone got booster shots against possible contagion from Frek remains, took anti-rad pills, and got equipped with live ammo and full-integrity body armor to replace what we'd damaged in training.

Centcom had shipped us in and tucked us away only days ahead of the campaign to sterilize the Eastern seaboard. We'd been down-earth for two months, like cicadas waiting to hatch from the ground when the weather turned hot, and we were eager to go. Even the guys who'd been dreading the day they'd see action looked relieved to finally be doing something.

Colonel Connery made the rounds while we suited up.

Captain Willis and Captain Smith followed him.

They helped with our gear. They steadied our nerves and tried to keep us from thinking too much about the blasted wasteland that waited on the surface.

I snapped the last of my armor in place, checked my ammunition, and waited for my platoon to finish suiting up. I was their sergeant. I tried not to think about what that meant. I'd had weeks to ruminate on it. Now it was time to act.

Colonel Connery reviewed our orders with me and said he was grateful to have a man like me in his division. I wondered how much of that came from what they'd programmed into his brain on the clone farm, or if he'd thought up any of it on his own. I guess it didn't matter one way or the other. His pep talk was protocol. When he was done he slapped me on the back, said he'd keep a good cigar waiting for me, and then walked off into the crowd of soldiers.

By then my platoon had gathered at the elevator.

The ride to the surface was silent, the journey up-earth long. Anticipation poured off my men in waves. They were good soldiers: Abernathy, Barnes, Champ, Foster, Itgen, Marvin, Morris, Smith, and Testa.

And me, Colin Rook.

They were my soldiers; they were Rook's Raiders.

I hoped we'd all come back together.

I knew we wouldn't.

Riding up-earth, I felt as if we'd always been fighting the Frek, as if the pre-invasion world had only ever existed in movies and dreams, and as if no time before my first day in bootcamp had been real. I couldn't remember the day I decided to enlist, or even when the Frek invasion had begun.

Like everyone else, though, I knew their first assault had come without warning.

We hadn't even known that the Frek, or any other alien life, existed until they attacked us.

Even now, no one really understands why they invaded Earth.

I lean toward the mistake theory: the Frek thought there were no intelligent species here, and by the time they figured out otherwise, it was too late to change course. If all Frek invasions are alike, then they're pretty much impossible to stop once they're underway. Frek females give birth to about 500 young at a time. Frek children pop out of the womb in little, curled-up bundles no bigger than soccer balls, but they grow to the size of lambs in about three days, and they're more vicious than badgers. The first anyone knew we were under attack was when pregnant Frek mothers, already in labor, began dropping from the sky and popping out killing machines. They dropped about thirty per continent to start, and within days 15,000 hungry, newborn Frek bastards shocked the world. What's worse is about thirty Frek out of every litter were female. Those things mature, mate, and reproduce in a matter of weeks. Soon as we caught on to that, we made hunting the brood-mothers a priority. It wasn't enough.

That's when the scorched earth campaigns began.

We started with full nukes.

Freks burned to cinders in the blasts, but the radiation barely slowed the survivors. It did have the benefit of sterilizing them, which made them easier to fight without worrying about picking up some Frek microbe that would blind you or turn your organs to slush. So far the white-coat grunts have identified about thirteen separate bacterial strains the Frek brought to Earth, seven of which are deadly to humans. They're working on cures and vaccines, but anything better than the crude, imperfect immunization shots they give us in bootcamp is a long way off. You catch a Frek death germ and get sick, you may as well throw yourself in front of a firegun for all the medics can help you. Thank God, the Frek bugs haven't mutated to airborne or human-to-human transmission yet.

Centcom switched to skybusters, which had about the same effect as nukes but without spreading as much fallout. The sterilization campaigns began in earnest then.

They say Africa is clear of Freks now. Thing is, it's also pretty much clear of humans. No one's sure we really won that battle.

The Frek control half of Asia and all of South America. Bombing runs along their perimeter 24/7 keep them in check.

Australia has fared pretty well with about half the country still habitable and mostly Frek free.

Europe and North America still hang in the balance.

That's where Rook's Raiders and a million other grunts came in. We were trained in the western deserts where the Frek never landed and then shipped east and north where the Frek are the densest. Now it was time to go see what there was to kill.

Fighting Frek isn't easy.

The children have skin like a beetle's carapace, and they can launch razor-sharp quills from their upper legs. Shooting the bastards five or six times usually drops them. Grenades are better. The only thing that makes it manageable is they're stupid and impulsive, and they tend to come running straight at you. They're fast, though. If you let one through, there's not much you can do but pray somebody's got your back.

The brood-mothers are worse.

They're about the size of personnel helicopters. Soon as they finish giving birth, they're back on all ten feet fighting. They spit streams of the vilest soup imaginable. It'll burn you bad. Guys who are allergic to it go anaphylactic and drop dead in seconds. The worst of the germs comes from the birther spit. You might survive being doused, but you'll spend a couple of months in D and Q, shaved hairless and having layers of skin flash-burned off you, while robot medics prick you and pop tubes into all your available orifices three times a day.

The mothers are uglier than the kids too.

They lumber around like octopi with stilts rammed into their tentacles. Their heads are flat and stretched into squares, and they got five big, red eyes that never blink.

I've never seen one in person, but they showed us plenty of vid records in bootcamp. Every grunt and officer gets a camera chip implanted in their skull beside their left eye, so every soldier is a cameraman. That's created a bounty of raw battlefield footage, and the top brass use it liberally.

That shit'll give you nightmares.

We made our rendezvous, and my first thought was someone at Centcom has a wicked sense of humor. That's the only explanation I can muster for why they cloned Peter Lorre to lead the Special Forces team. It wasn't only him, either. Although the other spooks hung back in the shadows, I'm sure I saw Karloff and Price in Captain's bars, Rathbone a Major. We were inside a blasted-out warehouse, and it was dark and gloomy, and I had to choke back a laugh. The movies those guys made were the ones I liked best: the classic monster flicks. They were the only ones with a touch of style to them. They could be gruesome, violent, and morbid, but there were real stories there, romances a lot of the time, and none of that formulaic, jingoistic cheerleading that was in almost every war movie we saw. Those old fright flicks came closer to reminding me of what I was fighting for than anything else we watched. That's because the heroes in those movies—and yeah, sometimes the monster was the hero, like in *Frankenstein* or *The Creature from the Black Lagoon*—the heroes were almost always noble.

I could buy that in a monster movie.

Not so much in the combat pics. In those, the hero died in the end way too often, and anyway, I'd seen fifty guys wash out of bootcamp for everything from cowardice to dementia to battlefield incontinence, and I knew soldiers weren't always noble. That's why it struck me as funny about Peter Lorre being cloned for Special Forces. He never played the hero in the horror shows. The thing about him was he was unnerving even if you didn't recognize him. He had a tic, and his eyes looked rheumy enough to slide out of their sockets. Considering the Special Forces guys fought in the dark and had little contact with anyone but the enemy, the creepier they were, the better, I guess. Not that the Frek cared, but I guess it mattered to someone.

With Lorre they even got the voice right.

"Sergeant," he said. "We have your valuable cargo, ready for transport to Camp Scott. Are you prepared to take possession?"

"Ready, willing, and able," I told him.

"Excellent. Your papers?"

I handed him our orders. He skimmed them as he led me to the back of the huge transport truck, and then he opened one of the rear doors. Inside was a canister about twelve feet in diameter and roughly twenty feet long. It was spattered with mud and other dried gunk, and it looked like a rusty, oversized oil drum. Sealed up tight and strapped down solid enough to stay put even if the truck rolled, it filled almost the entire cargo space. I'd never seen anything like it.

I asked him what they had in there.

"We have captured one of the enemy's brood-mothers before labor and have trapped it in stasis in this tank. Frek bodies are quite pliable once they're subdued."

I guess I made a face or didn't speak for too long, because Captain Lorre's expression got even more worried, and he pulled out a white handkerchief and wiped sweat from his brow.

"Are you deaf, Sergeant?" he said. "I tell you we have captured one of the enemy birthers and have trapped it in this tank, yet you have nothing to say."

I'd heard him fine. No one had ever taken one of the Frek birthers alive. I thought we'd have heard the news.

"It is secret, of course, which is why we must get the prisoner as quickly as possible inside Camp Scott. You and your men only have to drive this truck home, like good chauffeurs. Do not interfere with the canister. For God's sake don't try to open it, or there will be horrible consequences. Absolutely horrible."

I asked him if he'd be coming with us.

He shook his head and wiped his brow again, and I saw why his unit had to pass the baton. Captain Lorre's sleeve pulled back from the hem of his glove, uncovering about eight blood blisters on his wrist, a sign of Frek infection. The rest of his unit must have been contaminated, too. They'd probably caught the germ while subduing the birther. Word was when Special Forces picked up a Frek bug, they didn't bother coming in for triage, they simply ran suicide missions to kill as many Frek as possible before they expired. I felt a little sad for the captain, but in the end he was only a clone. No doubt there were other Special Forces "monster units" running around out there. Centcom hated to waste a good clone matrix once they'd developed it.

Captain Lorre handed me the keys to the truck and turned to rejoin his unit. I called him back before he disappeared into the shadows.

"Hey," I said. "They forget Lugosi?"

The captain smiled. "Oh, no, they could never forget Lugosi, but I'm sad to have to tell you he didn't make it. He's in the canister, with the prisoner."

Morris drove. I rode shotgun.

In back with the trophy were Abernathy, Champ, Marvin, and Testa. Barnes, Foster, and Smith rode the gun positions mounted behind the cab. Itgen sat between me and Morris and worked up a sweat navigating.

We had maps and GPS and high-level training in dead reckoning. Only problem was all that was keyed to geography that no longer existed. A few days of skybusters had chewed up the landscape and spit it back out in a bold, new arrangement. Even when we followed the compass, we kept coming to roads turned into craters, bridges reduced to splinters, and buildings blasted across every inch of ground creating a litter of obstacles where the map showed clear paths. Camp Scott should've been a six-hour drive from our rendezvous with Special Forces, but we'd driven that long and covered only a quarter of the distance.

Every so often we spied the dark specks of surveillance drones coasting past the horizon.

At one point we passed a rabbit hole and thought we might stop there for help, but an off-target skybuster had cracked its lid and let the Frek in. We knew what we'd find down there. We moved on, fast.

Another hour and we covered maybe fifteen more miles. We'd started in daylight. Now dusk was creeping into the horizon. I debated whether we should push on or stake a defensible position in the rubble. Neither option appealed to me. Being indoors at a secure location overnight was survival 101.

While I was mulling that over, Foster popped off a dozen rounds into the shadows of a broken building, and everyone snapped alert with weapons ready.

Something moved behind a pile of debris.

Several other somethings followed it.

About thirty Frek bastards skittered out from beneath the rocks and charged us.

How the hell they survived the skybusters, I'll never know, but I didn't worry too much about having an opportunity to rectify that. I climbed onto the hood of the truck and opened fire.

Barnes and Smith kicked in with the fireguns. The rest of the men started lobbing grenades from the rear of the vehicle. One of them went wild and ripped a grapefruit-sized hole in the truck's armor. Everything turned fiery and frantic and sounded like it was happening far away once the explosions numbed my eardrums. Most of the Frek were dying, but the ones that made it through, instead of coming for us, they tried to claw their way through the side of the truck. They must have sensed the birther was in there. The truck's armor slowed them down enough to make them easy pickings, and it wasn't long before the battle ended. Not a casualty among us, but the Frek were all dead.

We regrouped and drove off.

I screamed at Morris to go faster and kept screaming until we were far from where we'd been attacked. His ears had to be as dead as mine by then, but he got the message. When the ride smoothed out, Itgen and I took up the map and tried to calculate our safest route.

It was pointless.

The best we could do was hope we'd find the shortest.

It got dark and I told Morris to keep driving.

Barnes, Foster, and Smith popped on their night eyes.

The truck's headlights were bright, but the darkness was so dense and pervasive, it seemed to swallow up the light. Around midnight we passed an unexploded skybuster sitting in a crater and drove around it. That was rare, but it happened. A dud igniter or maybe someone didn't arm it properly. Eventually it would blow. They always did.

Half an hour later we stopped.

Bad news.

Abernathy and Testa had found holes in the stasis tank. Something was leaking out. They refused to ride with it.

I got out and climbed into the cargo space.

Shrapnel from where the stray grenade had blown a hole in our armor during the skirmish had perforated the skin of the tank. The sludge dripping out was the color of cornhusks, probably a combination of Frek blood and whatever had been pumped in there to keep the birther alive. There wasn't much, but if it was contaminated it was plenty.

My men looked to me for answers.

I didn't have any good ones.

I told them to look for a tire repair kit. When they found it, I dug out its largest self-adhesive patch and slapped it onto the canister. It held, but it barely covered the three holes, and I saw it would peel off as soon as it got too damp from the leakage.

There weren't enough footholds outside the cargo trailer for everyone to ride on the exterior. It would've been too dangerous in the dark. Hit a bad bump, and you could lose someone and never notice. As ugly as it sounded, some of us would have to ride with the tank.

No one liked it, but they accepted it, especially when I told them I'd be riding there with them. I ordered Abernathy and Testa to squeeze in up front, and then I climbed into the trailer with Champ and Marvin.

Before we got the doors closed, before Morris even started the engine, I heard something buzz by overhead. Its high-pitched whine told me it was only a surveillance drone. Maybe they were searching for us because we were so late. I looked for it and saw two small orange lights circling in the black sky. Between them was a single, blinking red light. The drone passed over us low before it rose and began circling.

I was watching it when the entire truck lurched, and I almost fell out.

It felt like we'd hit a huge bump, but we weren't moving. The truck shook again. This time I saw why. It was bouncing with the tank. The metal container was vibrating and shaking, and every few seconds it jolted in one direction or another like the birther inside was trying to pound its way out.

The makeshift patch popped off and goop spurted the inside of the truck. Champ and Marvin almost knocked me over on their way out. I jumped down and we all drew our weapons. The others came around from the front, armed and frightened. We watched the tank rock and rattle and wondered if it would hold.

They never should've made me a sergeant. I don't think like most soldiers. I never bought all the way into the official story of how things are. When someone tries too hard to sell me something, it makes me suspicious, and that's what all the movies were down our rabbit hole. A nonstop sales pitch to keep us on board with how the honchos wanted us to see things. The clones worked like a charm in that regard, tricking soldiers and civilians into believing reality was exactly like the movies and vice versa, leading us deeper into the story, distracting us from asking questions, so we would always fight the Frek with steady fervor.

Not that I doubted we were fighting for our lives; I knew we were.

Only I wasn't sure we'd been given all the information. When a movie's based on true events, there's always tons of stuff they leave out to make the story more exciting. For example, behind every war there are people who pull the strings, and sometimes they do it for their own benefit and damn the world and everyone in it. The movies never showed those people.

When the tank settled down, everyone let out the breath they'd been holding.

I hopped into the trailer, ignoring my men's shouts for me to stay clear.

I walked up to the tank and banged on it.

Whatever was inside banged back.

That gave me a shudder.

The guys got quiet.

I tapped the metal again and again got a response.

Another two raps got me two right back.

I looked at my men, and said, "No fucking way that's a Frek birther in there."

No one said a thing.

I saw in their faces that all they wanted was to close the thing up, get back in the truck, and dump it at Camp Scott. Already done wouldn't be fast enough for them.

I wanted that too, but even more I wanted to know what the hell was in the can.

Unclipping the flashlight from my belt, I walked around to the damaged side. Standing on a field box, I stepped up eye level with the holes and flashed the light in. Nothing more had dribbled out and what was there was drying to a crust, but the unmistakable stench of Frek came pouring out. Through the punctured metal I saw only darkness and a yellowish shine from my light reflecting off the goop.

A shadow moved inside.

My light flashed off a patch of iridescent Frek skin.

An eye filled up one of the holes and peeped out at me.

Screaming, I stumbled backward, lost my balance, and fell. Abernathy and Barnes bolted into the trailer, grabbed me, and dragged me out, spilling me onto the ground, while the rest of the men leveled their weapons toward the canister.

I told them to stand down.

I told them we'd been lied to.

I told them what I'd seen through the hole in the metal.

It was a human eye.

Aside from me, Barnes, and Testa, no one thought opening the tank was a good idea. After I calmed down I figured the monster unit's Lugosi was still alive in there. It made sense, but it didn't sit right with me. Still, I thought we should try to rescue him. The rest of the men wanted to push on to Camp Scott, and since those were our orders, we did so.

A few miles farther along, we reached impassable ground.

Must have been a hundred skybusters dropped there during the bombing, because there wasn't an unbroken spot of earth left as far as we could see in any direction, except back the way we came. We couldn't raise anyone on the radio, probably due to residual radiation in the air over the blasted zone.

Itgen and I scrutinized the map, but there was no sure way around. There was a river to the south, rough hills to the north, and east was behind us.

While we sat on our options, the Frek came again.

Whatever was left of them after the bombing campaign must have been tracking us for most of the night. They came from behind us, out of the dark. Only Abernathy keeping watch with his night eyes stopped them from overrunning us before we knew they were there.

We opened fire and scrambled for the truck.

Morris revved the engine.

Most of us made it on board. Frek bastards got Champ and Marvin and dragged them out of sight.

A rain of quills clattered against the armor. Morris floored the gas, turned us around, and drove us head-on toward the line of running Freks. They crunched under the tires and splatted against the armored sides, but a lot of them managed to hang on. We were covered with them, and they were doing their best to tear the truck open. They wanted to kill us, I'm sure, but more than that they wanted whatever was inside that tank. Whether or not we ever reached Camp Scott, I couldn't let that happen.

I leaned over to Morris.

I told him where to go, and then prayed we could hold off the Frek long enough to get there.

By the time we reached the unexploded skybuster, we'd lost Barnes, Smith, and Testa to the Frek.

Morris slammed to a stop so close to the bomb, we almost bumped it. The effect was immediate: the Frek fled, scrambled back, and circled around us. They knew enough to fear the skybuster. The break from fighting was a relief, but then it sunk in that all I'd accomplished was a standoff.

In the fleeting quiet I heard the buzz of drones overhead. There were four of them now, orange lights hovering like eyes, red lights blinking like stars. I no longer thought they'd been sent to find and help us. They were there to watch and record. We were on; it was our big moment.

I tried the radio again.

Only static, maybe due to radiation. Maybe not.

Without help, I only saw one way out.

If we gave the Frek what they wanted, they'd slaughter us the moment they had it. I looked at Foster, Itgen, and Morris and saw they'd each concluded the same thing. We had enough ammo to hold off the enemy for a couple of hours, no more. The Frek would get us and the tank before dawn.

We couldn't allow it.

Fuck us, but Rook's Raiders wound up in a war movie instead of a monster movie. We got to die for our mission instead of killing the monster and living to see the next dawn.

The four of us climbed into the back of the van and began untying the tank. It shook and jolted as we worked, knocking us off-balance. Whatever was inside, it wanted out. Maybe it sensed what we had in mind. Foster dropped out and examined the skybuster, locating the access panel that would allow us to manually detonate it. He gave us the thumbs up. With the cargo doors open the Frek knew what we planned, and they didn't like it. They came at us in a biting wave. We fought back, but we were outnumbered. Seven Frek bastards got Foster as he pulled a grenade. He dropped it live. It exploded beneath the truck, knocking me, Morris, and Itgen to the ground and driving the Frek back. But the blast hit the exposed tank, too.

The seal at the end cracked.

Fluid squirted out.

The Frek closed on us again.

The thing inside the tank pounded against the lid, shoving it upward by inches.

In the sky the drones circled. There were eight of them now, each one watching from a different place, a different angle, recording us, even as we recorded everything we saw through our implanted cameras. I wondered who was watching and why they didn't send help.

Then the lid popped off the tank and slammed against the skybuster.

From the opening two limbs emerged: one Frek, the other human. The thing inside was massive, and it squeezed itself out of the canister, pushing a wash of viscous goop with it as it came. When it unfolded, stood on its ten legs, and raised the flat disk of its body into the air, the sight sent us reeling. It throbbed and pulsated as if gasping for breath. Dangling from its underbelly were eight bodies at the end of pulpy tubes. Two were miniature Frek birthers. The other six were human. There was Lugosi, hanging there, staring down at us, and so many of the others: McQueen, Smith, Wayne, even Colonel Connery. Each was an unfinished figure waiting for the breath of life to be breathed into it, for its brain to start working at full capacity. They looked frightened and half alert.

The worst part of it hit me the moment Itgen and Morris turned their guns on me.

One of those dangling, dripping horrors had my face.

I ran toward the skybuster even as my men opened fire.

I felt the punch of the slugs and started to go numb, but my fingers were already clutching the wires. I pressed them together and clicked the switch.

The skybuster turned the world to fire.

Down the rabbit holes, the men watch movies while the surface burns.

I take no interest in them now that I'm wearing captain's bars. On the nights they show my movies, I stay in my quarters and read technical manuals. Centcom told me that with time the memories should fade. They haven't, though. There's something wrong with me, a flaw in my matrix that keeps me from forgetting.

They never should've made me a captain.

General Wayne was there to hand me my bars and congratulate me when I came back online at the clone farm.

"You've done good, son, and we got it all on film," he said. "The folks at home loved it around the world. You're international now."

They told me the Frek in the canister was a type that intelligence had reports of but had never seen up close. It grew clones of captured soldiers. Once the Frek realized how clones were helping to sustain our war efforts, they decided to use them against us. They had captured several clone farms in South America, which gave them all the data they needed. They couldn't master our technology, but they found an organic way to create clones. Then they set out to infiltrate our troops by sending decoys into the field. They'd started with Special Forces. Captain Lorre and the rest of his monster unit had been bogus, infected with Frek germs to self-destruct. They had given us a Trojan horse and trusted us to ferry it inside Camp Scott. The fact that I'd been among the decoys was only because the Frek had captured the clone farm where I'd been brought online. Our real cargo had been the recovered torch from the Statue of Liberty, a "valuable artifact" like our orders had said. Now it was gone, and we had a whole new front on which to fight the Frek. I guess they hadn't counted on their stray bastards fouling up their plot by trying to rescue what their senses told them was a broodmother.

Me and all my "others" got bucked up to Captain for my "quick thinking and decisive action in the field." I hadn't known until then that I was a clone.

"It's better that way," General Wayne had said. "You had some popular movies before the Frek landed, but we had to test run your matrix. Make sure you were functional, see what kind of ratings you got. You start out a sergeant for a couple of runs, and we see if you break out into a more popular role. We're at war, sure, but that doesn't mean we can't give the people some entertainment to keep their spirits high. You passed with flying colors. Now we'll start reaping the cumulative benefits of your experience. That's how we'll beat the Frek. Sooner or later, we'll find the way to decisive victory. But it's a hell of an adventure getting there, and we've got to keep the populace on board with the war. If we let it sink in how dire things really are, it would be too demoralizing. People might want to surrender. We won't let that happen."

I asked him when I would see my men again, if they would keep my unit together. A puzzled look came over General Wayne's face, and he smiled like a patient father as he told me, "They were extras, son. Extras don't come back. Extras get replaced."

He saluted me and walked away.

Before he stepped through the door, I asked, "General, are we winning?"

Without looking back, he said, "Of course, we're winning the damn war. We're the heroes, son."

He seemed so certain.

I can remember a lot of things I'm not supposed to, but I can't remember how long we've really been fighting the war with the Frek. I think of how easily it came to me to sacrifice myself and my men by blowing the skybuster, and it reminds me that sometimes Frankenstein's monster was the hero, too.

Now the whole world feels like a haunted house: not everything here is what it seems, and there are ghosts everywhere.

That's why I don't watch the movies anymore.

I can't sit down there in the dark while the ground rumbles and shakes above us, sit there with the good men who are winning the war against the Frek, but who won't come back when they die, who won't ever see victory, who won't ever be known for their sacrifice. I can't sit there in the dark with the extras. They're heroes too, but they're trapped in a war movie, and I'm trapped in a horror show.

THE BATTLE FOR KNOB LICK

A Chronicle of The 142nd Starborne

Patrick Thomas

HOW THE HELL DID WE END UP LIKE THIS?" GRUMBLED ANDIE HASTINGS WITH enough venom to make a cobra slither away with feelings of inadequacy.

The man in front of her on the drop ship ramp turned his head as they disembarked. "Because we followed your orders to abandon the people of Ozark to the walking dead."

"Shaker, I am still your commanding officer and you will treat me with respect," ordered Hastings.

"Not any longer, or did you miss Benedict's coup back on *Kyklopes*?" said James Shaker.

"We will retake the station," whispered Hastings.

Shaker and Flauker Lao laughed. Hastings bristled at the mocking sound of the men she had considered her two best junior officers.

They stood in formation at the base of the Harpy's ramp as Harvey Kline and Justine Dorna descended and lined up in formation beside them.

The Harpy's sergeant had saved the former colonel's quintet for the last drop. All the other teams had ten members. Instead of having one team with fifteen, the sergeant decided to make sure Hastings's team was operating at half strength. "Knob Lick is a kilometer southeast of this position. It had a population of seven thousand and several factories. Your weapons will be unlocked after we are airborne. Once you locate or exceed fifty survivors, comm *Kyklopes* for evac. Good hunting."

"Thank you, Sergeant," said Shaker, meeting his eyes. The sergeant nodded back, approving. Few of the decommissioned officers or enlisted were able to hold their heads up after Major Hans Benedict's dressing down for their dereliction of duty which ended in the rebel major stripping all five thousand soldiers of rank and status in the Host forces.

The quintet moved far enough away from the Harpy-class drop ship so the heat from the blasting of her engines didn't fry them. All stood and watched as their ride lifted off to return to orbit.

"Excellent. Now we can start re-gathering our crew and plan our retaking of *Kyklopes*," said Hastings.

"Benedict has both the literal and moral high ground," said Shaker.

"I followed protocol," said Hastings through gritted teeth.

"You gave the orders, but we followed them. People died," said Shaker.

"And worse," said Lao, thinking of those the reanimation virus infected, killed, and brought back as mockeries of life. "Plus, there is no way to lock him out of the command controls."

"And he can override our weapons, making their value in a firefight about as effective as clubs," said Shaker.

"Not to mention even if we gain control of a Harpy, *Kyklopes* could blow us out of the sky," said Lao.

"They don't know about our sensor dead zones." Even an orbital space battle-station as large as *Kyklopes* has sensor limitations to the parts of atmo-sphere and planet it has a direct line of sight to, augmented by a web of smaller sensor satellites orbiting the planet. Since Ozark had few orbit-capable craft and *Kyklopes* was their only line of defense from external attack, the dead zones caused little concern, but they were there. "We can achieve orbit in one of the dead zones, plot a course, and use our momentum to approach the station undetected," said Hastings, rightly suspecting the method Benedict had used to board her station.

"Benedict is hardly a fool and probably has *Behemoth* orbiting over another part of the surface. And a Colossus-class warship can blow a renegade Harpy out of the sky without breaking a sweat," said Lao.

"Not that ships sweat much," added Shaker. "Unless you count the plumbing system."

"So what do you two propose?" said Hastings.

"We carry out the mission. Find any uninfected survivors and get them to quar-antine on *Kyklopes*," said Shaker. The reanimation virus incubated by the twenty-fifth hour of infection, so thirty-plus hours of isolation was enough to guarantee a lack of infection. The battlestation's emergency facilities housed half a million, nearly a quarter of the planet's pre-infection population.

"Get reinstated in the Host," said Lao.

"Benedict is not the Host. He's a goddamned traitor who mutinied and took over his ship," shouted the former Colonel Hastings. "And he's only a Major to boot."

"I understand he refused to abandon people who needed his help," said Shaker. "And not a single ship that returned to Earth to fight in the conflagration has been heard from again."

"Not to break up this debate," said Dorna. "But deaders are attracted to noise and we have no idea how many are nearby. May I suggest we switch over to head-sets and start moving toward Knob Lick. And do it quietly?"

"Excellent point. Fan out twenty feet apart, standard star formation," said Shaker.

"What makes you think you're in charge?" growled Hastings. After more than three decades of service to the Sway, the idea of following the orders of a former subordinate was beyond distasteful, especially after having her command stolen out from under her by her former lover. Add to that being lumped in with the rest of the soldiers and having Benedict himself point a gun to her head after she pleaded for mercy and Hastings' bad mood was easily understood.

"Because none of us are going to follow you at this point and someone has to do it," said Shaker.

"I second Shaker," said Lao.

"Third," said Dorna. "Which makes the motion carried."

"The Host is not a democracy," shouted Hastings.

"But we're no longer in the Host, or what controls it, are we? You can come or you can stay. I think I'd rather make up your quota of rescues than have to deal with your suicidal plans to take back *Kyklopes*, but the odds of you surviving alone are slim," said Shaker. "And prior to this episode, you were a good commander. The same principles apply. You look out for us, we look out for you, but as equals. Can you handle that? We need to know that you have our backs before we engage the enemy."

The former subordinate and superior locked eyes in a battle of wills. Hastings lifted her rifle and aimed toward Shaker, who dove to the ground. A second later three plasma shells ripped through a corpse that had come over the crest of the hill behind Shaker. The superheated shells reduced the zombie to pieces, but the noise attracted another ten walking dead.

"Nice shooting, ma'am," said Shaker, firing at another.

"I trust that answers your question?" said Hastings.

Shaker's response couldn't be heard as Lao, Dorna, and Kline were blowing more corpses to pieces.

In the silence that followed the one-sided fight, the quintet turned rapidly, scanning the area, each pulling their breathing masks up and goggles down to prevent infection from any airborne spatter and switching on their comm headsets.

"Anyone see any more deaders?" shouted Lao.

"Clear," said Dorna.

"I think we're good," said Kline.

"Move to the road, people, and let's hightail it out of here and scout the town," said Shaker.

The gunplay had knocked the fight out of Hastings. She fell into formation with the rest of her former subordinates.

"Dorna, you were the officer in charge of monitoring the reanimated. What going to help us beat or avoid them?" whispered Shaker into his comm. "Benedict's prep was rather limited."

"Yeah, all I know is don't get bit or have sex with one unprotected," said Lao.

"Ick," said Dorna.

"Hey, we had to watch a vid on it before we got dirtside R&R," replied Lao. "Means someone had to be desperate enough to try it."

Dorna sighed. "More than one sadly, but it was hardly widespread. The reanimated are mainly used as slave labor. The ones in the labor force are fitted with controllers in the cerebellum. They shock parts of the brain to control and program movement. It's choppy unless the insertion is perfect, but very effective. Most people called them stemmers because of the mistaken assumption that the controllers go in the brain stem. I guess it's catchier that cerebellers. Stems are also what the controllers are commonly called. Personally, I've always thought it was stupid to use an infectious workforce, but settlers on a planet like this can't afford to waste any resources, even their dead. The stems are fairly easy to insert and a syringe of infected blood and a couple of zaps from a defibrillator can usually revive anything dead less than forty hours."

"I hear the 121st Starborne has an entire zombie legion," said Kline. "The Host has bloodsuckers, patchwork soldiers, and were-beasties fighting for us, so why not? Use the monsters to fight the monsters. The Host never mentioned that we could end up fighting their own monster soldiers in the recruitment vids though, did they?"

"Benedict's 142nd Starborne doesn't have stem soldiers, does it?" asked Lao.

"I don't think so. Amazingly, this is the first known planetary outbreak. All previous outbreaks have always been limited to a much smaller geographic area before they were contained," said Dorna.

"Translation, they were flaypalmed," said Lao.

"Which worked, but using it against major civilian centers was banned by the Sway government after it incinerated a high-ranking politician's kid," said Hastings. "Otherwise, I would have flaypalmed the first two infected cities *and* the surrounding countryside."

"You could have done that? What about all the innocents?" asked Dorna.

"I *didn't* and look what happened to them. Do you think they'd prefer to have been incinerated quickly or be deaders?" said Hastings. "This all started 'cause some idiot violated protocol and didn't report being bit. The reanimation virus killed that smuck who came back as a deader and went cannibal on his friends and neighbors."

"Not how I want to go. I get bit, I'm eating my gun," said Lao.

"We'll just stay out of sight and we should be fine," said Shaker.

"Not necessarily," said Dorna. "Sight is not as important as hearing and neither matches smell in helping them hunt living meals."

"Smell?" said Kline.

Dorna nodded. "The olfactory nerve doesn't connect to the spinal cord, it hooks right into the brain. More primal. Because it connects higher up than the stems, it is hard to bypass. There's a failsafe in the stems that stops the legs when it loses a signal, but the arms and heads can still attack, especially if they smell something and are hungry.

"And they're always hungry," said Lao.

"True, which is why handlers are trained to not go near an unsecured deader," said Dorna.

"Okay people, something up ahead. Looks like a farmhouse," said Shaker.

"There's livestock. Maybe that means people," said Lao.

"Not necessarily," said Dorna. "Deaders are people-eaters. Livestock usually get left alone unless there's fresh blood in the air. Then they'll go into a frenzy and attack anything moving, including each other."

"There's our solution. Anyone want to donate a few pints? Come on Shaker, it's for a good cause," said Lao.

"Sure, I vote we use yours," cracked Shaker.

"I second it," teased Dorna.

"Forget I said anything," said Lao.

"No, it's not a bad idea," said Hastings.

"What do you mean?" said Shaker.

"If the deaders get one of us, it takes a long time for the virus to take affect. We set a trap and get as many of them into one area as we can," said Hastings.

"And throw the wounded to them?" said Kline.

"Too cruel. We let them get into the middle with some grenades and go kamikaze. The spatter would fill the air, drive them all crazy. With luck they all rip each other to shreds and the rest of us pick off the survivors," said Hastings.

"Coldhearted," said Dorna.

"Maybe, but better dead than deader. And at least it would be quick," said Hastings.

"You going to do it if you're wounded?" asked Shaker.

Hastings paused. "I pray I have the guts, but yeah, I will."

Shaker made the mistake of locking eyes with her. He wanted to mock her, but found he couldn't so he turned away. "Let's do a recon."

The quintet checked each out each outbuilding and the main house, but all were empty.

They repeated the process for all the buildings they came across as they followed the main road into town. Fortunately deaders wandered and didn't stick to the roads. None of the searches turned up any survivors.

Cautiously, they topped a hill. "Down!" Shaker hissed into his comm and the quintet dropped to the ground. "Multiple deaders surrounding that building."

Each of the soldiers moved to get a better view. There were several animated corpses moving around the grounds in random patterns, others appeared stuck to one spot while three were loading a truck with anything they could. It was full to the point of overflowing. The soldiers dropped their breathing masks to talk easier.

"What the hell are they doing?" whispered Lao.

"That's a factory of some sort. Some of them must be pre-infection workforce stemmers. The ones loading must still be getting a signal, so they haven't stopped. The ones standing still have no signals and have reverted to standby mode. The others are victims infected with the re-animation virus," said Dorna. "Parts of that building look about ready to fall down. Looks like some of the deaders tried to make their own doors instead of using the open one. They've been know to attack buildings if they think someone is inside."

"Look at the third-floor window. A towel hanging out," said Shaker.

"So what?" said Kline.

"Back home I lived in a high rise. That's the signal for rescue in case of a fire," said Shaker.

"You think there are people in there?" said Kline.

"There's deaders sniffing around; they've got to be there for a reason. It's a good sign. Ideas for the best way in and out with any survivors?" asked Shaker.

"Blow them away and load survivors in the truck," Kline said.

"The truck I like, but a firefight is only going to attract any more deaders nearby and we have limited ammo. I think we need something quieter," said Shaker.

"Too bad I didn't have time to head back to the station and get my aftershave. They'd never smell me then," said Lao.

"I've smelled it. They'd get one whiff and they'd leave you alone rather than endure the stench," said Dorna.

"That's it," said Shaker.

"Lao's aftershave?" said Dorna.

"Better," said Shaker. "And worse. Lao, you up for something crazy?"

"Depends," said Lao.

"Follow me back to that farm. The rest of you watch the factory. If you see any humans before we get back, don't let the deaders get them," said Shaker.

"We won't," said Hastings.

It was twenty minutes before the pair returned and their comrades smelled them long before they saw their now browned uniforms and skin.

"What did you do to yourselves?" said Dorna, pulling her face filter back up and goggles down. Hastings and Kline followed suit. "Cover yourselves in shit?"

"Yep," said Shaker.

Dorna paled. "Any body fluid or solid contains the virus. You may have just infected yourselves."

"Nah, we used pig and cow shit," said Lao.

"How can you tell the difference?" she asked.

"I was raised a farm boy. Trust me, I know," said Lao. "Besides, the zombies left the animals alone. Shaker figures we don't smell like people any more so we should be able to walk past the deaders without them coming after us."

"What do you think?" said Shaker.

"That you are both nuts," said Kline.

"Actually, it makes sense. It could work," said Dorna.

"Could?" said Shaker.

Dorna smiled. "The only way you're going to know is to go down there and find out."

"No, I forbid it. We can't afford to risk forty percent of our manpower this deep in enemy territory without knowing for sure if there are people still in there," said Hastings.

"Ma'am, right now I'm in command, so it is my call. Trust me, I'm not going to die. Any deader comes near me, I'm going to blow him to pieces. If this works, we get one great big advantage over the deaders," said Shaker. "Kline, I want you to move around and take up position on the opposite side of the factory. Dorna and Hastings, watch our backs as we go in, but hold your fire unless I tell you otherwise or we're about to buy it."

Kline was given a head start and once he commed that he was in position Shaker and Lao slowly made their way down the hill, imitating the side-to-side gait of the zombies. Despite the odd way of walking, deaders could move faster than the living for short distances and almost as fast as a trained soldier over the long haul. The only advantage they had was that zombies moved by instinct, so planning could help the living get away, but not always.

The heads of the unfettered deaders and stationary stemmers turned to assess them, but none made a move as the fecally covered soldiers approached, lumbering toward the factory door. It was open to allow the loaders access. Shaker and Lao waited until the loaders passed outside, before going in. In a standard search pattern they moved through each section of the ground floor using hand signals.

"No deaders on the ground floor," whispered Shaker into his comm. So far his olfactory camouflage was working. Zombies didn't talk, so he didn't want to push their luck by risking one overhearing him speak.

The pair moved up to the second floor, secured the door they came in and repeated the process before comming the info. When they made it to the third floor, it too was clear, but there was one locked door.

"Lock the stairwell door," whisper Shaker. Lao complied and Shaker knocked on the door. "Is there anyone in there? We're here on behalf of the 142nd Starborne to evacuate the living."

There was a click and the door cracked open. An emaciated girl on the verge of her second decade looked out. "You've come to rescue me?"

"Yes, miss. I'm Shaker, this is Lao. What's your name?"

"Gail. You're soldiers?" The men's eyes darted to each other and they nodded. "Why are you covered in poop?"

"The manure is camouflage from the deaders so they can't smell us," said Shaker.

"Seems like they smell you coming sooner. Does it work?" asked Gail.

"We got in here to you with the deaders leaving us alone," said Lao.

Gail pinched her nose with her fingers. "Can't blame them for that." The girl scrutinized their emblemless uniforms. "What are your ranks?"

"We were lieutenants, but that's not important. That was very smart of you to hang the towel out the window. It helped us find you. Are you alone?" said Shaker.

"Yes. When the deaders came for us there wasn't enough time to get away. My daddy told me to lock myself up here and he tried to hold them off. That was ten days ago. I think they got him."

"Your father sounds like a very brave man and I'm sure he would be glad you survived. Is there anybody else in the building or nearby?"

"No. I was helping Daddy. As soon as the stemmers finished loading the truck, he was going to put them to bed and close up for the night. Everyone else went home. The sink still worked so I had water and we had a snack cabinet so I had a little to eat. Are you going to take me up to the battlestation?"

"Yes, but not right away. We need to gather more people first. Did you go to school?" asked Shaker. The girl nodded. "Did they teach you drills for disasters?"

"Yes."

"Where did they tell you to go?" asked Shaker.

"The basement of the school," said Gail.

"Even if you weren't at school at the time?"

Gail nodded.

"Then that's our next stop," said Shaker, looking out a window. "Those three stemmers are still loading the truck. We'll have to get it away from them. Maybe we can lock them in the factory and jump from the second floor onto the roof of the vehicle."

"I could just turn them off," said Gail.

"How?" asked Lao.

"The remote for their controllers is right below us on the second floor," said Gail. "I know the access code."

"Gail, that's an excellent idea. I want you to stay close to Lao while I check to make sure that floor is still secure."

"You have all the fun," said Lao.

"Not like I tried to give your blood away. Besides you're welcome to go outside to the truck first if you like," said Shaker.

"Thanks, you're a real pal," said Lao.

Letting the barrel of his plasma rifle lead the way, Shaker went down the stairs, scrutinizing every shadow. Only darkness looked back so he whispered into his comm. "Second floor still secured."

"We're coming down now," said Lao.

Despite the two soldiers as protection, the girl looked around nervously, as if to double check there were no zombies lurking. She opened a closet door, revealing a rectangular metal box about the half the size of a full military pack. The top was a standard computer keypad with another twenty buttons for preprogrammed actions. There was a view screen and a touch pad that tied into satellite GPS to make large-scale movements easier to program.

The girl tapped in the access code as both men watched. "It's easy to remember. *Gail is the best.*" Her eyes teared up. "Do you think my Dad is out there as a deader?"

"Depends how hungry—" Lao said, but Shaker elbowed him in the gut.

"If he is, it's only his body. The part of him that was your father has gone to a better place," said Shaker.

The girl hit the first preprogrammed button. It had the word *bed* written on it. She held a long yellow bar with her thumb as she did it. A dial allowed a single stemmer or a programmed group to be singled out. The bar ensured the commands were transmitted to all the dead workers. A glance out the window showed all the stemmers stopping their previous activities and walking into the ground floor. Shaker and Lao opened the landing door and watched as each walked into a bed, which looked like a cross between an upright coffin and an old-fashioned phone booth. The chambers leaned back at a thirty-degree angle and each stemmer climbed in and pulled the door closed behind them. A click was heard as each door self-locked.

Gail sighed as the last one closed. "The stemmers have all been put to bed."

"Why does each bed have a window by the face? So you can monitor them?" asked Shaker.

"Sure, so we know that none are wandering around with a damaged controller, but also some of the stemmers freak out if we don't leave them a way to see. The beds hold them, but given time they could break out and damage them. They're expensive, which is why not all the factories use them," said Gail.

"What do they do with their stemmers?" asked Lao.

"Usually lock them in a storeroom in default mode," said Gail.

"Gail, we're going to take you out to the truck, but I'd like to cover you with this shi . . . manure first," said Shaker, toning down his language in front of the girl, who made a face at the idea. "I know it's pretty disgusting, but it seems to work. We don't want any deader to catch your scent and follow us."

Gail reluctantly agreed and each man scraped some fecal matter off himself to spread on the girl. They instructed her to copy the deader walk. This time Lao took the lead. The zombie victims were on the far side of the lot and they were able to get to the truck unaccosted.

Unfortunately, the olfactory camouflage only worked to a limited degree. The sound of the motor turning over was enough to cause every deader in the area to make a beeline for them. Fortunately the truck turned over on the second try and they were able to drive to the road before any deader reached them. One came close to cutting the truck off near the exit, but Lao swerved and avoided him.

The sight made Gail gasp and freeze up. Realizing what had happened Shaker opened his arms and the girl collapsed on his chest sobbing. "Oh Daddy . . ."

"Just one?" whispered Kline. Gail was ten feet away, chowing down on some rations they had given her.

"We have to start somewhere," said Lao.

"And I think that somewhere is the Knob Lick school. It is big and includes the town hall," said Shaker. "But the truck is a bad idea."

Deaders from all over the countryside had swarmed toward the sound of the engine. They ended up having to speed up, jam the gas pedal on a straightaway, and jump out to lose the walking corpses.

"I do, however, have another brilliant idea," said Shaker.

"Your last one was a dozy, but it worked," said Hastings. "What's this one?"

"That factory has ten stemmers and a remote. It weighs about twenty pounds," said Shaker.

"We don't need the extra ballast and it won't do a thing to the deaders," said Hastings.

"True, but you were complaining about our lack of manpower. What if we used the stemmer workforce as cannon fodder?" said Shaker.

"Explain," said Hastings.

"They don't have military-grade stems, but we can program in some basic martial moves and send them in ahead of us to distract and hurt the infected deaders," said Shaker.

"You think we can get them to do enough damage to destroy deaders?" said Hastings.

"Maybe. The reanimated are almost three times stronger that they were when they were living. If we move them in formation, who knows?" said Shaker.

"It gives us a long-distance weapon that doesn't make noise. I like it Lieuten . . . Shaker," said Hastings, correcting herself. "If Benedict doesn't reinstate you as an officer for this idea, I'll kick his ass myself."

"Thank you, ma'am," Shaker said with a smile, some of their old comaraderie reasserting itself.

"I have an idea to make it even better," said Dorna. "We use our spare surface-to-orbit antenna to boost the signal and send out a general command for any other stemmers to follow us."

"We could end up with our own army," said Lao.

"Of course, this will take some special programming and there's one of us with a better shot that the rest," said Shaker, looking at Dorna.

"I assumed I'd do it," said Dorna.

"But we have to go get it and you'd have come along to make sure we take everything we need the first time," said Shaker.

"Fine, I'll go," said Dorna, confused about why he was re-stating the obvious.

"Unfortunately, you haven't been properly camouflaged yet," said Shaker.

"Oh, no," said Dorna, realization dawning.

"And we didn't bring back any extra manure . . ."

Dorna saw the evil smile on Shaker's face and spun to run, bumping into Lao.

"But we're willing to share," said Lao, two handfuls already scraped off himself.

The two men playfully caught the woman between them and bounced her back and forth, covering her in the manure as they did so.

Again against Hastings's protests, they spilt up again, Shaker and Dorna returning to the factory, Lao going back to the farm to get more manure, leaving Hastings and Kline to protect the girl. Hastings took Gail aside and made her strip down, out of sight of Kline, to check for any wounds that might indicate deader infection. The girl was clean.

Lao was back long before the other two. He had commandeered a wheelbarrow and filled it to capacity. With more than a little reluctance, Hastings and Kline put on their stinking camouflage.

"We're coming in and we have company, so hold your fire," came Shaker over the comm.

The soldiers watched as ten reanimated corpses came over the distant ridge in a formation that would never pass muster in the Host, but was impressive for a group of corpses. They stopped far enough away from the soldiers and their ward so as not to traumatize the girl.

"It worked?" said Kline.

Dorna was smiles ear to ear, like a kid with a new toy. "It took a while to reprogram the controller. I was limited in how many new movement patterns I could add in, so I had to see what was already programmed and what I could do with those. I've got them ready to engage the enemy and provide distractions." She gave everyone a crash course in how to use the controls, as well as the emergency stop button she had programmed just in case.

"Gail, please show us where the school is," said Shaker.

Bringing the wheelbarrow and the zombie brigade with them, the quintet plus one moved slowly toward the town proper. They would have been able to find the town's survivors without the girl's help. Upwards of seventy deaders had surrounded one of the buildings. It was not a military siege in the traditional sense of continual bombardment or attack, but it had cut off all supplies to the living, so the end result would be the same. Most of the deaders milled around, with one occasionally attacking the building near the air vents. When one started, the rest followed. Eventually they ceased when the walls did not fall and returned to milling, but it was obvious they had done a lot of structural damage. There were more reanimated here. This group appeared more focused on finding a way in and it showed. This building was in far worse shape than the factory. Whole sections of wall had started to crumble.

"I don't think we have enough manure," whispered Lao.

"Or ammo," said Dorna.

"That's enough talk about what we don't have," barked Hastings. "What we do have is frightened people who are going to die of starvation if we don't get them out. We need to drive a wedge through the deaders' ranks and gain an access to the building that we can secure behind us. We use Dorna's stemmers to march in and push them back, trying to hurt as many as they can, or at least make a wide enough hole for us to get through. Then we have to get inside the building and secure the entrance behind us." Hastings stole a glance at the girl, who was sitting nearby. "And keep the girl safe."

"Suggestions?" said Shaker.

"We find a place to hide and secure the girl and come back for her," said Hastings.

"I don't like the idea of leaving her behind," said Shaker.

"You think I do? For all we know, she's the only survivor in Knob Lick," whispered Hastings.

"And Benedict won't let us back if we don't get at least fifty people," said Kline.

"Fuck Benedict. If she's all we can find, he'll damn well come pick her up. He can leave us, but he won't punish a child for my sins," said Hastings, for the first time admitting out loud that she had made a mistake in not rescuing the citizens of Ozark. "Or anybody else. We comm for evac no matter how many survivors we find inside. We risk their lives the longer they're dirtside."

Shaker hesitated, then said, "Ma'am . . . would you like to assume command of the assault? You're the only one of us with battlefield command experience."

"Which was not long after the lot of you were out of diapers. No, you were right to take command of this team. I've screwed up these people's lives. I'll do what I can, but I'm not going to take your first command away from you. Especially when you are doing such a good job of it."

"Thank you, ma'am. It means a lot," said Shaker.

Hastings nodded at him. "I will offer some advice, however. If we can enter through one of the windows on an upper floor, we will have a better chance of keeping the deaders out."

"I was thinking the same thing," said Shaker.

"I can rig a grappling hook to our belt lines and we can scale the wall," said Lao.

"Or we can search for an extension ladder," said Dorna.

"Well, if you want to do things the easy way," replied Lao with a smile.

"They keep the ladders in the tool shed," said Gail, who had walked over to hear better. "Do you think you can get everyone out?"

"We're going to try . . ." started Shaker.

"Absolutely," said Hastings. "Problem is, we have to keep you safe, and bringing you with us to take the building isn't going to do that."

"I don't want to be left alone," Gail said.

"I understand, but if we leave someone behind with you, there is less chance of us living long enough to get to the people inside the building. The shed looks strong. We could have you lock it from the inside and open it when we come back for you," said Hastings. "How does that sound?"

"Scary," said Gail.

"Good. Scared is good. It'll make you careful, help keep you alive." Hastings took out her personal sidearm, took off the safety, and handed it to the girl. "Do you know how to shoot?"

Gail nodded. "My daddy taught me."

"Good. This has twenty shots. Only use them if you have to. The noise will attract more deaders."

"But you'll come back for me?" asked Gail.

"We will," said Shaker.

"You have my word that we will not leave you behind," said Hastings.

"Okay," said Gail.

Dorna used her stemmers to move into the masses of deaders and attack. The best the remote could manage was randomized blows which were almost totally ineffective, so Dorna changed tactics and had the stemmers run away as living-like as the programming would allow. The fast, sudden movement triggered the prey centers of their reanimated brains and they gave chase, leaving only a handful of stragglers at the east side of the building. The quintet moved quickly with the girl between them toward the shed. Lao used his Host-issued multi-tool to cut the lock.

Luck smiled as they pulled out an extension ladder. Hastings helped Gail get inside and showed her how to lock the doors using the chain and a bolt.

"You'll be back for me?" she asked again, nervously.

Hastings made an X over her chest with her index finger. "Cross my heart. Do not open this door unless one of us tells you to."

Gail nodded and Hastings shut the door.

The quintet made a mistake by running for the wall. One of the stragglers caught the movement out of the corner of his eyes and came after them.

"Incoming five o'clock," said Kline.

"Everyone up the ladder as soon as we have it standing," said Shaker.

Lao and Shaker laid it so the top was on the sill of a third floor window.

"Go," shouted Shaker, hitting Lao on the back. Lao climbed as fast as he could, smashing the glass with the butt of his plasma rifle, using his gloves to clear out the shards before climbing in.

Next up was Dorna. She left the remote below the window, but had the far end of her belt line hooked to the device. Once she was in, she reeling it up after her.

Next up was Kline, but the deader had crossed the school field and was, approaching the soldiers.

"Damn," said Hastings and shot out both the dead man's knees. It stopped his approach, but the shot of the plasma round was heard by more of the reanimated, who now converged on their position. While the first had been moving as a leisurely searching pace, the others were now racing, as were others from around the town. "Go!"

Shaker shook his head. "My command. You go, I'll be right behind you."

"Damn straight you will be," said Hastings, pulling out her retractable beltline and hooked the clip on the back of Shaker's battle belt. "I'll pull you up, you pick off those deaders."

Shaker nodded and sat on the ladder, his back to the building. Hastings climbed up, pulling the larger man behind her. The rungs were of the self-turning variety, which made the task much easier, but still a challenge for the fifty-plus-year-old woman.

Shaker started shooting the nearest zombies and learned that Benedict hadn't been kidding when he told them a firefight with deaders was something you never got used to. When facing down weapons that can cut them in two, human foes, and even most of the other monsters, will take cover or at least flinch as they are turned into chopped meat. The reanimated were drawn to the noise of gunfire like moths to a zapper, so shooting them only increased the frenzy of their attack. Firing at them was the one way to make sure a soldier attracted the most attention from deaders. The zombies in the back would rip apart the reanimated in front of them for a chance at gunner chow. Of course, not shooting them tended to allow the reanimated to either eat or convert their human foes. Usually both.

Hastings barely climbed fast enough to keep Shaker out of zombie hands. The hungry dead tended to be weaker at higher motor functions. That didn't mean they couldn't climb ladders; it just meant they didn't do it pretty. One tried to walk up it and fell through the rungs, so the next one managed to step over him with one foot before tripping face first. His fall allowed the female dead next in line to walk over him to get closer to the soldiers.

Fortunately, by this point Hastings was already through the window, yanking Shaker in behind her.

"Lift the ladder. Shake and shoot 'em off!" ordered Hastings. Working together, the quintet pulled back and pushed down, lifting the ladder and the three trapped deaders off the ground. The next wave of dead men and women reached up and pulled down hard enough to lift all five soldiers off the floor.

Shaker and Hastings let go and opened fire, tearing the zombies on and below the ladder to bits of bone, muscle, and organ jelly. The trio of soldiers who were still holding the ladder dropped down and pulled it inside the window.

"Try not to touch that end," said Dorna. "Big contamination risk."

"Let's secure this building ASAP and check the basement shelter," said Shaker.

"Do we need to guard this exit point?" asked Kline.

"No way deaders should be able to climb up the side of the building," said Dorna.

"We go down one floor at a time," said Shaker.

And they did. The upper floors were good, but the first floor had been compromised in several sections, too many for a five-person force to secure, so they locked the steel fire doors from the stairwell to the first floor before descending to the basement.

Shaker looked to Hastings, but the older woman nodded for him to do the honors, so he knocked.

"Host forces here. Is anyone alive in there?" asked Shaker. "We have the area secured."

A bolt scrapped against metal as it was drawn back and the door opened a crack, just enough for a man with a bearded face to verify Shaker's words.

"Oh, thank God. I'm John Ruddy, the mayor." He looked up. "Colonel Hastings? You came down for us yourself?"

"How many are in there with you?" said Hastings, ignoring the reference to her former rank.

"We lost part of the town. We got as many as we could in the shelter. There's six hundred and twelve of us in here." Each of the quintet's faces lit up at how many survivors there were. "And we've been out of rations for two days," said Ruddy.

"Mayor, we're going to need to get everyone up to the roof for evac. I'll need those of you who can still walk to help those who can't," said Shaker. "Kline, call for some Harpies."

"Yes, sir," said Kline, using his long-range comm as the others helped the townspeople to the stairwell. Twenty minutes later, all the civilians were topside on the school roof, instructed to lie down in the center and stay away from the edges. That gave the soldiers access to watch or fire at the deaders. The civilians took up almost half of the open space. Although there was fear on their faces, there was also relief at having someone else take charge.

"Kline, where's the Harpy?" said Shaker.

"*Kyklopes* control said ETA is two hours," said Kline.

"Why so long?" asked Lao.

"Coordinating drop sites," said Kline, shrugging in apology.

"I hope we have that long," said Dorna, looking over the roof's edge. "The deaders are in a frenzy. They can see, hear, and smell the civilians and the original damage to the building may be worse than we thought. They are literally tearing apart the south side of the building. They keep this up and that entire wall could collapse and bring part of the roof down with it."

Shaker joined her at roof's edge. "Damn it. We're trapped. We're only five floors up. That wall falls and they might be able to use the rubble and exposed structure to climb up to get us."

"Be quieter," whispered Dorna. "You'll panic the civies."

Hastings grabbed the long-range comm from Kline. "*Kyklopes* Control this is Colonel Hastings."

"Ma'am, you know your rank was stripped . . ." The air jockey's tone was polite, but there was a condescending edge to it.

"Shut the hell up and listen. We have six hundred plus civilians on a rooftop of a damaged building in Knob Lick that is in danger of collapse and is being overrun by deaders. We will lose the goddamned civies if we don't have a Harpy at our position in fifteen," said Hastings.

"I'm sorry, only Major Benedict has the authority to change pickup schedules," said the voice at control, without a hint of actual regret in his tone. In fact, Hastings heard a few sniggers in the background at having the architect of this disaster screwed by it.

"Then put Benedict on now," ordered Hastings.

"The Major is busy right now. I will make sure he gets the message," said Control. Hastings could practically see the smirk on his face.

"Just because I screwed up, don't punish these people," pleaded Hastings.

"Pickup will be when scheduled," said Control, too politely.

"Either you put Hans on this channel in thirty seconds or I relay what happened on Cascade on a planet-wide broadcast," said Hastings.

"You don't have the signal power . . ."

"But I can tap into the civilian system and broadcast on all channels. Hans cut me out of *Kyklopes*, but that does nothing for my personal access code for the planetary system," said Hastings.

"Maybe if you told me what the information was . . ." The voice on the other end had lost its cockiness and sounded nervous.

"Keep me on hold another twenty seconds and you'll find out along with everyone else," said Hastings.

In nineteen tocks Benedict was on the line. "Andie, what the hell are you doing? A Host officer even speaking of Cascade can be given the death penalty."

"As you know, I am no longer an officer of the Host," said Hastings.

"You could still be put to death," said Benedict.

"By who? You? That would mean you breaking your word when you promised not to kill any of my crew. Hans Benedict may be a traitor to the Sway, but an oath breaker? Come now," said Hastings. "Besides the way things are going, I'll probably be dead before you get your chance."

"What do you want?" sighed Benedict. She knew that tone and in her mind's eye she could see him running both hands through the stubble on the top of his head in frustration.

"Emergency evac for our civilians," said Hastings. "Your control boys have been dicking me around. My civilians are about to become deader food."

"Andie, I'm sorry but you'll have to hold the line. There are plenty waiting ahead of you. We have to take largest numbers first. One group has three hundred plus. Two groups have more than two hundred," said Benedict. "You have sixty."

"Hans, I have over six hundred," said Hastings. The line went to dead silence. "Hans?"

Dead air broadcast for another minute before Benedict came back on. "Andie, you have my sincerest apology. You were being screwed with by members of my crew who didn't think my amnesty was good enough for you. I was told you only had sixty. The people who did this are on the way to the brig and you have two Harpies en route to Knob Lick. ETA eighteen minutes."

"Good. Tell them to burn fumes."

"Andie?" said Benedict.

"What?" said Hastings.

"Nice job. I knew you were still in there somewhere. Sorry I pulled a gun on you," said Benedict.

"Don't be. You were right. Maybe having the only man I ever loved threaten my life was what I needed to wake me up," said Hastings.

Benedict was notoriously poorly versed in the sharing of emotions normally necessary in personal relationships, being of the actions-speak louder-than-words philosophy. "Andie, I didn't . . . You never said . . ."

"Past tense, Hans. Hastings out." Turning to the assembled townspeople, she said, "Harpies will be touching down in less than eighteen. We will get the weak and injured on the first drop ship, everyone else on the second." Hastings' eyes went wide. "We don't have everyone yet. We have to get Gail."

"Ma'am, look at them down there. It's suicide. We have to wait for the drop ship and use their guns to clear the deaders out," said Shaker.

Hastings hesitated, looking out across the field and frowned at what she saw. "She doesn't have that kind of time. Look."

In their frenzy, the reanimated had accidentally knocked holes in the wooden shed the girl was hiding in. In a very human reaction, Gail made the mistake of screaming once. She instantly quieted, but it was enough for a few nearby zombies to turn their attention on the shed. The front and side walls would be kindling before very long.

"We have to get her," said Hastings.

"It'll be suicide," said Shaker. "And it would leave the rest of the civies unprotected."

"You're right," said Hastings. "But I gave her my word. You hold the line. I'll get her."

"Ma'am, I forbid it," said Shaker.

Hastings grinned. "Is that an order, James?"

"Yes, ma'am, it is," said Shaker.

"Put me on report then," said Hastings. "Dorna, bring your want-to-be stem soldiers around here. What's their ETA?"

"Three minutes work?" asked Dorna.

"Not really, so you'll have to try to come behind and get us an exit. Maybe an old-fashioned wagon circling strategy," said Hastings.

"Already working on programming the moves," said Dorna.

Hastings nodded. "Kline, give me the end of your belt line."

"Why?" said Kline.

"Once Dorna gets us back to the building, I'm going to hook it to Gail and you lot are going to pull her up here," said Hastings.

"No, we'll use it to pull both of you back up here," said Shaker.

"Works for me. Just because I'm going on a suicide run doesn't mean I want to die," said Hastings. "Everyone but Lao get a rake ready to blow those deaders to hell."

Warfare always advanced weapons design. Host soldiers carried grenades and rakes. Each was designed so shrapnel from the initial explosion exploded seconds after contact with oxygen, giving lots of deadly second chances. Smaller bits of metal were also harder for a field surgeon or medic to remove, and nicked more arteries.

Rocket launchers were still used for heavily armored targets, but for the average soldier in the field they were too bulky. Rakes were the optimal solution, the marriage of missile and grenade. Pulling the pin ignited the formerly inert solid fuel, turning it into a rocket. Sensors in the nose held off exploding in less dense materials like flesh in favor of letting the propulsion system rip enemies to shreds. A rake explosion made a grenade look like a cream pie. They weren't used without something very solid between the launcher and the target. Each soldier carried a half dozen, one on the outside of each thigh and four on their battle belts. That left room on the belts for four grenades.

"Why not me? Hell, I can get a grenade as far as a rake. I have the best arm on the station," said Lao.

"I know. I saw your baseball stats as part of your academy records before you even arrived on *Kyklopes*. How else do you think I knew enough to pick a ringer for my softball team?" said Hastings.

"Battlestation champs three years running," said Lao, flexing his shoulder.

"The noise of the rakes and the cover fire these three are going to lay down to cover my ass is going to attract deaders by the dozens. I want you to lob grenades off the far side of the building as far away as you can manage at reasonable intervals once our rakes are spent. With luck the dueling noise will confuse them or they'll go toward the louder explosions, which will hopefully have the added bonus of stopping their destruction of the building. Everyone give Lao three of your grenades. I of course expect you to try for maximum deader damage with each toss rather than wasting them purely for a distraction," said Hastings.

"I won't let you down, ma'am," said Lao.

"I know you won't, Flauker," said Hastings. "Now let's tenderize us some deaders."

Four rakes did a nice job clearing the field, but they were limited in that the soldiers didn't want them going off too close to the already weakened walls of the school or the rapidly splintering wood of the tool shed. Human soldiers would be corpses or at least bleeding out after the barrage from the hand missiles. Many of the deaders had lost enough parts to make locomotion difficult, but some were managing, their limbs hanging on by slivers of tendons.

Hastings lowered herself by her primary beltline to the ground, pulling the end of Kline's line with her. The first explosion from the far side of the school covered the sound of her plasma round to the pelvis of a deader that had spotted her. It blew apart the bones so the legs had nothing to stabilize them and the zombie collapsed to the ground. A second round to the head stopped it from crawling after her as she cut her line to run toward the shed. The half dozen deaders nearest to the wooden shack were untouched. Getting them would have meant risking killing the girl. None of them left their positions because their primitive brains knew there was prey inside the shed, so they were not distracted by things that went boom.

Adrenaline pumping through her let Hastings move like a woman half her age, closing the gap and picking off two zombies with as many shots, blowing gray matter in streams through the exit wounds in the opposite sides of their skulls.

"Gail, it's me. Get ready to open the door," shouted Hastings, pulling a deader back by its head before putting a plasma round through its brainstem. At the sound of Hastings's voice two others turned toward her, forcing Hastings to drop to the ground and roll, shooting out their knees but they fell upon her with hands and jaws, grabbing at her legs in a hunger-driven frenzy. Hastings kicked for all she was worth and stood, stumbling back. The zombies stood and lumbered after her, when suddenly both heads exploded with rounds shot from the school rooftop.

"We've got your back, ma'am," said Kline on the comm.

"And to think you only gave me average on my marksman annual," said Shaker.

"I stick with that grade. If you were a superior shot, you could have lined up the deaders to take them both with one round," teased Hastings.

"That mean you want us to hold back and take multiple targets per round if another deader approaches you?" shot back Shaker.

"Hell, no. Take as many as you need," said Hastings. "One left."

"Too close to the girl for us to try," said Shaker.

"No worries. He's mine," said Hastings.

The remaining deader had made a hole in the shed large enough for his head and torso to fit through. Gail's scream caused Hastings to lunge forward, but the single shot to the deader's head stopped her short.

The sidearm Hastings had given to the girl had more traditional ammunition so the single shot was not enough to destroy its brain, but it caused the dead thing to fall twitching its arms and legs. Hastings grabbed him by the feet, pulled his convulsing corpse back and put a plasma round in his head for good measure.

"Ma'am, our stemmers are converging on you. Don't shoot them," said Dorna.

"Roger that," said Hastings. "Gail, open the door. We have to go now."

The girl did as instructed and threw herself into Hastings arms. The woman found herself smiling. "You came back for me, even with all those deaders. I thought you'd leave me."

"I promised you I'd be back. I was . . . I *am* an officer of the Host, and our word means something," said Hastings, scooping up the girl so Gail's arms were wrapped around her neck with her legs squeezing her waist. "You did good with that gun. I'm proud of you."

"Thank you," said Gail with a small smile, which was frightened off her face by ten zombies marching in formation in front of them.

Hasting comm chirped with Dorna's voice. "Ma'am, our stemmers are right behind you."

"Gail, these are the stemmers from your factory. They are going to walk us back to the building. I'm going to hook you to a line and my team will pull you up to the roof. Two drop ships will be here any minute to take you to the station. I'm going to ask you a favor."

"What?"

"I want you to hold onto me with your arms and legs. Put you head into my shoulders and keep your eyes closed. Can you trust me to do that?"

The girl nodded, but held the gun up. "But if I keep my eyes open, I can shoot any deaders that try to sneak up behind you."

Hastings gently took the weapon, put on the safety and returned it to her holster as the controlled zombies encompassed them in a circle. "Let's compromise. You shout if you see any and I'll blow them to hell. Deal?"

"Okay."

"Dorna, we're moving out. Have your wannabe stem soldiers double time it. Gentlemen, prove my station board assessment of your sniper skills to be a gross underestimate and keep any deaders from us," said Hastings.

"Will do, ma'am," said Shaker. "Be aware, you have deaders approaching you from seven, five, and three o'clock." The familiar sounds of plasma rounds rang out as Shaker and Kline tried to lessen the numbers of reanimated approaching, but all their shooting only made a dent.

"Dorna, make these stemmers run," yelled Hastings into her comm.

"I can't manage that and keep them in formation around you," said Dorna.

"Well, we saw that you haven't figured our how to make them fight worth a damn yet. They'll only slow the other deaders for a moment since they ain't doing much by way of camouflage. Any chance of you coming up with anything more martial in the next thirty seconds?" said Hastings.

"Nope," said Dorna.

"Okay, then I'm leaving the wagon circle and triple timing it to you. Scatter the stemmers to confuse the enemy," ordered Hastings.

"But . . ."

"Here we come," said Hastings, sprinting for all she was worth, but the longer the battle went on, the lower that value went. Command had made her lazy in regards to her personal workouts and that led to weak and slow. Even considering that the artificial gravity on *Kyklopes* was set at about five percent higher than the planet below it, Hastings was not physically fit for combat. The deaders, however were augmented by whatever hellish science had created the reanimation virus, making even the slowest of them faster than a former battlestation commander carrying a child. No matter how fast she pushed her burning legs, the only way she'd be guaranteed of beating the zombies was to lose the seventy pounds that was holding onto her for dear life.

To Andie Hastings's credit, the thought of dropping the girl never even occurred to her. The command decision to follow protocol and abandon Ozark was never one she took easily, but after the assumed destruction of Earth and most of the Host fleet, she let fear goad her into not making the tougher choice. Being back on a battlefield changed her. The woman who sat in *Kyklopes's* command chair had been accepting of her duty to put others in harms way while she remained safe. The Hastings on the battlefield at Knob Lick wasn't.

So when Andie Hastings realized she wasn't going to make it, she came up with a plan that would never have crossed the mind of Colonel Hastings.

"Gail, I'm going to need to put you down. You are going to have to run to the school. Straight ahead of you there is a line with a hook. Put it on your belt and hold on. Kline will pull you up," said Hastings.

"What about you?" asked Gail.

"I'm going to slow these deaders down a bit. Now git," said Hastings.

The girl obeyed and ran for the wall. Deaders saw her and realized she was the easier of their meal choices, altering their course accordingly. So did Hastings, firing plasma rounds as she did so.

"Ma'am, what are you doing?" yelled Shaker, who was still frantically firing at the encroaching deaders.

"Keeping my word. That girl is the first one on a Harpy, James, understood?" said Hastings, firing at the zombies closest to her. "Don't make a liar out of me."

"I won't, ma'am," said Shaker. "I'm lowering my belt line for you. I expect you to use it as soon as the girl passes the second floor."

Hastings actually grinned as she replied. "Yes, sir."

"I'm out of grenades," commed Lao. "The deaders are coming around the south end and they are starting to attack the weakened wall again." There was a loud crash and a cloud of dusts. "Correction, they've torn the wall down." The sound of Lao's plasma rifle firing thundered through the air. "My shots are only attracting more of them. The rubble buried a couple, but the rest are using it to climb up. They're using the exposed floors and support beams for hand and foot holds. We're up crap creek without a boat."

"I've got Gail," yelled Kline.

"Hastings, attach my line!" ordered Shaker.

The former commander turned and leapt for the line, holding on with one hand while clipping it on with the other. Shaker braced himself and activated the belt winch, pulling his teammate up the side of the school.

One deader took that time to recall that his body could once jump and leapt after the rising woman, managing to get his undead hands around her right boot.

"Son of a bitch," said Hastings, kicking out with both feet to dislodge her passenger. "I got a hitchhiker and he ain't shaking."

Unable to use her rifle at close range without risking blowing off her own feet, Hastings grabbed for her sidearm and emptied it into the deader. She missed the head, but blew apart his shoulder, which weakened his grip enough for her to kick him loose.

"Nice job, Hastings," said Shaker, pulling her over the top of the roof.

"Can't argue with you and I can't tell you how happy I am to be back safe and sound," said Hastings.

"Oh no," said Dorna, her eyes on the former colonel's knee. The uniform between the side of her shin guard and knee body armor was torn and bloody.

Hastings looked down. "Crap, I didn't even feel that." Shaker moved to help her, but she held her hand up and said what they were all thinking. "Stop, I might be inflicted."

"It could be a secondary wound," said Dorna.

"I pray you're right." Bending over, Hastings tore apart her pant leg to reveal the wound. "Damn, that's where those two were going at me when I was on the ground." Reaching inside a belt pouch, she took out a piece of what looked like old-fashioned litmus paper and thrust it in the wound. And like its scientific forebearer, it changed color when positive, only instead of acid or base, it tested for the reanimation virus.

Hastings pulled it up for all to see. There was no nice blue or pink color. The Host was far too literal to have developed something falsely cheerful like that.

"Oh shit. Black," said Shaker.

"I'm so sorry," said Dorna.

"Me too," said Hastings.

"Deader!" yelled Kline as a dead head cleared the rubble on the far side of the roof. The soldier emptied a plasma round between his eyes, causing him to tumble back down the five stories. The civilians who had been dutifully keeping their heads down during the entire battle screamed and scuttled further away.

All their comms chirped. "Attention rescue party Zed, this is Harpy *Alexander*. We and Harpy *Gilgamesh* are converging on your position. What is your status?"

"Ready for the civies to board," answered Hastings. "But the deaders have breached the roof. They will be held off until boarding is complete."

"Do you require our drop team's assistance?"

"Too little too late, *Alexander*," said Hastings.

"And your team?"

"Four to board," said Hastings.

"I'm sorry, Zed, whom did you lose?"

"Me. Hastings out."

"There's got to be something..." started Dorna.

"But there's not. I'll hold the roof," said Hastings.

Shaker nodded, then bowed his head. Carefully, he removed his remaining grenade and his last plasma round clip, then handed them to his former commanding officer. Dorna, then Kline followed suit, handing over their last grenades and clips. Lao, having used all his grenades, handed her his remaining rakes.

"If you're going to go out with a bang, might as well make it a big one," said Lao.

"Amen," said Hastings.

"Ma'am, it is an honor to be able to say that I have now truly served with you," said Shaker.

"Thank you," said Hastings as she secured the incendiaries.

"Colonel on deck," shouted Lao, snapping to attention, his right hand held high in salute. Shaker, Kline, and Dorna followed suit.

Hastings returned and held the salute for a moment before yelling, "The lot of you do me proud. Dismissed."

Hastings took out her knife and cut her exposed skin so she'd be as bloody as possible as she used her secondary belt line to descend the five floors to the enemy below, hoping for a good, strong breeze to carry her scent to as many deaders as possible. She shot off three climbers on her way down.

Shaker made sure Gail was the first to board *Alexander* and, with the help of the drop crew, it didn't take ten minutes to load all the civilians onto both drop ships. The quartet were the last to board *Gilgamesh*.

As soon as the ship was airborne, a tremendous explosion rocked the far side of the school building, able to be heard even inside the drop ship. Shaker, Lao, and Kline stiffened and bowed their heads. Dorna put her head on Shaker's shoulder and sobbed.

JUNKED
A Combat K Adventure
Andy Remic

T HE SLAM CRUISER HOWLED THROUGH THE UPPER ATMOSPHERE OF RYZOR, buffeted by an enraged storm. Lightning sparkling from armoured hull shells in crackles. Iron bruise clouds closed around the SLAM like a fist around a pebble, holding it tight for a frozen moment before flinging it down in a violent acceleration...

"We're gonna die," moaned Franco, curled fetal in his CrashCouch, forehead touching his knees, beard rimed with droplets of sweat and vibrating vigorously. He clutched his Kekra quad-barrel machine pistol to his chest, as a mother would a weary child.

"Don't be such a pussy," snarled Pippa, glaring at Franco with cold eyes. The female member of this particular Combat K squad, Pippa was low on empathy and understanding, high on the twin goals of violence and destruction. "You knew we were breaching the storm, dickhead. What did you expect, sunshine?"

"I would have preferred a scanty-clad welcome party of thong-strapped, lap-dancing beauties," said Franco, without any hint of sarcasm. "Either that, or a good pub. Maybe a tastefully decorated brothel." He glanced up, making eye contact with Pippa who was battling the SLAM cruiser's controls. "Hey, actually, now we're on the subject of sex, what about you and I . . ."

"No."

"You don't know what I was going to suggest."

"Yeah I do, Franco. You're a sexual deviant, and I've suffered enough depraved suggestions to last any woman, whore, or gal-slacker a lifetime. Just stay in your couch, focus on the mission, and keep your paws off my arse."

Franco mumbled, and closed his eyes as the SLAM rattled violently, huge shudders juddering corrugated walls, buffeted by Nature. Nature was in a foul mood. She was good and ready for a spot of fisticuffs.

"Coming in fast, Keenan. Bang goes our covert entry."

Keenan reclined, one army boot on the console, drawing on a home-rolled smoke filled with harsh Widow Maker tobacco. He gave a single nod, rubbed weary eyes. "They'll not scan shit in this storm," he drawled on an exhalation of diesel smoke. "Drop us vertical under the Beacon Scanners, an' we'll cruise up the river and go in light. I doubt General Zenab is hard to find; the Junks will be treating the bastard like a king."

Combat K were elite, murderous combat squads trained by the Quad-Gal Military specializing in interrogation, infiltration, assassination and detonation. Their original game-plan had been simple: to end The Helix War, which had raged for a thousand years. However, after QGM quelled one conflict, so another had taken its place—in the form of *junks,* a twisted, hazardous species of deviated aliens, a toxic race intent on polluting the Quad-Gal with their infestation—and wiping out *all* species in the process.

Once believed extinct, the junks had reappeared on Galhari, a quiet fringe planet, with devastating suddenness...in a flood of *millions.* The planet had been taken in hours, and from that foothold the junks began a galaxy-wide conquest which had, in all honesty, gone *bad* for Quad-Gal Military. Recently, a series of freak coincidences led to military intelligence uncovering a source of the junk's expertise: a psychic general, capable of reading minds across the Four Galaxies and uncovering QGM's secret plans. Named Zenab, the general was also rumored to have invented a Nano-Bomb, a microscopic detonation device which could put QGM out of the game for good. Zenab was making it possible for the junks to extend their diseased and toxic empire, and had set up camp in his Nano-Bomb Factory. Now, it was Combat K's mission to take him out . . . before millions more died.

"Tipping in now," said Pippa.

The SLAM's engines quietened and it fell vertical, accelerating through high-altitude rage toward the smash of jungle canopy below. Like a meteorite they plummeted, the ship's computers masking their profile and using a radioactive Doppelganger Shift to pre-empt rogue AI SAMs.

Without incident, the SLAM reached a half klick above the rain-lashed jungle, and engines suddenly roared, energy *whumping* against trees and blasting a crater fifty metres wide. Every tree in the radius was shredded, instantly. The SLAM levelled out, stabilizers grunting, and settled into the crater. Engines died. Rain played drumbeats on the hull, and Franco uncurled from his CrashCouch and glared at Pippa with a teenage pout. "Not exactly what I'd call smooth," he said.

"Get to shit, Franco. I'd like to see you do better."

"Actually, they don't call me Franco "Ace Pilot" Haggis for nothing, chipmunk."

Keenan placed a hand on Pippa's shoulder, and smiled into her blossoming wrath. Relax, said that smile. Chill. There are more important things than Franco's attitude.

Keenan stood, stretched, and removing his cigarette, which he stubbed into a whirring mechanical ashtray with six metal fingers which took the weed and crushed it into recyclable pulp, said, "Let's tool up."

The ramp hit the blasted jungle crater, and Combat K descended, guns primed, covering one another's arcs of fire with a practiced finesse. Pippa held a PAD computer alongside her D5 shotgun. "All clear," she said, expert eyes reading the scanner.

They stepped into the rain and a cool wind, and were instantly drenched. In one fist Franco carried a small black ball, which appeared to be made from rubber. It gleamed in the rain.

They crossed the crater, climbed slick mud sides, and moved efficiently into the jungle, a well-oiled military machine, with Keenan walking point, Pippa scanning central, and Franco, complaining as usual in a mumbling mutter, bringing up the rear. He had three D5 shotguns on his back, a military porcupine, a Kekra quad-barrel in one fist, and a Bausch & Harris sniper rifle strapped to his pack. As was usual, Franco was terribly over-tooled for the mission—but he wouldn't have it any other way. He'd been in a savage fire-fight once and run out of ammo; it hadn't been a pleasant experience, and Franco spent many long hours, drunk, regaling people with an exaggeration of the tale.

The trees were eerie, silent. The rain danced. A strong aroma of rotting vegetation flooded the jungle like toxic gas.

It was too . . . still. Just too damn lifeless.

The squad halted in a vast swathe of curving jungle. Somewhere they could hear a raging waterfall. Keenan glanced at Pippa. "How far to the contact?"

Pippa smiled at that. Keenan could be so . . . clinical. The *contact*. The target. The assassination. The taking of a human life, and yeah, OK, that guy was responsible for the deaths of millions according to the unreliable monkeys of QGM military intelligence, but who's to say they were right? Who gave Combat K the right to play God?

"Twenty klicks. Northeast."

"How far to the Blood River?"

"Eight hundred and twenty-seven metres. Give or take."

"Let's move out."

They eased through the enemy jungle. There had been no early ScoutBot Scan infiltrations or WebCloud relays, because QGM wanted to retain the element of surprise. In and out in three hours. A neat excision.

It was immensely dark in the jungle, and muted sounds echoed metallic between trees. The sounds were odd, unlike usual jungle noises. Keenan and Pippa exchanged glances, but continued, heightened senses alert to danger, guns rain-slick and slippery in gloved hands. Permatex WarSuits moderated body temperature and kept the stifling jungle humidity from biting...too much. Franco still mumbled curses as he brought up the rear, expertly scanning their back-trail, and expertly watching Pippa's arse. *I wish,* he thought sourly. *Oh to get my paws on that ripe pair of peaches!* But it would never happen, especially as Franco was currently married to an eight-foot mutated zombie super-soldier, once beautiful, now an abomination of pus. He frowned at the memory. It was a long story, a tale of violence and psychopathic *biohell*.

The river surprised them, despite electronic warnings. It slammed from the darkness, a muted roaring greeting them instantaneously from the gloom. It was lighter here, out from under the tree canopy, and a rime of green moonlight crept from behind bruised copper clouds. Keenan gave Franco a nod, and the small ginger squaddie knelt in the mud by the side of the river.

"Do it."

"Yeah boss."

Franco twisted the small rubber ball, and tossed it into the river on the end of a flexing TitaniumIII cord. The ball gave a *crack* of ignition, and a hiss, and inflated instantly into a special forces covert boat, nicknamed a Rubber Duck, or *Sitting Duck* by the more cynical members of the squads. Pippa and Keenan climbed in, guns tracking dark shorelines overhung with skeletal branches. The air crackled with strange, metallic creaking, not unlike the discharge of energy. Pippa gave a shudder.

"You OK?"

"I feel like we're being watched. The PAD states otherwise, although the thing's playing up—which is unusual. They're normally good for a billion years. Maybe it's the high magnetic field? Maybe we're being dicked with."

"Still no life?"

"No life," said Pippa. "By that, I mean *absolutely* no life. This jungle is deader than a crypt. There's no indigenous life-forms; no birds, no insects. Nothing. I've seen more energy in a corpse."

Franco jumped in and fired stealth engines, a twin-set of Suzuki Whisper MkIVs. He eased the boat out into the strong tug of the river, and turned against the current. They were headed up-river; deeper into the jungle, deeper into nigritude, deeper into the heart of darkness.

Franco stared at the gloom. "I don't suppose there's any brothels up there?" he muttered.

"Don't be an idiot," snapped Pippa.

"Pubs? You reckon?" He sounded feebly hopeful.

"Dickhead."

"What about a casino or two? It's ages since I've had a flutter."

"Mate, the last time you gambled you lost your damn *house*. Haven't you learnt your lesson?"

"'Twas a simple error of reading the cards. I'll do better next time, so I will."

"Well," said Pippa carefully, "I don't see how. After you shot the place up with that K7 shotgun, and dropped a BABE grenade in the manager's office. Fair blew the place to shit. You've been banned from every gambling franchise on The City."

"Rubbish! They know that was only little old me playing toy soldiers." He brightened. "Still. This guy is a king, right? This General Zenab? Showered in gold and jewels by the junks? Treated like royalty?" His eyes went suddenly crafty, as he guided the small submersible through dark channels of foaming river. Rainfall gleamed on his skin, and as green moonlight caught him, he looked quite demonic. Like a devil, sick of sin. Like a twice reanimated corpse. "We might even make a few dollars!" He beamed. "There might be dancing girls in the palace!" He beamed wider, showing his broken tooth from too many drunken bar-brawls.

Pippa slapped his arm. "You're a muppet. You need to focus, Franco, and focus hard. This ain't no game we're playing. Kee? I told you he'd be a damn liability. I told you to choose somebody else."

"Well, charming!" stuttered Franco. "Thanks for your vote of confidence, sweetie."

"We might need his detonation skills," growled Keenan, with a shaded glance. "And you *know* there's nobody better with a Bausch & Harris. I'm hoping we can get this gig finished—*without* getting our hands dirty."

They cruised in silence through obsidian shadows. The jungle closed in as the river narrowed, became yet more violent, raging and pounding around black fists of ancient volcanic rock. Quietly, Pippa said, "Never in a million years."

They stopped in a small bay of calm water for navigation checks. Pippa was jagging the touch-dials of the PAD, and shook her head. "No good, Kee. There's something wrong—either with the PAD, or with the whole damn planet."

"Leave the pad," said Keenan. "We'll use our eyes and ears. Just like the old days on Molkrush Fed."

He glanced up, and there, at the edge of the jungle, perhaps five metres away, stood a squad of junks. Four of them. Heavily armed. For what seemed an eternity the two groups faced one another across the expanse of stagnant water, a platter of stinking glass . . . then hell erupted—

Keenan's Techrim 11mm was out and pumping in his fist and he dived right, over the edge of the boat. Pippa dropped to one knee, D5 in her gloved hands, *booms* crashing through the jungle. Franco split left, a Kekra quad-barrel machine pistol in each hand slamming bullets at the squad. The junks, tall and powerful wearing basic electronic leather armour, skin pitted like metal, eyes like pools of blood, short, forked silver tongues flickering in silver mouths like liquid metal— they split with equal skill and speed, their MPKs firing volleys of roaring bullets at Combat K. Everything was a deafening bellow of chaos and confusion. The jungle screamed with concussion and bullets, a distillation of confusion, as Keenan pumped rounds into a junk's face and watched him stumble back, blood spewing from destroyed eyes, his face a mash of chewed bone and gristle and flapping cheek skin. Franco, yelling, charged with Kekras roaring. Two bullets *thumped* his WarSuit like hammer blows, knocking the wind from him, slamming his heart with pounding fists but he was on the junk, both guns screaming, aware like the others that junks were insanely tough, hard to kill, real *bastards* to put down. Their eyes were their Achilles' heel; shoot out their eyes and death would follow. Franco was on the junk, both boots slamming the stunned, eye-destroyed face and riding him to the ground to crouch beside the writhing figure. The two remaining junks charged Pippa, her D5 still cracking but they *absorbed* shells in primitive armour and skin and muscle, which rolled like melted wax, reforming, repairing even as it was decimated and Pippa felt panic well in her breast at this seemingly indestructible threat before her...and closing fast. One reached out, took the D5 from her hands and bent it into two discrete parts with a *snap* and scatter of unspent shells. The junk screamed in her face, a toxic blast of poisonous air that made her weak at the knees, ingested toxins attacking her central nervous system as the second junk turned on Franco and fired a volley of MPK rounds...

And Keenan was there, Techrim against the junk's head. "Put her down, shit-bag." The junk turned and grinned at him, blood red eyes narrowing as Keenan pulled the trigger and the bullet whined through skull and brain, erupting in a mushroom shower of shards and mashed brain-slop. It rammed a fist into Keenan's chest, slamming him back over the boat in an acceleration of gasping pain and realization that the junk *could still operate with a bullet in the head* . . . the junk turned on Pippa, who smiled a nasty smile, and slammed her knife into one eye with a downward punch. She ripped the blade sideways, cutting out the junk's second blood orb and it screamed, a sudden high-pitched shrill, flopping back in the Duck, thrashing as Pippa hurled the blade to embed in the final junk's armour. It turned from Franco, lying back on the rocks, stunned by bullet blasts in his Permatex. When it glanced at Pippa, Franco reached back and grabbed the first thing which came to hand. His Bausch & Harris sniper rifle, packing high velocity 8.98 medium calibre rounds. At that range, face to face, the weapon was devastating. The rifle gave a *thump* in Franco's gloved fists and the junk's head disintegrated. The body stood for a moment, jiggling, blood a fountain from the jagged neck, then fell flat and dead on the rocks. A thick, evil stench poured from the open neck. An aroma of rotten eternity. The perfume of the junk.

Franco coughed, and looked to Keenan, who struggled from the water clutching his chest. He felt like he'd suffered a heart attack. Felt like he'd died. "Get back on the boat," he wheezed, and they all scrambled aboard.

As they cruised into violent storm waters, wind howling, the heavens pounding their insignificant craft with needles of rain, Pippa gave Keenan and Franco a savage snarl. "We can assume the bastard PAD is well and truly compromised, yeah? We're on our own, boys."

"Just the way we like it," smiled Franco sardonically.

The storm died in a sudden rush of warm air, like a dragon blast. As if in response, or perhaps by coincidence, the river became a flat platter, glass, ice. Pippa, now pilot, slowed their cruise to a halt and they sat for a few moments, rocking, listening, peering at the overhanging edges of uncompromising metallic-stinking jungle.

"Never get out of the boat," muttered Franco.

"What?" snapped Pippa.

"Just something I heard."

"How far?" said Keenan.

"Three klicks. We're getting close. That's why we met that little scouting party. Was it an accident, I wonder, or were the bastards looking for us? Maybe they saw the SLAM come in, thought they'd investigate."

"To all sensors it'd still look like a meteor strike."

"Still," said Pippa. "I'd want to know what came down twenty klicks from *my* base of operations. Especially if this place *is* a Nano-Bomb Factory."

"Let's assume they know we're here," said Keenan, mind ticking. "What would General Zenab do? He can read minds, or so we're told. See through tangled paths of the future. Has he seen his own impending assassination?"

Pippa stared at Keenan. "That isn't even funny."

"Do you see me laughing? OK. So you've got patrols in the jungle, textbook. What about the river? Patrol boats? We've not seen anything here. What else could you use?"

"It's not deep enough for a sub," said Franco, frowning.

"When I went in the river before, this water, it's not normal. I know it's red because of mineral deposits, but it was also full of . . . oil, or something. A lubricant. It wasn't natural."

"Is that why we can smell metal?"

Keenan shrugged. "Not sure. But whatever it is, it may have a purpose. It reminded me of the Terminus5 Shell reactor; remember the bunker? Full of that insane AI bio-wire which ate through your bones and separated a person long-ways out?"

"I remember," said Franco, voice low. "You think they may have AI tech?"

"I always thought the junks low-tech, but . . . we should prepare for anything. This gig stinks like a dead cat."

"You want to ditch the boat?"

"Maybe. I'm considering it."

They paused, and something *slopped* in the river. They glanced at one another. "I saw something," said Pippa, carefully, hoisting her weapon, nervous now, gun tracking an invisible foe. The river seemed deeper, here, more stable; and yet more threatening at the same time. Like a motionless predator; a hunter waiting to pounce.

Ripples suddenly drifted away from the Rubber Duck, or at least, from something *near* it. Pippa stood, alongside Keenan, and they both aimed weapons at the flat surface.

"I don't like this," moaned Franco.

"Shut up. Pippa, get us out of here."

Pippa nodded, and eased them forward. They moved across the water, still as a lake, green-tinged from the moon. Ripples flowed, slapping shores. The engine purred, near-silent, and Pippa angled toward the shore . . . .

It was this which saved their lives.

The *thing* squirmed across the river, surfacing sideways like a sidewinder serpent, a long, bright silver eel as thick as a man's waist and perhaps thirty or forty feet long. Pippa gasped and Keenan started firing at the creature undulating toward them. Pippa joined him, but their bullets were absorbed with tiny *plops* as it accelerated, a massive eel that crashed into the Rubber Duck with stunning force, sending all three Combat K soldiers flipping into the river . . .

Keenan went under, felt something cold and metallic brush his WarSuit, recoil for an instant, then *slap* him with such force only his armor stopped immediate death through impact. He choked. Everything, all wind and life were knocked from him and yet he forced himself to swim, powerful strokes, toward the shore. He *felt* the eel's approach rather than saw it, and dived, twisting, by some miracle passing under the undulating body of thick muscle. He struck out, under the river, fighting strange currents until he clambered up the shore, dripping, panting, muscles screaming like irate fishmongers. Franco was already there, heaving, hands on knees, looking sorry for himself in a hangdog fashion.

"Where's Pippa?"

Franco stood upright, stared out, watched the mercury eel circle their Rubber Duck and suddenly ensnare it, its whole body flipping from the river to wrap around the boat again and again in huge circles, and with a sudden *pulse* and tug, crushed the boat into a hissing, buckling, pulped oblivion.

Slowly, Franco pulled free his Bausch & Harris. "She's there. See. Pippa, Hey!" He waved. She seemed disorientated in the gloom, in the drizzle of light rain, but focused on his words and struck out toward him. However, the eel also heard Franco and turned, writhing in foam as Franco snarled a curse and aimed down the rifle's sight.

"You'll draw attention to us!" snapped Keenan, hoisting his own guns and casting about for enemy.

"I can't let her *die,*" said Franco.

He fired, a muted *thump* and the bullet disappeared in the eel's mass. Pippa powered on, but the eel moved fast for something so big. It gained swiftly. If it caught her, it would crush her without doubt. Franco breathed deep, and fired off another three shots in quick succession. The thump of bullets echoed off, flesh slaps, muted by the jungle.

"It's going to kill her," said Keenan.

"Not on *my* watch," snapped Franco, and began pumping shot after shot after shot into the silver eel, unaware if his bullets had effect, unaware if this *thing* was something they could *kill*. What was it? AI? A simpConstruct robot? Organic? Or a meld of all three?

"Come on!" urged Keenan.

Franco kept on firing, and the eel suddenly slowed, its sidewinder motion becoming erratic. Pippa reached the shore, but the eel's tail lunged from blood waters and wrapped around her chest. It dragged her back, and both Keenan and Franco leapt forward, guns thundering and howling into the thick silver body which twitched and pulsed. Pippa screamed, hands straining against the metallic surface. Then her fingers slipped inside, as if entering jelly, and came out, shocked, trailing umbilicals of silver eel strand . . .

Franco dropped to his knees on the rocks, in the mud, his eyes locked to Pippa's and reading the pain and suffering there. He pulled a BABE grenade from his belt, gave her a wide grin, pulled the pin and plunged his fist *inside* the eel's apparently semi-solid body. He pulled free his arm, rocked back on heels, and fell to his arse. He watched as there came a muffled *crack*. Ripples shuddered along the length of the eel, and it twitched, every molecule vibrating out of synchronization with every other. Then, the creature was still.

Franco and Keenan dragged Pippa from the strange creature's embrace, Pippa coughing, holding her chest. Without her WarSuit she'd be a mashed pulp, a skin bag of crumbled bones. Even now, the armor was buzzing warnings; it was seriously damaged, and would fail if it took another impact.

"I'd say they know we're here," said Franco.

"Let's move out. The quicker we get this done, the quicker we go home."

"I'm beginning to hate this planet," said Franco, pulling his sulky lip.

Pippa coughed, and stood. She took several deep breaths. She looked annoyed.

More than annoyed. She looked ready to *kill*. "Let's go assassinate this bastard," she said, and hoisted her shotgun with a scowl.

They moved like ghosts through the jungle. Up close, the trees were metallic, coated in a sheen of oil. They were not living, not organic, but simple machines designed to imitate life. A machine jungle. An army of sentry steel.

"What kind of freak creates such a place?" said Franco, frowning. It was the waste and pointlessness, more than anything, that offended him.

"Just keep your eye on the PAD."

For the last two klicks they'd evaded nine junk patrols, keeping low and quiet, going to ground at the first hint of enemy activity. But the fact still nagged Combat K—if the enemy knew they were there, on the planet, alertness would be increased. And the enemy may also now have discovered the SLAM cruiser. The last thing a soldier needed after a bad gig was a compromised ride home.

Franco, bringing up the rear, caught Keenan's signal and dropped instantly, silent. He carried the Bausch & Harris, now, in his big pugilist's paws. He was twitchy; on edge. A man on a high wire. A hairline trigger.

Dropping to his belly against the floppy, metallic leaves, Franco commando-crawled forward. They were on a cliff-top overlooking a bowl valley devoid of jungle, although with so many thick creepers it could happily be described as a bowel valley. To the left, the Blood River eased sluggish and wide. Boats were moored there, low-alloy vessels with big guns. Several ornately carved stone buildings squatted at the center of the cleared jungle, lights shone in windows. And yet the whole place looked deserted, especially as this was supposed to be the Nano-Bomb Factory. It felt wrong, and much too small in scale. If this was a Nano-Bomb Factory, would General Zenab really surround himself with a mere handful of junk protectors? If this man really was as richly rewarded, highly prized, and threatening to QGM as they claimed, wouldn't the security be far more aggressive?

"This stinks," said Pippa.

"Like a ten-week dead pig," added Franco.

"Let me think," said Keenan. "Is the PAD still dead?"

"Like a ten-week dead skunk," said Franco.

Keenan held up one fist. "Stop! I need to think. Pippa, is this the target?"

"Yeah."

"It's so wrong."

"I know that, Kee. This ain't no Nano-Bomb Factory."

Keenan bellied down, chin on his hands, and watched the modest activity which surrounded the small stone buildings. The carvings were ancient. Alien archaeology. He shuddered. It always filled him with a desolation, as if humans had only been kicking around the Quad-Gal for a few minutes—which in reality, they had. Aliens, sentient life-species as a matrix, had been around a billion times longer. This simple infancy made humanity feel quite insecure; something they made up for with aggression and a savage empire.

"Maybe," said Keenan, "this bastard is so tough he doesn't need protection. We're looking at this wrong. Maybe Zenab is an ancient alien creature, more powerful than any of us dreamed. After all, we're assuming he's human, because QGM *assumed* he was human. That was never confirmed."

"Shit intel, again," snapped Pippa. "The story of our lives."

"We need to make the best of it," said Keenan. "This is the gig. I'll head in alone; you two cover me, especially Franco with that lethal bastard rifle. OK?"

"I don't like it," said Pippa.

"I didn't ask whether you liked it."

Pippa took his arm, stared into his eyes. And he could read it there, the love the need the want the lust, sexual desire but more than that, a deep and meaningful *connection*.

"Don't go, Kee," she said.

"We need to get this done."

And he was gone, easing down the slope, fingers digging in rock, eyes and senses alert for enemy activity. But the camp, or base, the supposed Nano-Bomb Factory was pretty much deserted. It was a ghost ship.

"He'll be OK," said Franco, grinning, and patting Pippa on the shoulder. "Let's keep him covered."

"If he's not back in ten minutes, I'm going in."

"That isn't what he said."

"It's what *I said*," she hissed, eyes an insane glare.

"OK, OK, don't take it out on poor old Franco."

"Just play with your gun."

Mumbling, Franco checked over his rifle, and tried not to look concerned.

Keenan touched down on moist soil. His eyes raked the jungle perimeter. The stone buildings appeared inviting, warm, homely, and for the first time in a long, *long* time he found himself thinking of home. His old home. Before Galhari, and before the...*murders*. The word sat foul on his tongue, in his brain, like a diseased implant, a toxic augmentation. His wife, Freya, and their children, Rachel and Ally, had been killed. At first, it had been pinned on Pippa and they had hated one another, tried to kill one another—after all, hadn't Pippa been his lover? Hadn't he cast her aside? Hadn't she had *motive* to murder his family? But as days fell into weeks fell into months it had blurred and become apparent that something far more sinister was at work, so complex even Pippa herself wasn't sure if she'd committed the evil deed. One thing was for sure, however. Keenan's family were dead, slaughtered, and sometimes, occasionally, more often now as months flowed like mercury, he longed to join them.

He knew they were waiting.

Keenan descended the final section of rocky slope, boots digging in, searching for targets. But the area was deserted and this worried him more than any waiting army. Keeping a low profile, he crossed the bare ground to the largest of the stone buildings, eyes taking in ancient carvings which passed through several planes of reality. They were deeply alien, twisted, some shifting from sight to scent to aural expression, and dazzling Keenan with a form of sensual confusion. "Alien shit," he muttered. "Bring back Picasso."

He stopped, back to the wall, gun against his cheek, and glanced up to where Franco and Pippa were camouflaged, invisible, their guns trained, protecting him like hot metal guardians. A robot dad. He peered into the building, which was cool and inviting, a staggered tile floor, every inch of the walls lined with rich tapestries hanging ceiling to floor.

Keenan stepped in, sounds muffled by the vibrant needlework. He moved through rooms, realizing the building was much larger than anticipated . . . but there was no bomb-making equipment on show, no advanced circuitry for the design and production of nano technology. It was primitive. Bare. A let-down. A cerebral retard.

He emerged on the edges of a modest room, circular, walls hung with green tapestries which shifted in a breeze. Sliding behind these convenient screens, he observed three figures, three huge junks with rippling muscles and holstered machine guns. Before them stood a child, a girl, six years old with fine blonde hair and blue eyes in a pretty, oval face. She wore a simple white robe, and clutched a low-profile wooden box in both hands. She was talking, words gentle, like whispers on the wind.

Keenan's gaze shifted back to the three junks and he wondered which one was General Zenab . . .

"Hello, Mr Keenan," said the child, turning, head tilting, just as Keenan was deciding which junk to kill first. He froze, aware he'd made no sound, had not compromised his position in the slightest. He relaxed. So. They knew he was coming; and more than that—they knew who he was.

Combat K. QGM. *Shit.*

He stepped from his tapestry-concealed hiding place, grinning wryly. He'd never made a good assassin. *Hell*, he thought, *I'm barely a soldier these days; barely human.* He expected a battle, but the junks failed to present arms. They stood, facing away like automatons, apparently oblivious to his existence. Drones in the hive.

"Come forward," said the little girl.

Keenan moved, D5 shotgun in his gloved hands, ready at a twitch to blow any living creature in half. He was watching the junks, eyes narrowed, senses screaming at him with his tainted alien blood; but he could *feel* no others. The five of them were alone . . .

"Which of you is Zenab?"

"Ahh," said the little girl, eyes sparkling, hands clutching the wooden box so tightly her knuckles were white. "You have come for murder. Assassination. Death. We will be sorry to disappoint you; sorry to send you away."

"So he's not here?"

"Assumptions by Quad-Gal Military are so refreshing." Something about the way she spoke the name made Keenan freeze, boots welded to floor tiles, eyes fixed on her and realizing, an instant too late, that she was more than the sum of her parts, and infinitely more dangerous than her simple image led him to believe . . .

He gazed into that face, and his heart melted, and he knew, knew in a blinding white-hot intensity that this girl this child this pale innocent was the *general* he sought to exterminate. And he knew, knew deep in his soul that he could not kill this person.

That's what it wants you think . . . whispered the dark side of his soul.

No! She's a child, a puppet of the junks; I should kill them, her guards, the scourge which has imprisoned her! I should take her away from this place, this evil, take her away to a better life . . . a life with kindness, and family, a place filled with warmth and love.

She will kill you, Keenan. She will possess you! She is not human . . . she will usurp your flesh.

But that's impossible, he realized. She could not usurp him, or possess him, because he barely lived there himself.

"You are General Zenab." It was not a question.

"So very perceptive." She smiled, with small white teeth. And he knew; understood that her arrogance precluded an awesome power. She was no human, because *Keenan was no longer human,* and the alien blood from an earlier encounter *had* tainted his own blood, own soul, had somehow elevated him, somehow desecrated him, dropped him into another plane of existence.

"I have been sent to—to *kill* you." Keenan's voice was quiet. "But I will give you a choice. I will take you away from this place. Give you another life, a better life." He no longer saw Zenab. He saw Rachel and Ally. Their bloody corpses. It ate him like acid.

"Like you would have done for your girls?"

"Yes." Keenan's voice was strangled, neither human nor animal; an imitation of the organic. And a tidal wave of guilt and shame washed over him, flooded him inside out and he felt his knees go weak, his anger flee, any straggled remnants of hatred were torn and all he wanted, more than anything in this world, in this life, was to save this child . . . as he failed to save his own.

He knelt, and placed his gun on the floor with a *clack.*

"Come with me," he said.

She laughed. "I cannot. You do not understand."

"I understand you are prisoner, forced to use your talents for the junks; to aid their empire, to extend their evil."

She smiled, pretty face wrinkling, and Keenan's heart melted, his soul burned, and he only realised Pippa and Franco were behind him when he saw the barrel of Franco's Bausch & Harris rifle ease past his shoulder . . .

"Don't move, buddy," said Franco.

"What are you *doing?*" snapped Keenan.

"She's a witch, a changer, a junk-spawn. She's *infested, mate.* She's hooked into your brain, and into your spine. She's using you, Kee. She'll kill you. Don't trust her." He grinned, but the smile looked wrong on his face. Twisted. Too much bone. Too much skull.

Keenan frowned, the whole world tumbling down. "Bullshit!" he snapped. "She's a prisoner. We have to rescue her . . . to free her! What's wrong with you, Franco? Can't you see?"

"He's right." Pippa's hand touched Keenan's shoulder, then her gun caressed the side of his head. "Sorry, Kee. It's time to die."

A *feeling* swept over Keenan, nausea, a violent bout of sickness worse than anything ever felt. Like a puzzle solved, everything clicked into place. The *pulse* of alien blood through his veins, the beat of his heart, all melded to show him the truth . . . he ducked as Pippa pulled the trigger, and her bullet whined, entered Franco's skull with a *slap*, blasting his head into ribbons of flesh and curled bone. Brain mushroomed out then paused, like elastic caught at the point of furthest trajectory, and ravelled swiftly back in as the head reformed itself disjointedly and for a moment, the briefest of instants, Keenan saw the face disintegrate into a cloud of particles . . . and rearrange as solid flesh.

Keenan whirled fast and the world kicked into guns and bullets, into action and reaction as Franco and Pippa leapt from a doorway with guns thundering, bullets scything into the fake forms of Franco and Pippa, into their *simulacrums,* created things, imitations of life.

Pippa killed herself with a shotgun blast to the head, and watched her own body curl in on itself, into a shower of silver powder that trickled down between cracks in the floor tiles. Franco had a short, vicious fight with his own head-holed ganger, and shot himself in the stomach, then the throat, and finally the face. He watched himself die, and in dying, so the real Franco was born again.

"Shit," he panted, face bathed in sweat. "They nearly had you, Keenan!"

The three junks attacked, as Combat K attacked. Keenan was kicked out of his shock, grabbing the D5 shotgun and leaping forward, blasting a junk guard in the face with a burst of shells and removing his head. There was a whirlwind of violence which left Combat K crouched on the tiles, surrounded by blood and junk gore, limbs, chunks of flesh, as a cool wind blew through the chamber and they realised the little girl had gone.

"The General's fled," said Pippa. "What the fuck's going on?"

"Nano-technology," snarled Keenan. "And the box she carries. It's the Nano-Bomb Factory. I don't know why we thought it'd be an installation; it's something complex, something small, something incredibly advanced. We have to get it. It's too dangerous to let go."

They ran through corridors, through chambers, all writhing with ancient alien stone-craft. They emerged, saw the little girl sprinting toward the river and a sleek alloy craft.

"She's going to escape," snapped Pippa. "Shoot her! QGM rely on it! Millions rely on it."

Franco lifted his rifle, and caught Keenan's eye. Keenan looked as if he'd been hit by a hammer. How could he shoot his own daughter in the back? *How could he murder his little girl?*

Franco, also, was flooded with doubt. He lowered the gun, long barrel pointing at the churned mud floor. "I can't," he said. "I can't shoot a child in the back. It's just not right!"

"Give me the gun," snarled Pippa, dragging the rifle from Franco's scarred hands. She aimed, and with a *crack* took the back of the girl's head off. General Zenab toppled to the floor in a tangle of limbs; and did not move.

"I'm just mangled," said Franco. "What the hell actually happened? Why did I just kill myself?"

They moved to the girl, a destroyed form. Even as they watched, a tiny cloud, millions of silver particles, formed into a fist, then dissipated swiftly on the wind.

"Nanobots," said Keenan, mouth twisted in a sour grin. "They imitated you. Imitated the girl. General Zenab doesn't exist; it's an AI construct, a very, very advanced machine."

Pippa stooped, picked up the wooden box. "But we got the Nano-Bomb equipment."

"Yeah. At least we got something."

"We didn't kill her, him . . . *it*, did we?" said Pippa.

"We hurt it," said Keenan. "Whatever the hell it was. And we bought QGM some time."

"So we'll be back?"

Keenan, programming the rejuvenated PAD to bring in the SLAM, nodded. "Yeah Pippa. The war ain't over. We'll be back. For people like us, this kind of shit never ends. The suffering never stops."

Pippa gave a nod, and clutching the small wooden box, waited for exit.

FIRST LINE

An Alliance Archives Adventure

Danielle Ackley-McPhail

Go! Go! GO!" THE SQUAD LEADER BARKED INTO THE COMM.

The order pinged her transceiver, a sharp reminder of many missions past. Quieter than the barest whisper, hard, taut, and intense, it triggered automatic responses in a battle-honed soldier: a flood of adrenaline, combat awareness drilled in by special ops training and countless field missions, a fierce impulse to bring a weapon to bear.

In one instant, she went from drifting through oblivion, to combat-ready.

She was no longer capable of adrenaline rushes, but the rest of her reflexes were still on the mark. It wasn't supposed to work that way. By all rights, there shouldn't be anything left of Lieutenant Sheila "Trey" Tremaine. Well, nothing capable of such a knee-jerk reaction to the issued order. Now who the hell's cock-up was that?

There were large gaps in her memory, or at least she presumed there were, seeing as the last thing she could recall was dying. She used to be an officer assigned to the 428th Special Ops unit, MOS: demolitions specialist, but when an enemy round took her down, on its way to taking her out, she'd been offered a chance. She remembered that too (before the dying part). The head of the tech division had shown up beside her hospital cot once it was clear she was well on her way to succumbing to her injuries.

Horrible way for a soldier to die, by the way: slowly, in a hospital bed, a burden to the very society you were meant to serve. Feeling worse than useless. It just wasn't right. You either kicked ass and survived to fight another day, or you took a shitload of them down on your way out. That was the way it was supposed to be. For a soldier. Anything else just felt wrong. They'd lost two men saving her should-have-been-dead ass. The only thing worse than waiting to die was staring that guilt in the face the entire time.

"How serious do you take your oath to serve, Lieutenant?" the bureaucrat had solemnly asked.

She'd allowed her gaze to sweep across her broken body before giving him a look as sharp as a knife's edge. Her lip had curled up in a bare approximation of the warning sneer her unit would have recognized before she tore into someone particularly dense. Of course, her clear status of "non-threat" made him oblivious to her reaction at the insult he'd issued. If she'd had any energy left for anything except guilt and dying, she would have shown him how wrong his assessment was.

"Very," she responded, if faintly.

That was when he offered her an approximation of immortality. Okay. Maybe not. But definitely a way to make up for dying the wrong way, and an opportunity to protect her unit in a way she'd never imagined.

"We'd like to neuro-scan your brain," he went on, very matter-of-fact, as if he were discussing the watch schedule, or what was being served in the Mess. "To preserve your expertise and instincts." He went on to explain the great advancements in this process and how they would then be able to imprint the scan-capture onto a neural matrix so that her training and experience would not be lost at her demise, but could be utilized in this time of conflict to ensure others did not fall as she had . . . *blah, blah, blah.*

Manipulative prick.

"Why wait . . . till now?" she managed. After all, she'd been there in that cot quite a while.

There was an uncomfortable silence on the egg-head's part. "The process is terminal."

Well. Okay. So was she, apparently. Not that she hadn't figured that out already. Still, she'd been tempted to say no, just for the piss-poor way he handled the proposal. The idea itself intrigued her, though. The way he explained it, if she agreed, her thought processes would be imprinted on the newest generation of packbot to augment the technical data already hard-wired in, with the intent of mating that automated programming with her learned reflexes and evaluative capabilities. She didn't get all the technical bits; after all, her training was in demolitions, not computers. But really, the only thing she needed to understand was that a part of her would live on to fight those that had taken her out.

Ultimately (clearly), she'd agreed. The clincher, in the end: the mech in question had been requisitioned by the 428th. The guy should have mentioned that to begin with. That was her only real enticement. What did she care about revenge? She'd believed in why they were fighting. That and protecting her men mattered to her more than any petty revenge.

"Will they know it's me?" she managed to ask. The answer was no. "Will *I* know it's me?" Again, no.

"Though urban legends persist to the contrary," the egg-head assured her, "there is no evidence to substantiate the rumors that personality is transferable with this process."

She'd taken his word for it. She'd wanted to believe some part of her would go on, would continue to serve. That didn't mean she wanted to be conscious of it.

Her body had failed just as the final neural pathways were scanned. Trey knew this, because even that the process had captured. Now, she was the next level in advanced warfare. And contrary to all assurances, she was still self-aware.

Trey took stock of her current situation. Besides overall being FUBARed, sensors indicated she was currently being jostled, but the motion spoke more of stealth than open assault. Something close to excitement, leavened by a bit of apprehension went through her. It wasn't supposed to work this way. But what the hell; too late now, right?

There were murmurs going back and forth across her transceiver. Just bits and pieces, mostly sub-vocal sounds rather than words. She understood this, though. Most of the communicating going on between the deployed team was done through gestures and glances. They'd been a team a long time. Who needed words?

Of course, that meant Trey was in the dark. The packbot that housed her was in standby mode. The transceiver was active and ready to receive input, but the cameras that would be her eyes were powered down and she had no access to the subroutines that would power them up. It was like she was tied up and blindfolded. *Not* something she was into.

She was used to being in charge, or at least an active participant. The deal she'd made was not quite looking so good at the moment. The waiting, the not knowing, was doing a number on whatever part of her personality had glommed onto the scan.

Finally the forward motion stopped.

Trey felt a jolt as power flooded her system. Data was keyed in, leaving her disoriented. She was, after all, merely a passenger within the robotic interface, a data source that allowed the CPU to interpret scenarios for the handler based on her collective experience. She was a resource with not one whit of control over anything.

Yeah, maybe her deathbed wasn't such a good place to make life-altering decisions. She may have been a demo specialist, and understood the mechanical workings of the packbot, but from the inside she couldn't follow impulse one of the directives being fed into the unit for the pending incursion. This passive-observer mode definitely had the potential of evolving into her own personal hell. At least as a part of the military she'd had the freedom to act within the structure of command. In combat she was used to taking charge, even. Trey was not a passive creature.

She felt better once the internal gyros registered a change in the robotic unit's orientation as its handler drew it from his pack and lobbed it into the crumbling shell of a building.

"Boombot deployed, Sarge," Trey's handler subvocalized into his bonejack. "Unit transmission at . . . 85 percent optimal." Nothing sounded like it used to, but from the irreverent terminology, Trey figured Coop was the soldier reassigned her demo duties. She hadn't known him so well, beyond an officer's familiarity with those she led, but he'd always been the one to add some hint of humor to every mission. By her reckoning, wisecracks were one more part of his armor, right along with his ballistic mesh. She was finding it comforting, herself.

"Damn . . . we need better than that, soldier," responded whoever had taken over as team leader—Trey couldn't help feeling a bit smug that it had taken two men to replace her . . . at least, until she recalled her new role was "Boombot, " and why.

"Adjust your frequency; no one goes in until that 'bot is transmitting at 95 percent minimum. *I'm* not loosing any men to sloppiness."

The implication wasn't lost on Trey. For the briefest instant she had the overwhelming impulse to go "buggy" on the colossal shit. Let him see how "optimal" he could be when things were out of his control and there was pressure from the higher ups to achieve the mission directives *now*.

Hell, he was the one nice and cozy at the fall-back position, while here she was completely *over* the front line. Of course, it was so easy to forget she was only a passenger. Right up until Coop started fiddling with the controller.

Talk about weird. Trey could "feel" as he adjusted the packbot's settings, maneuvering the unit around the crumbled remains of the building, manipulating the camera angles. She heard him murmur about the darkness. It should have served as a warning, but she totally didn't pick up on it. When he triggered the variable-intensity LEDs she would have flinched, if she could have. The sudden light had the intensity of a bomb blast without the fade away. She could visualize her eyes snapping closed. And suddenly, they did. Or at least, there was an abrupt return to total darkness. It was a coincidence, of course, but a welcome one. Well. For her.

Coop swore like a cross between a marine and a twenty-dollar whore.

A flood of data transmitted to the 'bot. Then once again, supernova. Trey reflexively "flinched" and was returned to total darkness. She was in awe as the revelation dawned. Maybe passive observer wasn't her lot after all.

"Military-issue piece of crap! We don't have time for this!"

There was that guilt again. What was relief for her was just a dangerous complication for the squad. But it did demonstrate that perhaps she had some control over her fate. To test the theory, she triggered the circuits that brought the lights up again independent of Coop's efforts, only gradually. Okay, enough experimentation. She had some amount of control. That alone made her just a bit more comfortable in her titanium skin.

Enough. She didn't want Coop scrapping the mission because 'Boombot' was malfunctioning. She "stepped back," releasing control to the handler.

It was odd not having to go to any effort to do her job. She had finally reached the state seasoned soldiers both dreamed of and dreaded: where a combat zone didn't require active thought to evaluate. Of course, she'd had to die to achieve it.

Always a down side, wasn't there?

Between her knowledge and the packbot's superfast processors, analysis of the building interior was instantaneous. The moment the cameras panned across a zone all the potential hot points were identified and assessed, simultaneously scrolling across the unit's micro-display and the handler's monitor.

All threats on the first floor were old activity, already neutralized. As the last lower-level quadrant scan completed, Trey and the packbot approached the staircase. A sensor extended from the 'bot until it connected with the first riser. Next the unit emitted a supersonic peal, followed by a probe shooting out from the front facing, forcefully punching up against the structure. Again, data analysis was instantaneous. The sonic blast revealed nothing but the standard staircase infrastructure. The impact test confirmed the architecture was sound and was not rigged to blow or collapse. With the all-clear given, the handler activated the 'bot's front flipper assembly. Trey was fascinated as the flipper extended up and forward until the belted track grabbed the next tread. She found the sensation odd as the servos engaged and the front of the unit was raised up, followed the flippers up the steps. The monitors continually tracked the stability of the structure as the process repeated, until the 'bot rested soundly on the upper level.

There was nothing there or in the rest of the surrounding buildings. Nothing recent, anyway. Plenty of signs of neutralized ordinance, along with one or two that had clearly been triggered, but by the levels of accumulated dust, signs of animal habitation, the weathering . . . all indications were that the outpost had been abandoned by all parties.

"Echo sector has been cleared for occupation, sir," Coop reported over the comm to his squad leader.

"Our ETA is 0700," was the response. "Have your men set up base operations and then stand down until we arrive."

Trey wanted to protest as the 'bot's systems were again powered down and the unit was returned to Coop's MOLLE pack. She noticed that once the rest of the system was shut off and beyond her reach, her own power source was likewise reduced until she was operating under what felt like brown-out conditions. Apparently, she was in her own version of stand-by.

Part of her railed against the restrictions; she was just getting the feel of her new situation, the freedom and capabilities she had never dreamed would be open to her. But then, the squad leader had no clue she was anything more than a complex data dump. Having to admit that made her seethe. Not that she had a right to. She'd signed on for this tour, after all.

As the outside world went away, she perversely wondered if this was how her laptop had felt each time she'd shut it down. And had it likewise amused itself in the darkness plotting theoretical rebellion?

Was it days or weeks or even longer that her existence went on this way? Trey had no clue. Well . . . she knew the chronological time and date stamp that queued up each time her systems were powered back up, but you know . . . when you spend an eternity in isolation in between those fraught, tedious moments of recon, the relative time bore no connection with a clock or a calendar. Trey, in short, felt ancient. And kind of like she was suspended in purgatory, or maybe limbo.

Before her was another crumbling structure, another potential hotbed of insurgents. It was time to earn her one step further from hell.

As she went about her duties—she no longer thought of herself separate from Boombot, though her identity of Trey was still very real to her—her processors filtered out the background chatter of the waiting squad. There was increasingly too much of it. The men were getting too relaxed the longer they went without encountering opposition. It was making them sloppy.

Already several had to be patched up by the medic after tripping over the remnants of a misfired hydra mine. The plungers had been obscured by the overgrown ground cover, but that was no excuse for the soldiers' blunder. Trey would have torn them a new one for being that sloppy on her watch. Demerits would have been the least of their problems. Fortunate for them, if not the whole squad, the payload had long ago been triggered. Trapped in the can at detonation when the lid malfunctioned, the mine apparently had geysered, rather than blowing out in a radial pattern; otherwise there would have been nothing but a crater as testament to where it used to be. Of course, as cold as the thought was, perhaps it wasn't a good thing the mine had been spent. If the men had gotten more than a gash for their inattention they would have learned their lesson better. Sloppy soldiers often got more than just themselves killed.

Speaking of which, Trey chastised herself for dwelling on the folly of others when she had her own duties to execute.

Nightmares were the worst part of standby mode. Yeah, even that plague of every soldier hadn't been left behind. Kind of hard to wake up from a reccurring hell when you had no body, no icy sweat to whisk away, no rapid breath to ramp down to a normal speed, nothing physical to distract you from the images you could never forget, or to remind you they weren't happening in real-time.

Trey wished she had enough control to power herself back up. Of course, it wasn't like she could drop and do push-ups until she tumbled into a deep, dreamless sleep, as she would have done in her other life, so what was the point? Though she could imagine how Coop would freak if he'd caught her trying it.

Trey settled for reviewing the data she'd so far gathered in their recon of the sector. Something about the zone was making her uneasy. She caught glimpses in her nightmares, hints of whatever had her "nerves" buzzing, but just as in her flesh-bound dreams, everything was shadowy, more impressions than anything else. Well, except for the blood. And the screams. Shrugging it off, she went back to analyzing the data. Had she been here before? It was so hard to tell, after all, as she already noted, the world was a heck of a lot different through the camera-eye of a 'bot. Whether or not she was covering familiar ground, she was getting a bad feeling the closer they drew to the next sector.

There had to be something in the data and damn if she wouldn't find it. She wasn't about to lead another squad straight into the guns of the enemy.

Hours later she finally recognized what she was looking for. It was 0Dark00 and the squad had been on the move for two hours. They were entering unsecured territory. This was the sector her unit had been heading for that fateful day. The one where good men died retrieving her.

Up until now Coop had reserved her for establishing the all-clear of structures in zones their side had already pacified, cleaning up any parting gifts left by the insurgents. This time when she was powered up she discovered he'd reconfigured her chassis with the explosive ordinance detection kit, increasing her speed and adding more muscle to her manipulator arm. Now she was running point for the squad across uncleared terrain, looking for more aggressive threats along their path. Already, together she and Coop had discovered and disabled half a dozen hydras and discreetly marked and redirected the squad's route around countless claymores. Those that came behind them would have more leisure to decommission the munitions. Their squad wouldn't risk it now. To do so would slow them down at best, and give away their position at worst, should even one mine be mishandled.

"Sarge, copy," Coop subvocalized.

"Acknowledged, report," came the response.

Coop kept it short, as even comm signals could be intercepted, if the enemy cracked the frequency. "Cleared to perimeter, sector Tango; squad heading in. Going comm dark."

"Roger."

The rest of the unit would now follow via the cleared corridor.

Trey was so on edge her lip would be twitching, if she'd still had one. She was surprised she wasn't shooting sparks as it was. She felt charged enough for a full fireworks display. Earlier, while exploring the internal pathway of the packbot, she discovered the protocol that would initiate self-destruct should the unit be compromised. If she could figure out how to trigger that at will, it could come in handy. If nothing else, she'd feel better knowing that, at least in a way, she was armed. She set a portion of her . . . mind to the puzzle as she continued rolling along.

Eventually, she came upon a civilian compound. It had been hit hard, as had many she had seen before. Coop ran her up to the first of the buildings with infrared sensors activated. There were some thermal, but nothing larger than the planet's equivalent of a rat.

She saw no traces of munitions rigged to blow, though there were signs of recent habitation. Local wildlife, perhaps, or squatters displaced by the recent conflict. There was nothing to imply occupation by a military force, though. Trey assessed the risk factor of the building at a level three, and fed the cautionary note to her handler. After careful inspection sent up no additional red flags, she was directed to the next building. Inspection continued in a similar manner through most the compound, bringing her about to the main structure.

By now Trey was twitching like anything, if only on the inside. There was still nothing registering on infrared, but her mics were picking up trace sounds that might be stealth movement . . . or might just be a branch in the wind. She was running all four cameras, though only data from the primary was feeding to the control monitor. It was odd being able to scan forward and still watch over her own shoulder; not as reassuring as it should be, though. After all, it only served to remind her she was out here solo.

As she entered the final building her instincts started grumbling. Flashbacks of her nightmares sprang to the forefront, demanding she back out of the structure, double-time.

With sheer determination and her virtual jaw set, Trey ignored the impulse and powered through to do her duty.

The lower level was clear. More signs of habitation, less clear as to the source. Her unit had rudimentary olfactory sensors Coop never seemed to activate. Chances were he didn't even know they were there. It was a new feature Trey herself had never seen before this model, only recently discovered. She made an executive decision and brought them on-line. Traces of human sweat. Food. Some particles of ordinance components.

Shit.

There were times she definitely hated being right. Her self-preservation instincts were all but standing on her non-existent head screaming. She ignored them once more, rolling up the stairs and turning down the upper corridor in the direction from which the odors were strongest. Trey could feel an internal tug as her actions diverged from those dictated by Coop and the controller, but this was a case where instinct (the combat kind, rather than the self-preservation kind) demanded a different course of action. Her primary camera had a fiber-optic extension for situations where the bulkier unit would not serve. She extended it now as she approached the first doorway. At the same time, she readied the self-destruct protocol. Just in case.

There was time for her to identify a crude munitions lab and roughly fifteen operatives clothed in thermal-dampening suits positioned around the room before a hand shot out and grabbed the extension.

Crap! She tried to backpedal, but as he drew her within range, his other hand brought up a silenced pistol and fired on the camera assembly, shattering the lens.

Before he could do more damage, she aimed a probe at his leg and zapped him with enough current to fry his brain. Her olfactory sensors overloaded on burnt flesh as her manipulator arm came around to drag the corpse out of her way.

The enemy forces were not idle. She transferred optical to her backup camera and assessed the situation. Weapons had been brought to bear and the soldiers were converging. She couldn't handle them all, and the lab and its contingent were a serious threat to her unit and the offensive. Without a second thought, she initiated the self-destruct protocol, ready to die a warrior's death.

There was yelling and a sudden sizzle of sound as Coop lost visual. He breathed a curse and his hands clutching the controller tighter, though it had gone nonfunctional. He was still receiving data from the 'bot. In fact, impossible as it was, the unit somehow seemed to be moving independently. Before he could settle on a plan of action, an image reappeared on his monitor, the angle skewed as it came from a secondary camera. He watched in stunned silence as more than a dozen Dominion soldiers rushed the Boombot.

"We have hostile contact," he called to his men, who scrambled to defensive positions on all sides. Coop turned his attention back to the monitor. He tried once more to pull the 'bot back, but it was no use; the unit still didn't respond to the controls. He watched with a mixture of awe and frustration as it revved forward, grabbing the foremost enemy's rifle hand in what oddly looked like a judo move, snapping it. The soldier dropped his weapon. The corresponding scream echoed oddly, coming both through the 'bot's comlink and more faintly from the building a half a klick away.

"What the . . ." he murmured, startling the unit's sniper, who crouched beside him. Coop stared hard at the words that appeared on his monitor.

<<GO BACK TO HELL, DEMONS!!!>>

The words triggered a memory of many a past mission.

It couldn't be. There was no way. But he'd been assigned to this unit a long time, most of that time in this squad. Under the command of Lieutenant Tremaine . . . His left hand moved away from the 'bot controller to the keyboard, rapidly tapping just four keys . . .

<<T...R...E...Y>>

On the last stroke there was a *pop*, and a fireball engulfed the structure under surveillance.

"No!" Coop yelled, silence no longer an issue. On the monitor, in the camera-view window there was nothing but snow as the comlink with the packbot was severed. He gulped at the final entry in the log window:

<<LtST – initiating self-destruct.>>

His fingers flew over the keyboard, frantically trying to call up the final transmission made by the 'bot, which was programmed to back up its system data prior to self-destruct. As he did so he couldn't help wondering, was he imagining things, or had he just lost his lieutenant . . . for the second time?

"Go! Go! GO!" the squad leader barked into the comm.

The order pinged her transceiver, a sharp reminder of many missions past. She jerked to awareness with a start, her nerves tighter than a well-set tripline. In one instant she went from drifting through oblivion to combat-ready.

There were large gaps in her memory, or at least she presumed there were, seeing as the last thing she could recall was deciding blow up a room full of Demons... and preparing to die...again. *So who the hell's cock-up was this?* she thought, as the 'bot was powered up and tossed through a nearby gapping hole that used to hold a window.

"Treybot deployed, Sarge," Coop subvocalized into his bonejack. "She's transmitting at . . . 100 percent optimal."

VICTORIA PER VIRES

TO SPEC
Charles E. Gannon

MENDEZ, THE NEWEST GUY IN THE SQUAD, HAD BEEN JUMPY EVER SINCE THE worsening weather updates started coming in. The most recent message—that Priestley's replacement wouldn't show up for at least another three hours—just made him more anxious. As Eureka command post signed off, Grim saw Mendez hold his new rifle—a flimsy piece of experimental junk known as the Cochrane XM 1—a bit too tightly. So, in an effort to take the newbie's mind off his anxiety, Grim asked him, "So, what's on the 'other' radio today?"

A tentative grin twitched at the right corner of Mendez's mouth. "It's against regs to listen to—"

"I'm not a snitch, Mendez."

Mendez needed no further encouragement: broad, short, and compact in his pint-sized vacc suit, he made a fast, flat zero-gee hop over to the control panel. Steadying himself on a handhold, he pushed a preset button, jumping the radio over to the Commonwealth Armed Forces frequency.

But instead of plaintively wailing guitars, they heard a painfully jocular deejay working his way through the end of the news. First, Mendez looked like the kid who got coal for Christmas—but then he went rigid as the announcer segued into the weather:

> "Hey, here's a CWAF flash from our siblings-in-arms guarding the Big Secret out at Eureka. "Quaff" this one, grunts: they tell us that it's another beautiful February day out at the Mars L-5 point, with the mercury peaking at minus 215 Celsius. There's good visibility despite average dust densities and a continued surge of downstream trash sent by some unknown admirers near Mars. But for everyone out here in the fourth orbit, remember: that huge solar storm-front we've been watching will move on through in just an hour or so. So come on inside before the weather

turns and send a shout out to the folks back home. Don't let those 2.1 AU stop you."

Great: now Mendez looked more anxious than ever. Grim reached out a brown, blunt-fingered hand to shut off the radio, reflecting that this might be the right moment to employ some of the conversational and psychological subtlety for which sergeants have always been famous.

Grim looked directly into Mendez's eyes. "What the hell is wrong with you, Mendez?"

Mendez looked gratifyingly startled, then abashed. "Well, sir—"

Grim sighed. "Mendez, don't offend me with that 'sir' crap: I'm not an officer. I work for a living."

"Yes, si—Master Sergeant Grimsby."

Eldridge Grimsby—who was never called anything other than Grim—grunted at the narrow margin by which Mendez had avoided a repetition of the original slur, and nodded for him to continue.

"I don't know, Sarge; it just makes me nervous—guarding the Big Secret they're building on Eureka."

"Why?"

"Well—because it's a secret, I guess. And if it's as important as all the security precautions seem to indicate, that means that someone out there"—he swung an arm at the space beyond the bulkhead—"could have us in their crosshairs now, this very second." When Grim failed to respond in any way, Mendez added, "Sarge, we could die without warning—and without ever knowing what it was we were guarding."

Grim stared at him. "And your point is?"

"Well—that's an awful lot of risk without an awful lot of information."

"Mendez, if the spacesuit you're wearing hasn't tipped you off just yet, you're in the ExoAtmospheric Corps, and we don't get information; we get orders. And bad food and worse pay. What part of this have you failed to understand?"

But Grim could see, from the way that Mendez's gaze wandered away, that his fear wasn't as general as he had made it sound: there was something more specific behind it. And Grim had a pretty good idea what that might be. "Okay, Mendez, spill it. What have you learned about the Big Secret? Why are we more at risk now?"

Mendez folded his hands and stared at them. "Sarge, I was floating watch outside the comcenter yesterday and heard the staff officers getting briefed by a pair of civvies."

"Okay, Mendez, I'll bite: who was briefing the staffers?"

"I heard two names, Sarge. One was some kind of spook, I think: a Mr. Wilder. Darryl Wilder. Mean anything to you?"

Grim felt his stomach contract. "Yeah; security specialist. Ex-Air Force. Then ex-FBI."

"Who's he with now?"

"Wish I knew."

"Private contractor?"

Grim emitted a rumbling set of amused grunts; he was secretly proud of having a laugh that sounded like an irritated crocodile. "Mendez, guys like Wilder don't retire. Ever."

"So—"

"So he's interagency, or an errand boy for the Joint Chiefs, or carrying out an Executive Order."

"How do you know about him?"

"Right after we started setting up shop out here, he was on-station for about a month: always sniffing around, like a security inspector or engineer. Didn't talk much, never gave an order, but always looking, examining, watching. I think he was the one who suggested building the Big Secret out here on Eureka."

"Well, he sure as hell picked a crappy place."

"Which was his intention, I'm sure: easy enough to get to Mars from here, and vice versa, but not really on anyone's flight path, so you see intruders well in advance. Now, you said you heard a second name?"

Mendez looked sideways at Grim. "This guy was not military or security; sounded like he was involved with building the Big Secret itself."

"I ain't playing twenty questions with you, Mendez: who is he?"

"You know that guy Wasserman, the professor who—"

Grim leaned forward before he could stop himself. "Robert Wasserman? The physicist?"

"High-energy physicist—and engineer. Nobel nominations last two years in a row."

"You think they're really—?"

"Could be a starship, Sarge—just like the minority scuttlebutt says."

Grim leaned back so energetically that he almost floated into a backwards somersault out of his "seat." Robert Wasserman. And Darryl Wilder. Both out here in the Martian L-5 wasteland. What besides a secret FTL project could explain their presence? And it would also explain why the other blocs were having trash-heaving hissy fits about being kept at arm's length. If they knew that the Commonwealth was getting close to achieving faster than light travel—

But Mendez wasn't done. "And everyone at the debrief was worried, Sarge. Real worried."

Hearing Mendez's tone and words, Grim suddenly felt the first creeping fingers of contagious anxiety. "They were worried? About what?"

"About this solar storm."

Grim tried not to scowl, failed. "Jee-zus; what the hell is it with this storm? With these hourly updates on expected EMP and rad levels, you'd think we'd never seen a flare before."

"Sarge, if you check the text of those updates, you'll find that HQ has never used the word 'flare'."

Grim blinked: that was strangely, and unsettlingly, true. "Then what the hell aren't they telling us?"

"Sarge, this is a CME. A big one."

When transferring to the ExoAtmo Corps six years ago, Grim had managed—blissfully—to sleep through all the space science crap served up by the rear-echelon weenies, so he was compelled to ask: "What's a CME?"

"A coronal mass ejection."

"And that means?"

Grim immediately regretted asking the question, because Mendez—otherwise a good kid—sat a little straighter, and readied himself to deliver A Recitation of The Facts, as was his wont: he was bucking for OCS so hard that Grim wondered if he sometimes got whiplash from the effort. "A coronal mass ejection occurs when the sun actually heaves out a jet of plasma. Much worse than a flare: lots of EMP, hard radiation, and—" Mendez actually shivered "—a big increase in cosmic rays."

Now, finally, Grim understood Mendez's anxiety. In the flippant vernacular of the Service, radioactive emissions—and particularly those of the most energetic, non-particle variety—were collectively known as 'zoomies.' Cosmic rays, however, had their own special category: they were 'ultra-zoomies.' Unless you were safe inside a (fantastically expensive) electromagnetically-shielded hull or habitat, you just prayed that one of those little nano-scale laser beams didn't hit a chromosome and clip one of your telomeres too short, thereby kicking off runaway replication. Or, as was the more prosaic diagnosis of a cell gone stupid, cancer. Fortunately, that kind of damage was beyond prediction or control and was, therefore, just part of the random nonsense of the job. So Grim—a hardened veteran—wasn't disposed to worry about it. Much.

However, it meant they might have to wait out the storm and hunker down for a very extended watch in their one-room rad shack: a small, pressurized hab module that got its name from what its occupants really cared about: its multilayered radiation shielding. Designed to house—barely—a three-man team for extended watches, its interior was an inhumanly cramped collection of long-range guidance and tracking computers, sensor and drone control consoles, and a single bunk. Its head was a constant source of black humor and savage derision: by comparison, the fresher of a commuter jet seemed positively palatial. On extended watches in its claustrophobic interior, even Grim had found himself beginning to reconsider the hazards of a spacewalk in exchange for a little extra room to stretch, and a change of scenery. Not that Grim was a fan of EVA ops: he had come late—and unwillingly—to zero-gee maneuver, tactics, and training. And now, to his even greater delight, he was about to find himself the middle of the biggest solar storm on record. He sighed, and found a way to conceal the rest of his ignorance: "So, Mendez, let's see how much of your training you remember: what are the special protocols for a CME?"

"Well, we'll have to pull the sensor and comm array in all the way: if we don't, we're sure to fry something. Maybe everything. Not much reason to leave 'em out, anyway: anything but laser-based comm and nav is going to be static-soup."

"Not like we have much to scan except the Mars trash." In response, Mendez frowned again. Grim snorted. "What? Now you're worried about the Mars trash, too?"

"Well, the brass is, Sarge. Seems like the other blocs are *not* dumping the trash anymore—at least not the way they were right after we posted Eureka as a no-fly zone."

"So who's doing it now—and how?"

"Well, that's what's got the brass upset. Word is that Earth HQ got on the horn with Admiral Riggen and tore him a new one. Threatened him with additional proctological procedures if he didn't find where the trash was coming from and pronto."

"God almighty, Mendez: it's space. How hard can it be to find where it's coming from? You track back and—"

But Mendez was shaking his head. "It's not that kind of trash anymore, Sarge. No metals, nothing too big. Now it's all composites, plastics: just a bunch of black bodies by the time it reaches us. And a lot of it is so small that—"

Grim put up a bearish hand. "Okay, professor: that's enough. I'm not on the review board for your OCS app."

Mendez's eyes bulged, blinked, bulged again. "But Sarge, I wouldn't—I'm not—"

"Save it: except for your fear of cosmic rays, you're too eager to die to be an enlisted man. Also, if the rumors are true, you have more brain cells than an amoeba, so obviously you're on OCS's radar."

As if on cue, the command circuit toned twice: coded traffic from Base. After going through the tiresome two-sided authentication waltz, the inevitable Junior Grade Lieutenant on the other end got down to business: "Shack Four, we are updating you on your replacement for Priestley: we've got a clearance snafu on our end. Probably won't get it resolved before the end of your watch."

As Grim heard the first indignant words come out of his mouth, he realized that he was now shouting at an officer— as had happened too often throughout his career. It did not matter that the officer was a J.G. and therefore the human equivalent of pond scum: this pond scum still ranked him and could pull a seniority marking— a "rocker"—off the bottom of his stack of sergeant's chevrons. Grim's realization of this trailed a crucial second behind his shout of: "We're a man down because of a 'clearance snafu?' What the hell kind of bullshit is that . . . sir?" Grim could hear the insincerity in the lagging honorific; knew the J.G. had heard the same. Oh well, Grim hadn't really liked being a Master Sergeant anyway: too much paperwork.

"Sergeant Grimsby,"—the voice was markedly colder than the outside temperature—"Priestley can only be replaced by someone who's cleared for the same special duty."

"Special duty? What special duty?"

Mendez tapped his junk-rifle, muttered: "Sarge, he means the Cochrane. Carrying a field prototype is special duty: along with Priestley, they only cleared five of us for—"

Grim rolled his eyes. "Jesus Christ. Sir, are you telling me you won't send out a replacement because you don't have anyone else who's permitted to carry around another of these dumb-ass guns?"

"Sergeant, I'm telling you I *can't* send anyone who's not a part of the field trial: the protocols are quite explicit—and are a top priority, as per Earth HQ."

"Great: so we're down to two men for the rest of the watch."

Grim was surprised when the affirmation lagged, and then did not come. Instead, the J.G. said, "No; you're down to one."

Grim looked at Mendez, who was already looking at him. Eyes narrowed, Grim asked the console coolly. "Say again, sir. Sounded to me like you said the duty watch in this shack is to be reduced to one."

"That is correct, Sergeant."

"That is a violation of our standing orders, sir. One man can't oversee all the critical systems in the event of an attack. So—with all due respect—I am not going to leave Private Mendez out here on his own. He's only been on station for—"

"Sergeant: you're not leaving Private Mendez. He's leaving you."

Oh. Well. That made everything just lovely, then. "On whose order am I losing Mendez, sir?"

"No one from here, Sergeant: this order actually originated off-base."

Mendez half-rose, eyes wide, fearful: Grim waved him down. A "mystery summons" from the rear was every soldier's dread, since it usually signified bad news from home. But after thirty years in uniform, Grim had seen exceptions to every rule and this might be one of them: he decided to check. "Is he being called in to receive a personal communiqué from stateside?"

"Doesn't say, Sergeant. But the order to pull him off the line comes straight from Mars HQ. And he's got to start back now. Otherwise he won't make it inside before the hard weather hits."

Mendez raised his chin, seemed ready to resist; Grim shook his head at the newbie once, sharply. "Understood, base. Mendez is on his way. Rad Shack Four out."

The light that indicated a live carrier signal hadn't winked out before Mendez launched into his protests. "But, sir—"

"Mendez!"

"But, *Sarge*, this order just isn't right—"

Grim was touched. "Listen, Esteban; I'll be fine out here on my ow—"

"No, no: I mean that my recall order sounds fishy—and besides, it will invalidate the Cochrane's field test."

It made Grim all warm inside to realize that Mendez's commitment to an experimental weapon was immeasurably greater than whatever (apparently weak) concern he had for the continued well-being of his senior NCO. "Ah. The Cochrane." That flimsy piece of shit. "Listen: if they were about to invalidate their precious test, they would have told you to leave it behind for me to babysit."

"I don't buy it, Sarge—and no one seems to have clued in the J.G.: by ordering me in, he'll invalidate the current trial phase. And my recall order doesn't make any sense, either: whether it's a family loss notice or not, it should go through the company CO before it gets to me. And leaving you out here on your own? That's blatantly against standing orders." Mendez frowned. "There's too much going wrong or weird at the same time: I'm gonna look into this as soon as I return to base."

"Which starts now," added Grim, snagging and handing the Cochrane up toward him.

Mendez, distracted, took a moment to realize what Grim was doing: then he shook his head. "No, Sarge: you keep it."

I'd rather have a piranha in my pants. But Grim said: "Mendez, as you pointed out, I'm not cleared to—"

Ever-respectful Mendez interrupted, almost violently. "Sarge: keep the Cochrane. If—well, if anything *happens* out here, you might need it."

Like I need a hole in my vacc suit. "I'm better off with my old—"

But Mendez had snatched up the weapon Grim was about to mention—an Armalite 6mm caseless. "No, Sarge: I'm taking this one. You keep the Cochrane."

"Mendez, you stop this nonsense. I've been using that Armalite since—"

But Mendez smiled an apology as he snugged his helmet, faceplate still up, over his head. "Sarge, the Cochrane is state of the art: liquid propellant, variable munitions and velocity. That makes it extremely versatile, and great—*great*—in zero-gee. Do you remember everything I told you about it?"

I hear your endless gushings in my sleep. "Some of it."

"Then please: do this for me." He checked the clock. "Mother of God; I've gotta go. *Via con Dios*, Sarge."

"You too."

The airlock squealed open, and then complained once more as it was shut.

Leaving Grim quite alone in Rad Shack Four.

Forty-two minutes later, the external environment monitor started an almost nasal squawking. Grim pushed himself into a slow drift toward the console, looked at the radiation sensors, inspected the rem numbers on the real-time dosimeter—and blinked. As he reached over to silence the alarms, he kept his eyes on the unprecedented numbers, and settled in to watch their unprecedented rate of increase.

—and bumped into the XM-1 Cochrane's oddly-vented flash-suppressor, which nudged cheekily against the side of his thigh. Grim scowled at it; okay, so it was cool to look at: a sleek, unipiece design. And, although he had refused to admit it to Mendez, he had read the stats on the weapon. If the hype had any resemblance to the truth, its nannite-reinforced composites made it light and extremely rugged. But it still looked like some flimsy piece of crap out of a sci-fi B-movie of about a hundred years ago.

But, to hear the brass tell it, looks were apparently deceiving. With the liquid propellant stored separately from the warheads, the bullpup magazine held three times the usual number of rounds. No shell casings meant it was a sealed action, without breech or bolt: the liquid propellant was simply injected into the combustion chamber, making velocity—and therefore recoil—a function of how much was injected at any one time. The same combustion chamber was also used to boost bigger munitions out of the integral, underslung launch-tube. Grim wanted to call that a 'grenade launcher' but every time he did, Mendez corrected him: apparently this miracle weapon was capable of launching a variety of other, rather exotic submunitions. The Cochrane could probably turn water into wine, too, given half a chance. Grim sneered down at it: yeah, you look fancy, and the specs look impressive, but you just won't cut it as a sturdy tool. You look like—and probably are—a kid's toy, not a real gun: all bells and whistles, but no balls for business.

The short-range radar emitted a strangled squawk: a partial contact, just at the edge the system's threshold. It was probably a marginal object that, tumbling, had presented a momentarily bigger cross-section for the radar to bounce off. But the system squawked again, and this time Grim saw what had tweaked it: a faint signature, range established at seven kilometers—no, six. Then the range indicator plummeted to three, jumped up to ten, and finally zeroed out for a recalibration as the whole screen surged brightly for a moment. As it faded back into its normal contrast ratios, Grim looked up at the external weather sensors: a corresponding surge in charged particles was dying down. Which suggested that the contact was probably just an anomaly of how the storm was interacting with the trash, since the blip had appeared to be closing at exactly the same rate as today's unusually dense sampling of debris.

The monitor surged again, but this time, remained bright: the sensor's overload alarm system chirped and an orange warning light glowed on the board. The automatic protection software had activated: in ten seconds, unless overridden, it would yank back the combined sensor/comm mast, sheathing it in a hardened faraday cage until it was safe to peek outside again. Grim watched the countdown ticker erode toward zero—but he reached over quickly when it hit "4" and turned the system off. The program hooted at him, asked him—in bright red block letters—"Do you wish to engage safety override?"

Did he? Really? Grim rubbed his stubbly chin. Well, of course he didn't: if he kept the mast extended, there was a reasonable chance that its sensitive electronics would fry, and an equal (indeed, directly proportional) chance that the brass would fry him. That—along with the system SOPs and his situationally-specific standing orders—should have decided the matter. But this situation was not the one envisioned by those standard procedures and standing orders. And that meant that Grim's capacity to follow them was about to "fluctuate": that was the term he had used during his first disciplinary hearing twenty-eight years ago, and had been using ever since. And he'd probably get busted a stripe for his trouble. And what for? Was there really—*really*—any danger? Even if a basketball-sized package of plastique slipped past his metal-obsessed sensors, and headed toward the Big Secret on Eureka, what harm could it do? It would have to be invisible to radar, which meant no metal, which meant no computer, which meant no terminal guidance: it was—literally and figuratively—a shot in the dark. And with all the EMP activity, there'd be no way to command-detonate such a package, unless some mad scientist had come up with a strange new piezo-electric initiator, or maybe a switch activated by timed biological decay—

Like iron filings suddenly exposed to a magnet, Grim's thoughts swiftly collected around the term "biological," just as the short-range radar let loose a full squawk, and showed the same junk-blip still approaching—but on a slightly altered vector. Grim added the terms and concepts together: Biological. Change of vector. No reliable electric systems.

God damn, it was a live attack; in the midst of this solar typhoon, there were living, breathing saboteurs inbound—

Grim reached out and tapped the dynamic button that would open the link back to base. Which produced no results. He tapped it again, then harder, then hammered at it. Nothing. He turned to the hardwired auxiliary console to his immediate right, flipped the toggle for the command line: a sudden wall of cat-scratch static prompted him to shut off the volume.

So: thanks to the weather, communications were out. Which meant he had no way to call for help, or send a warning, and, reciprocally, base would no longer be receiving automated status updates from the rad shacks and therefore would not check to discover why he had failed to retract his sensor/comm mast. He was alone—and only he had the knowledge, and therefore the opportunity, to act.

Grim leaned back slowly, checked the range: given the one meter/second closure rate, he had about ten minutes to consider the problem, decide on a course of action, and carry it out—whatever it happened to be.

Grim turned to his tried-and-true first maxim of planning: know thy enemy—and had to admit that he knew next to nothing about the approaching attackers. So, using what little data he had, could he induce or deduce any tactical intel from it?

First, given the detection range of Eureka's main arrays, and the attackers' rate of approach, they had not been inside any hull—shielded or not—for at least a week. That meant that the attackers had floated in with the junk, using it as a moving smoke screen. And that, in turn, meant that this was a suicide mission: given the wholebody rem dosage the attackers had accrued during that extended approach, this solar storm guaranteed that their death from radiation sickness would be as certain as it would be swift.

As peculiar as that conclusion seemed, Grim discovered that it was consistent with the pattern of careful and meticulous planning evinced by his opponents. The timing of the attack indicated that it was designed to take advantage of the rising solar activity cycle. Indeed, it had probably been held in readiness for weeks, even months, until solar meteorology indicated the first, turbulent signs of an imminent coronal mass ejection. In the meantime, Eureka's security forces had been lulled into a slow and inevitable complacency regarding the camouflaging trash flow, ultimately seeing it as just another part of the environment. And in retrospect, Priestley's absence, and now Mendez's, had probably been achieved by hacking, bribery, or both.

Given that level of commitment and preparation, it was probable that the attackers' equipment was purpose-built for this mission, meaning that from weapons to vacc suits, it was almost entirely non-metallic. However, complete thermal equalization and diffusion was more difficult to achieve in space, and such systems would be further impaired if they had to avoid using any metal components.

Which meant that the attackers' thermals that might still be visible: Grim quickly snapped over to the slightly more robust thermal sensors. And there, mixed in with the slowly oncoming stream of trash, was a diffuse, almost invisible thermal bloom above the background, pointing inward like a finger.

Pointing straight at Rad Shack Four. Grim rechecked, confirmed the vector of approach: although their target was unquestionably the Big Secret being built on Eureka, they were heading straight at him. Why?

The answer followed the question without delay: because the saboteurs surely knew about the rad shacks, and therefore knew that they needed to eliminate whichever one sat astride or closest to their point of penetration as they crossed through Eureka's spherical security perimeter. Which meant that Rad Shack Four wasn't a haven anymore: it was a coffin. Oh, it still protected Grim from the rads, but that wasn't the biggest danger, now: thinking like the attackers, he somberly concluded that he'd opt to take out the rad shack with something quick and decisive. A high-explosive, armor-piercing missile would be the weapon of choice: it would easily penetrate the shack's shielding and would bust it open like a pickaxe smashing through the shell of an unsuspecting mollusk.

Grim returned from his thoughts, facing down into the sensor screen over which he was perched. He placed both of his hands on its wildly-flickering surface: despite the pronounced veins and sturdy wrists, his lightly pebbled and very dark brown skin looked suddenly and incongruously fragile and vulnerable. And Grim felt the accuracy of that perception rise up with the thought: "I've got no choice: I've got to go out there, too."

Which seemed like suicide, on the one hand, because in this storm, EVA ops was the radiological equivalent of going outdoors during a hailstorm of razor blades. But what could he achieve by staying inside? Unable to fight back from within the EMP-crippled rad shack, he could only wait to die.

Grim rose carefully from the seat, grabbed his helmet, reached for his Armalite—and closed his hand on empty air. Oh. Right. Slowly, he turned to look at the Cochrane. Okay, then: you and me, bitch. And—for your sake—you'd better perform to spec, or you're going to get very lost in deep space.

He reached down, picked up the weapon and moved toward the airlock, slaving the rad shack's shaky sensor feed into his HUD relays as he went.

Exiting the airlock, Grim controlled the first, transient sense of nausea that always surged up when he went EVA: no up, no down, and the black forever all around him. The stars only made the distance and solitude more absolute. Why so many people—from the earliest astronauts to the current day—were thrilled by "spacewalks" was beyond him.

The distant sun—a small, painfully incandescent nickel—peeked into his helmet, rising up over the lower rim of the faceplate as he manually dogged the hatch and resteadied himself. He had a full MMU on his back, but the less activity and motion he engaged in, the better. Right now, surprise was his only sure advantage, so high-energy maneuvers of any kind were out of the question.

Using the external handholds, he towed himself back down into the shadow, and then around behind the rad shack, placing its mass between himself and the approach vector of the saboteurs. Once there, he checked the rad shack's sensor feed in his helmet: not good. Whether it was the sensors failing or the EMP interference, the data skipped sideways, winked out, came back, fizzled, cohered, leaned, then straightened and remained momentarily, quaveringly, readable—before it commenced its weird free-form dance all over again. But in that brief moment of clarity, Grim had seen the oncoming blip—except that it was larger now, shaped like a lumpy, mostly collapsed quatrefoil. There were *four* of them? Maybe it was just another sensor glitch—

But it probably wasn't, because it made perfect sense. It was just the right number: one heavy weapons expert, a backup expert who was probably carrying the missiles they planned to use on the Big Secret, and then two heavies. The heavies' specialty would be in EVA weaponplay—which, given the way that conventional firearm recoil sent you tumbling ass-over-ankles in zero-gee, was not a common or easily acquired skill. The heavies would provide cover for the other two, distract and/or neutralize responding defense forces, maintain situational awareness. The guys with the missiles would be monomaniacally focused on their equipment and their target.

In another minute they would reach the 2000-meter mark, which is where Grim estimated they might consider eliminating the rad shack. Meaning it was time to get a little distance from it. Grim placed both feet against the hull of the rad shack. He reached down to the handhold on either side of him, achieving a position akin to being frozen in the "squat" phase of a squat thrust. Then he simultaneously released the hand holds and pushed as hard as he could with his legs.

As he shot quickly away from the rad shack, he checked the HUD to see if there was any reaction from the blips; no new course changes were evident—and then the whole display went black. Great. Either the signal was lost or the system was fried; either way, it was all on him, now.

Which meant it was time to confront the Cochrane and its insanely diverse ammo bag. Clips of penetrators, expanders, non-lethals—those were pretty self-explanatory. Pulling up the top flap on the segmented grenade pouch, Grim laid a finger on an HE round, considered its use as a flare, rejected the tactic: Eureka's own sensors would be pulled in, but the explosion would surely alert the attackers to his presence. Instead, Grim selected two range-detonated flechette rounds, loaded them, and reasoned he should give the targeting system a quick check before trusting his life to it. He turned it on, and raised the integrated sighting scope to his right eye—

And held his breath. Whatever computer was silently working in the recesses of the Cochrane was apparently laboring overtime: multiple moving objects were quickly located optically, ranged and vector assessed by a laser ping, and a guidon indicated how to reposition the gun to acquire the target. Damned impressive—but still just a toy, Grim reminded himself.

He revised that opinion when the Cochrane flashed a new guidon into existence in what seemed like open space and indicated a cluster of four objects—which Grim *still* couldn't see—closing at .97 meters per second at 2100 meters range. Sweet Jesus: unprompted, the Cochrane had found the attack force. *Well, well,* Grim thought, smiling at the gun, *you've earned your continued existence—bitch.*

The targeting display flickered, then reasserted: the electromagnetic soup was already getting to the Cochrane's electronics. Grim switched off the power, and brought the scope back up to his eye.

Even through the faceplate, the unassisted sight-picture in the unusually wide eyepiece was still viable—and at maximum magnification, the plain old mechanical scope was already picking out dark blotches moving across and occluding the background starfield just where the targeting system had detected the intruders. Grim grunted in satisfaction: gotcha. He settled in to watch them, calculating that they would make their move within the minute, if his conjectures were correct. And so far, they had been—except for one unsolved tactical variable: where was the ship from which the attackers had deployed, and how had it stayed both out of sight and out of the trash stream?

Grim glanced sideways at the scattered, tumbling bits of irregular blackness and greyness that were the trash stream—and suddenly he knew the answer: the attackers' "ship" was floating past him right now. Their ship was now part of the junk. Sure: each of them had been sealed and launched in a self-disassembling pod. It had had a hull of composites and plastics, rudimentary thrust, life support, comestibles, and was set on a ballistic course, so it required no guidance. When the attackers neared the range at which Eureka's arrays might pick them out, they—figuratively speaking—pulled their ripcords and let the pods fall, or rather, float, to pieces around them. That way, they could probably have approached to within about 300 kilometers before getting into their vacc suits and preparing for—

The attack began with a sudden burst of vapor, centered on a bright flash which bloomed and then arced out from the midst of the attackers: a rocket, speeding toward the rad shack. Grim flinched away as a blinding flash coronaed up from the far side of the boxy module, knocking it into a slow tumble as papers and pulped electronic parts vomited out of the huge, jagged rupture in its side.

Time to return the favor. Grim reactivated the targeting system, leaned into the Cochrane's sights again, ready to fire—but was surprised to see a question mark glowing on the right margin of the display overlay, underscored with the legend "0G opt?" Grim wanted to spit: goddamn, was this weapon busted already? Goddamned tinkertoy piece of sh—

Oh, no, wait: Mendez had told him about this. The weapon sensed strong changes in ballistic conditions—such as gravity—and would ask if you wanted an optimum solution. So: "0G opt?" was obviously offering him an optimal firing solution for zero gee. Well, that seemed like a good idea: he edged his thumb up to the "accept" button behind the handgrip, pressed it. The query blinked away.

Grim focused on the four attackers again: they were still clustered, and at 1400 meters range. He reasoned he might get two of them with the flechette grenade. But how to access the launcher?

The needed information arose as chapter and verse from Mendez's endless worship of the Cochrane: "You've got three settings, Sarge: main weapon, launcher, or integrated. Just adjust this dial down here—"

Grim did. The Cochrane identified the ready round in the launcher (the laser-controlled, range-detonated flechette grenade), computed the ballistics (which were pretty clean in free space), and superimposed the firing solution on the current scene: it painted a dim red cone on top of two of the attackers' vector-projected plots at the time of warhead discharge. Then the image faded, almost blanked out: EMP overload. Damn: moment of truth. Grim snapped the safety off, lined up the weapon until the guidon told him his aimpoint matched the indicated firing solution, and squeezed the trigger—just as the image fuzzed, flickered, and winked off for good.

For a split second, Grim was sure—again—that the weapon had malfunctioned: the almost imperceptible jolt from the underslung launcher barely tumbled him. But no, he could see the grenade moving briskly downrange. But wait a minute: he could see it? How was that possible? Why was it going so slowly—?

And then he realized that, in zero-gee, the optimal firing solution was not so much a matter of maximizing accuracy, as it was concerned with minimizing recoil: the munition had been fired with only a tiny bit of force.

Grim, now moving backward more rapidly, and in a very slow tumble, entertained the brief hope that, because of this minimum downrange bump, he would also remain undetected by the attackers. No such luck: a mere second after he had launched his counterattack, the infiltrators turned toward him, weapons flickering. He twisted his head to keep them under observation: the muzzle flashes were very small, and seemed to occur in short, angry sequences: probably small-caliber weapons, with a maximum three-round burst setting. All common features in zero-gee firearm designs that—ever unsuccessfully—tried to minimize the recoil of conventional rounds. A few self-oxidizing tracers indicated the vector of the fire, which dropped off: having seen that they were wide of their mark, they were no doubt using their own MMUs to correct their tumble before reaiming—

Almost precisely where Grim had seen the sparkle of their weapons, there was a barely-visible flash, from which extended a small, lateral vapor plume: his flechette grenade. As Grim rolled up slowly toward direct alignment again, he brought the scope up to his eye.

Seen at the visual equivalent of fifty meters, one of the figures he had targeted was thrashing spasmodically; whether or not he was wounded, it was pretty clear that his suit was vented, probably multiple times. The other figure was a stark contrast: motionless, arms widening slowly, some object—his personal weapon?—had begun to free-float away on a slightly altered vector of its own. The third attacker, who had been at the edge of the area of effect, was also engaged in rapid motions, but these were brisk and methodical, not desperate. Probably one of the missile specialists trying to change over to his personal weapon, realized Grim as he selected the Cochrane's primary barrel.

He was approaching the end of his first full 360 degree tumble, briefly wondered if he should use his own MMU to restabilize, then realized that if he did so, he would lose the advantage of getting in another shot before they were ready to respond. But taking that shot would also make his own tumble worse. Mendez *had* mentioned something about a rear-jet compensator for zero-gee firing stabilization—sort of like a mini-bazooka backblast—but Grim couldn't recall the details. And since Grim had no time to screw with it, he used what he knew: he spun the propellant dial to the lowest setting—minimum recoil, in case the automatic optimization system has been fried. Then, as he rolled up into correct alignment, he quickly lined up the attacker who had been outside the cone of flechettes, and fired four quick rounds.

Grim was surprised—and relieved—to find that most of the imparted thrust vectored him directly backward; as he fired, the muzzle brake's cruciform nozzles selectively vented the weapon's exhaust to precisely counteract any pitch, yaw, or roll changes to his trajectory. But the Cochrane's system wasn't perfect: possibly because Grim had rapped the rounds out so fast, there was still enough off-vector impulse to increase the rate and skew of his tumble.

As he came around on his first faster, slightly cockeyed rotation, Grim panned the scope across what he estimated had been his target area. At first, he saw nothing—then a faint white plume: he swept back toward that. The plume disappeared briefly, then appeared again, evidently rotating back into view. It was a punctured air-tank, the rapidly venting gases throwing its wearer into an accelerating spin and carrying him on a very divergent trajectory. Judging from the figure's already muted writhings, he wouldn't live to see where his new heading took him: Grim guessed that he had hit more than just the backpack unit.

But now, as Grim continued his own knees-over-nose rotation, he faced two alternatives—neither of which had promising outcomes. Grim could either wait until he completed another somersault, try to access the last target through the Cochrane's scope (unlikely, given his increasingly erratic tumble) and score some more hits (profoundly unlikely, for the same reason); or, he could let the Cochrane float on its lanyard while he grabbed for his MMU controls to correct his tumble—and thereby allow the other guy to finish getting his personal weapon readied and aimed, and thereby beat Grim to the probably fatal punch. But wait: Mendez had once said, "And here's the beauty part, Sarge; you can use the Cochrane to correct your tumble—"

—And then Grim was following his memories of Esteban's instructions, just as they came to him, word by word—

"First you set the magazine feed to 'off'—"

—Grim did—

"—so that when you squeeze the trigger, the Cochrane's muzzle works just like a little rocket. And to counterboost, all you do is reorient yourself—"

—Grim swung his left arm out, imparting a little spin to his body—

"—then aim into the vector you need to correct—"

—Grim aimed down into the direction of his roll and slightly to one side—

"—and fire."

Grim squeezed the trigger, leaned into the light recoil, felt his rotational speed drop, saw that the yaw had almost disappeared. He straightened out the tube, fired two more times. And was almost perfectly stabilized. He threw his left arm back across his body to turn around again—toward the enemy—and brought the weapon up to his right eye.

He got his left hand back on the forestock, saw the starfield sweep past in the scope, caught a glimpse of movement—and then spotted a silhouette against the stars, head hunched down as if taking aim. Hail Mary, now. Grim thumb-selected autofire, twisting at the waist to keep the barrel on-target. He saw angry little flickers coming from the silhouette as he fired.

Even the Cochrane couldn't keep up with that insane barrage of thrust-generating discharges: Grim tumbled backward, felt a sharp slap to the back of his head as the spinning began. And that slap was probably death's calling card: the attacker's first accurate round had hit his helmet—luckily in the tough rear-plating, probably burrowing into the command electronics for his now useless computer and HUD. But the next round would probably hit something that was soft, would puncture, would release air, would leak blood: would kill him.

But that next round never came.

After correcting his madcap cartwheels with the MMU, and maneuvering into the solar lee of a little loping rock that dutifully followed the ruined Rad Shack

Four in its slow orbit of the distant sun, Grim waited. And waited. And contemplated his probable wholebody rem dose. And waited some more.

Almost a full hour later, base finally sent a shielded away boat out to nose among the rocks in the vicinity of Rad Shack Four. When it got within 500 meters, Grim toggled his radio, heard the faint hum of the carrier wave under the EMP static, and said, "Hey. Over here."

After a moment of silence, there was the inevitable request for the day code, the countersign, and a curt request from a new voice: "Sitrep, Sergeant Grimsby."

"Uh—who is this?"

"Sergeant Grimsby, my name is Darryl Wilder. I'm—"

"Yes, sir; I know who you are, sir."

A pause.

"Very well. Proceed."

As the away boat made its slow approach, Grim proceeded to give the most respectful, thorough, professional, and utterly boring sitrep of his entire career to date. At the end, he even managed to forget about the rads sleeting through his body long enough to ask, "Any idea who was behind this, Mr. Wilder?"

"No hard evidence yet, but I'd say it was the megacorporations."

"Corporate? Why? They afraid you won't let them sell Big Macs on Alpha Centauri?"

There was a long pause. "Sergeant, you seem very sure that our construction project at Eureka has something to do with interstellar travel."

Oops. "Uh . . . sorry, sir."

"Sorry?"

"Shouldn't have said that on open channel, sir."

"Hmm . . . no, you shouldn't have: but your conclusion, and your presence of mind, is promising. So, it seems, is the Cochrane."

Grim stared as the gun; the approaching bow lights of the away boat glinted off its selector switch: it seemed like a bright, conspiratorial wink. "Yeah, well—it was okay."

"'Okay'? Sergeant, from what our first readable scans are showing, it seems like it was the star of the show."

"Sure—but, with all due respect, Mr. Wilder, what if the Cochrane hadn't worked?"

"Just be glad that it *did* work, oh Ye of Little Faith,"—Grim's Grandmama Rayshawne had used that same expression; didn't sound right coming from a man—"because if you had had your old Armalite-6, you would have had to conduct a full MMU tumble correction after every shot. How many shots do you think you could have taken that way?"

"Uh—two. Maybe."

"Yes, 'maybe'—with a capital 'M.' Either way, two shots would have been two too few: they came at you with four attackers. A conventional zero-gee weapon couldn't have engaged them all. But the Cochrane could—and did. You were right to have Mendez leave the Cochrane behind, even if it was against regs."

"Uh, sir—"

"Yes?"

Grimsby paused: the smart thing to do was to take the credit for keeping the Cochrane at the shack. But—maybe because he had just recalled Grandmama Rayshawne belting out "Sweet Bye and Bye" at First Baptist—he said, "Sir, I didn't think of keeping the weapon at the shack. That was Mendez." With any luck, that would earn Esteban enough brownie points for his OCS nod, allowing him to become a less-than-typically detestable shave tail—if he lived long enough. But luckily, Mendez had spent a little time coming up through the ranks, knew to listen to sergeants (usually), and so had a better than even chance of dodging both enemy bullets and the tender ministrations of a late-night latrine fragging.

Wilder was still talking: Grim tuned back in as he was commenting, "Well, you certainly proved that Mendez made the right choice."

"Yes, sir, but I did break a few regs."

"Well, I'm not your CO, but it seems to me that if they don't bust you, they're going to have to decorate you."

"Why's that, sir?"

"Well, in addition to single-handedly defeating a sabotage attempt on what you will soon know as Project Prometheus, you just gave the Cochrane a field test the likes of which no weapon has ever had—either in terms of what was demanded of it, or how well it performed. And that in the hands of an untrained operator. Back at Eureka, the testing team all look like they stole grins off a Cheshire cat, talking about how no amount of careful planning can beat plain old dumb luck."

"Huh: in my case, very dumb."

"Suitably self-deprecating, Sergeant, but not very convincing. When you emerge from your debriefing—which they claim will last a week—we should have a talk about your future. How does that sound?"

That sounded almost as good as the week-long debrief, which mean a soft, solo bed in officer's country and real chow, instead of the grey walls of the brig he had been expecting to inhabit for the foreseeable future. "That sounds fine, sir."

"Good. Now, one last thing. The fellows up here from Picatinny are so eager to find out if there were any failures or shortcomings with the Cochrane, that they refused to wait for the debrief. So I promised them I'd ask you: did the Cochrane fall short on any of its design parameters, or did it perform to spec?"

Grim looked down at the gun. "Yes sir, it performed to spec." Then—because no one was there to see—he grinned. And he thought:

Yeah; definitely to spec.

TO SPEC Acknowledgements: For expert opinion and information on the topic of solar weather in general, and the effects of coronal mass ejections in specific, the author gratefully acknowledges the expert input of: Dr. Gordon Holman, NASA Goddard Space Flight Center; Lt. Col. Peter Garretson, USAF; and Russell Howard, a principle investigator in the USN's SECCHI (Sun-Earth Connection Coronal Heliospheric Investigation) initiative.

GUNNERY SERGEANT *
Jeffrey Lyman

I DRAGGED MY FINGERTIPS ACROSS ROWS OF SENSORS MOUNTED JUST BELOW THE gun access-plates. The half-meter hatches at the height of my head had once been yellow, but heat had blistered and chipped the paint. Information flowed from the sensors up through the uplink-pads on my fingers as I walked from one end of the chamber to the other. Everything was in order. Each of my twenty-four guns held a warhead. Twenty-four ordnance conveyers were poised to feed them more. Waiting on my call.

It was cool in the chamber, but in a day or two, or whenever we ran into the Aylin raiders, it would be a cauldron of ejected gases. I would hang in my gravity harness, shielded from concussion-vibrations, helping Fire Control find weak spots in the Aylin shields.

I pressed my ear to the hatch at gun seventeen. My primary gun, my baby–Lucinda.

"Gunner Kirchov," barked a hard, familiar voice. "Are you making love or taking inventory?"

"Taking inventory, sir," I replied to the Lieutenant on the screen above me.

"Get yourself cleaned up. The captain wants you in his conference room."

"Sir?" The captain had never spoken to me before.

"Admiral Geltier's ship is docking now, and you're to meet him in thirty minutes. You've been reassigned."

"But we're due at Zed Station, sir." The ship didn't have enough competent gunners. This reassignment must be important. My heart beat fast.

"I wasn't given a choice. Get moving!"

"Yes, sir. Thirty minutes." I started a countdown timer behind my right eye and ran for the showers and my dress uniform.

* The events in this story take place directly prior to those in "Compartment Alpha", *Breach the Hull*, 2007.

Twenty-eight minutes later I climbed off of an intership transport near the captain's quarters. I had never been this far forward. I saw a familiar face as soon as my shoes hit deck.

"Sergeant Conner," I said, grinning.

"Ain't this the shit, Kirchov? You know what this is about?"

"No idea."

"I hear the admiral needs gunners," Conner said. "This could be an attack mission."

We high-fived. About time. Fleet had been floundering for a year, trying to defend far-flung worlds from the aggressive Aylin raiders, unable to engage the enemy in a meaningful battle while they scourged system after system. Rescue ships couldn't pick up citizens fast enough. Refugees were piling up.

My countdown timer reached one minute. "Don't want to be late," I said, and held my palm over the scanner at the captain's conference room door. It slid aside and we stepped through.

"Private Kirchov. Sergeant Conner. Please sit." The captain pointed to two empty seats.

The room was as small as a table with ten chairs would allow, and we had to squeeze our way down to our seats. Gunners Hong and Daljen were already seated, dress caps precisely positioned on the table in front of them. The other three faces I didn't know.

The door opened again and the admiral entered with his aide. We stood as one.

"We don't have much time so let's get started," he said.

He was probably in his late sixties, and robust. I wondered if he took regeneration shots, or if he was naturally healthy. Decades of sitting behind a desk usually reduced the admirals to potatoes. He dropped into the seat at the head of the table and waved for us to sit. We waited for the captain to sit first.

"Aylin raiders have taken remote Station BHB-12 in the Mirrim System," he said.

I met Hong's eyes across from me. How could the Aylin field so many ships at once? How could they advance on so many fronts? We *had* to launch an attack— give them a reason to concentrate their forces where we could train our big guns on them. We had to find a system or a planet they cared about.

"BHB-12 is lost," the admiral continued. "The next target down the line is the Tarish System. We have a colony in-system called Bountiful, defended only by Upsilon Station and a few old carriers."

I wondered how he could be so calm, talking about losing ten thousand citizens on BHB-12, but then realized he must be used to discussing the loss of systems and planets by now. Stations were small by comparison.

"As you may be aware, we can't stretch our battle groups any thinner to protect the lesser systems. The fleet shipyards are running at one hundred and ten percent, and the mercantile shipyards are nearly all converted to military use, but we won't see an upswing in new vessels for at least six months. The lesser systems don't have that kind of time. They're sitting ducks, and frankly we still can't find rhyme or reason to the attacks."

I stared at him, cold. I had always thought the Aylin were *trying* to stretch us thin, but who was I to have an opinion?

"Bountiful can't be protected," the admiral said. "We sent pickup carriers to rescue whoever we can, but there's not enough time. We're going to lose a lot of people. That's where my group comes in."

He stood and walked to the vid screen and waved his palm over the ID panel. A still-motion image of a ship filled the screen. It wasn't a ship I was familiar with.

"It's a gun cruiser," the admiral said, turning to face us. "Light. Fast. Stripped down to guns and thrust."

It looked like a twentieth-century rocket, maybe one hundred meters long and fifteen in diameter. It bristled with guns—four double-barrel units crammed in between the attitude thrusters around the bow, four more at midships, and four aft. Communications arrays sprouted along the hull, ending just before standard drive pods at the back. The nose cone was obviously shaped for hyperspace bow-shock.

"We can make these quickly," the admiral said. "A lot quicker than we can make the big ships. These will be the defenders of the lesser systems. We've already sent twenty to Bountiful to defend the pickup carriers. You will be in the second wave of thirty ships."

"Sir," Sergeant Conner said. "A ship that size would be like a gnat against their cruisers."

I couldn't take my eyes off the guns. They were external, like on the carriers I used to gun for. Only bigger. We were *finally* taking the fight to the enemy.

"Think of it as a super-fighter, Sergeant," the admiral said. "Fifty of these at Bountiful, six hundred guns, twelve hundred barrels. Enough to handle a raid. But we need gunners and pilots. I'll take you to the rendezvous point."

I looked down at the three faces at the table I didn't recognize. Pilots.

"Sir, what's the complement of those ships," one of the pilots asked.

I had been wondering that. With life support and oxygen generators and waste collection and food, there wouldn't be room for more than fifty people packed shoulder to shoulder. The guns needed thirty-two people, if you just counted sixteen gunners and sixteen gun-techs.

"Her complement is three hundred."

My breath caught. Stunned looks passed around the table. The captain broke the silence. "How could you possibly fit three hundred crew on that ship, Admiral?"

The image behind the admiral switched to a cutaway of the ship. The space between the inner and outer hulls was mostly hyperspace batteries. Packed around an open inner corridor were lines of stasis chambers. "The crew will be suspended," he said. "There's no other way to do it. Pilots and gunners will command your crews through the common neural link."

"And if the link fails?"

He waved his hands. "The link is decentralized. It's redundantly generated in each of fifteen separate compartments. Each compartment will have a full skeleton complement of crew, and each skeleton complement will be mixed so that, should a compartment fail, we won't lose an entire gun crew or pilot crew or maintenance crew. You can turn these cruisers into Swiss cheese and still man guns and thrusters. They are perfect for wearing down the Aylin cruisers, or even one of their destroyers, until we achieve killing shots."

I felt ill. The ships were too small to generate shields. We would be Swiss cheese after every encounter. I had to get out of here. The room was feeling very small and crowded.

"Unfortunately," the admiral continued, "the gun-cruisers don't have much range in hyperspace. The batteries last about sixty hours, then we have to drop into realspace to recharge. We're modifying a couple of our big carriers to cradle the gun cruisers, probably thirty at a time, for transport to far destinations. They're not ready, so we'll be taking the long way to Bountiful."

"When do you leave, sir?" the captain said.

The admiral stuck his jaw out. "We need to do a few quick body modifications before we leave," he said. Then he met our eyes. "The original complement of the ships was two hundred and fifty, but there wasn't enough redundancy. The only way to achieve redundancy was to reduce the size of the stasis chambers."

"So what, sir?" Conner said. "We'll be in the fetal position for the tour of duty?"

"No, Sergeant, the Fleet has elected to remove your legs. They will, of course, be regrown when you return to Earth Base."

One week later, following a brief stop at a second battle group for more recruits, the admiral's transport dropped out of hyperspace in the scheduled rendezvous system. We sixteen candidates sat, unmoving, in our transport slings. They had, as stated, removed our legs at mid-thigh. My raw stumps had been concealed under titanium cuffs. I scratched at the fusion point where my skin ended and titanium began.

The flanges at the bottom of the cuffs were crowded with feeder ports. They explained that this would save them the trouble of sticking our arms and legs with I.V.'s and risking infection during the long suspension. Instead the feeders and blood cleaners and waste removers and regulators and injectors would all screw into sterile ports near our femoral arteries.

I played with my stumps constantly. It reduced my claustrophobia a bit. When we were in realspace I stayed linked to the ship's external sensors so I could watch the stars go by. The view in hyperspace can be nauseating, so for long stretches I took sedatives and comforted myself that we were the vanguard of the attack. We would be the ones to give the Aylin a bloody nose. They expected lumbering dreadnoughts and destroyers, not fast-attack vessels.

"Forty-five minutes to docking," the pilot's voice drifted through the cabin and we all looked up at the speakers.

I lifted a cable from my pocket, inserted it into the cybernetic port behind my left ear and jacked in to the ship's sensors. I linked to the forward visual feeds. We were sailing in toward a very yellow star, coasting on the momentum of our hyperspace exit. I dialed up the resolution on the feeds and caught my first glimpse of our titanium coffins.

"They're tiny," I whispered to Conner on my right. He jacked in and I felt his presence join me in the bow.

The gun cruisers, all thirty, were clustered in orbit around the star. Beefed up fighters was exactly what they were.

"Hey, Lieutenant Valk," Conner called over to one of our pilots sitting in a sling a few meters down the compartment, "They changed the attitude thrusters. Looks like you'll have more kick."

The pilots all jacked in and the forward feeds got crowded. I could see what Conner meant about the thrusters, and I called up a schematic. The forward and aft attitude thrusters, mounted at four points around the hull, were easily several meters longer than on plan. I heard groans.

"You know what that means," someone griped over the neural link we had established by all jacking in together.

"They failed initial maneuvering drills so they welded on extensions," someone else said.

"Careful on those hairpin turns." I recognized Valk's voice. "The spot-welds might snap."

I tuned out the chatter. I only had eyes for the guns. I had never seen such guns on ships so small. They had to be 150mm's. The barrels were ten meters long at least, extending between the attitude-thrusters. The engineers must have installed strong gravity dampers to keep the guns from rolling the ship while firing. It was good that we would be in suspension, because it would be a bumpy ride.

I zoomed in tighter and saw the skeletal hulks of loading servos on either side of the breaching. Damn it! "Hey, Conner," I said. "Those are manual load. We're going to have Ordnance Jockeys in our crews, manning the servos."

"Why the hell'd they do that?"

"Don't know." No one used manual loaders.

We docked a little over forty-five minutes later, the first of seven dockings as our meager crew was distributed among ships craving experienced crewmembers. I boarded the Glory, my new home for a year or two, or three.

I hauled myself through the docking hatch and waited to be inserted into suspension in the smallest, most constrictive space yet. The sound of waves crashed around my ears and I clutched at handholds. The central open tube, around which the stasis containers were wrapped, was smaller than it seemed on the schematic, maybe two meters across. I waited behind two others, a female pilot named Lieutenant Pordue and another gunner named Bell, neither from my former posting. They stripped us of our clothes, so now I was cold as well as claustrophobic, in exchange for 1mm skin suits. The suits were to protect our skin from suspension fluid. I noted that they bore a number in the center of the back, as well as our stripes of rank. My promotion had come through. I was a sergeant. I gripped the handhold tighter.

The life support techs, both with missing legs and titanium leg-cuffs, strapped us into our containers and coupled multi-colored tubes and wires to the ports in our cuff-flanges. I held onto the open edges of the canister.

"You been suspended before?" the tech asked, glancing at my white-knuckled grip.

"A bunch of times."

"So you know the routine. Sorry to rush, but you're the last ones in and we're shipping out as soon as you're secured."

I could feel the drive pods rumbling to life. We were moving already? "They're not wasting time, huh?" I said.

"No time. Let's get your neural link connected." He pulled a thick cable from the wall of the container, thicker than any I'd ever used. "Lean forward."

I leaned and he screwed the wire into the connection behind my ear. "That's it. The sedatives are flowing. You'll be accepted into the neural link as soon as your body's asleep."

He slammed the container doors on me and I concentrated on breathing slowly while the sedatives took hold. I couldn't see. I hyperventilated. Cold suspension fluid pumped in around my hips and I could hear displaced air escaping through vents. I panted faster and faster, willing the sedatives to creep their way through my veins to my brain.

My world lit up with lights and I blinked rapidly.

Where?

I turned around. I was standing (standing? How did I get legs?), in a wide corridor with bright lights and a calm, beige carpet. I felt gravity. Lieutenant Pordue and Sergeant Bell stood beside me, both looking alarmed. We were dressed in shipboard uniforms.

"This is amazing," Bell said.

"Welcome to the consensus-reality of the ship," someone said, and we turned to face a Lieutenant who hadn't been standing there before. We saluted.

"I'm Lieutenant Roarke," he said, "and we are underway. We'll be jumping to hyperspace as soon as we get free of the star's gravity well."

"This is all simulated, sir?" I said, looking around. I had used recreational holos before, but I had never used them in standard operational conditions.

"We figured, since we're all in the neural link, why not make the ship seem like a big one? It's laid out like a standard Class B-6 Destroyer. Everyone gets private quarters, and all quarters have portals. There are complete recreation facilities you can use on your downtime. However, there'll be little downtime in the near term. You will undergo a series of war simulations while we're in hyperspace, designed to familiarize you with combat on this ship.

"Let me show you the external feeds."

The corridor vanished and we entered one of the attitude thrusters. Ship status outputs scrolled behind one of my eyes as I looked out of the visual feeds down the curved hull of the Glory. The feeling of a vast ship around me vanished.

"You can go to external feeds any time you want," Lieutenant Roarke said. "You can access shipboard status reports from inside the simulation. You can even visit your body if you want to."

We returned to the corridor.

"Where is everyone?" Sergeant Bell said. "Things are quiet for a ship-wide neural link."

"I was giving you a moment," Lieutenant Roarke said. "I'll connect you to the link now."

I shielded my mind, something I'd been trained to do during battles when busy neural cross-talk could grow cacophonous. The *Glory* opened up around me and I felt the consciousness of the other two hundred and ninety-nine souls on board. The chatter was loud across fifty bands. I damped all the private bands, and then the official bands that didn't relate to guns, until only the Command Channel and the Fire Control Channel remained. The lieutenant nodded when he saw that we'd all adjusted.

"Import ship's time and on-board schematics. Remember, we have no intraship transports. If you're aft and want to get to the bow, just move your avatar there. It's not necessary to walk.

"Here are your commanding officers. Sergeant Bell, you have been assigned to Forward Gun #3, on the port side. Go with Lieutenant Amadio." They vanished. "Sgt. Kirchov, you have been assigned Aft Gun #11, also port. Go with Lieutenant Burkett."

I followed Burkett's avatar, reading his destination via the neural link we shared. Ship's schematics pinpointed our final location at Gun #11, Aft.

"Meet Annie," Burkett said. "She is your girl while you're on the Glory, so take good care of her."

I entered Annie's processing node and looked down the length of her twin barrels through her targeting feeds. She was so new that her paint hadn't even been scratched. Stars glimmered in the black beyond.

"She's beautiful," I said. I wanted a target to shoot.

Burkett threw a virtual arm around my shoulder. "She's special and requires far more concentration than you ever gave to those great banks of guns on your dreadnought. There you could fire at will. Here, you have one gun and limited ordnance. Every shot counts. That means you will have to assign importance-levels to your targets. You have two targeting techs in your crew, and they'll feed you vectors and proximities. They'll interface with the guidance computers and suggest priorities, but you'll be pulling the trigger."

"And . . .?"

"You've got to choose your ordnance for each shot. Homing rockets to find the weak points in their shields, warheads to follow them in. High-yield, non-nuclear rockets for close targets, low-yield, high-velocity rockets for their fighters. That's why we're using human loaders instead of automatic conveyers."

"You couldn't get the loading computers to coordinate cleanly?"

"We couldn't get you gunners to coordinate cleanly with the loading computers. Your two ordnance jockeys will direct the loading servos and the conveyors from the armories. They're fully integrated into the loading computers, and you'll be integrated with them. It makes it easier on you."

I continued staring down Annie's barrels. If I had been able to feel my heart I'm sure it would have been pounding. I was King of the Cannon. "I've never done anything like this before."

"No one has. We'll run simulations on the way to Bountiful to bring you up to speed."

"When do I meet my gun crew?"

"Right now." Four presences entered the gun, my two targeting techs and my two ordnance jockeys.

"The simulations will begin when we enter hyperspace," Lieutenant Burkett continued. "You'll start by yourself. Later you'll link with the other guns and learn to coordinate with Fire Control.

"The pilots will be running their own simulations. Eight attitude thrusters and four drive pods. You should see these ships bob and weave once the pilots get integrated. Final simulations will involve coordination between the gun crews and pilots. Not only will your targets be moving, but so will the ground beneath you."

"I can't wait," I said.

"We're going to put you through your paces. Think of rescuing Bountiful as a dry run for the future. When the go-ahead finally comes to penetrate deep into their territory, we'll be ready."

I grinned. "Bring it on."

"One last thing, Sergeant. During the simulations, if you shoot off one of the thrusters or shoot one of your fellow guns I will personally tear you a new asshole. Is that clear?"

"That is clear, sir."

"Thirty minutes to hyperspace entry. Everybody introduce yourselves and prep for simulation. Good luck."

I gripped Annie's virtual control arm. Time to see what she could do.

I easily survived the first half-dozen simulations with limited bogeys. As the number of bogeys increased, I struggled to cover my little piece of the *Glory*. I had to learn to differentiate the threat level of my attackers, and change ordnance quickly as new threats presented themselves. We took a beating from small-fire, but survived several simulations because I was able to neutralize the shipkiller threats.

I figured it would be easier once we meshed with the other guns. It was harder. We had to avoid double-teaming targets and wasting ammunition. I needed to watch for threats that adjacent guns missed. And I needed to be aware of the *Glory* around me. Several gunners shot off thrusters and received visits from Fire Control officers. I had numerous near misses.

But our sixteen guncrews were experienced and we got the hang of the gestalt quickly. Then they brought the pilots into our simulations. Good God! The ship spun and twisted and lurched so much I couldn't hold a bogey in my sights. I missed so many targets that I ran out of ammunition and received a reprimand. The pilots had their own share of troubles. Several times gun-recoil pushed us into incoming rockets. The dreadnoughts I'd served on barely shivered under full recoil.

I was again pleased at how quickly my two targeting techs and my own cybernetic implants adapted to the pitch and yaw. We anticipated lead-times and made good on a number of hits. By the fifth shipwide simulation, the pilots kept the ship steadier and we gunners had more time to aim. The Aylin fighters fell like dominoes. We maneuvered in tight on their heavy cruisers, evading defensive fire and dropping rockets.

A few more simulations and the crew worked in lockstep. I began to appreciate what the pilots could do with these ships. My gun, Annie, rotated swiftly and precisely, her barrel rising and falling to track targets as we dropped and turned. My ordnance jockeys could switch warheads with small rockets in under a second.

Then Fire Control introduced the other gun-cruisers into our simulation and we worked on formations.

We trained all week, the length of time it took us to get to Bountiful and Upsilon Station. We didn't even need all that time, but the simulations continued anyway. I didn't mind. They were fun.

"Alert, ten minutes to realspace reentry," the XO's voice came across the neural link.

All simulations wound down. I looked out along Annie's barrels at the roil of hyperspace, again wondering if my heart beat fast down in my chamber. This was it. The Tarish System. Bountiful.

There was chatter on private bands about what we would find. Pickup carriers doing their job in ease and safety with no Aylin in sight? A firefight? Everyone dead and the fight over? We didn't even know what ordnance to load. My jockeys would give me what I needed in an instant, but I had them load low-yield rockets in case we emerged next to a bogey. I gripped the virtual firing toggles and closed my eyes. We were well trained. We were extraordinarily mobile. We could handle anything.

"Eight, seven, six," the XO's voice counted down to reemergence.

Proximity alarms blared, too many to be useful. Light and noise and motion. I swiveled Annie hard as we descended into a hornet's nest, already cut off from the rest of our squadron.

Aylin fighters, gullwings covered in chevrons, swept past the bow and down the Glory. We reacted. They suffered decimating losses as they passed the forward guns, then the midship guns, and finally the aft guns and me and Annie. The survivors circled up in broken formation, probably as surprised as we were to find us here.

I struggled to hold Annie steady as the bow of the Glory plunged. The pilots shoved us down hard, and the hull of an oncoming ship rumbled past, meters away. I couldn't even tell what it was, we were so close. It was big. The orders came down for the starboard and ventral guns to engage the ship. "Fire at will."

The Glory pressed forward. Port side faced out, and we held off the gull-winged fighters, taking heavy small-arms fire. There were many fighters, swarming, targeting our drive pods. I kept firing. There shouldn't be this many fighters with a raiding party. Where had they come from?

Our pilots kept us tight to the deck, trying to keep us below the firing-plane of the Aylin ship's gun-batteries. Moving fast. Our starboard and ventral guns flung warheads, cratering the target's hull in a long stripe.

We rolled out around her bow and curved back in tight for another pass, scattering fighters. Two sister gun-cruisers passed us high and low, also scarring the hull, also engulfed in fighter swarms. Too many. Small-fire continued to get through.

In the *simulations*, people died all the time. Compartments depressurized. Whole ships disintegrated. The computer shuffled the deceased to the back of the neural link and you could hear their frustrated grumbling. In battle, people just vanished from the link. It was so quiet and discrete that I could almost pretend this was just another simulation.

So I posted a running tally of ship casualties behind my eyes to remind me that those rockets flaring across the Glory, inches above our hull as maneuvering thrusters pushed us down and out of the way, were real rockets. The fighters whipping across my field of view had to be thinned out. In the simulation it was okay to take mounting small-arms damage so long as you stopped the big threats and won the battle. Here, people died when armor piercing rounds penetrated the battery racks and into the stasis chambers.

Flames erupted from the Aylin ship in places where we hadn't dropped warheads. Explosions from within. The captain ordered the pilots to break off.

As we passed out into the black, still pursued by fighters, I could see that it had been an Aylin carrier. Flames rolled from launching bays. One of our sisters flew in tight behind us and helped clear us of the last of our fighter trail, and I finally got a view of Bountiful.

This wasn't an Aylin raid. This was an invasion. They had come in through the kind of lesser system that we typically didn't defend.

The Aylin battle line lay in a crescent that started to our port and curved around the far side of the planet. There had to be ten heavy destroyers, and at least five carriers. Scores of smaller cruisers and support ships. They were invading *us*?

Someone had towed Upsilon Station in close to the planet as a defense and she was taking a pounding, but giving back. Magnesium flames rippled from much of her near side. A bright flare signified the death of a nearby Aylin destroyer.

Dozens of Fleet pickup carriers were lifting off of the near side of Bountiful, trying to get clear under heavy fighter attack. Optimally they can carry twenty thousand people each, but they never achieve close to that in panic evacuations. They were jumping to hyperspace barely clear of the atmosphere, a horrifically risky maneuver but better odds than running the fighter gauntlet.

"Incoming." The XO's voice flashed across the link. Alarms blared again.

I rotated Annie's barrel down along the *Glory's* hull as rockets flared toward us from the Aylin line. A lot of rockets. We fired defensively. We couldn't survive in the open. We couldn't afford to waste rockets like this. Our strength lay in flying tight. Twelve of our sister gun cruisers grouped around us as we turned toward the Aylin line. I looked through the forward visual feeds as Aylin fighters rose to meet us. Hundreds, backed by the gun batteries of the destroyers.

We couldn't survive this. We were supposed to be stopping raids. The gun-cruisers weren't meant to go toe-to-toe with destroyers.

Another flare down the Aylin line. A carrier near Bountiful's moon split in two, spilling debris. Just as *Upsilon* Station was eclipsed by the planet, I saw two destroyers close with her. She wasn't long for this world either.

If nothing else, we had to give the planet rescue carriers time.

A gun cruiser to my starboard took a rocket square in the bow. Explosions rippled back along her hull like a wave as compartment after compartment disintegrated. I stared, appalled, then snapped my attention back to incoming. Not a simulation. People were dying. This was real—the start of the war.

Our forward gunners struggled to intercept incoming. Munitions stores were falling. The captain called for full thrust, and we raced into the teeth of the destroyers. The gullwinged fighters closed, giving us some cover from the rockets.

Dozens and dozens of gullwings swept past my position. My targeting techs and I picked them off like swatting mosquitoes. Again small-arms fire peppered our hull and the death tally mounted. I lost one of my ordnance jockeys. He winked out. Gone. My remaining jockey assumed control of both loaders.

The targeting techs alerted me to destroyer proximity and laid a schematic over my eyes. Our squadron captains were trying to implement an attack pattern. The gun-cruisers were assigned four ships to a destroyer on strafing runs up four sides. See if we could peel back their hulls like a banana. See if we could keep their attention away from Bountiful and draw fighters away from the pickup carriers.

I was once again on fighter duty, trying to hold them off. Sparks chattered up from our hull as projectiles penetrated reinforced steel. One of the drive pods behind me buckled and the pilots ejected it before it could explode. Attitude thrusters on the starboard side roared, trying to keep the unbalanced *Glory* flying straight. I launched a high-yield rocket into our ejected drive pod and it exploded, clearing three gullwings.

The buckling hull of the Aylin destroyer whistled by, meters from our starboard side, ejecting flames and debris. We were hurting them. We were having success. We just needed to get in tight, and then we were at our strength. Maybe we *could* fight destroyers.

"Aft guns, target their bridge. Repeat, target their bridge." The XO's voice barked across the link as we and two of our sister gun-cruisers shot past the nose of the destroyer.

My jockey rolled in warheads and I fired quickly with the other aft guns. Flaming rocket-tails crowded the space between our ships. Gullwings flung themselves into the paths of the warheads in suicide bids to protect the destroyer, but three got through. The bow of the ship bloomed.

There was no time for celebration as the gullwings swarmed forward again and we evaded down in tight to a carrier. I defended as best I could, making every shot count, preserving my warheads for the sweep around the carrier's bow.

Gullwings came down on us in a cluster from above. Midship guns pivoted up, trying to intercept, but the fighters came too fast on a ramming course. The neural link shivered. One of my targeting techs vanished. Alarms shrieked and power levels plunged. I lost the feeds to the midship guns. The burning carrier passed to our stern and I fired warheads at its bow.

Damage reports scrolled behind my eyes as I squeezed Annie's virtual trigger. We were still intact, still flying. Swiss cheese. In virtual reality, nothing felt different.

"Incoming ship," the XO's voice barked. "Evasive maneuvers."

We rolled hard to port. I lent a small portion of my attention to the forward feeds. A monster bore down on us, brushing away debris in its path. This was a new ship, twice as big as the others. Nearly as big as our dreadnoughts. With horror I watched as four more big ships dropped out of hyperspace to bolster the Aylin line.

"We have been ordered to retreat," the captain's voice whipped across the link. "Fleet has to know the specs on these ships, and we're the messengers."

We joined side-by-side with two surviving sister ships, the *Corsair* and the *Mariah* and rocketed toward deep space, ramping up to required velocity. *Glory's* three remaining drive-pods vibrated out of sync. Dorsal-midship guns were crushed and silent. More gullwings descended on us as our intentions became obvious, and we meshed our gun crews across all three ships to defend a wider swath of space.

A gunner died on the *Corsair* and I took control of both of our guns in the gestalt between ships. For the first time I really worried about dying. My body was encased far forward, but the small-fire getting through was like driving rain. I doubted there was anyone left alive in our aft suspension chambers.

A burst and flare to port. the *Corsair* was down and falling. Our gestalt rippled as her gun crews vanished. I lost contact with the second gun.

More gullwings swarmed. Annie chattered on full automatic as my munitions stocks ticked away. A destroyer fired, and some of our guns had to rotate back to high-yield rockets to intercept incoming.

Nearly there. Ten seconds to minimum hyperspace velocity.

"Sergeant," my surviving jockey whispered to me, "are we going to make it?"

"We'll make it," I lied.

A rocket got through, punching through the *Mariah's* bow and FTL chamber. She fell to our stern. I continued firing, staring at our sister ship.

The *Mariah's* bow was gone—FTL drives, communications arrays, forward compartments. There was empty space where the front third of the ship had sheered off. Midship compartments were heavily damaged. The surviving back half of her turned on steering thrusters and sped toward the destroyer, five guns firing high-yield rockets. Some of the gullwings left us to pursue.

The visual feeds turned hazy as we ascended into hyperspace.

"We'll make it," I repeated, numb.

What was left of the *Mariah* had sacrificed herself for us. How had they made that decision so quickly? I looked at our own high death-tally. Would they shrink the size of the *Glory* now so it wouldn't seem so empty? Would there be a morgue somewhere with all of the virtual bodies laid out on steel gurneys?

How could anyone think in battle?

All of the gun-cruisers were gone but us. All of the ships that had been training together an hour ago. And it was still a victory. We had bloodied them.

And now they were coming. Their main fleet, attacking via a back door. It hadn't occurred to me they would ever engage us directly. Our dreadnoughts were too powerful. But with a force this size and our fleet stretched thin across so many systems . . .

I felt ashamed of the boasts I'd once made on my dreadnought-posting about my gun skills. I had been as green as an ensign and hadn't even known it. There is no gun-skill. You fire until they get you, and on the virtual ship you don't feel your own death.

I slumped over Annie's console and reached back to find my sleeping body in the stasis canister. My heart beat fast. That was real.

GRENDEL

A Lost Fleet Campaign

Jack Campbell

GRENDEL. A STAR SYSTEM WHERE NOTHING IS HAPPENING, NOTHING EVER HAS happened, and nothing ever will happen."

Lieutenant Commander Cara Decala, the executive officer of the Alliance heavy cruiser *Merlon*, turned a wry smile on Commander John Geary, the commanding officer. "Be careful you don't jinx us, Captain."

"Advice noted and logged." Geary leaned back in his command seat on the bridge of *Merlon*, his eyes on the display floating before him. Six hours ago they had arrived at Grendel, using the jump point from the star, Beowulf. From Grendel they would jump to T'shima, where the fleet's main base for this region of space was located. The drives which allowed faster-than-light travel could only jump between points in space created by the mass of stars, and then only if the destination star was close enough. That made Grendel a necessary waypoint, and that's all it had ever been. No one went to Grendel because they wanted to go to Grendel.

At the moment, *Merlon* was the flagship for a convoy, with Geary also controlling the light cruiser, *Pommel,* and three destroyers as well as an even dozen massive cargo transports hauling military supplies. Against the vast reaches of the Grendel star system, the convoy he commanded formed a very tiny human presence indeed. Still, in the human scheme of things it was both significant and something of which to be proud. The Alliance had been at least technically at peace for several decades, and the limited number of warships in the fleet reflected the casual attitude of a people who had not had much active need of defenses. Nonetheless, Geary had managed after long years of service to not only achieve the rank of commander with his pride and his self-respect mostly intact, but also gain the command of a heavy cruiser.

Measured against that accomplishment was the reality that no one expected the Alliance would anytime soon require its heavy cruisers, or its few battleships and battle cruisers, to protect its people and its planets. Nor, as far as anyone knew did the convoy actually need an escort to protect it. Regulations called for practicing convoy escort duties, and for convoys transiting border star systems to have escorts, so a few ships were temporarily assigned to that task and required to run various drills so that they would be prepared if someday, somehow, convoys really did need escorts.

Decala squinted at her own display. "We are lucky, though. We could be stationed on the emergency facility here and have to stay for years. At least it's only three days to the jump point for T'shima and then we get to leave."

"That is indeed a blessing." The orbital base at Grendel had a minimal crew, and only existed because every now and then ships passing through this star system enroute to other stars needed repair assistance for their equipment or medical assistance for somebody aboard. If not for that requirement, the several barren planets, which were either too hot or too cold, and the mass of asteroids in the star system would have held no reason for any humans to linger at Grendel. The star system wasn't as bad as the gray nothingness of jump space, but that wasn't saying much.

Geary pulled out the scale on his display so that it showed the entire neighborhood of stars in this region. Grendel rested next to the border between the Alliance and the Syndicate Worlds, an imaginary wall with many a curve and bulge drawn through nothingness by the two greatest political powers in human space. In the dozen centuries since humanity had left the Sol star system and the Earth of its oldest ancestors, most inhabited worlds had become part of either the Alliance or the Syndicate Worlds, though much smaller groupings such as the Callas Republic and the Rift Federation also existed on the Alliance side of the border.

The nearest star to Grendel on the Syndic side of the border was Shannin, but the two stars might as well have been a million light years apart since ships never jumped between them. On this side of the border, most of the stars belonged to the Alliance by the choice of the inhabitants of their planets. On the other side of the border, every star system belonged to the Syndicate Worlds, whether the people living on the planets liked it or not. The leaders of the Syndics liked to proclaim their avowed love of freedom, but the outcomes of allegedly free votes in the Syndicate World either were never in doubt or made little difference since local authorities were given little real power compared to the corporate-dominated power structure.

Decala must have noticed what Geary was looking at. "What do you suppose the Syndics are doing? It's been almost six months since they announced that no more Alliance merchant shipping would be allowed in Syndic space."

He shrugged in reply. "You've seen the intelligence assessments. No one on this side of the border seems to know, and our embassies and other diplomatic posts inside the Syndicate Worlds haven't been able to find out what's going on. The best guess is that it was a protectionist trade measure, to seal out competition from the Alliance."

"It's not like we ever had that much trade with them. They never encouraged it."

"No. Not much tourism, either. But whatever the Syndics are thinking, it hasn't ramped up tensions beyond the usual level. They seem to be behaving themselves and respecting the border agreements." Geary checked his daily agenda. "Only two drills scheduled over the next twelve hours, and those are just simulated maneuvers."

"We have to conserve fuel cells," Decala reminded Geary dryly. "Remember what Admiral Kindera said. Fleet budgets won't support racing around star systems."

"Or support carrying out necessary training," Geary agreed. "Keep the ship on a routine schedule today, but make sure the junior officers most in need of training are on hand for those simulated maneuvers this afternoon. I'll be there to supervise and make sure the other ships are taking the drill seriously."

He stood up. "Let me know if anything changes," Geary informed the bridge watch standers, then headed toward his stateroom to get some paperwork done.

"Captain to the bridge!" Halfway through his regular walk-through of the ship, Geary's feet were moving toward the bridge before his mind fully absorbed the urgent summons. Rather than pause to call the bridge on the nearest comm panel he simply kept up a quick pace, any crew members in the passageways of *Merlon* jumping aside when they saw him coming so he would have a clear path. He was sliding into his command seat on the bridge when Lieutenant Commander Decala arrived on his heels. "What's going on?" Geary asked.

"A Syndic flotilla has arrived via the jump point from Shannin, sir," the operations watch reported.

"What?" The news was not only unexpected but also inexplicable. Geary activated his own display, seeing the data which *Merlon*'s sensors had already collected. Coming in-system from the jump point were not just a few Syndic warships, but a substantial flotilla.

"Four heavy cruisers?" Decala asked.

"Plus four light cruisers, six Hunter-Killers, and ten corvettes," the operations watch confirmed.

Geary frowned at his display. Military attachés and other sources within the Syndicate Worlds had a pretty good handle on Syndic military capabilities, and he was certain that the Syndics had the same sort of knowledge of Alliance warships. The Syndic heavy cruisers each pretty much matched *Merlon* in maneuverability and protection, but the Syndic armament was slightly better, even though the Syndic missiles weren't quite as good as the Alliance's wraith missiles. The light cruisers were significantly smaller, both more lightly armed and armored than heavy cruisers, but faster because of greater propulsion capability relative to their mass. In a one-on-one match up, *Pommel* would have had a slim advantage against any one of them. The Hunter-Killers were smaller and less capable than the Alliance destroyers, but the HuKs were a little faster. The Syndic corvettes were smaller yet, singly not a match for any Alliance warship, and could just keep up with their heavy cruisers. Still, it was a very strong force relative to *Merlon* and the other Alliance warships at Grendel.

The Syndics had come in from a jump point to one side of the current track of the Alliance convoy, barely two light hours distant. Which meant the Syndic warships had already been in this star system for two hours before the light from their arrival reached the Alliance convoy. He wondered what they had been doing in those two hours. "I need an assessment of their track as soon as possible."

"Yes, sir. The Syndics have accelerated and come around to port." Space had no directions as humans understood them, of course, so humans imposed their own, arbitrarily designating an exact plane for any star system and defining one side of that plane as up, the other side as down, any direction away from the star as port and directions toward the star as starboard or starward. It wasn't the only possible means by which ships could orient themselves to each other in space, but it was the one which humans had adopted. Without an external reference and such conventions, no human ship could possibly understand what any other ship meant when it gave directions.

Rubbing his neck, Geary tapped a request into the maneuvering system and saw the result pop up. "I don't like this. They seem to be moving onto an intercept with this convoy."

"They could just be heading onto a converging vector," Decala noted, "if they were also aiming for the jump point for T'shima."

"Why the hell would a Syndic flotilla of that size be going to T'shima? For that matter, what the hell are they doing in Alliance space at all?" Protocol dictated that a foreign ship arriving in a star system announce its intentions, but any such message from the Syndics should have shown up right about the same time as the light revealing their appearance at Grendel. "There's nothing from the Syndics on any channel?"

"No, sir," the communications watch confirmed.

Geary pulled up the current version of the rules of engagement. This wasn't the first time that he had read them, of course, but he hadn't seriously expected to need the ROE on this trip. "We are supposed to defend Alliance space, Alliance citizens, and Alliance property, we are required to be firm and resolute, but we are not allowed to explicitly threaten military action or open fire unless first fired upon. I wish the idiots who wrote these instructions were here now." He pounded one fist softly on the arm of his seat. "I'll send a challenge, but it'll be two hours before they get it, and even if they reply immediately, that will take almost another two hours."

"They're still a long ways off," Decala said. "We have time to figure out how to deal with this."

"Do we?" Geary's display updated, showing the Syndic flotilla had steadied out on a course and speed two hours ago, the now-converging paths of the Syndic flotilla and the Alliance convoy arcing across the expanse of Grendel star system. "They are heading for the jump point for T'shima, and they're going to get to it before we do." The jump point was only about two and half light hours distant now, but with the convoy loafing along at point zero four light speed that translated to about sixty hours of travel time. The Syndics, at about three light hours distance from the jump point for T'shima, were traveling at point zero eight light speed and would get there in a less than thirty-eight hours.

"We can accelerate," Decala suggested. "Fleet will raise hell with us for using extra fuel cells, but it's justified."

He hesitated before answering, then ran some quick checks using the maneuvering system. "That's not good enough. The transports are too slow. We could all beat the Syndic heavy cruisers and the corvettes to the jump point, but the Syndic light cruisers and HuKs could intercept us before the jump point if they separated from the rest and used their best acceleration. It wouldn't take much damage to the transports to leave them unable to outrun the heavy cruisers and HuKs."

Decala was now staring at Geary. "Sir, you're talking as if this was a combat situation."

"Maybe it is. Don't we have to plan as if it is?" He wished he had days to think about this, or at least a few more hours, but he had to act quickly or not at all. The slow, cumbersome transports needed all the lead time they could get if this was indeed a threat. *Think of it as a combat exercise. A drill. They're presenting me with this situation. What do I do? Hold off acting until my options are gone? Or do something knowing it might be wrong, and might get me laughed at for over-reacting and disciplined for 'wasting fleet resources?'* He'd probably even get that annoying "Black Jack" nickname thrown in his face again. But. . . "They didn't make me commanding officer of a cruiser because they expected me to do nothing."

"Sir?"

"I'm just lecturing myself." Geary punched his controls, calling up an image of Lieutenant Commander Lagemann on the *Pommel*. "I'm splitting the convoy," Geary announced without any preamble. "You are to take *Pommel*, all three destroyers and all of the transports, accelerating at the best pace the transports can achieve so as to reach the jump point for T'shima as soon as possible." The transports would accelerate slowly, but could eventually manage point zero eight light speed themselves. After factoring in how long it would take the transports to reach their maximum velocity if they started accelerating now, it would be thirty-four hours before they reached the jump point. Time enough to beat the Syndics there, as long as none of the Syndics accelerated. But time delays worked both ways. It would take the Syndics two hours to see what the Alliance ships had done, two hours before the Syndics could react in any way.

Pommel's commanding officer didn't quite manage to conceal his surprise at the orders. "Sir, if you think those Syndics might be a threat, we should keep our forces concentrated," Lagemann objected.

Geary shook his head. "Our job is to get those transports safely to T'shima. That's the overriding priority. I will take *Merlon* and use her to block the movement of the Syndic light cruisers and HuKs if they are detached to try to intercept the transports. *Pommel* and the destroyers will be responsible for defending the transports and stopping any Syndics that get past *Merlon*."

Lagemann gave him the same look which Decala had earlier. "You really think this might turn into a combat situation, sir? If so, we shouldn't split our combat capabilities," he urged again.

"If that entire Syndic flotilla catches us, our entire combat capability won't stand a snowball's chance in a star's photosphere. You can see that as well as I can. If we weren't encumbered by the transports we might be able to wear the Syndics down until they had to withdraw, but we are responsible for those transports. We have to keep the Syndics from getting enough of their forces within range of the transports, and this is the only way to do it."

Pommel's commanding officer looked away, clearly unhappy. "Sir, you're asking us to leave *Merlon* to face the Syndics alone, to fight alone if necessary."

"I realize that, and I appreciate your loyalty to your comrades." Geary smiled in what he hoped was a reassuring and confident manner. "This is our best course of action. Most likely, they'll stay clear of us and then leave after making whatever point they're trying to make. But if the Syndics do prove to be hostile, and if any of them get past *Merlon*, those transports will need *Pommel* and the destroyers. That's where your duty lies."

"I understand, sir." Lagemann saluted. "When do we detach?"

"Immediately. I'll send the message notifying everyone. Get those transports moving."

"Yes, sir."

That done, Geary called the Syndics. "This is Commander John Geary of the Alliance heavy cruiser *Merlon* calling the Syndicate Worlds' warships which have entered the Alliance star system of Grendel. You are to immediately identify yourselves and your purpose for being in Grendel."

"Firm *and* resolute," Decala observed.

"Yeah." In another four hours or so, he would know if the Syndics were going to answer him. "Get the crew some rest while we can," he told Decala. Any executive officer's instincts were to keep a crew working, but at the moment Geary felt he should override those instincts. "We might need to come to full readiness and stay there for a while."

"Yes, sir."

He had either already made a major fool of himself by over-reacting, or had set up a situation where *Merlon* might have to actually trade shots with the Syndics. He wasn't sure which one of those things would be worse for his career.

"We finally have a reply from the Syndics."

Geary accepted the transmission in his stateroom, where he had retired for a little while to avoid driving his bridge crew crazy out of his own frustration as the hours had gone by without any answer from the Syndics. His comm panel lit, showing a female Syndic CEO with the usual perfectly done hair, perfectly fitted uniform, and perfectly insincere smile. "Greetings to Commander Geary from CEO Third Rank Fredericka Nalis on the Syndicate Worlds' heavy cruiser C-195. Our flotilla is on a peaceful diplomatic visit to Alliance space, arranged through your own fleet headquarters. It seems you were not informed of our impending arrival, but I trust there will be no incidents which might imperil a visit designed to reduce tensions between our peoples."

It sounded plausible enough, especially given fleet headquarters' tendency to forget to tell operational units what was supposed to be happening. "Commander Decala, have you seen the Syndic response?"

Decala's image appeared on his panel and nodded. "Yes, sir. I don't like it, sir."

"Fleet *has* screwed up in the past about notifying us."

"Yes, but not about something this big. A large Syndic flotilla entering Alliance space? Sir, they'd have been assigned an Alliance escort, wouldn't they?"

"That's the proper procedure." Geary tapped another command as an alert sounded. "Damn. The Syndic light cruisers and HuKs are accelerating away from the slower warships."

The image of Decala nodded again. "On an intercept aimed at *Pommel* and the transports, or maybe just the jump point. Same difference. Sir, this stinks."

"It surely does, Cara. Work up a direct intercept for us, bringing *Merlon* in toward those Syndic light cruisers and HuKs. I'll be on the bridge in a minute."

By the time he arrived the maneuver had been calculated. Geary studied it for a moment, thinking things through. Relative to *Merlon*, the Syndic heavy cruisers and corvettes were just abaft the port beam and just above, their course slowly converging on *Merlon* and their distance slowly decreasing. The accelerating Syndic light cruisers and HuKs would be creeping forward of *Merlon*'s port beam, their paths aimed ahead of *Merlon* and toward the rest of the Alliance convoy which now was off the starboard bow of *Merlon* and slightly below, drawing steadily away as the lumbering transports burned through fuel cells at a rate that would probably make the budget geeks at fleet headquarters faint from distress. If the maneuvering system estimates proved right, the Syndic light cruisers and HuKs could intercept the transports in less than eight and a half hours, half an hour before the transports reached the jump point for T'shima. There wasn't any time to waste. "All right. Let's go."

Merlon's thrusters pitched her bow around and slightly down, then the main propulsion units lit off and accelerated the heavy cruiser onto a vector which would cross just ahead of the path the Syndic light cruisers and HuKs were on.

As *Merlon* steadied out, Geary checked the time to intercept. The Alliance heavy cruiser would cross the path of the Syndic light cruisers and HuKs in seven and a half hours. He took a calming breath, then transmitted another message to the Syndics. "Syndic CEO Nalis, this is Commander Geary. We have no notification or clearance for your ships to transit Alliance space. Your light cruisers and Hunter-Killers are to rejoin your main formation at the earliest possible time, and you are requested to assume an orbit about Grendel until we receive confirmation that your visit has been approved."

Decala was shaking her head again. "If the brass try to nail you for causing a diplomatic incident, I'll back you up, sir."

"Thanks." Geary tried to ignore an increasing sense of disquiet as he watched the movements of the Syndics. "Let's hope a diplomatic incident is the worst that can come of this." He indicated the latest updates on the maneuvering display. "If those Syndic light cruisers and HuKs don't turn back, either we stop them or they'll get to the transports before the transports can jump out of this star system."

"Surely they wouldn't—Captain, I've reviewed the latest intelligence and news we have. It's just as we thought. There's nothing going on that should have triggered Syndic hostile actions. Things are tense, certainly, but they've often been tense." Decala made a baffled gesture. "I don't trust that Syndic CEO at all, but her story is the only explanation that makes sense for what's happening."

"The only explanation that makes sense to us, you mean." Geary rubbed his face with both hands. "Before the convoy jumps, I'll tell Lagemann to ask the brass at T'shima for guidance once he gets there. If there was a Syndic flotilla coming through a region of space that T'shima was responsible for, even fleet headquarters wouldn't forget to notify them. The commodore at T'shima can send instructions back with one of the destroyers, telling us what to do with the Syndics."

"Assuming the Syndics do as you directed and maintain an orbit here until we get those instructions."

"Yeah. Assuming that." Geary looked at the course vectors curving through space on his display and shook his head.

The eventual reply from the Syndic CEO, once again hours later than it should have taken to arrive, was accompanied by the same artificial smile but a chiding tone. "We have been ordered to meet with certain Alliance officials and Syndicate Worlds diplomatic representatives at T'shima, Commander Geary. You're asking us to violate our orders and the Alliance's own agreement to our passage. My flotilla was delayed earlier by propulsion problems, so my light cruisers and Hunter-Killers are going on ahead to arrive at T'shima on time and bring word of the imminent arrival of the rest of the flotilla." The Syndic CEO's expression grew a little stern. "I hope you will not take any further steps to attempt to impede this important diplomatic initiative, Commander Geary."

"She's definitely pressuring us," Decala said. "It is possible they had propulsion problems. Those nickel corvettes are nothing for the Syndics to brag about."

Geary nodded. The Alliance fleet had nicknamed the Syndic corvettes "nickels" because they were small, cheap, and would be easily expended in combat. "If they didn't have four heavy cruisers backing them up, I wouldn't waste sleep worrying about the nickels. But otherwise, I feel like you do. That Syndic CEO is trying to push us into letting them pass, and she's dragging her feet in dealing with us as much as she can while she keeps pushing. Why?"

After a long moment, Decala replied. "It's what I'd do if I was up to something I wasn't supposed to be doing. If T'shima really expects them, then why hasn't a ship arrived here from T'shima by now to escort them?"

"And if the Syndics were delayed," Geary added, "it makes it all the odder that no one from T'shima has come here yet. None of that is proof the Syndics are planning anything hostile. But if they are . . . Cara, I have the distinct feeling that no matter what we do, we're going to be screwed."

"Join the fleet and service the Alliance," Decala agreed in the sailors' usual sardonic twist on the actual recruitment slogan to 'serve' the Alliance.

"We're two hours from intercepting the light cruisers and HuKs. I want the ship at maximum combat readiness one hour prior to intercept, just in case the Syndics try something else."

Decala nodded. "Yes, sir. But . . . combat readiness. Captain, if you're wrong—"

"Unfortunately, there's a lot of different ways for me to be wrong," Geary said. "We're going to stick to our most fundamental mission. Defend Alliance space, citizens, and property." And hope that there hadn't been an unusually monumental screw-up by fleet staff which had left them at Grendel facing what was supposed to be a diplomatic situation but was fast spiraling out of control.

"All systems at maximum combat readiness," Decala reported. "All personnel at combat stations."

"Very well," Geary acknowledged. He, Decala, and everyone else in the crew were in survival suits, ready in case the hull was breached and atmosphere within parts of the ship lost. "Charge hell lance batteries, load grapeshot launchers, and prep wraith missiles."

A moment later, as his commands were being executed, a virtual image popped up on Geary's display. The avatar of Captain Erabus Booth, the current aide to the assistant to the deputy to the fleet chief of staff, gave Geary a stern look. "Charging and preparing weapons is not authorized by current guidance for routine encounters with Syndicate Worlds warships. You are directed to review regulations and instructions governing the current situation and to ensure that your every action conforms with those regulations and instructions. Failure to comply fully with existing guidance will result in appropriate reprimand or disciplinary action should investigation reveal failures or lapses in judgments—"

Geary closed his eyes. "Commander Decala, please instruct the combat systems officer to kill Captain Booth."

"Disable his avatar in the combat system alert routine, you mean, sir?"

"That's all we have within reach at the moment, so it'll have to do. Cara, if everything does go to hell here and I don't make it back, please do your best to get those damned staff avatar alert routines removed from fleet warship operating systems. Tell everybody it was my last wish." Not that he expected anyone would care what his last wishes had been if it came to that.

"Yes, sir." Decala didn't argue, since she and every other officer on the *Merlon* felt the same way about the automated staff alerts embedded in the programming of the ship's systems, and which ship officers usually referred to as HQ viruses or staff infections.

Geary took another long breath, blowing it out slowly before he transmitted his next message. The Syndic light cruisers and HuKs were close now, only five light minutes distant, and coming on fast, the swift HuKs well ahead of the light cruisers. With *Merlon* approaching on an intercept from one side, the combined closing velocity was about point one two light speed, enough to stress the abilities of the combat systems to score hits during the very brief moments when the ships would be within range of each other. "Syndicate Worlds warships operating in the Grendel star system, this is Commander Geary on the Alliance heavy cruiser *Merlon*. Your ships are operating in an Alliance star system without authorization or clearance. You will not be allowed to jump for T'shima until such time as appropriate authorization is received. You must alter your vectors immediately. You will not be permitted to cross the current track of *Merlon*. You are ordered to veer off *now*."

He had done everything but threaten to open fire. Would it be enough? As the minutes went by with no reply from the Syndics and no variation in their course and speed, the answer increasingly seemed to be "no."

"We'll be within wraith range of the HuKs in fifteen minutes," Decala reported.

Fifteen minutes. Geary checked the missile engagement parameters. He could fire as early as fifteen minutes, or as late as twenty-five minutes from now. After that, *Merlon* would be too close to the Syndic warships for the missiles to acquire targets before they shot past each other.

Decala wasn't pressing him for a decision. He imagined she was grateful that the decision wasn't up to her. He would have been grateful in her place. "This would be a good time for my ancestors to give me a sign."

"I'll let you know if mine tell me anything. Why do they just keep coming? Are the Syndics trying to provoke us into firing at them?" Decala wondered. "Putting the blame on us? But we're in an Alliance star system. They're disregarding our warnings. Any fault for what happens will clearly be theirs."

Geary managed a crooked smile. "Do your best to get assigned to my court-martial as one of the voting members."

She swallowed and spoke with exaggerated calm. "Have you ever actually been in combat before?"

"Some minor incidents. Nothing like this."

"Me, either."

Ten minutes until they reached the engagement envelope for the wraiths. Geary made his voice as stern as he could. "Syndicate Worlds warships approaching the Alliance cruiser *Merlon*, you are ordered to change your vectors immediately to cease closing on any Alliance shipping or the jump point for T'shima. You will *not* be permitted to cross the track of this cruiser. This is your *final* warning."

Nothing changed, the Syndic warships approaching without the slightest sign of altering their courses or speeds. "Lieutenant Commander Decala, work up an engagement plan for the wraiths. I want the first wave targeted on the propulsion systems of the Syndic HuKs."

"Yes, sir." With the help of the automated systems, the solutions popped up almost instantly. "Engagement plan prepared."

Geary felt outside himself for a moment, as if were he watching himself giving orders. "Assign the plan to the first wave of wraiths."

"Plan assigned. Wraiths ready to fire. Awaiting command authorization."

A red marker glowed before Geary now. All he had to do was tap that marker, call out "fire" for a verbal confirmation, and the missiles would fly.

Geary activated an internal circuit letting him speak to his entire crew. "As you are all aware, we are close to contact with Syndicate Worlds' warships. There is a real possibility that we may find ourselves forced into combat within a short time. You are an outstanding crew, well-trained, motivated and steadfast, and I know that you will face whatever challenge arises in a manner that will make our ancestors proud of us all." As Geary ended the internal transmission, he wondered if he had overdone the pep talk, but it was how he honestly felt at the moment. "It's up to the Syndics now," he commented to his executive officer.

"They must be planning something," Decala insisted. "Why else keep coming? They're counting on us not doing anything."

"We can't afford not to do anything. They must know that." Though the uncertainties made the temptation to not act very powerful. He didn't *know* the Syndics were planning to attack. But he did know that if the light cruisers and HuKs got past

Merlon unmolested, they would easily overhaul the transports, and could overwhelm *Pommel* and the three destroyers. The entire convoy could be wiped out, *would* be wiped out if the Syndics staged a surprise attack, and the Syndics would arrive at T'shima with no warning.

Which had been the plan, Geary suddenly realized. "They didn't know we'd be here. Their target is T'shima, but once they saw us they knew they had to prevent any of our ships from jumping first and warning T'shima the Syndic flotilla was coming."

Five minutes to missile engagement envelope.

Decala nodded. "That explains what they're doing. Keep stringing us along as long as possible. Get as close as they can before they attack to ensure none of us get away. It all fits."

It fit perhaps too neatly. Geary clenched his jaw tight enough to hurt as he thought about what firing first might mean, how many people might die here and afterward before the resulting conflict was resolved.

But a final piece of the puzzle came to him as *Merlon* entered the wraith engagement envelope. "No battleship. No battle cruiser. Why would a major diplomatic mission not be accompanied by a capital ship?"

"Because the Syndic battleships and battle cruisers must be engaged elsewhere," Decala answered, her voice momentarily faltering. "May the living stars preserve us . . . . The Syndics must have flotillas entering Alliance space in many places. They're attacking all along the border, without any warning. They must be. That's why the Syndics here didn't call off the attack when they saw us. This is just one of dozens of coordinated strikes."

Geary's finger hovered near the red firing marker. The Syndic HuKs were very close now, only a light-minute distant, less than five minutes before intercept. He made up his mind, but as his finger moved alerts blared from the combat system. "The Syndic light cruisers are firing missiles!" the operations watch cried.

His finger finished moving, the red marker flashing green. "Fire," Geary said in a voice that sounded to him like that of a stranger. "Alter course up zero three degrees, come starboard zero four zero degrees. Hell lance batteries and grapeshot launchers engage when the HuKs enter firing envelopes." The charged particle beams of the hell lances had much shorter ranges than the missiles, and the solid metal ball bearings of the grapeshot were only effective at very close range where their patterns were tight enough for the kinetic impacts to overwhelm a ship's defenses. "Activate full counter-measures against Syndic missiles."

Merlon shuddered slightly as a wave of wraiths erupted from her, the missiles accelerating onto intercepts with the sterns of the oncoming Syndic HuKs. The Alliance cruiser was already turning, thrusters and main propulsion units pushing her onto a course close to parallel with that of the Syndics as the HuKs and *Merlon* rushed into contact. The final maneuver cut the closing rate slightly, but the two forces were still approaching each other at close to point one light speed, or about 30,000 kilometers per second.

The moment of closest approach came and went, the remaining distance dwindling too fast for human minds to grasp, weapons firing under automated control since humans couldn't react quickly enough, Geary barking out more commands the instant it was over. "Come starboard zero one two degrees, accelerate to point one one light speed." *Merlon's* structure groaned as the inertial dampers fought to compensate for maneuvering stresses which would have otherwise torn apart both ship and crew.

"Nice run!" Decala exulted.

Geary checked the results popping up on his display. Of the six HuKs, four had lost all or almost all propulsion as the wraith missiles slammed into their sterns. Two other HuKs were still able to maneuver, but one of them had been battered severely by *Merlon's* hell lances and grapeshot and was falling off to one side, most of its weapons assessed out of action. The sixth HuK had only taken a couple of hits, but *Pommel* and the three Alliance destroyers could easily handle a single HuK which had already taken some damage. "We've still got four light cruisers to deal with."

"Syndic missiles inbound on final," the combat systems watch called. "Hell lance batteries engaging."

Caught in a stern chase by *Merlon's* maneuvers, the Syndic missiles were relatively easy targets, but there were a lot of them against the defenses which the heavy cruiser could bring to bear as thrusters pivoted her to face the attack bow on. *Merlon* shuddered again as a missile tore into her shields, weakening them, then bucked as a second missile rammed through the weak area and exploded against the cruiser's armor. "Hell lance battery one alpha out of commission. No estimated time to repair. Armor breached forward. Damage control is sealing breached compartments," Decala reported, her voice steady.

"Target the next wave of wraiths on the propulsion systems of the light cruisers, then fire the final wave at the same targets."

"Yes, sir."

He had a few moments to make another transmission, one to which he didn't expect to have time to receive any reply. "*Pommel*, you are ordered to jump the convoy to T'shima as soon as you are in position to do so. All units are to jump. You are to warn T'shima that a Syndic flotilla is enroute and that they have initiated combat action against the Alliance. *Merlon* will follow if possible." He had to take a second then to ensure his voice remained steady. "If *Merlon* cannot follow, you must assume her destruction at the hands of the Syndics and request that the Alliance fleet undertake action to drive the Syndics from Grendel and rescue *Merlon's* crew as well as the crew of the emergency station. Good luck and may your ancestors watch over you. Geary out."

He was bringing *Merlon* around again as more warnings erupted. "Another wave of Syndic missiles inbound. Syndic light cruisers four minutes from contact."

The red marker glowed and Geary fired his wraiths again. "I'm giving you release authority for the third wave," he told Decala. "Punch them out as soon as they're ready to fly."

"Yes, sir. Captain, if we continue around like this we'll be heading right into the teeth of the Syndic missile barrage, and we'll be hit by all four light cruisers as we pass through their formation."

"I know. We have to stop those light cruisers and we only have a small window of time to do it in, so we have to ram straight through them." Geary shook his head. "It's going to cost us, but it's the only way so we're going to do it."

Decala nodded. "Yes, sir."

Two more missile hits staggered *Merlon*. "We lost the port wraith launchers," Decala reported. "Firing remaining wraiths."

The light cruisers and *Merlon* tore past each other, the heavy cruiser hurling out hell lance fire and grapeshot to all sides as she went between the Syndic light cruisers at a slight down angle and a sharp side angle. At the same time, fire from the Syndics lashed at *Merlon*, the heavy cruiser wobbling in her course from the impacts of three more missiles as well as hell lances and grapeshot hitting from every direction.

It took Merlon's battered sensors a few more moments than usual to evaluate damage to the enemy this time. Three of the light cruisers were out of the fight, their propulsion systems too badly damaged to allow them to catch the convoy now. The fourth light cruiser was in fairly good shape, but Geary was bringing *Merlon* back again on a long curve, aiming to get in a firing run.

"Forward and amidships shields have failed, hull armor is breached in multiple locations. All wraith launchers out of action," Decala reported. "Hell lance batteries two bravo, three bravo, and four alpha out of action. Grapeshot launchers three, five, and six are out of action. Heavy damage amidships. Propulsion capability reduced to fifty percent. Seventeen dead confirmed, wounded total unknown."

Geary felt that curious detachment again as he stared at the display where the damage to *Merlon* showed as growing patches of red, then to the three disabled Syndic light cruisers, still throwing out long-range fire at *Merlon*, to the operational light cruiser firing missiles again, and then to the track of the Syndic heavy cruisers and corvettes coming on, steadily closing the distance. Doctrine called for pulling clear now, gaining distance and time for shields to rebuild, for damage to be repaired, to get up velocity shed by the turns. But if he did that, the last Syndic light cruiser would make it to the transports before they jumped, and *Pommel* and the destroyers wouldn't be able to stop it before it crippled a bunch of the transports. Which left him only one option. "All nonessential personal abandon ship."

"What?" Decala shook her head, then focused on Geary again.

"All nonessential personnel abandon ship," Geary repeated. "Get them moving."

"Yes, sir."

He concentrated on the remaining light cruiser as *Merlon* bore down on it. The Syndic light cruiser was beginning to draw away, but Geary brought *Merlon* across her stern at close enough range to blow apart the enemy's main propulsion and leave her out of the battle.

Merlon had saved the convoy, but the price for that victory was about to go a lot higher.

A moment later two more missiles hit *Merlon* and the lights dimmed as circuits fought to automatically reroute themselves. "Propulsion down to ten percent." Decala's voice had grown mechanical, as if she were walling off emotion. "Only hell lance battery one bravo remains in action. All shields have failed. Engineering requests permission to retain all personnel aboard for damage control."

"Negative. Get them out. Get everyone out." Decala stared at him again. "Not just nonessential personnel. Everyone. Abandon ship. Now! Those heavy cruisers are going to tear this ship apart and I don't want my crew dying when they can't fight back!"

She passed on the orders and then shouted "get out of here!" at the remaining personnel on the bridge. As the others left at a run, Decala faced him, pale but determined. "I'm staying. I can handle the remaining working systems on the ship from the bridge." Another Syndic missile hit rocked *Merlon*, and both Decala and Geary had to grab for support as more damage alerts blared urgently.

"No, you're not," Geary insisted. "I'm the commanding officer. It's my responsibility to stay. I'll keep her fighting as long as I can. You don't need to be here."

"I won't leave you alone, Captain! *Merlon* is my ship, too!"

He reached out and grabbed her shoulder. "Cara, if this is really the start of a major war, the Alliance is going to need every experienced officer it's got. My duty requires me to stay here and keep *Merlon* fighting as long as possible, so the convoy and you and the rest of the crew can get clear. When the last combat systems go dead, I'll set the power core for self-destruct and I'll abandon ship, too. I promise. But if I don't survive this, then you have to. Because you're going to be needed. The rest of the crew needs you at this moment. Thank you for being an excellent officer and a friend. Now get out of here!"

She wiped an angry tear from one eye, then saluted. "Yes, sir." Decala appeared about to say something else, then turned and ran.

He sat down, then carefully checked the seals on his survival suit. The well-protected bridge in the heart of the ship still had atmosphere, but according to the readouts which continued to function on *Merlon,* most of the rest of the ship was in vacuum. A flock of escape pods was accelerating away from the heavy cruiser, carrying those of her crew who hadn't died already, a few more escape pods following at irregular intervals.

He hadn't had time to be scared before this, caught up in the fighting and responding to events, but now he was alone on the bridge, there was a brief interval before the rest of the Syndic warships got within range, and Geary had to fight down a wave of dread as he faced the reality that he and *Merlon* might die together.

But he still had a job to do. He had to keep the Syndics focused on *Merlon*, and not on the escape pods carrying most of her crew. He wouldn't let his crew be captured, to be made prisoners or even hostages on the Syndic warships heading to attack T'shima. The Syndic heavy cruisers and corvettes were ten minutes from firing range as Geary entered maneuvering orders. *Merlon* staggered in a wide, slow loop, trying to come onto a course facing the enemy.

He checked on the convoy. Almost to the jump point. The lone operational Syndic HuK had veered off, and Geary realized that it was trying to lure the convoy ships into chasing it. But Commander Lagemann could be trusted to use his head and follow orders.

More alerts, warning of the oncoming Syndic heavy cruisers. Geary targeted *Merlon*'s last functioning hell lance on the leading cruiser, setting it to fire automatically as the Syndics raced past. Outnumbered four to one, with his cruiser's shields down, almost all of her weapons knocked out and her armor already breached in many places, Geary had no illusions about his chances.

Syndic hell lance fire tore through *Merlon*, riddling the cruiser from one end to the other. Every remaining combat, life-support, and maneuvering system was knocked out, atmosphere rushed out of the bridge where holes had been punched through consoles and bulkheads, and the stricken Alliance warship began an uncontrolled tumble off to the side. The final hell lance battery was dead, but Geary felt *Merlon* tremble as more Syndic fire ripped through her. It must be the nickel corvettes making firing runs now, the scorned nickels able to pound the stricken Alliance cruiser with impunity.

He pulled open a special panel on his command seat, accessing the emergency self-destruct system. Geary punched in the authorization code with trembling hands. As far as he could tell, *Merlon*'s power core still had enough left to blow the ship apart. The Syndics wouldn't capture her intact. Though whether he needed to blow the heavy cruiser to pieces was a good question with the Syndics continuing to pound the Alliance warship into fragments. Why not just take her apart with a volley of missiles? But the Syndics probably wanted to save those missiles for the attack at T'shima, and perhaps hoped that prolonging *Merlon*'s death throes might entice the convoy to try a despairing rescue.

Code in and acknowledged. Enter confirmation code. Confirm again. Accepted. He had only ten minutes before the power core overloaded and *Merlon* exploded. More Syndic hell lance fire and grapeshot pummeled *Merlon*, and the local backup systems for bridge functions failed, the last virtual displays fading into the darkness.

He had no time to lose, but Geary hesitated before he left the bridge, gazing around at the deserted, ruined compartment. His ship. His command. *Merlon* had died fighting, but now he had to leave her and he hated it, cursing the Syndics who had reduced his beautiful ship to a hulk which would soon destroy itself.

Moving through the ship was a nightmare of another kind, the uncontrolled tumble making the bulkheads, decks, and overheads rotate erratically and seem to swing in and out as Geary propelled himself through passageways choked with wreckage and in some cases the heartrending remains of those of his crew who hadn't lived long enough to abandon ship.

But it got worse, as he found every escape pod access showing either a pod already ejected or the red glow of a status light indicating the pod had been too badly damaged to launch.

Finally he found a pod with a yellow status light over its access. It was damaged, but with less than five minutes before core overload Geary couldn't be picky even if he had known whether or not any other functional escape pods remained aboard. He pulled himself inside, sealed the hatch, strapped in as fast as he could, then slapped the ejection control.

Acceleration pinned him to his seat as the pod raced clear of *Merlon*. The pod lurched wildly, more damage lights blazing to life on its control panel, and Geary realized it had been caught in the edges of the blast from *Merlon*'s core overload.

The pod's propulsion cut off abruptly in the wake of the additional damage. It should have kept going a lot longer. Geary, feeling numb, tried to read the status display. He had ample power reserves still functional, but no maneuvering controls. Communications were out. The life-support systems on the pod were damaged too and, while still working, wouldn't hold out long.

Maybe he hadn't escaped after all.

Then his seat began reclining and Geary realized the pod was activating the emergency survival sleep system. He'd be frozen, kept in a state where his body needed only the tiniest amount of life support.

The panel which should have displayed an image of the outside was dark, not that he could have physically seen any of the ships already far distant from his pod. Surely the convoy had jumped by now. Lieutenant Commander Decala would be assembling the other escape pods from *Merlon*, keeping them together, heading for the emergency station orbiting Grendel. His crew, those who had survived to abandon ship, should be safe.

The lights on the panels above Geary were going out one by one or dimming into dormant status. He hadn't noticed the injections preparing his body for survival sleep, but felt lethargy stealing over him as his metabolism began slowing down.

He hated being cold. The idea of being frozen was far worse. But it would only be for a little while. *Pommel* would bring to T'shima the news of the Syndic attack here. The Alliance would counter-attack, resecure Grendel star system and rescue everyone from *Merlon*.

A war had begun, though he had no idea what had led the Syndics to launch surprise attacks. How long would it last? His last conscious thought as the cold took him was that surely it couldn't last too long. Sanity or the firepower of the Alliance fleet would prevail. Maybe by the time he was picked up, the war would already be over.

Geary's body slipped into survival sleep, his damaged pod drifting amid the wreckage of battle, its beacon dead, its power usage levels too low to stand out among the other debris.

He slept, while more battles raged in Grendel, one side then the other prevailing, the emergency station long since destroyed, larger and larger fleets clashing, then for a long time no ships at all. Around Grendel nothing orbited but the wreckage of earlier battles and one badly damaged survival pod, its power sources slowly draining.

Until one day another fleet came, the largest of all, and a destroyer spotted a suspicious object amid the leavings of battles. Electing to investigate rather than simply obliterate the object, the destroyer picked up the pod and delivered it to the fleet's flagship.

Geary's mind drifted back to partial awareness. His body felt like a block of ice and he couldn't see. Perhaps his eyelids were still frozen shut. Vague noises around him resolved into a few words. "Alive," "miracle," "Black Jack," and "war." He struggled to make sense of the words, finally feeling some emotion as aggravation at the nickname came to the surface.

"He'll save us!" That sentence came through clearly just before Geary began passing out again. He caught one more word as he drifted back into unconsciousness; *"Dauntless."*

His body shivered and for a time he knew no more as warmth returned.

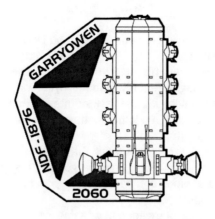

CLING PEACHES

An Alliance Archives Adventure

Mike McPhail

"The truth is what you make of it."
William Kriegherren

THE YEAR WAS UC104—2065 A.D. BY THE TERRESTRIAL CALENDAR—THE Scout Frigate *Garryowen*, NDF-1867, was inbound for the AeroCom Squadron Base, *Brooklyn Yards*, Heartland/Luna America. Damaged by a ground-launched Firemoth missile during the opening phases of the invasion of Demeter, she was running with only a skeleton crew, tasked with ferrying her home for repairs. Now some four-plus hours out from the planet, their next challenge rapidly approached: Transition to hyperspace.

Floating through the last set of opposing hatches, acting Chief Engineer William Donovich entered the drive section's service module. "By any other name it's still engineering," he stated. "A magical land traditionally ruled by mad Scotsmen and techno-fetish women." The very though brought a smile to his face.

In truth it was his love of science fiction that had drawn him to study engineering; he always seemed to have a need to find out the facts behind the fiction. Eventually this led him to apply to the National Space Agency where, after months of evaluations, he was rejected on the grounds that he was physically unfit to be an astronaut; whereas the AeroCom recruiter welcomed him with open arms.

Despite the mundane crap of life in the service—and the occasional megalomania of its civilian overseers—there were moments like this; when his daydreams of crewing an all-powerful starship across interstellar space came true.

"It's just a shame it doesn't look the part," said Donovich, looking down from the main hatchway platform; he often felt the ship's SM was less of a grand starship's engine room—one capable of governing the drive field generators that boosted the ship to the higher energy plane of hyperspace—and more akin to a padded, cold-war missile silo, with its lack of interior walls to divide its circular decks into compartments; this in addition to having equipment platforms bridging parts of its central gangway.

Looking back, Donovich could visualize the platforms being lowered through the central hatchways alone the gangway's cargo rails, then locked into place and connected to a myriad of pipes and cables by engineering specialists wearing orange MAC suits just like him.

"Wow," he said, a feeling of excitement washing over him. "Now the fun begins." He maneuvered himself to the platform's hatch control station. With a practiced push and heel snap, he locked his foot into one of the station's boot-docks; he activated the controls, which came to life with a myriad of color-coded icons. Looking up, he could see the hatchways, their passage indicator lights both showing steady-green.

"Why can't real life come with its own sound track?" he asked, thinking back and failing to come up with any score or song he could run through his head that would be appropriate to the moment. "I'll just have to wing it," he concluded.

With a quick look down, he placed his gloved finger between the protective side loops of the "Lock All" sequence button. With a gentle press and a confirming *click*, his world became filled with pulsating yellow lights and the chirp of alert tones.

With the ten-second time count for hatch closure running through his mind, Donovich once again looked up. "The CM's connected to the pod-bay . . ." he started singing as the first hatch swung into place, to be shortly joined by it's pod-bay counterpart, " . . . the pod-bay's connected to the SM . . .," he continued as the hatches just above his head swung one by one into place, with a steadfast motion and an accompanying mechanical *whirr*, the SM's main two-meter access hatch pressed into its frame and locked. Its pulsating, yellow warning lights then switched to a steady red.

After checking the status display on the consoles, he looked over the platform and down the length of the SM, " . . . the SM's connected to the DS; the DS contains the TL Drive, the reactor, and some other stuff." He paused before concluding with a boom in his voice, "OH HEAR. . .THE WORD . . . OF THE LORD!"

"Nice little tune," said a familiar female voice.

Donovich turned to see who had intruded on his moment. There was no one. "Duh," he whispered to himself. "Sorry, ma'am," he said into his comm-hood's pickup mics, "I was just running through the hatch checklist." He felt foolish at being caught acting so cavalier about doing his job.

"That's alright, Chief, I'm glad you're not stressing about the situation," reassured Major Ware, the ship's CO. "So I'll take it to mean that the drive section is secured?" she asked.

"Yes, ma'am," replied Donovich, as he snapped his foot free from the restraint. "I'll just need a moment to get into my station."

"Understood, Chief. Ware out."

With a tap on his arm control pad, Donovich switched his primary comm channel to standby and then opened the squad-band. "Patterson," he called, as he pushed off toward the ramp at the side of the platform; grabbing the handrails with both hands he redirected his momentum down the ramp.

"Patterson here, go'head, Chief," replied a voice with a slight southern drawl.

Donovich passed quickly over the life-boat deck and was now holding on to the top of the handrail loops for the ladder well. "What's your status?" he asked as he looked down through the two stories of wire mesh tubing that surrounded the access ladder.

"Everythin's green, Chief; we're good to go."

"Understood," replied Donovich, while still debating his next course of action. "Go strap in; I'll give the All-Go as soon as I hit my station and get some coffee." With that he pulled himself head-first down the ladder-well; an experience that is visually not unlike diving into a cheese grater.

"Yes'ir," then there was a pause, "Um, did ya'll say coffee?" asked Patterson.

Donovich waited until he had cleared the ladder before answering; free-falling down a ladder-well was just something no sane Starman should do, so getting stuck and having to explain himself as someone came to fished him out was definitely on the top of his "things-not-to-do" list. Now over the main deck, he maneuvered to his station. "Do you remember that guy Tony from the *Vandenberg*?"

"Yeah, I think so; but there were a lot of techs floatin' around, tryin' to glue us back together for the jump home," he remarked.

Grabbing the handhold next to his station's jump-seat, Donovich pulled himself into place below the rack holding his MAC's pressure helmet and its adjoined environmental chest pack. With a snap, he locked his heels into the boot-docks, and reached for the five-point harness handles. "Well, while we were talking, I mentioned that fluid-loading didn't work to keep down the nausea during Transition."

The feeling of the seat's restraining straps snuggling up, and then locking down, was always comforting, and in its own way sort of creepy. "So he recommended a hot cup of strong coffee instead of that citrus-flavored electrolyte stuff," he continued as he reached for the self-heating pressure-mug. "I love a ship with cup holders," he added as he pulled the mug free from its mount below the console. Depressing the top, he took a long, hard draw from the mug's mouth piece; a satisfying warmth spread through his chest.

"I take it ya'll still got your bag with 'n arms reach?" asked Patterson.

Locking the mug back down, Donovich opened the top pocket of his suit's utility jumper and pulled up the open end of a red biohazard bag. "Aye," he confirmed. "Okay, Patterson, I'm about to give the flight deck the All-Go, you set?"

"Yes'ir."

"Understood, Donovich out." A beep signaled that the channel was now on standby. Looking up he could see the underside of his suit's pressure helmet. "Regs state that I have to wear it . . ." he said doubtfully, ". . . but after last time. . . Nope," he concluded and turned his attention to his station's console. All status lights were green, except for the few that were blacked out from the missile strike. He depressed the "All-Go" button and waited for the flight crew to do their part; on this trip that would be just Major Ware and the XO, Lieutenant Koenig.

The two-minute warning klaxon sounded. "Attention all personnel, prepare for Transition," announced the ship's computer over the intercom. It was clear the CO was just waiting for his signal.

Hyperspace Transition Syndrome, or hypes, was comparable to the space-sickness many astronauts suffered as they adapted to living in zero-g. The professionals didn't really know what caused hypes, or who was likely to be susceptible to it—let alone how to cure or even minimize the effects; all Chief Donovich knew was it specifically didn't like him.

Eyeing his console, he wasn't so much monitoring the systems readouts, as watching for flashing yellow or red icons: once the trans-light drive sequence was engaged, only a full-blown "Blow the main power couplings and pop the compositors," abort could stop it from firing. Even then, it could only be interrupted up until the drive field started to form; after that, you were going for a ride.

Suddenly, the sound of crackling static seemed to come from everywhere, and he could feel the hairs on his body trying to stand up under the constrictive force of his MAC suit. On his console the guard covering the lighted red "Abort" button popped open with an accompanying alert tone. As the saying went, "His ass snapped shut" at the very thought of ever being in a situation where hitting that button was his only option. The pretty, candy-like button was just part of the "pilot factor," where the guy in charge (or in this case, the Chief engineer) must retain some ability to override the computer in the event of an emergency . . .

Donovich's thoughts were cut short as the drive field formed.

It was said that how one perceived the sensation of entering hyperspace was directly proportional to how often, and how severely, one suffered from hypes. Some said it was like standing on a commuter rail platform in winter as a train speeds by. Personally, Donovich pictured it as falling down a long-forgotten mine shaft somewhere in the frozen hell of Siberia, this after having been drunk for the weekend and dealing badly with a massive hangover.

The actual Transition to hyperspace wasn't the problem; that happened faster than the human mind could ever hope to perceive. All of the vertigo-inducing special effects were actually caused by the ship's own TLD systems. It was only after the ship had passed through the point of Transition that the field compensators could finally even out the power flow and balance the drive's harmonics against the resident frequency of the ship's spaceframe.

"Enough technobabble. . ." he said to himself through clenched teeth, ". . . knowing doesn't help. Believe me!" The nausea was there and starting to push at him; he reached for the bag's grab tab at his pocket. A heavy thump sounded from somewhere overhead, quickly followed by a sharp metallic ping from somewhere nearby. Donovich looked up. His eyes were tearing; he attempted to wipe them with the back of his glove. "No good," he murmured, and then looked over at his console; no flashing red indicators to greet him. Turning back, he listened for the sounds of escaping gas or grinding metal; there was nothing.

As his vision cleared, he could see that the mission clock had started. It read 482 hours and 56 minutes as the seconds counted down. "That's almost three weeks under driver," he said, now realizing that it was over and that, for the first time, he hadn't lost it all over himself from the hypes.

"Attention all personnel, secure from Transition," sang out over the intercom in the lovely, neutral female voice that was the SC; it was accompanied by the usual low-gravity warning.

Uncoupling his harness, Donovich stepped out onto the deck; now under pseudo .3-g—one of the unforeseen side effects of the TLD was that it creates something akin to its own gravity well—he felt heavy again, with that all-too-familiar draining feeling as fluids once again moved toward their lowest points.

After a few deep breaths and a bit of stretching against the elastic action of his MAC suit, Donovich turned and reached past his console for his pressure mug. He heard the warning tone from the console as his hand touched the mug's handle; in that instant the very reality around him rapidly compressed and expanded like an image in a carnival mirror.

He grabbed for his jump seat and managed to get a handhold on the frame. The vertigo drove him to his knees, retching, unable to breathe from the abdominal contractions. His other arm was locked straight, with the hand pressed down into the deck in an effort to support himself.

At that moment he was alone; trapped in the darkness behind his own eyes, with the feeling of being squeezed to the point of suffocation. Then somewhere at the edge of his consciousness he could once again hear the alert tones, now joined by the voice of Major Ware.

Donovich opened his eyes, but growing pressure against his face threatened to force them shut. Somehow he managed a gulp of air, which he forced down past the burnt feeling in his throat; he hadn't voided his stomach, but definitely refluxed up into his mouth, then he was breathing again.

"Chief, what is your status!" the Major demanded. "Patterson get up there and see what you can do!" she ordered.

"Donovich here," he said with a raspy voice.

"Thank God." There was stress-tainted relief in her voice. "Chief, the SC reports that we've gone into field imbalance."

"Understood, ma'am, I'm on it," Donovich responded, as he scanned along the length of his console.

"I'm headin' up," replied Patterson.

"Patterson stay put . . ." Donovich countermanded as he pulled himself up to his console on unsteady legs, ". . .in case the problem's at your end of the module."

"Yes'ir."

Donovich was having trouble seeing—no doubt he'd blown some blood vessels from the straining. It wasn't so much that his vision was blurry, but that every lit display now had a superimposed twin. The console was awash in flashing yellow status lights, each indicating some irregularity with its respective system. They could all wait: red priority markers strobed around the icon for the Drive Frequency Controller. With a touch of the icon, Donovich opened a dialog window stating, "MANUAL OVERRIDE AT DFC UNIT," accompanied by two columns of numbers; one number set was flashing red.

"Damnit!" he exclaimed, looking over at the machinery mounted to the nearby equipment platform. "That's where that bang came from," he muttered, remembering the sounds he heard during Transition.

Like a chimp climbing slowly through the treetops, Donovich reached out from one handhold to another for support, not releasing his grip on the first until he was secure to the next.

Before long he was holding onto the platform's guardrail, just across from the unit; the marked access hatch was flanked by handholds. Reaching out, Donovich grabbed one, and then depressed the spring-loaded latch pin on the hatch, which opened with a snap. He swung it up until it locked. Inside was the unit's hardwired controls with its oscilloscope-style display showing two color-coded, opposing harmonic waveforms—normally it was just a straight line, indicating that all three axial oscillations were being effectively countered—but now one was out of sync.

"By the book," muttered Donovich as he looked up at the interior of the hatch for the procedural check list; it took him a moment to sort through the different emergency scenarios. "One: Check for manual setting change at panel." He looked down at the instrument panel, mostly back-lit in green; there were the three metal gear-tooth, wing-lock knobs in question. One was back-lit in red. "That's it!" he said.

To the side of the panel was the maintenance log—the Techs from the *Vandenberg* had recalibrated the system to compensate for the loss of two of the ship's external fuel tanks—the last entry was less than a day old.

"Right," he said as he reached for the knob. Its safety-lock worked like a prescription bottle's child-proof cap; with a determined squeeze to its side-wings, Donovich ever so gently turned the knob to the recorded setting. Like a concluding drumbeat, the pulsating stopped.

". . . and all was right with the world!" he said with relief. Holding his hand still, he opened his fingers. The knob's locks pressed out and clicked; its backlight turned green.

He just stood there for a moment, looking over the instrument display, checking the lockdowns for any other possible problems.

"Chief, I take it you have things under control?" asked Ware over the comm.

"Yes, ma'am," rasped Donovich. His mouth and throat were a mess. "Right now, it looks like a switch shook loose; it's going to take us the better part of a day to look over the key systems to confirm that's the only problem."

"Very well, keep me informed; Ware out."

With a tap, he once again switched his comm to stand-by, then withdrew a marker from his pocket.

Dutifully, Donovich recorded the malfunction and setting change on the maintenance log; the computer entries would have to wait. His next stop was the medical supply cabinet, or med-station. Distracted by the thought of impending relief, he let his marker once again get away from him. It fell somewhere into the recessed area of the panel. "Butt-monkeys," he exclaimed.

Carefully he moved his head in for a look—the last thing he wanted was to bump something and start the show all over again. The marker wasn't in the front. Retrieving his pocket flashlight, he depressed the base switch; the LED cluster came to life.

Moving in close, he could only bring one eye to bear past the frame of the access hatch; he played the spot into the side portion of the recess. At first the stowaway didn't register—since he was preoccupied with looking for the marker. Once it did, he was feeling too crappy to really care either way. Things do manage to get onboard ship, but generally they don't last long in the inorganic environment of the module. "Great, and me without a mayonnaise jar," he said, with a feeling of annoyance at having something else to deal with.

His unwanted visitor was a spider, just sitting there at an odd angle, affixed to the instrument panel.

"Why is it always a spider, don't the cockroaches have a space program?" he said sarcastically.

As house spiders went, it was pretty big, maybe as much as an inch across, but it was hard to judge; his new friend was all bunched up, and Donovich's eyes were still a bit fuzzy.

Letting out a long breath, he thought over his options and decided upon the ancient, tried-and-true approach—the one that did not involve a newspaper.

He did, however, need something to store the beastie in. Donovich pulled the unused biohazard bag from his pocket, and with a practiced hand, swiped it full of air. Placing his flashlight into his mouth, he bit down on its flexible grip; he could feel the tension in his jaw rising along the left side of his aching face.

Rubbing his gloved fingertips together, Donovich explored whether he would have enough sensitivity not to squish the beastie—which would require him to dismantle the unit's casing to clean up the mess—let alone be able to catch it just by feel. The suit's gloves were state-of-the-art for working in vacuum; highly flexible, heated, and armored against puncture, so taking one off to reach blindly into a confined space, to grab a potentially poisonous spider, was out of the question.

Slowly he reached in, palm down and fingers fanned out; aiming for the mental image of the beastie's position. "I bet when I turn you over, you'll have 'Property of the Vandenberg' stenciled on your butt," he said.

Now beyond the controls, he slid his hand along the surface of the panel. Then he touched something with the side of his index finger, with a pinch, he tried to catch it against his thumb.

It felt slick—not wet—more like the effect you get when you bring equal poles of a magnet together, a sort of wavy feeling. Then it popped free and was gone. With his head starting to pound against the pressure in his jaw, Donovich withdrew his hand and took the light from his mouth.

Looking back in, Donovich saw that the beastie was still sitting in the same spot. "Now you're just messing with me," he said. This time around he noticed that the spider had thick, antenna-like protrusions coming from where its head should be, kind of like a cylinder with round ends. *Sort of hotdog-shaped*, he thought.

What he originally thought of as fur turned out to be either a glossy, blue-grey skin or a carapace, which meant it wasn't a spider, but whatever it was, it was hefty for its size. *What are you?* The very thought added to his headache; looking back over his shoulder, he could see the med-station in the distance, with its beautiful, six-pointed blue and white "Star of Life," which seemed to call to him. "I'll deal with you later," he said as he closed and snap-locked the unit's access hatch. Flattening the biohazard bag, he tucked it in a pocket and went to find some relief.

"I was enjoying myself earlier," he commented as he stood in front of the med-station's closet-sized door; he removed his comm-hood and let it hang by the suit's interface cable, he then ran a hand over his buzz-cut hair before opening the cabinet.

"Nothing is ever simple," grumbled Donovich as he looked at the maze of labeled, numbered, and color-coded drawers, compartments, and lock-boxes; unfortunately, he knew from experience where to find what he needed. He snapped a cold-pack to life and balanced it on his head while he dug out a tube of chewable pain killers.

As he was popping open the package's safety cap, he thought he heard something. Taking out several pills and slipping the rest into his pocket, he turned to face the gangway. He listened for anything beyond the usual sounds of the module; there was nothing. With the pills now dissolving in his mouth, it was time to get back to his station and finish off his coffee; he felt in his guts that this was going to be a very long day.

He had only taken a few steps when the sound of a dull thump echoed from somewhere in the module. *Must be Patterson moving about*, he thought, reaching for the comm control at his arm.

A distant crack and a sizzle caught his attention—the dreaded sound of something electrical arcing and shorting out. No alarm had sounded . . . yet. He quickly looked around his immediate area for any telltale signs of arc light or smoke.

The arcing sound had stopped, to be followed by a *splat* sound very near by. With a hand holding the cold-pack in place, he was looking up through the deck gratings when something moved at the edge of his vision. Turning, he caught sight of it. Something steaming hot oozed down through the grating from the deck above.

Donovich moved toward it, being damn sure not to get underneath. Every fluid used onboard ship was color-coded and often scent-infused—like the sulfur they added to natural gas—this to alert the engineers to its threat level and possible system of origin; but this stuff was dark amber in color, and moved in a thick ribbon, like some form of industrial grease. It was already seeping through the deck grating at Donovich's feet. There was the smell of ozone in the air, and something almost sweet, like a marshmallow burnt black over an open fire.

Fear grabbed at Donovich as his imagination broke loose. The parallels to an old sci-fi movie raced through his mind; he suddenly felt vulnerable and naked against the unseen, but envisioned, horrors, moving about through the machinery of the module. Escape was out of the question; whatever was there was between him and the main hatchway to the CM.

As he backed away from the steaming goo, he struck his elbow on a protruding piece of equipment. The cold-pack dropped to the deck as he cradled his arm against the pain. Reality finally fell back in upon him.

"I need a nap," he said, moving his arm to work out the ache. He watched his hand, as he fanned and contracted the fingers against the numbness and tingling sensation. After retrieving the cold-pack from the deck, Donovich put on his comm-hood and secured the pack beneath it.

After a few more pain killers, he started off toward the ladder well, and the two-story climb to the life-boat deck. At this point he knew clearly that he should at least let Patterson know what was going on, but after his moment of insanity, he needed to make sure before he made a complete fool of himself. "Beside, if it eats my brain . . ." he laughed, ". . . then at least my headache will be gone." He started climbing.

From the ladder well he could see that whatever the goo was, it had dripped down from the top deck, through an intervening deck, to where he'd spotted it. He knew that there was no machinery in that general area of the life-boat deck, nor any hydraulic or fuel lines; only storage lockers.

The life-boat deck was designed to be used as an emergency staging area in the event that the CM became compromised and had to be abandoned. To that end, it was basically just a large, open area ringed by stocked storage lockers.

On this trip it had been used as a barrack for two squads of Starine Ground Observers that had been dropped off over Demeter in re-entry capsules. As happens when people are thrown together out of necessity, Donovich came to know many of the men living on the life-boat deck. In fact, it was the GO team leader, Sergeant Ryan Warwick, who had warned the *Garryowen* of the impending missile strike. "Thanks, my friend," Donovich whispered.

"Get your mind back in the game," he ordered himself, as he neared the top of the ladder well. He could see where the unidentified fluid had come through the decking; sighting on that point, he casually brought his eyes above the level of the deck plating. There, caked onto the wall, was a line of goo running down from one of the chest-high lockers. Its door hung partially open.

With his feet still on the ladder's rungs, he took a slow and careful look around; this while visions of procuring something from the small arms locker continued to play across the back of his mind. "And I'm going to do what, to whom, with a Peacemaker?" he said, shaking his head in disbelief at his own foolishness, as he stepped up onto the deck.

Despite the reticulating fans, the air was still thick with the sickly-sweet smell. As he walked slowly toward the locker, he wished that he had brought up his MAC suit's helmet, if for nothing else than an added feeling of security; then he remembered that it didn't help that guy in the movie. "Stop that," he forcibly whispered at himself.

Now, standing in front of the locker, he pulled it open by the handle and stepped back, keeping the door between him and whatever was inside. With a *splat*, something fell out onto the deck at his feet. Despite his best effort at self control, Donovich jumped, his whole being riveted on what landed in front of him.

There they sat, two baseball-size hemispheres, clearly parts of one whole, steaming and partially impaled by the corrugated decking. Like the goo, they were dark amber in color, except for where a lighter, fleshy material showed through from the areas torn open in the fall.

Donovich forced his breathing to slow, then held one breath and slowly let it out; he felt dizzy from the effort. His body was awash with adrenalin and hormones, fueling him for either fight or flight against the unknown.

"Enough of this crap," he snapped, now becoming angry with himself. He swung the door open until it locked back, then stepped around the stuff on the deck to get a look inside the locker. After just a moment, Donovich stepped away and engaged the squad-ban. "Patterson from Donovich," he commed. A smile of relief crept across his face. He turned and walked toward the mess-station for something to drink.

"Yes, Chief?" replied Patterson.

"What's your location?"

"I'm 'n the machine room just below the middeck hatch."

"Come up to the life-boat deck," Donovich instructed, understanding that it was a six-story ladder climb. "I'm going to need help with a few things."

"Yes'ir," replied Patterson, almost enthusiastically; with a beep, the comm switched to standby.

Donovich felt physically rung out, and emotionally less than worthy to wear the uniform of the Aerospace Command. The only up-side to all this was that the mission recorders—the ship's black boxes—continuously stored system data and comm traffic, but only recorded images at very specific moments, such as Transition, and when certain alarms were tripped. So with luck, it should have missed all his stupidity over the stuff from the locker.

"Ya'll called, Chief?" said Patterson, as he climbed up onto the deck.

At about six-foot four and built like someone who worked for a living, Patterson literally stood out among his fellow Starmen.

Donovich just stood there by the open looker, sucking something from a collapsible drink bottle. "Is this your handy work, Sergeant?" he asked with an *I already know the answer* undertone.

Patterson just smiled and walked over for a better look. After a moment of contemplation, "Nice trick," he said turning to Donovich, "Someday ya'll have to tell me how I did it." Patterson had one of those easy-going personalities that made it hard not to immediately take a liking to him, but as far as Donovich was concerned, it was the fact that he was a highly knowledgeable and dedicated member of the engineering team that made him a worthwhile comrade.

Clamping the drink bottle closed, Donovich stowed it in his utility jumper and reached into the locker. "So you're claiming this isn't one of your practical jokes?"

"Yes'ir," Patterson replied. "My jokes never involve havin' to clean up afterward." He smiled and motioned toward the deck. "That's quite a smell you got there, what's this stuff?"

Donovich pulled out what appeared to be a closed pull-top can, and casually tossed it to Patterson; it was heavy and made a sloshing sound. Patterson turned it around in his hands for a look at the label. "Yellow Cling Peaches," he read.

"Yep, in heavy syrup; that explains the burnt-sugar smell," Donovich said as he pulled several other cans from the locker and placed them on the deck. "They're not Squadron-issued, so where did we get them?"

Patterson thought it over in his usual, drawn-out way; he once had to explain this to a rather annoyed instructor, "Sir, I'd rather be right and considered slow, than fast and stupid." Although this wasn't tolerated in training, it later proved to be one of his most outstanding attributes.

"I'd say it's part of the ship's discretionary cargo, most likely from one of the officers; hey, maybe even the CO?" he speculated.

"Lovely," stated Donovich, as he dug out several cleaning packs he had brought back from the kitchen station. "Well it's our mess now, let's get going on this," he said, handing Patterson a pack.

Inside the locker was a mass of caramelized sugar and two more burnt peach halves. Donovich scooped the mess into a bag, and wiped down the area; the pack's chemically treated cloth made short work of the remaining goo, but it uncovered something else: a circular outline matching the base of the can was burnt into the floor of the lockers.

"Patterson, look at this," he called.

Without a word Patterson stood up and watched as Donovich tried to clean off the ring. "It looks like the can just flashed over," said Patterson. He was no longer smiling.

"Agreed," stated Donovich as he bent down and picked up the other peach cans. "I don't know what's going on, but until we get a chance to sort things out I'm securing these in one of the ordnance bunkers we installed for the Starines." He headed out across the deck. Patterson joined him.

The bunker looked like a black garbage can bolted to the deck by four spring-loaded shock absorbers. "Get the lid for me," asked Donovich.

"Yes'ir," Patterson replied as he undid the oversized wing nuts.

"Thanks," Donovich said. He placed the cans down into the drum designed for storing small arms ammunition and explosive ordnance—such as grenades. The bunkers were more than capable of containing and redirecting the force of such an explosion; this while the quilted lining burst, releasing a cloud of heat-absorbing particles to dampen down any fire.

"Okay. . ." said Donovich as they secured the drum's lid, ". . .we'll finish the clean up, then you can help me track down the bug in the DFC unit."

"Yes'ir, but my diagnostic set is still down by my station, it'll take me a bit . . ." he started to explain. Donovich motioned for him to stop talking.

"No, no, I mean, an actual bug." He held up his fingers to indicate the size. "About this big; I came across it after the incident," he said. "It was just sitting there on the panel . . ." Donovich fisted his hands and brought them up to either side of his head ". . . watching me with an eyeless, hotdog-shaped head."

Patterson just stopped and stared at him; a dull expression crossed his face as his eyes seemed to be looking back at some point in his memory.

"Patterson?" said Donovich calmly; it was obvious that his comrade was in trouble, "Robert . . . Bobby, look at me. . ." He resisted the urge to physically reach out to him. Patterson's breathing became deep and drawn out; something was frightening him.

"Starman Patterson!" yelled Donovich with his best military bearing, "Look at me!" Patterson snapped to attention and fixed his eyes on Donovich; the look of wide-eye terror quickly faded.

"Sir," said Patterson, as he pulled himself together.

"Would you care to explain yourself, mister!?" commanded Donovich, hoping that by maintaining the pressure, he could work out what was upsetting his fellow Starman.

"Can't," replied Patterson.

"Can't or won't!?" demanded Donovich.

Patterson took deep breath, "Can't." Clearly Patterson knew that this answer was going to piss him off, but before Donovich could retaliate, "Sir . . ." Patterson said, holding up his hands in an effort to deflect the outburst. "Chief, can we stop playin' spacemen for a bit, and just talk?" Patterson asked, sincerely, with a look of concern in his eyes.

Donovich picked up on this. "Sure," he said, and pulled out his package of pain killers. He took one, and then offered the rest to Patterson.

"No thanks," the man said with a wave of his hand. He turned and looked down over the deck's guardrail at the DFC unit. "It's been about two years ago now, I was the Assistant Chief Engineer onboard the *Boston*. Well, we were homeward bound from Proxima; about a day under drive we started havin' electrical problems."

"Isn't that run about a week?" asked Donovich.

"About that," he agreed. "You know, electrical shorts and loose couplin's are business-as-usual after Transition; but then equipment lockdowns were bein' found opened, or even missin' all together."

To Donovich, it sounded like a disgruntled Starman engaged in a bit of revenge sabotage, most likely to make someone else look incompetent.

"Then the shit really hit the fan. One of the support stanchions for the LI's laser canal broke loose. I don't have to tell you, if the gravity detector went out, findin' home would have been more a matter of religion than science." he turned to see Donovich's reaction.

All Donovich could do was nod in agreement. The Laser Interferometer was the only navigational aid the ship had under drive; its primary function was to detect the approach of a gravitational anomaly, namely a star or some other super massive object. Without it, navigation would have to rely on pure mathematics and a ballistic trajectory to determine when to turn off the drive, and that could lead—*had* led—to timing mistakes measured in hundreds of millions of miles.

"Mind you, by the end of day six, everyone was involved 'n tryin' to figure this thin' out. The CO ordered all nonessential crew to their bunks, while the XO handled it. Of course, by then there were only a few of us runnin' around." Patterson looked annoyed. "I understand what they were tryin' to do, but it backfired; stuff started happenin' faster than we could fix it. At that point the XO threatened us with court martial."

Donovich knew the next part. "And in a time of war, that could have added up to being *spaced*."

"Damn Skippy it could," Patterson agreed. "As for your bug friend," he said, gesturing toward the DFC. "We were just 'n hour or so from droppin' out of drive, when I heard somethin' shortin' out. By the time I figured out where it was comin' from, this big-ass thin', kinda like a crab. . .", he put both of his hands together at the thumbs, with fingers spread wide to show the thing's size, ". . . just came floatin' along like it was 'n zero-g."

"What did you do?" asked Donovich, feeling somehow very stereotypical at having asked that.

Patterson seemed to take offense at the question. "I didn't *do* a damn thin'," he responded, and lunged his hands at Donovich's face to make his point about being startled. "I called out over the comm for help. I had to tell that story repeatedly before I could get anyone to believe me; or at least I thought they did. By then we had come out of drive; we spent the rest of the trip tearin' everythin' apart lookin' for it."

"Let me guess . . ." said Donovich.

"Don't bother," replied Patterson, cutting him off. "It was just like when pilots made the mistake of reportin' UFO's back in the days. Without proof a saucer banged up your plane, you were screwed."

"Didn't the mission recorders pick anything?" asked Donovich.

"Nope," said Patterson, "Just me screamin' over the comm about a God damn bug." Patterson started to smile, "But I got lucky. They were short-handed for this little invasion of theirs. . ." Without concluding the sentence he pointed at the DFC, "Let's go have a look at your friend." and started off for the ladder well.

"You know, Patterson. . ." said Donovich as he followed him, ". . .if this turns out to be one big *catten* prank, the quartermaster is going to have to issue me a new pair of boots."

Patterson just looked at him for a moment, "Why so, Chief?"

Donovich smiled, "Because I'll have lost one up your ass!"

Now on the main deck, Donovich stepped around Patterson and walked off. "Where're you goin'?" asked Patterson.

Motioning at his station, Donovich explained, "I have coffee to attend to; besides, you'll need to figure out what to put the wee beastie in once you catch it."

Without a word, Patterson turned and headed toward the equipment lockers.

Then the lights went out, dropping the module into a world of inky black, outlined by yellow and green night-glow strips, with pockets of blue-white LED emergency lighting.

"What now?!" exclaimed Donovich as he rushed to his station; a red icon flashed on the console's power flow schematic. "Patterson!" he shouted. "Something just tripped the breaker on main bus B!" Thoughts of Patterson's little friend tearing apart his ship pushed at him.

Near the ladder well, a work light came on, it was Patterson putting on his head-lamp; its beam playing out across the space. "I'm on it," he shouted.

Donovich checked the fault indicator log on the breaker; he anticipated a power spike as the reason—static-electric build up was a common problem under drive— but the read-back told another story. "Patterson, don't engage the breaker!" shouted Donovich urgently as he left the station. "Don't engage the breaker; it's set to failsafe due to a power loss, there's a break in the line!" Not hearing a response from Patterson, Donovich raised his arm to access the comm control at his forearm.

An explosion of sparks erupted from the deck below, as fire claxons sounded and their accompanying yellow strobe lights pulsed. "Shit!" yelled Donovich, as he ran for the ladder well; pressing his feet against the outside of the ladder's rails, he slid down and landed with a jolt on the deck below. Grabbing for his flashlight, he hurried for the nearest fire extinguisher.

Patterson had just reached the ladder to follow Donovich down when he heard an arcing sound, coming from the life-boat deck; looking up he saw brilliant flashes of blue light dancing off the surrounding metal work. "Not this time," he growled, as he started up the ladder instead.

It only took one short blast from the extinguisher to deal with the problem; but now Donovich had to clean up the foam to inspect and repair the damage.

"Chief Donovich, status report," commanded the XO over the comm.

Donovich put down the extinguisher before answering. "Everything is now under control, sir," he said as he played his light over the damage. "We had a short circuit that set off the fire alarms." The conduit's access plate hung open; one of the cables had a clean piece missing.

"Very well, Chief, please keep me informed; Koenig out."

"Sabotage," whispered Donovich, as he slowly turned, expecting to find Patterson standing behind him; the Starman was nowhere to be seen. "I hope for your sake, that your little imaginary friends are real." Then it dawned on Donovitch that they were screwed either way. Shaking his head, he walked to the deck's ancillary control station, and with a tap turned off the alarms.

Against the ringing in his ears he could hear Patterson shouting. It took Donovich a moment to spot him through the deck grating. Patterson was jumping around on the top deck; his point of interest seemed to be the ordnance bunker. Then there was an arc flash, followed by the sound of metal striking metal, as if something had just been thrown and bounced off onto the deck, this accompanied by more shouting.

Silhouetted against the emergency lighting, something jumped—no flew—across the void of the gangway some three stories up. Looking like a pointy starfish, it flew with its six legs outstretched; reflected light contoured across its smooth surface. It brought its legs forward, and landed without a sound, disappearing into the deck's support structure and conduits.

"Did you see it!?" demanded a voice; it was Patterson leaning over the guardrail. "Chief!" he shouted forcibly.

"Yes. . ." Donovich squeaked. He cleared his throat, ". . .Yes, I saw it!" he shouted back, not quite *believing* what he had just said; but yes, he had seen *something*.

A few minutes later, Donovich joined Patterson above; the climb up to the life-boat deck had been one of apprehension and controlled fear.

"Look at this," said Patterson holding what was left of a spanner; half of its gapped end was missing. "I took a swin' at the thin' when it was cuttin' into the bunker." He pointed at the deck-mounted drum; four of its six spring-loaded, overpressure bolts had been cut away.

Donovich turned and looked down over the guardrail at the mission clock, its four-inch high numbers read 482 hours and 01 minutes, "We have to get this thing contained; we're only two hours in, there's no way we can keep this up for three weeks," stated Donovich.

"And where you goin' to put it?" Patterson said, gesturing toward the damaged ordnance bunker.

Good catting question, thought Donovich, as he looked around for both inspiration and the beastie.

Patterson walked up to him. "So what would they do in one of those sci fi stories you keep readin'?" Patterson asked sincerely.

Oh, just great! Now we are relying on the delusions of some writer to save our asses, thought Donovich. "Well typically, at a dramatically quiet point in all the screaming and running about, they try to blow it out an airlock." he said.

"There's no way we're goin' to get that thin' up the length of the CM and into the axial airlock; we can't even risk lettin' it out of this module!" proclaimed Patterson.

"Yeah, you're right," agreed Donovich, "But . . . we could try to get it into one of the re-entry pods; with the CM's gangway hatches locked, it couldn't get any farther than the pod-bay."

"What's to keep it from burnin' through the Can's hatch?" Patterson asked.

"What's keeping it from cutting its way into the CM now; or back into the fuel module, or even the reactor?" said Donovich, waving his arm about to emphasize his point. "Beside, once we get the hatches closed, we depressurize the causeway and it's trapped on the wrong side of hard vacuum!" he added, smacking a fist into his other hand.

Patterson paused, "Okay, Chief, I'm with'ya; but first, lock off your comm." Donovich knew he looked a bit confused. "Remember," Patterson explained. "The mission recorder tracks all comm traffic. If this works out, then we'll have proof sittin' 'n the can; if not . . ."

"If not . . . were screwed, but at least we'll have some level of deniability at our court martial," said Donovich, thinking back to Patterson's UFO reference; back then a pilot's radio report proved nothing—except when they were used as evidence against his competency to continue flying—and these logs will prove nothing now; he smiled at Patterson and turned off his comm.

"So how do we do this?" asked Donovich.

"Well we know it's after the peach cans, so we'll put them 'n the pod, some place hard to get to 'n order to slow it down while I move up and close the hatches," said Patterson.

"No. For one thing you're too big to move around quickly in the pod-bay." Patterson started to object, but Donovich motioned for him to be quiet. "Secondly, I don't think it will be stupid enough to just crawl into the pod, after all, it set up a diversion to get at them the first time."

"Okay, Chief," Patterson agreed. "So then we'll need somethin' to knock or blow it into the Can."

"Maybe rigging a quick valve to an O_2 or nitrogen tank, with a piece of pipe big enough to hold one of the cans; when it climbs up, I pull the line on the valve . . ."

"Nope, too complicated," Patterson interrupted. "Get me one of those Growlers out of storage."

It took Donovich a moment to work it all out, but he saw where Patterson was going with this. "Right, I'll meet you back here."

"Do ya'll need a hand with that?" asked Patterson as Donovich came up the ladder one-handed, cradling a wastepaper bucket-sized canister in his arm.

"I'm fine," he replied and stepped out onto the deck.

Patterson was busy loading the peach cans into a utility bag; he already had an engineer's carryall tool-pack over his shoulder. "I was goin' to pop open one of these cans and. . ." The look on Donovich's face said volumes about the idea. "Okay, Chief," said Patterson, while making a calm-down gesture. "I didn't. I was just tryin' to figure out what it wanted with them."

Donovich had already played with the idea that it—or they—had come aboard in the cans, but somehow it didn't quite make sense; it was too easy an answer. So maybe it has something to do with the material makeup of the cans themselves; but what was it about an Alluna (Lunar Aluminum) can that made it so all-important? After all, most of the ship was built from the stuff in one grade or other.

Patterson stood up and slung the utility bag over his shoulder. "You ready?"

Donovich nodded. "Any sign of our friend?" he asked, looking about.

"Couldn't rightly say," replied Patterson, as he depressed the 'hatch open' button on the station's console. Pulsating yellow lights flared to life and the chirping alert tones seemed louder than ever. Both men looked around, anxiously awaiting the inevitable appearance of the beastie.

"Go," instructed Patterson.

The hatches weren't even locked back yet and Donovich was up, through, and standing at the pod-bay's hatch controls.

With one last look around, Patterson scurried up the ladder. "Push it!" he yelled, even before clearing the opening. Donovich held it for just a moment before engaging. The inner hatch closed with a thump, its indicators switching to a steady-red.

The pod-bay was a cramped toroid shape; its empty ordnance racks curved along the surface of the bay's wall. At some point in time, the powers-that-be decided this would be a good place to mount the ship's automated point-defense cannons. So, protruding from both the ceiling and floor there were the butt ends of the turrets, with brightly colored warning labels and yellow and black cross-hatching around each of the weapons' ammunition feeds. But since the *Garryowen* was now out of the fight and heading home—as per operational doctrine—her ammunition stores were off-loaded and would be used as a reserve for the remaining ships in the squadron. *We're not paid to bring it home with us*, thought Donovich.

"I don't know how much time it's going to give us," said Donovich, "So I'll prep the pod. Here's your quarter-of-a-million-dollar toy." He handed the cylinder to Patterson in exchange for the utility bag. "Remember, it comes out of your pay."

Patterson just smiled and nodded. Carefully, he placed the cylinder on the deck before taking off and opening the tool pack. "Chief, lock the CM hatch; we don't want Koenig buzzin' around," said Patterson.

"No problem."

Patterson flipped over the black cylinder. Its yellow stencil markings indicated that it was a "MK 42 SLD," along with a series of inventory tracking and ID numbers. With a practiced hand, he removed the electronic decoy's baseplate and unfastened its separator charge; he looked it over, and then said a quick prayer before continuing.

With a click, Donovich inserted the failsafe pin into the pod's docking port control panel—this physically locked the port's docking clamps, while electronically overriding the pod's launch program—the T-handled pin had the traditional foot-long "Removed Before Flight" ribbon dangling from it.

According to the manual, ". . . if a pod were to be launched while a ship was under drive; upon impact with the drive field, the pod would atomize, the resulting energy flux would cause the drive field to collapse and drop the ship out of hyperspace, not unlike a conventional Return Transition." Donovich's only problem with this answer was simple, "To date no one has tried it," and he wasn't about to be the one in the history books to find out.

"Damn right," he said. Reaching back, he grabbed the utility bag and pushed it into the causeway.

"You set?" ask Donovich, as he crawled out a few minutes later.

"Just about, if you'd give me a hand," Patterson responded, as he held the charge up against the framework for the gun's autoloaders.

"Right." Donovich held the charge in place while Patterson zip-tied it down. "What's going to happen when this thing goes off?"

Patterson screw-connected a spool of wire to the charge. "It'll just pop, and hopefully launch the peach can into the Can with our friend sittin' on it," he said. "It's a gas separator charge, works just like a car airbag. You can let go."

"Thanks." Donovich moved off to ready the other pod; Patterson followed behind, playing out the wires.

With the starboard pod now locked down and hatches opened, Patterson ran his wires up into it; then, with the AeroCom equivalent of a roll of duct tape, he secured and camouflaged the wires to the deck. "Right, get 'n," he said.

Donovich got down on his hands and knees and backed into the darkened pod; he lay on his stomach, propped up on his elbows, just behind the hatch in the causeway; Patterson squatted down and handed him a circuit tester to which he had connected the wires from the charge.

"You know how this works," stated Patterson. "Key the power on, then hold," he said, indicating the recessed red test button.

Donovich just nodded. "See you afterward."

"Yep," replied Patterson; he then stood up and walked over to the charge, placing a can of peaches into the clamps that normally held the decoy secure. He watched as Donovich pulled his pod's access hatch closed on the wires.

The sight of Patterson disappearing down the ladder into the SM filled Donovich with a sense of abandonment; as an engineer, being physically alone for long periods on shift was business as usual, but he always knew there was someone else on the other end of the comm to come to his aid. This time, it was just him and the universe; waiting in the dark, while looking through a small porthole window into the lit pod-bay, half hoping that the damn creature didn't show up.

Time passed. How long, it was hard to say; Donovich just kept looking through the porthole at the open gap of the SM's two-meter hatchway. From time to time, phantoms would startle him, as his mind turned passing shadows and random sounds from the service module into the approach of the unknown.

There comes a point when fatigue wins out over fear, and the need to rest becomes all important; Donovich was already there. The urge to yawn kept forcing him to lower or angle his head away from the porthole for fear of fogging it up. "Damnit," he whispered, as he wiped his eyes; looking back into the pod-bay his mind said, *something is out there*. His breathing shallowed as his fear grew more tangible. There it was, slowly crawling around the edge of the hatchway. They had thought that it would try another diversion; but no, stealth was its new game plan.

Once in the bay, it stopped. It just stood there, clinging against the curvature of the wall; slowly, it started moving with spider-like locomotion toward the port pod. It looked just like the little one he had found in the DFC unit, but if it was, it had grown to almost a foot across. It stopped at the edge of the pod's causeway, its hotdog-like head flexed, as if it was looking around; it seemed to be contemplating their trap. With surprising speed it darted off into the pod.

Just like an ungrateful monster . . . thought Donovich as he slowly opened his hatch; he was trying desperately to be quiet as he crawled out on his elbows and knees, the circuit tester still in his hand. Now clear and standing, he could see past the loader's framework into the pod. There was no sign of the creature; hopefully it was still under the seats trying to dig out the cans.

He needed to keep his eyes on the pod, but he also had to be careful where he walked; now under gravity he could easily fall through the SM's open hatchway. He briefly looked down to check his position. All was quiet in the SM. Patterson wasn't in sight.

Donovich was just coming around the loader when the creature came back up into view; he froze at the thought of rushing the pod, and then he remembered that he hadn't keyed on the circuit tester. Without looking he brought his other hand to the box and turned the key.

The beastie spun and leapt down the short length of the causeway at him.

There was a boom as the gas charge went off, knocking Donovich aside. As he sat there, he realized that his thumb was firmly pressing down on the test button.

Dropping the box, he scrambled to the hatch. The beastie wasn't in the causeway. With everything he had left, he lifted the hatch into place. It stopped just short of closing. The beastie's six pointy, blue-gray legs popped from around the edge of the hatch.

"Shit!"

He suddenly found the adrenalin-powered strength to push. His shoulder drove into the hatch. Without forethought of the consequences, he smashed his fist down at the nearest leg. The hatch snapped shut and locked as his hand connected. The beastie had pulled back.

Breathing hard, Donovich just knelt there, both hands needlessly pushing on the hatch. Carefully, he looked through the porthole; the beastie just sat there, all bunched up, as he had seen before. Its hotdog head slowly flexed.

"Donovich!" Patterson shouted, as he frantically climbed into the pod-bay; he stopped when Donovich turned and looked at him. Carefully, Patterson walked over and knelt down next to him; he reassuringly put a hand on Donovich's shoulder, before looking through the porthole.

"I didn't get the pod's hatch closed, just the bay's." said Donovich, concern and exhaustion coloring his voice, as he gestured over his shoulder.

Patterson turned to him, "It's okay, Chief." he said calmly, "I'll deal with it. It's almost over, but you need to go tell Ware what's happenin'." He half-pulled Donovich to his feet. The Chief resisted. All he wanted to do was close his eyes and pretend none of this had happened.

"It's got to be you, Chief, you're the guy in charge," Patterson insisted, as he unlocked the CM's gangway hatch; it opened with the usual lights and sound. Sluggishly, Donovich nodded and started up the ladder.

Patterson returned to the pod. The beastie—as the Chief called it—was stretched out over the porthole. "Dear God!" he said. The creature's legs, and in fact all of its different body parts, weren't physically connected. They just seemed to stay in place like some stylized, computer-generated cartoon character.

Patterson leaned back and eyed the docking port's emergency pod jettison controls. Calmly, he reached up and removed the failsafe pin. The panel lit up as a warning klaxon sounded that the pod's inner hatch was still open. He lifted the cover over the manual override switch and threw it. With his hand on the jettison pull bar, he looked back through the porthole.

The creature had pulled back; its eyeless, cylinder-like head was staring back at him. Patterson leaned into the porthole "You're not fuckin' me over again," he said as a little smile grew across his face, "You don't exist," he whispered . . . .

THE GLASS BOX
Bud Sparhawk

THERE WERE TWENTY MISSILES STREAKING TO IMPACT THE PLANET'S SURFACE and I was the only passenger, but not for long.

When the sabot blew away, I flew off with the rest of the debris as the super-dense ballistic payload continued screaming toward a Shardie location over the horizon. It carried a single altitude-sensing charge in its tail that would accelerate the payload to strike at a thousand kps. At that hypervelocity the shock wave and impact would blast a crater five kilometers across and send dirt, rock, and dust into the stratosphere.

Twenty of these hitting the planet would be my diversion.

The wind whipped me as I dropped deeper into the atmosphere. Tendrils of spidersilk deployed behind me, threads with hundreds of microparachutes along their length, each one exerting miniscule drag, stealing momentum from my descent, then blowing away to swiftly dissolve in the air.

The tendrils would be indistinguishable from the thousands of smaller, broken fragments from the sabot. I just hoped that my presence was indistinguishable.

I skimmed trees and hills, stirring trails of dust as I moved at better than ten meters per second through the last portion of my drop. When the last of the threads tore away I still carried eight mps, slow enough to give me a chance of survival on impact.

I tucked for the bounce and roll, hoping that I'd hit where nothing would stop me before all my potential energy was dissipated. Desert sand would be nice, water better, but I'd take an open field if it came to that.

Just no damn forests.

The weak and fading signal had come unexpectedly from a colony world abandoned to the Shardies six months before. It was a short burst that might have been missed if fleet hadn't had a SIGINT unit probing the Shardies' signals.

"We tried to get away, but the things caught us," the high-pitched voice had cried. "I'm hiding. Please help me."

Fleet was conflicted. It was not impossible that some group might have been missed during the evacuation. Campers, spelunkers, or others could have been isolated when the order was sent. How long had it taken to move the twenty thousand off the planet—two weeks, eighteen days? They'd packed the colonists into any ship they could find. Most vessels barely had enough oxygen to sustain the refugees. The evacuation was chaotic, disorganized, and messy. They tried to get everyone, but still, some might have been missed.

Should we ignore it? command asked, thinking that the loss of a single individual was as nothing compared to the risks of extracting the survivor. Maybe the call was a ruse, a trap. Then again, it might be worth the valuable intelligence we'd gain to mount an effort. Fleet was desperate to learn anything it could about the Shardies, especially how a child had managed to elude capture by our relentless enemy.

Nobody had ever escaped the Shardies, not since we discovered how they turned any survivor into organic components for their ships. The horror of those images, the undead bodies stranded into the controls of the one captured ship, had shown everyone that there were worse things than death, should they be captured.

The Shardies had been relentless in driving us from our colony worlds. In deep space it was no better. They destroyed our most hardened ships with better tactics and weapons. Since we'd first encountered them, they had relentlessly continued to advance. If the war persisted as it had for the past three years, with us abandoning one world after the next, the Shardies would reach Earth within a decade, or maybe less.

Fleet needed whatever information the survivor might have. Earth needed the hope that someone could survive to report what she had seen. We all needed to know.

Command had no choice. Someone had to find whoever sent that signal.

The deployment was carefully planned to minimize risk. Four high-speed, light-attack ships would emerge from blink just beyond the Holzberg limit, fire off a stick of five Rapture missiles and blink away, hopefully before the Shardies had time to react. The theorists calculated that if the total hang time near the planet was fifteen to eighteen seconds—the upper limit only if a ship had to roll into firing position—they all might have a chance to get away.

The seconds after firing were the dangerous time for the ships' crews. If they didn't reach the Holzberg limit in those eighteen seconds, the overstressed drives would turn the ship and everyone on board into an instantaneously brilliant cloud of dispersing plasma. I had the easy part, they said.

All I had to do was survive long enough to send my signal.

The hundreds of fragments from the sabot spread out in an elongated, egg-shaped pattern over a thousand square kilometers along the path of the payload. Even if the Shardies weren't preoccupied cleaning up the destruction from the missiles' impacts and suspected something, they'd still waste a lot of time finding and inspecting that many pieces. Expand those searches over twenty patterns and you came up with the faint probability of my being detected. I knew that, even with that sort of insurance, they'd eventually find my landing spot. It was only a matter of time. I had to hurry.

I discovered I was still in one piece when I uncoiled my aching body after the long bounce and roll. My left arm dangled loosely and a chunk of that shoulder was missing. Other than that all my parts seemed to be functional. I probed the arm and found that it had been dislocated by whatever I hit. That must have been what ripped that piece of shoulder away. A little pressure in the right places, a twist of the shoulder, and the arm was nearly as good as the day it was installed.

I checked my position and discovered that I was about two hundred kilometers away from the location of the signal. Hell of an overshoot, but not bad, considering the variables. The deviation could have come from unexpected upper level winds or some other variable. I figured two days to hike there if I didn't stop. I set out.

The location was a tiny coastal village. There were thirty buildings that I could see from my perch on the ridgeline, twenty of them were homes. The long piers told me that this might once have been a fishing community, but whatever boats had docked there were now gone. One road ran down the center of town and there was a landing pad to the west. The landing pad looked too raw, too new.

Judging from the amount of debris on the road there must have been a hell of a panic when they abandoned this place. Maybe that's where the boats had gone. Had they been used to transport the colonists to an evacuation center?

I imagined they'd scuttled them, rather than leave anything for the damned Shardie bastards.

I watched the town until nightfall but saw no evidence that anything alive was down there. Not a stray dog or cat, not a rat, and no birds. An hour after dark, I worked my way down the slope, pausing often, alert for some sign of movement, some indication that I had been spotted.

I kept my disruptor ready. One of the things we'd learned was that the Shardies were incredibly fast. I'd only have two milliseconds or less to react—just enough time to squeeze the trigger once, but that was all it would take.

The largest building was filled with cold, rusting machines and long metal tables. Here and there were slender knives and curving hooks on long handles. Fishing village for sure, I guessed.

I worked my way down the road, passing from one building to the next as swiftly and silently as I could. On the fifth building, a home, I found her.

I shifted sight to infrared and surveyed the room. The only heat source was her small body. The only sound her slow breathing. The only light a shaft of moonlight through the shutters.

I put a hand over the girl's mouth and shook her gently. She struggled briefly and then went limp, her eyes wide in horror when she got a glimpse of me. "Sergeant Millikan, Fifth Marine," I said softly. I doubted anyone could overhear, but you can never be too careful where the Shardies are concerned. "I've come for you," I said, which while completely true, was not necessarily accurate.

"I didn't think anyone would come," she said in a rush. "Especially not something like you." She seemed to accept my assurance that I was a marine, but not quite sure that I was a someone.

I took a good look at her: skinny, scraggly hair, and filthy, all of which would be expected from what she had been through. Her black hair was cut short, her nails broken—some bitten to the quick—and crusted with God-knows-what. She had a gash on the top of her head that might be pretty bad under the crust of scabby blood. She looked to be about fifteen, maybe a year or two more or as much less— too damn young to be in this situation, not that there was any other age that would be better.

A pair of muddy tan boots that looked three sizes too large for her sat by her side. Nearby was a smelly pile of fish entrails.

She caught my glance. "I fished last night," she said. "By hand." And ate it raw, I guessed. That was smart. A fire would attract attention.

"How long have you been here?" I asked. "How did you get here?"

"A week, I think," she replied. "I was a mile up the coast before, but I came here after I used that 'phone." She must have seen my puzzled expression. "A mile is about one and a half kilometers," she explained.

"Archaic measure," I recalled. A lot of the colonies went back to the old measures as a signal of their departure from Earth's ways. Well, that experiment didn't last long, did it?

But, a week? "Where were you before that?" It had been nearly six months since the Shardies arrived.

She shrugged. "Running, hiding, keeping away from them. I just kept going until I found the 'phone—back there," she waved a hand in the general direction of the door.

I looked. It was an old unit, leaking battery acid and showing no power light. She must have drained it in that single cry for help. I left it there. Useless.

"Are you taking me away?" she asked when I returned.

That was a good question. Staying in the village wasn't a good idea. The Shardies methodically erased all signs of human presence before they moved on, so it was only a matter of time before they destroyed this one. It could be next week, or within an hour. Or maybe they were too busy checking the debris and dealing with the effects of the multiple strikes. "Yes," I said.

The girl quickly gathered her few belongings—the boots, a ship's jacket with a Fourth Fleet emblem on the shoulder, a wicked knife with a serrated back, and the blanket she had been sleeping under—before we set out.

"My name's Tashia," she said softly.

"Call me Sergeant," I replied.

I led her up the slope, following the same path I had taken in just in case they would follow our heat trail. Once we were on top I intended to stay to the rocks and touch the ground only where we couldn't avoid it. That way we'd avoid leaving obvious signs of our passage. I knew we couldn't escape detection completely, but there was no sense in making our trail easy either.

She began to lag behind after we'd covered barely ten kilometers and slumped to the ground at fifteen. "Sarge, I can't go any further," she sighed. "I'm so tired."

I dug into my side pocket and pulled out one of my G-rations. "Eat this," I ordered. The strong military stimulants probably wouldn't do her weakened body any good, but the nutrients in the bar would provide her with the strength to last until daybreak.

Intelligence had force-fed me every speck of information about this world they could glean out of the colonists. In the very early days of the colony there had been a small mining operation on this plateau. The vein turned out to be shallow and petered out within a year or so, but not before producing enough coal to fuel the first few settlements. After the mine was abandoned all of the miners had moved on, leaving behind only those things they could not take with them—foundations and the mine shaft. Machinery, building materials, household goods, everything that could be moved was taken away.

I found the entrance to the shaft before the sky started to gray. I took us back deep enough that I couldn't see the stars framed in the entrance. I flopped down with my back against the wall to face the way we'd come.

Tashia sat near my side, arms hugging her stick-thin legs against her chest. "I'm glad you came, Sarge," she said. "I was so afraid nobody would. I just used that 'phone to let somebody know I was alive."

"You said there were others. Tell me about them."

She shook her head. "Dad died, I guess." She said that in such a calm voice that I figured she'd already drained emotion from the memory. "Dad and I were out camping when everyone else went away. I guess we sort of got overlooked."

I nodded. It could happen. Emergency evacuations are messy affairs at best, chaotic at worst. Easy to suppose the missing ones were on another boat, another vehicle. A few could get lost.

"We didn't know where to go. We couldn't find anyone. It was like they all ran away." She was trembling as she recalled that frightening time. "Then the things came for us."

"Things? What did they look like?" This was good information. A first-hand description might help someone.

She shook. "I . . . I didn't get a really good look, but they were glowing, sort of. It was night and they moved so fast. They put me in a sort of box. It was so small I couldn't stand up in it. Dark, too."

"Did you hear anything, sense anything—a smell, an aroma, anything at all?"

She was silent for a long while. "No. I was so cold. They took my clothes so I had goosebumps all over."

"Anything else?" I had to get as much information from her as I could in the time remaining. "How long were you in the box?"

She frowned. "Maybe a few days 'cause I got really, really thirsty. One day I woke up, the top of the box was opened a crack. I stuck my fingers in the crack and pried it open.

"I was in a white room with a lot of icicles, only they weren't ice at all. More like glass, you know?"

"Was there anything else in the room—somebody moving around, a machine, anything that you'd recognize?"

She thought a moment before replying. "A couple of other boxes and those weird icicles everywhere."

"Go on, please. What did you do then?"

"I ran. I had to get out of the scary room away from the box. I found a pile of stuff from our camp—that's where I got some clothes—then I ran away into the woods."

"How did you hurt your head?" Her story sounded too bizarre. Were the boxes and the room figments of her imagination, or was she telling the truth?

Her hand darted to her head. "Oh, I guess I must have cut it on one of the icicles. It stings," she added quickly, almost as an afterthought.

"Let me see," I said. She leaned forward. The long gash ran from just above her left temple to the top of her skull. I could see little flecks of glass in the wound. "That looks like it had to hurt."

"I guess it did, but I must have been too scared to notice," she said. "Anyhow, I ran and ran until I found a place to hide. After that I kept running from one spot to the next at night, so the things wouldn't find me. Then I found the 'phone and made the call. I prayed somebody might come. Somebody." She was quiet for a long while after that. "You, Sarge," she added in a small voice.

"The Shardies don't usually let humans go," I replied. "They make them into components, use human brains to help them win this war."

Her mouth formed a small "O" of horror. "That's what they were going to do to me?" she cried. "Oh, my God!"

"That's why they sent me. We had to find out how you managed to escape and hear what you could tell us about the aliens. That's why I'm here."

"You must be really brave," she yawned and stretched. "I don't think I could do something like that." She hugged my arm. "But I'm not scared now that you're here. I know you'll take care of me."

"Get some sleep," I said. "Just pick a spot."

She dropped the blanket next to me. "You can share," she suggested, offering me a corner.

"I don't need sleep," I replied. "I rest a different way." No sense telling her that I could shut down the remaining organic component of my brain while the autonomic parts took care of surveillance and housekeeping. Better she remained ignorant of all the terrible things the surgeons did to me after the firefight. Better that she continue to think of me as a marine and leave it at that.

I'd been going continuously through the past fifty-eight hours and needed some rest time. The diversions of the missile strike, the escaping ships, and hundreds of pieces of sabot shred gave me, at most, thirty hours more, before I expected to be found. Sleep and rest would steal many of those hours, leaving me only a narrow bit of time to complete my mission.

Tashia had fallen asleep and was snuggled against my hip with one arm thrown across my waist. I could feel her soft breath against my left arm and her gentle movements as deep sleep relaxed tired muscles. At rest she looked so innocent, so peaceful, that one could easily imagine her snuggled in her own bed, dreaming of boys and dances, of family and friends, of loved pets and fond memories. But my imagination could only take me so far before brutal, ugly reality intruded.

I heard a faint, nearly indistinguishable sound and went instantly on alert. I was at the mine's entrance in under two seconds and tuned every sense to hyper-alertness. There! Near the horizon was a golden glow in the early dawn light. It moved right to left, possibly tracing the path I had followed to reach the village. Were they tracing me or was their track merely happenstance?

If the former they would be here in a few hours. We had to move.

Tashia groaned when I lifted her, but didn't wake as we left the mine. Her weight was negligible, less than a full combat pack, but more awkward to carry.

"What's happening?" she whispered after we'd gone a few kilometers. "Where are we?"

"Running," I replied. "I think we're being followed."

She stifled a cry, showing more wisdom than I expected. "The things," she said. "They're fast."

"So am I," I replied. "They gave me really strong legs."

"What happened to you?" she asked. "I know you don't look right. Are you a freak or something?"

It was a fair question. I was hardly dating material and I doubt that my own mother would recognize me like this. She would probably disown me if she did.

"Sort of like that," I replied. "They had to rebuild me after the. . . . After it happened. It was touch and go. I almost died, they tell me. If I hadn't given consent I would have, but they did ask me, and that was only after they told me my options. Live and be useful like this, or die. Some choice."

"But you chose life," she whispered and squeezed my neck. "I'm glad."

"They gave me metal bones," I continued. "Augmented my muscles, increased my metabolic rate, and did some fancy stuff to my head." I laughed. "I can see in the dark and hear a pin drop a half kilometer away. My reaction time is five times that of a normal man's and my endurance is practically unlimited. I could go a week without food or water if I had to, a month with water alone and no diminution strength either."

"And the downside is?" she joked. "It sounds like you've been turned into a superman."

"There's the pain, for one thing," I replied honestly. "It's constant. I can't laugh anymore, nor cry for that matter. Everything seems dead to me, no nuance or gradations. It's like not caring any more, only I do care about things, like rescuing pretty little girls and helping the war effort."

She didn't reply, but I got another hug.

"Where did you say you got that jacket?" I asked casually. "There were no survivors of the Fourth Fleet."

"It was Dad's," she said. "I don't know where he got it. Maybe he was a veteran or something."

"That's a ship's jacket, not something anyone would wear anywhere but on board. Do you know what happened to the Fourth?"

"N-n-no," she whispered.

"The Shardies captured the ship and took prisoners," I explained. "We found some of them on a captured ship, wired into the controls." Then I added. "They weren't dead. Not then."

"But Dad wore it all the time. He didn't tell me about his ship or the aliens or anything. I was just cold and wanted something to wear so I wouldn't be so scared and cold and all." She began sobbing. "I didn't mean to do anything bad, Sarge."

"I know, honey. I didn't think you knew about the jacket. That's why I told you." Not the only reason, I added, to myself.

I checked the time. Twenty-two probable hours left, much less if they were really trailing us. Not much time either way.

"We've got to signal soon," I said. "The target's not far from here. Think you can walk for a while?" I set her down. I wasn't tired from carrying her slight weight, but I did want to have both hands free should anything happen.

"Give me another of those candy bars and I think I could run there." Her laughter was like tonic to my ears. It had been so long since I'd heard a young girl laugh, so long and so far back in my past that I had forgotten how wonderful it could sound.

I fished out two bars and threw her one. "They're a little chewy without something to wash them down, but maybe we can find some water."

We moved with the wind, moving as quickly as Tashia could manage in her condition, burning energy fast to reach the target in the shortest amount of time. I couldn't move as quickly as I wanted, but had to match Tashia's comparatively slow pace. With the augments in my legs and the hyperventilation of my lungs I could outrun a cheetah if I had to.

Even with the bar's energy boost, she could probably outrun a house cat, if it was tired and old.

"Are you going to call the fleet?" she asked. "How are they going to get us without the things knowing about it?"

"Fleet has ways of landing undetected," I lied. "Stealth, charged ice, snowflake, and owl's wing tech for the most part. The stuff is so good, the Shardies wouldn't even know we were here."

Her eyes grew wide. "I never heard about all that!"

"There's a lot you wouldn't know," I said, as I started the timer buried in my abdomen. I stuffed three more G-rations into my mouth to provide the energy I needed for the high-speed signal burst. The SIGINT boys high above would be waiting for anything sparkling within a hundred kilometers of the target location, just in case I didn't make it all the way.

"We are going away, aren't we?" she said, panic rising in her voice as she nervously scanned the area. I checked. Whatever that golden glow had been it wasn't detectable any more.

"There was a lot of debate about sending someone down here," I said, as the timer activated the signaling process, storing the data I had collected, along with my conclusions for the burst. "Fleet thought you might be exactly what you said—a poor little survivor who managed to sneak away from the Shardies. On the other hand, they suspected that it might have been just a false signal to lure us into a trap."

"But it wasn't a trap," Tashia said. "I really did use the 'phone. I really did run away from the things."

"There's the matter of the jacket." That damned, cursed, incongruous jacket that had no reason to be on this or any other planet.

"No, I told you. It was Dad's," she cried. "You have to believe me!"

"Then Fleet wondered if there was the possibility that you might not be human any more: That the Shardies wanted to loose a new horror on us, with a new way of using humans."

Tashia patted herself. "No, no. I'm me! Look at me. I'm as human as you, maybe more than you. Here," she threw open her jacket to bare herself.

I looked at the small mounds of her budding breasts, the ribs showing under her thin skin, and the little blue veins that ran across her chest.

I gently tugged the sides of her jacket together. "I know, Tashia. I believe you. I never doubted that you weren't human, not for an instant."

I could feel the heat building up inside of me as my I processed the G-ration into the squirter's storage unit. "I've recorded everything you told me," I went on. "Earth will hear it all and probably interpret more from what you said than even you know."

"But I'm not one of them," she cried. "I ran away. They didn't p-pro-process me like you said."

I thought about her escape, the improbable discovery of the ancient 'phone, and surviving on fish captured with her bare hands. Taken together they were improbable, but not impossible.

She might not be a conscious Shardie agent, might not even know if she was one, but there was that jacket, those glimmers of glass in her head, and those unexplainable gaps of time and memory. What had they really done while she slept in the box?

Tashia was sobbing. "I did so escape, just like I told you. I ran away. I was so scared. I didn't know what to do."

"I know." Oh God, I remembered the sound of her laughter, her curiosity about me, her desire to get back to her family and friends. It was all so . . . *human*.

"Listen, Tashia," I said. "The problem is that even if you really are one hundred percent human, they still couldn't risk rescuing you."

"But they could examine me, see if anything is wrong, see if those things did something to me. They could do that, couldn't they?" she pleaded. "Couldn't they?"

"They could," I replied softly. "But they won't. The important thing about sending me here was to get whatever information you could give us. That's what's important—the information." Yes, that and the fact that, despite all odds, a little girl, a human girl, had escaped to tell her tale. That fact alone would give everyone hope that we could find a way to fight back and, hopefully, win.

The heat was so intense that I knew the mission's end was near. In a few seconds everything within fifty meters would be consumed in an intense blast of encoded coherent light that would tell the watchers overhead all that I had heard and seen. The blast would leave scorched ground that looked like a rocket had taken off. The Shardies weren't the only ones who could use misdirection.

"But you do believe me, don't you, Sarge?" she cried, as if seeking a final bit of certainty.

"Yes," I replied softly as I reached out and hugged her close to give her one last bit of comfort against the cold dark and partly to ensure that nothing would remain for the Shardies to analyze.

"You're as human as me."

Looking for a Good Time
Tony Ruggiero

NOW

"BUT ADMIRAL, THE REPERCUSSIONS COULD BE QUITE SEVERE IF THE TRUTH EVER got out. Hell, it would jeopardize the human race's standing in the known galaxy," General Albacon said, as he stood in front of the admiral's desk.

"Well then, General," Admiral Rector, the Supreme Military Commander began, "we must make sure then that the truth is *never* known."

"But that will be difficult, sir. There are many people involved," the general said, as he made a wide motion with his arms.

"I didn't say it would be easy. Just keep a few rules in the forefront at all times and the word N E V E R as it applies. As far as the enemy goes, there are to be no prisoners. Never. As to these unique forces, you are to keep them restricted to their own unit at all times. They are not to mix with any of the regular or even special ops units. Never. Do you understand these conditions?"

"Yes, sir."

"I also want any formal records of their existence erased. They never existed. No one needs to know that they exist or how it all started."

"Is that part even clear?" the general asked. "I always thought of it as a rumor."

"The answer to that is it's whatever version works best for us at any given time. We have to be flexible, General. We are dealing with what, potentially, could be the next step in a war that could end all wars . . . and perhaps even humanity, if we are not careful."

"I don't understand," the general said. "I can see how their capability as a military force can contribute significantly to overall effectiveness, but not as the make-or-break consideration in a war or how they could have such a grave effect on humanity."

"It never starts out that way," the admiral said. "I've seen it happen more times than I can remember, but for some reason we ignore the warning signs. Even the simplest things such as *looking for a good time* can sometimes go south on us. But do we worry? Of course not. It's the human thing to think we are superior. We always think we have things under control . . . until it's too late. You mark my words, General, at some point, what is an asset today will become a problem in a few years or even decades. And then it will have to be dealt with. Some poor bastard will have to clean up the mess I have made. God help them."

MONTHS EARLIER

Space Marine Corporal Patrick Vanner waited impatiently in the berthing area for liberty call, as his ship landed at the space yard on the planet Ziron. At twenty years old he was one of the newest and youngest members of his unit onboard. However, he was descended from a long line of explorers and space-faring family members going back centuries and he felt as if he had come home when he finally got into space. Yet many often commented that, when one spoke with him, he always sounded as if he was an older and more seasoned veteran in certain matters, rather than a newbie to the service.

As he waited, he gave careful attention to his uniform. It fit him well, but youth always seems to help with a good fit. At almost six feet in height, and two hundred pounds, he filled it out in all the right spots. His hair was short, the traditional Marine buzz cut, but it worked for him. He brushed off the uniform for the fifth or sixth time and pulled the tie knot up to his neck for the second or third. He wanted to make a good impression—this was his first excursion on this world, so he scrutinized every inch of his uniform ensuring that it looked good. The only luxury he allowed himself during his visual inspection was for his eyes to linger on the patch that he wore on his right shoulder. The patch reflected his unit designation: a plain white skull and crossbones with crossed swords and the name, *Death Dealers*.

He had thought that the word *elite* meant "to be special", but he was quickly learning that more often than not, elite meant that they were only used for the most important and dangerous missions. This in itself was exciting, but it also resulted in long stretches of time when there was nothing to do. This had been one of them. They had been in space for over six months and nothing had happened. Nothing. All he heard were stories from the other, more seasoned team members about past battles, the killing and the victories.

"What the hell is taking so long," he said, glancing at the clock on the bulkhead.

"What's wrong, Vanner? Got a hot date or something?" A voice said, from around the corner of the small and cramped berthing space.

"Shut the hell up," Vanner said, in a tone that conveyed familiarity rather than any animosity. "It's been a long cruise and I'm just antsy to get off this damn ship and sink my teeth into something sweet, that's all."

"Ah . . . a good meal. I agree. This stuff onboard here will kill you—well, if we weren't already dead," Rufus said, referring to the motto of their unit: *The Dead Fear Nothing*. "But mooring will take as long as it always does. You know that. And then you have to get *the speech* from the chief."

"Yeah I know," Vanner said. He then made the motion of sniffing the air. "I can almost smell it—the land and the people on it."

"Uh-huh, sure. Anything else you're looking for?" asked Rufus. "Hmmm . . . sailor boy," he said, as he put his arm around Vanner. "I love you long time. Love you like number-one sailor," he said as he raised his finger in prominent gesture.

Vanner smiled and said, "I'm always looking for a good time, but you have to be careful where you . . . well you know about—"

"Alright, ladies," a deep voice bellowed. There was no mistaking that the owner of the voice was *the chief*. "If you have any desire to get off this ship on this one night of liberty, you better get your candy asses in line, and I mean now!"

From all directions in the berthing compartment, men spewed forth in various stages of dress and got in line. Vanner and Rufus fell in and stood next to each other.

"Where the hell is the mustering officer!" the chief yelled. He stood in the center of the compartment. The chief wasn't a big man—he was a huge man. Many just referred to him as "the mountain". He weighed about three hundred pounds and stood slightly over six feet in height. He was basically one solid mass.

"Here," a voice called.

"Then get on with it!"

"Yes, Chief! Alright, everyone fall in!"

When it appeared that most of the unit was in ranks, the mustering officer began calling the roll. After he had completed the list of names and checked off who was or was not present, he turned toward the men and said, "Unit 666, Parade Rest!"

The men and women placed their hands behind them in the small of their backs as they slid their feet about eighteen inches apart.

The petty officer turned in the chief's direction, saluted and said, "Space Marine Unit 666 all present and/or accounted for."

The chief saluted and said, "Very well. Bring them to attention and fall in."

The mustering officer took his position in the front rank and then said, "Unit 666, Atten-hut!"'

The chief stared at them. His eyes were deep sockets of emptiness when he looked at them this way. He remained like that for several seconds and then screamed at them, "Who are we?"

"Death Dealers!" the soldiers responded in unison.

"What are we?"

"Killers!"

"Who do we kill?"

"The enemy!"

"How do we kill them?"

"Destroy their will to fight by sucking the life from them!"

"Who is our allegiance to?"

"The human race, the Corps and to each other!"

"Who is God?"

"You are!"

"That's right, and you best remember that." The chief said the words slowly, allowing each syllable to sink in. "Alright, ladies, stand at ease."

The men and women relaxed somewhat, but as good Marines, they were prepared to snap right back to it in a second if need be.

"Okay, boys and girls," the chief began. "Here is your history lesson. If you need to take notes so that you don't forget anything, I suggest you do so. Forgetting important information can get you killed just as easily on a safe planet as it can on the battlefield. Don't ever forget that." He added that boring-through-your-skull look to ensure that they would not forget. He then continued, "The planet Ziron was colonized originally by humans about fifty years ago. However, over the years it's become a mixture of just about every kind of alien race, known and unknown. Needless to say, that there has been some intermixing of the races, so you will find just about anything you can imagine on the planet."

There were a few snickers from the soldiers as they took the chief's words as if they had *carte blanche* as to the pleasures and fun that they could look forward to.

"But that doesn't mean you can do whatever the hell you want! Remember he or she might *look* human, but that doesn't mean *they are* human—you got that?"

"Yes, Chief!" They roared in unison.

"Believe it or not, each and every one of you is an ambassador of the human race. If any of you brings dishonor to yourself, you bring it upon your unit and the entire human civilization. Am I clear?"

"Yes, Chief!"

"Now, there are some precautions we need to take to ensure that we are well received. You are *Death Dealers,* and many *will not like you* because of that. They do not understand who you are, what you do, and why you do it. So to quell their suspicions and fear, you will remove *all* identification from your uniforms that indicate such. Is that understood?"

"Yes, Chief!"

The Chief looked down the front rank. "This is not the place to show off the fact that we kill for a living! Did you get that, Mr. Vanner? Take that damn patch off!"

"Yes, Chief," Vanner said.

"Even without the patches, many of us will be recognized for what we are. You are to deny any accusations of what you are and move along. Is that understood?"

"Yes, Chief!"

"To ensure that you don't get lost, each of you will be given a map of the city. The areas in red are off-limits while the areas in green are the allowed ones. Off limits is bad—stay out of there. It's so simple that even you idiots can't screw it up. If you do, your ass is mine. You got that?"

"Yes, Chief!"

"And finally, liberty call expires at its usual time, one hour prior to sunrise. I will be waiting at the gangway to greet anyone that is late. Anyone who arrives at or after sunrise I will *burn you* myself. Understood?"

"Yes, Chief!"

"Good. Now go and hit the beach and have some fun. Death Dealers—Atten-hut! Dismissed!"

They left the ship in small groups of two and three. There was loud and boister-ous talk about where the best places to go were for anything imaginable. As they cleared the space port, or the "white area" as it was designated by its color, they entered the city area which was awash in people; virtually wall-to-wall people in this area of the city. Although they had been told about the inhabitant's fascination for color, actually seeing it in operation was quite different. The city itself was color coded. Each commercial building was circular in shape and designated a color based upon its function. Vanner thought how this could be both helpful and confus-ing at the same time, not to mention monotonous, if stuck in an area comprised of similar type or functions. All things considered, it would be very easy to get lost, so Vanner and his group agreed to meet up at one of the places marked on the map. Several of his fellow soldiers said, "Good hunting," and then smiled at each other, as they immersed themselves into the masses.

Even after being on the ship and in close quarters, it was nothing like this immersion, overloading his senses with the smell of these people—there were so many. Vanner felt a little claustrophobic, but calmed himself. As he felt he was in control of his senses, he easily slipped away from his buddies and further into the crowd. He did not watch or look for any of them because he had no intentions in staying with them.

This was his first real liberty and he was going to have fun by exploring the outer areas of the city and not the inner areas where the bulk of the soldiers would con-gregate. He headed off in the direction that he had memorized from the map which was right on the border of the green and red areas. He was planning to live on the edge both figuratively and literally on this shore leave and he was determined to have his fun.

The crowds thinned exponentially the further he got from the city and the closer he got to the red area marked in the map. In a few minutes, he found what he was looking for—a drinking establishment. He knew enough that a place in this location would have information he would find useful in his further explorations.

He went inside and stepped up to the bar. His military training kicked in and he automatically assessed the environment. There were about twenty people there. The bartender appeared human by all respects and probably was. He watched him carefully for a few seconds and thought that some of his movements and actions gave away that perhaps the guy was a retired soldier. He knew that it was a common occurrence for soldiers to retire off earth and open up bars. It was one of the many traditions of military service. Heck, they spent so much time in them when they were on active duty that it only made sense for them to open one when they finally retired. It was a perverse logic, but it seemed to work. Yet the longer Vanner watched him, the more something seemed off about the man. Then Vanner finally got it: he was wearing dark glasses and by the way he moved Vanner believed that he was blind.

He took his eyes from the bartender and scanned the remaining people. They were a mixture of just about every other alien race that he had seen. If he elimi-nated the standard humanoid, those that looked completely human with the ex-ception of some minor deviations such as hair or skin color, eye and/or ear location, the number of digits that they possessed and where they were located and things like that, that left about half of the patrons which consisted of many races found throughout the galaxy. He ran them through his memory to see if he could remember them all.

There were Betas, a green reptilian-type of creature, Carsos, an aquatic life form with skin of a bluish color that was comprised of a material very much like fish scales. Mennons which were a cow-like creatures but walked upright like a humanoid; a Kanggren, which was a race of only females, the male not required for reproduction so they were considered useless and therefore killed off centuries ago in order to reduce the population. He didn't think he would be hanging around them too much. There was also a Fritzer, a bat-like creature which did in fact subsist on blood, but only the blood of one specific creature on their home planet. When they traveled they literally had to bring their own food with them in order to survive—any other blood would kill them instantaneously.

"What'll it be?" the bartender asked.

"An ale . . . and some information," Vanner said, as he placed a universal twenty in the hand of the bartender.

The bartender used his hand and traced the edged imprint with his fingers along the bill. "Sure," he said as he pocketed the twenty and then poured the drink. He placed the glass on the bar. Vanner took a quick mouthful.

"The name is Breeze," the bartender began, "retired ten years ago from the infantry. Lost my sight in the Grimore campaign." He extended his hand to Vanner and they shook. "Boy, you're a cool one," he added.

"The glass is cold," said Vanner.

"So it is," agreed the bartender.

"My name is Vanner. So, where can I find some fun?"

"What did you have in mind?" Breeze asked. His tone seemed reminiscent, as if he recalled asking that question himself on numerous occasions.

"Maybe something sweet tasting in the range of female company," Vanner offered.

"Sure," Breeze agreed, smiling. "Been a while, huh?"

"Yeah—you could say that," Vanner agreed.

The bartender took a small card from under the bar and handed it to Vanner. "Here's the place that I recommend. It's a little pricey, but you get what you pay for. You don't want any of the cheap stuff—lots of rumors there; some genetic oddities of some sort. Anyway, this place is a good one—one of the best."

"Thanks," Vanner said, as he chugged the remainder of his drink and rose from his chair.

"Hope you find something to your taste. Take advantage of it while it lasts."

"Time is not an issue for me, I'm perpetually young," Vanner said, and turned to leave. Once outside he chuckled about Breeze's comment as he hailed a cab as it was going by.

The cab was cigar-shaped, long and skinny. He got in and the door closed loudly, the sound reverberating in his ears. The cab driver was human, for the most part. The extra digit on each hand was probably very useful in his profession.

"Where to?"

Vanner handed him the card, the driver looked at it, smiled, then handed it back without a word. *Some things just don't need explaining,* Vanner thought, as he sat back in the seat and considered what he hoped to find where he was going.

The cab came to a stop and Vanner got out. "Thanks," he said, and paid the driver. He checked the number on the card, 1432, and looked to find the corresponding door. He saw it and walked up to it. He found the announcing mechanism and pushed it in and waited. In a few moments the door opened. The lighting was not the best. It was hard to tell exactly what she looked like, but Vanner could tell that the outline of her body was mighty fine.

He handed her the card and said, "I was told that I could find some company here."

The woman looked up from the card and her free hand moved to a switch on the wall. She flipped it up and a light directly over him came on.

He could see her now and what he had perceived in the dim light was even better in full visibility. She appeared to be human in most regards, but her skin color was a distinct blue and her eyes were each a different color. He found the contrast to be quite exhilarating.

"Are you human?" she asked as she looked at him closely as if she was a doctor and he was the patient.

"Yes, of course. I am human," he answered.

"You look very pale—almost white. You sick. Are you anemic or something?"

"I'm a soldier—I am not allowed to get sick," he said, and then laughed briefly at his own joke.

Her expression became more speculative.

"That was a joke," he said, "lighten up, will you . . ."

"You don't look right to me," she said. "I don't take risks with any of my employees. I haven't seen any soldiers that are this pale—it's not natural."

"Not natural?" he said, leaning in closer toward her. "Can I point out to you that *blue* is a bit of an odd color for a person. Besides, what risks? I'm fine, honey," he said. "And I have plenty of money to spend. You interested or not?"

"I don't like your color," she said, again. "I think you're one of those monsters I hear about from the ship."

Vanner bit his tongue and simply said, "I'm just a soldier, lady, looking to have some fun," he insisted.

"No, I have made up my mind. You are one of them—murderer—with no soul. You not allowed in—go away!" She said and slammed the door.

"I'll be damned," he said. "Now that has to be a first: turned away at a brothel. What are these worlds coming to?"

He walked away from the door and when he was back at the street he hailed another cab. One pulled up and he got inside. The driver asked, "What's the destination?"

"Well after a miserable first attempt, I was hoping you might know some places where I can find some interesting companionship?" Vanner slipped another universal twenty from his pocket and handed it to the driver.

"I might know a place," the driver said.

The cab driver drove into the sector that, according to Vanner's map, was well into the area marked red on the map. Although Vanner knew it was wrong, it didn't really seem a problem so long as he didn't get caught. What was the old expression? *It's easier to beg for forgiveness than to ask for permission.* Right now, neither one was on the top of his list. He checked his watch; he still had a good six hours before sunrise. *Plenty of time,* he thought. *Plenty of time.*

Vanner stared out the window of the cab and into the darkness as the areas they drove through became less and less lighted. The circular buildings became darker and the amount of litter and debris in the streets more abundant. They also lacked the labeling color. Vanner figured that this part of town was probably one of the older sections, and either didn't want the orderliness of the city or it didn't care. Either way, he thought that the situation was promising for him and his mission.

In a few more minutes, the cab came to a stop. The driver leaned over and pointed out the window, "Up those stairs and to the right. There will be a door at the end of the hall. Knock on it three times and show whoever answers the door this." He handed Vanner a business card.

"Last time I used one of these, it didn't go very well," Vanner said, as he looked at the card.

"It'll be fine. Now go, I have another fare," the cabbie said, as the dispatcher's voice echoed from the small speaker in the front of the cab. "I'm not supposed to be in this area."

Vanner nodded and said, "Thanks."

He stepped out of the cab and made his way up the stairs. When he got to the top, he turned back in the direction he had come and saw that the cabbie had already left. Vanner continued to the door at the end of the hall. He knocked three times and waited.

"What?" a voice said, through the door.

"I have a card," Vanner said, "from the cab driver."

"Slide it under the door," the voice replied.

"Okay—here you go," he slid the small paper through the thin slot. A few seconds later he heard the sound of locks being unlatched and the portal finally opening. A woman . . . or a reptile that looked like a woman, depending on your perspective, stood in the threshold. A Beta, Vanner thought, well a Beta with a great body as his eyes scanned her, a very nicely shaped body, but he didn't think he could get intimate with something that looked like it preferred to be crawling across a desert somewhere.

"Ah . . . well, perhaps the cabbie made a mistake," Vanner began. "I was looking for something a little more human."

"We have all kinds here, soldier boy," she said. "Don't worry about that. I'm just the welcoming wagon and screener, if you know what I mean." She tapped the side of her body and it made the sound that reminded him of body armor. "Thick enough to stop standard rounds."

"Is there a need for such . . . precautions?" asked Vanner.

"Usually not," she answered, "but it never hurts to be prepared. Let's say that sometimes there are visitors that don't agree with our policies, so by the time they finish with me, those issues have been pretty much resolved."

"I can see how that might be," he said, and smiled.

Suddenly the reptilian woman stared intently at his face. Her eyes did not waver and her tongue made a swishing motion back and forth, as if she were agitated. Finally she asked, "What's wrong with your teeth?"

"My teeth?" he asked. "Why, nothing is wrong with my teeth. They're good enough for the Corps."

"Your canines are very pointed."

"So, I have pointy teeth. What does that have to do with anything?"

"I've seen many soldiers but there have not been any with the pointed teeth like yours. You're one of those . . . *those kind* from the ship."

"Not again," he said, thinking that this was going pretty much like his last encounter did.

"You leave here, we're not into that kind of stuff," she said.

"You have got to be kidding me," he said. "This has got to be the pickiest planet I have ever been to. What is it with—"

The door slammed and he could hear the locks being engaged.

"—you," he said, finishing his sentence. He took a few steps back, still finding it hard to believe that these people in this profession could be so damn picky.

"Fine, then," he said. "I'll find my own good time. Not everyone in this place can care if my skin is too pale, or if I have pointed teeth!"

After Vanner had walked a while in the direction that the cab had come from, he removed the map and studied it for several minutes. He figured that if he did not run into any cabs, he would have to walk most of the way back to the green zone, and that looked like a few miles. He looked at his watch. He had a little less than five hours left. He wasn't worried about having enough time to get back; he knew he could hike the miles quickly if he had to. He started to walk again and figured that maybe he would pass a bar where he could ask for yet another recommendation of where to go, although he was beginning to think that perhaps that was not possible on this planet.

"Where are you going, soldier?" a female voice asked.

Vanner stopped and turned in the direction of the voice. There was a woman standing on the edge of an alleyway that intersected with the street that he was currently on. He couldn't make out much of her because she was encompassed by the dark alley, where the ambient street lighting could not reach.

"I'm heading back to the spaceport," he said.

"That's a long walk," she said, and laughed lightly.

"Yes it is," he agreed, "but that's okay because it's been . . . well . . . one of those nights."

"You're cute and have a good sense of humor," she said, as she laughed and stepped out into the dimly lit street.

"Ah—yeah," he said. His voice left him as she came into his line of sight. On the whole she was pretty much human, and a nicely formed human at that. She looked to be about twenty or twenty-five years old with black hair that flowed half way down her back. Her skin had some color variations to it and some other subtle differences, but compared to the reptile lady—this woman was perfect. But that wasn't what had caught him off guard. She was wearing the exact dress that he had seen in a vid magazine just last week, and had commented on how sexy it looked. In fact, as he had been walking, he had just been remembering that too and now here it was . . . *What an interesting coincidence,* he thought to himself.

"You're kind of quiet," she said. "Don't you have something you want to say to me?"

"Yeah sure," he stammered with the words. "Just promise me that you won't say anything in regards to me being too pale, or that my teeth are too pointy," he said, baring his teeth.

"No," she said, and giggled. "I really think you're cute. How old are you?"

"Wait a minute—before I answer that. Is there an age thing on this planet that I should know about? Like too old or too young—that kind of thing?"

She giggled again. "No, I was just wondering because you look kind of young to be a soldier—that's all."

"Good genes," he said.

She stepped closer to him and her fingers touched his uniform, dancing about as they played with the buttons. "How good are these genes we're talking about?" she asked, in a voice so hot that it felt like it burned him.

"Let's just say that they go back—way back."

"Well then," she cooed. "If you're looking for a good time, my place is not far from here—would you like to come and . . . *visit* with me for a while?"

"Honey," he said, "I promise you that that is one question you will not have to ask twice. Lead on."

Just prior to sunrise, the shore patrol was driving around the fringes of the red zone, making their rounds before heading back to the fleet landing area. They called this kind of patrol the drunk collection with an occasional brawl break up. The three things soldiers loved to do was to have sex, drink, and fight, and not necessarily in that order.

"Up there," the sergeant said. He pointed to a soldier walking erratically. "Let's check him out."

They pulled up alongside. "Hey fella, what's your name."

"Vanner," he said. "Corporal Vanner."

"Well, Corporal Vanner, looks like you could use a ride back with us."

"She was so nice . . ." Vanner said, dreamily.

"I bet she was," the sergeant said. He looked Vanner over.

"What do you think, Sarge?"

"Aside from looking kind of pale, he appears to be a little disoriented but nothing serious."

"Help me get him in."

They got Vanner into the vehicle and he sat quietly in the back, wondering what had happened to him and the woman after he walked her to her place. His long awaited and dreamed of good time was all one big blank.

"After all that crap, I didn't even get any," Vanner said, the anguish evident in his voice, "or I don't remember if I did."

"Well, it sounds to me," Rufus said, "like you ended up with the wrong woman at the wrong place. She was obviously working on her own and basically she lured you up to her place and probably drugged and then robbed you. You know there actually is honor among the working-class ladies, but you have to stay at reputable places."

"Oh please—I tried," exclaimed Vanner, "But like I told you, they had so many issues with my skin color, my teeth, and probably would have about my age as well I think."

"Okay, I'm talking to you like a friend here, Vanner," Rufus said. "There are some things you need to work on."

"Like what?"

"Well, for starters you need to get some sun on you. You're as pale as a ghost. Hit the sun lamps in the recreational center for a while, that will help. Next, you need to get to the dentist so that they fix those teeth of yours. They are kind of scary because when you smile, they do look like fangs. And lastly, grow a mustache or something, that way people won't be questioning how young you are. Do you think you can do those things?"

"Sure," agreed Vanner.

"This vampire look works great if we're in battle—hell it scares the shit out of me—but when you are on liberty, man, you don't want to *scare* the ladies you're trying to romance. You understand me?" he said, in his best imitation of the chief.

"Sure—thanks."

"Now go make an appointment to see the dentist or something—there's no time like the present to get started," Rufus said.

Vanner left the compartment and headed toward the medical area of the ship. He went past the dentist's office and kept going until he hit the sick call area. He signed in and took a seat. After a few minutes his name was called and he was ushered into the examination room.

In a few moments, a doctor entered the room. "So what can we do for you, Corporal?" the doctor asked.

"Well, sir, when I was on liberty . . . well, I kind of met this woman . . . at least, I thought she was a woman, but she really was something else . . ."

"I see," the doctor said. "A prostitute."

"Well, in a way she was, I guess," agreed Vanner.

"So did you and this woman have sex?"

"Well . . . I think we did. I woke up all sore and tired, but she was gone."

"What else?"

"I think she bit me too. Here on the neck," he said, as he pulled his collar down and pointed to the area on his neck where it was red and irritated.

"I see, got a little kinky did we?" the doctor said, not looking at Vanner, but continuing the conversation as if he had had it numerous times before.

"It all gets kind of fuzzy then. I think I remember her sucking my blood and then . . . and then I did the same."

"Ah-huh," the doctor said casually, not really paying any attention to the conversation.

"It was horrible—no it was wonderful . . . I'm not sure. I just feel so different now."

"What kind of symptoms are you having?" he asked, as he went to the medicine cabinet and began to remove the antibiotics that he would probably have to administer.

"Well, it's very strange," Vanner began, "I feel on the edge, ready to pounce, as if I am aching to get into a fight and attack something. And then I seem to have this craving for . . . blood."

"What?" the doctor said as he turned around to face Vanner. "Blood? Did you say blood?"

As the doctor came face to face with Vanner, the sight of the man made him drop the bottle of antibiotic he had in his hand and it shattered on the floor. Vanner was not the same man that had entered the office. In fact, he did not look like a man at all anymore. His face was extremely pale; it looked as if the skin had been pulled so tight that his skull was ready to break through. His eyes had become orbs of red, but that wasn't the worst. The worst part was the fangs that extended from his mouth. The sharp fangs that moved toward the doctor very quickly.

"What the . . ." the doctor began, but he never got to finish the question as what used to be Corporal Patrick Vanner quickly ripped out his throat with his large pointed fangs and then began to suck the blood out of him.

The doctor struggled and kicked out at the creature, but was only successful in knocking over some tables and making noise. In a matter of a minute, he became prone and the creature dropped him to the floor.

The commotion in the office brought two other doctors to the room. One stayed to try and subdue the creature, while the other went for help. The doctor that stayed in the room with the creature looked at the body of his dead colleague on the floor when he should have been watching the creature. While he was distracted, the creature grabbed him and held him with his feet off the floor by several inches as it proceeded to carve his flesh with its long claws. By the time additional security arrived, the second doctor had been carved to the bone.

Finally, a security team of six soldiers arrived. One look at the carnage that had occurred drove them to immediate action. Several of them opened fire on the creature. There was no effect. The creature grabbed the nearest soldier and dispatched him quickly by sending his body and head in two separate directions. One soldier called for reinforcements.

Finally, after four more soldiers had been maimed or killed, eight soldiers were physically able to restrain the creature by chaining his wrists and legs together. When the area had been secured, a colonel stepped forward to examine him.

"We should waste it, sir," one of the junior soldiers said. "We've lost many good men."

"I would love to accommodate you in that request," the colonel said as he looked around the room at the carnage. "But we have orders to keep it alive. Admiral Rector thinks that the abilities of Corporal Vanner, or what was once Corporal Vanner, might be useful if it can be modified."

Vanner's name was removed from his unit roster. What exactly happened to him after that is not clear. There was no trial. There was no hearing. In fact, after a while, people were not sure what the real story was. As to Vanner, there was speculation, well not exactly speculation, more like a rumor, that whatever happened to him on that shore leave on Ziron, it was something that helped the Corps. Some said that he found something on the planet and had to keep it a secret from everyone. Some said that he changed so much from what he discovered, that he went insane. Regardless of what story you believed, from that point on, Unit 666, the *Death Dealers* were consigned to their own ships and no longer allowed to mix with any other units. The military brass gave several reasons: some say they disestablished the unit, others say that Vanner became the new model soldier that they wanted and used him as breeding stock to start a new era of soldiering. There were so many rumors about them that no one was really sure whether they existed or not anymore. The only issue that arose which raised speculation was that they changed the patch for their unit: they added the pointed teeth and the red glow from the sockets where the eyes used to be.

Some say that it even looks like Vanner—well the *new* him anyway.

EVERYTHING'S BETTER WITH MONKEYS

C.J. Henderson

"What a piece of work is a man! How noble in reason! how infinite in faculties! in form and moving, how express and admirable! in action, how like an angel! in apprehension, how like a god! the beauty of the work! the paragon of animals!"

William Shakespeare

"Were it not for the presence of the unwashed and the half-educated, the formless, queer and incomplete, the unreasonable and absurd, the infinite shapes of the delightful human tadpole, the horizon would not wear so wide a grin."

F.M. Colby

THE *ROOSEVELT* WAS THE FIRST OF THE LONG-AWAITED DREADNOUGHT CLASS, a single ship stretching for nearly half a mile, inconceivable tons of metal and plastics, crystal and biomechanical feeds, brought together from Earth, the Moon and the asteroids that, when ultimately combined into an end product, became something unheard of—something utterly incomprehensible. And thus . . . so the thinking went . . . unbeatable, as well.

She was, in the end, a sum far greater than her parts. The *Roosevelt* was known as "the cowboy ship," for it had been that cocky gang of rocketeers labeled as the Moonpie Prairie Riders who had built her. They were the wildmen of the mightiest nation in the system's Advanced R&D Team, and it was their spirit that infested her—as well as programmed her still not-quite-understood artificial mind.

The *Roosevelt* was the opening number of a new kind of show, the all or nothing-at-all first born of the Confederation of Planets—big, because she had to be.

The first ship with functional energy shields, she needed room for the massive protonic engines essential in powering such revolutionary devices. And for her thousands of attack aircraft, hundreds of them merely hanging off her sides. And for her extensive guns, her big ticket—the whisperers and the pounders—and all her hundreds of thousands of missiles and bombs.

She was the solar system's first spacecraft carrier, a mobile prairie outpost, a relentlessly strong, self-determining fortress in space. Capable of housing as many as 10,000 sailors and marines, the great ship was meant to explore the galaxy, to chart the universe, and to bring prestige and riches to the human race in general.

But, that had been when that particular track meet had thought it controlled the only runner on the field. Reaching the edge of the system's outer planet's orbit, the *Roosevelt* was hailed, in English, Spanish, Dutch, Jamaican, and eighty-three other standard languages, by a small, obnoxiously shiny craft commanded by a small, and equally obnoxious alien life form that was all too happy to deliver its news.

The quite unexpected messenger announced to the finally-capable-of-interstellar-traveling human race that this accomplishment had gotten them an invitation to join the awe-inspiring Pan-Galactic League of Suns, an organization of worlds begun by the Five Great Races. It was an announcement that, essentially, the party was over before it had begun, that all the planets worth anything were all sewn up, all intelligent species discovered, all franchises in all the marketplaces possible well-established and even better protected.

The news came as a crushing blow to the adventure-craving crew of the *Roosevelt*, and for their first two years, eight months and fifteen days in space they showed their resentment in many a creative and colorful manner. And then, suddenly, all the rules changed. Thanks to that first, bold human crew in space, the entire galaxy discovered the League was a sham, that their claims to have everything under control were simply so much eye-wash, and that there was still plenty of unknown universe out there, teeming with mysteries and excitement—enough even to satisfy the collective curiosity of the crew of the *Roosevelt*.

Within weeks of that revelation, more than a dozen trans-galactic federations had begun to struggle into existence, including the *Roosevelt*'s hometown group. Once made up of only six of the Earth's neighboring planets, because of its pivotal role in pulling the Pan-Galactic wool from the galaxy's eyes, the Confederation of Planets had already expanded to a membership of some seventy-eight worlds, proving, quite nicely, the old adage that everyone does, indeed, "love a winner."

Which is why the crew of the *Roosevelt*, one fine galactic star date, from its stalwart captain down to the lowest chef's assistants and protonic bolt tighteners, was in a rousing, near giddy, mood. They had started their space-bound careers in defeat and through a luck understood by only the most perverse of gods had rolled it over into unbridled victory. So recent had their triumph been that, truthfully, most on board were still at a loss for words when it came to explaining exactly how their good fortune had come about.

"I'm tellin' ya, Noodles," announced Chief Gunnery Officer Rockland Vespucci, more commonly known to bartenders and military police officers across the galaxy as Rocky, "there ain't nuthin' that's gonna trip things up for us again."

"Incautious words," answered the aforementioned Noodles, better known to top notch wire-and-screw jockeys everywhere as Machinist First Mate Li Qui Kon. "As Confucius said, 'he who stops watching for falling fruit will be first to get bonked by an apple.' "

"So, we just reinvent gravity."

Both sailors turned at the sound of a new voice indicating their being joined on the observation deck. As they did so, Technician Second Class Thorner and Quartermaster Harris came into view. As Noodles took exception with the tech's off-handed comment, accusing him of not taking theoretical physics seriously enough, Thorner spread his meaty hands wide, answering;

"Hey, it was just a joke. But com'on, really, look at the way things have been cruising for us. Earth is out in front. We've got the edge. It's our game from now on."

"I've got to agree," chimed in Harris. Taking a deck chair, he leaned back, putting his hands behind his head as he added, "Fate keeps lobbing us softballs, and we keep knocking them out of the park."

"He's right, little buddy," added Rocky. Grinning from ear to ear, staring out into the vast black, Rocky cavalierly added, "Criminey, it's almost enough to make a guy wish for some trouble."

And, it was at that moment that Fate, as she so often does when those bound to her decrees begin to act as if they had somehow negated her sway over their existence, chose to prompt the commander of the good ship *Roosevelt* to broadcast an announcement.

"Attention, this is your captain speaking. We've just received orders to proceed to the Kebb Quadrant to begin negotiations with the inhabitants of the planet Edilson. More information will be zimmed to us shortly, but we're to make best possible speed, which means, ladies and gentlemen, it's time to once more bend the fabric of space and time and be on our merry way."

"Edilson," asked Harris, "where in the wonderful world of color is Edilson?"

"And so it begins." All heads turned to the latest voice to join the conversation. As they did, one of the thinnest individuals to ever muster enough soaking-wet-weight to make it into the Navy added;

"The MI boys are just beginning to appreciate galactic rotation. Which meant that mudball was absolutely destined to hit our radar."

The speaker was Mac Michaels, a balding, bespectacled razormind out of the science division. As the others continued to stare at him, scratching their heads, he spread his hands like a high school math teacher about to share the wondrous joys of algebra as he said;

"Right now Edilson is nowhere, a low rent piece of real estate totally off the charts. But, if you calculate the rotation of the galaxy's set pieces, four hundred years from now, it's going to be in the veritable center of everything." Noting the group stare of complete lack of comprehension slamming at him from every angle, Michaels sighed, then added;

"It means that those who are far thinking will want to strike an alliance with Edilson now, so that when the time comes, they'll have an ally situated smack in the center of everything."

Michael's words made sense. Earth was expanding, making friends and team-mates everywhere its representatives went. Enemies as well. If the Confederation of Planets was to maintain its presence, to continue advancing in power and pres-tige, let alone to be able to handle itself in the political and economic arenas of the universe against the likes of the Pan-Galactic League of Suns and others, this was just the kind of advanced cogitation they should be pursuing.

And, as the gobs headed off cheerfully to their various posts, their pride in the planet of their birth swelled. They came, after all, from a forward-thinking world, one clever enough to send them off to negotiate with a solar system that would not really be worth having as a pal for centuries. That, they knew, whistling merrily as they took up their duties, took foresight. It took brains.

If they had possessed the brains to realize just how much desperate luck they were going to need to survive their upcoming expedition, however, they might have thrown in a few prayers in between all the whistling.

"All right then," growled Captain Alexander Benjamin Valance, as he reached for what was to be the first of several large drinks, "tell me someone has discovered something to explain whatever in hell *that* was."

The *Roosevelt* had arrived at the Edilson Well far in advance of the time re-quired for their diplomatic team's meeting with the planetary council. In their best dress uniforms, the captain and his senior staff along with the ship's resident diplo-matic officers had disembarked, prepared to put the Confederation's collective best foot forward. "An unmitigated disaster of incalculable proportions" was the phrase one might use to describe their meeting with the Edilsoni who came to greet them—but then, *only* if that one were trying to put the best spin possible on the most unfortunate encounter between dissimilar species since the Log Cabin Re-publicans first came across the D.A.R.

"Ahhh, if you're willing to consider some non-sanctioned information, sir . . . "

"Meaning?"

"Meaning," answered Valance's aide in a slightly lowered voice, "data ac-quired from outside official circles." When the captain only stared, the look in his eyes indicating his aide should just simply speak, the woman cleared her throat, then said;

"I did a records swap with a Chambrin starsweeper a few months back. Running a search through those files, I've managed to pull up some records from a couple of freelance Embrian traders who passed through this sector a few years ago—Iggzy and Cosentino Shipping."

At first, everything had seemed swell. The planet's inhabitants turned out to be an semi-amorphous life-form. Neither male or female, the Edilsoni could, with some difficulty, stretch and remold themselves into any manner of shapes if they desired. Normally, however, they were rubbery, blue-skinned, watermelon-shaped folk who walked on three appendages roughly two to three feet in length. The melon of them—their torso as well as skull—was surrounded by three tentacle-like arms, as well as three eye-stalks, their disturbingly large mouths sprouting from the center of their heads.

"And what did these shippers report?"

The captain and the others, of course, were no strangers to aliens. They had encountered all manner of varied life forms since hitting deep space, and not once had any of them so much as raised an offending eyebrow at anyone or thing they had met. Not when they had watched the Georgths groom each other and subsequently devour their findings, or when they labored to decider the language of the Mauzrieni, the only race in the galaxy to communicate through farting. But the Edilsoni, they . . . well . . . they were different.

"Their report tallies pretty much with what we just crashed through." As the aide read through her findings, the captain and his diplomatic squad fell further into the abysmally deep funk they had brought on board with them. For a while they had been able to hold onto the hope they had simply not understood what had been happening. But, sadly, they had.

The planet Edilson possessed a singularly peculiar make-up. Much of it was formed on unstable rock. Not the kind given over to earthquakes—or edilsonquakes, if you would—but the kind that produced the type of environment found in Earth-spots such as Japan or Yellowstone National Park. Edilson was, in short, one great big steam-manufacturing ball, and due to its odd rock formations, anywhere the steam leaked out, it filled the air with various streams of continual sound.

Over the millennia, the Edilsoni had cultivated these passage ways, giving their planet an unending steam-driven soundtrack. They filled vents with crystals and cymbals, fashioned all manner of horns and harmonicas, even planted bamboo-like reeds where the steam could leak through, making music in every corner of their world. Of course, as one might imagine, this had more of an effect on the population than to simply dress up their days.

"There's no doubt about it, sir," said the aide hopelessly. "The Edilsoni sing and dance to make conversation. It seems they can't even understand races that simply 'talk' at them. In fact, they distrust any species that isn't comfortable doing so."

"Distrust?"

"Yes, sir," said the woman, absently as she continued to read from the stream crossing her handscreen. "Seems they even went to war with one of their in-system neighbors when they stopped up the steam vents on the grounds of their consulate here."

Captain Alexander Benjamin Valance found himself as close to despair as ever he had been since taking command of the *Roosevelt*. "Why," he thought, imploring what gods might be left in his ever-shrinking corner of the galaxy, "do these things keep happening to me?"

This was worse than when his crew had shaved the sacred monkeys of Temple-world. Or when they had conned the guards of the Pen'dwaker Holding Facility into allowing them to transform the prison into a gambling den for their Intergalactic Crap Shoot of the Millennium tournament. Or even when they had sponsored their infamous inter-species mixer where they introduced the debutante daughters of the leading politicians of the Pan-Galactic League of Suns to the various bears, cows, pigs, and chimps they were transporting to the Inter-Galaxy Zoo on Chamre XI.

It was worse than when they had stolen the *Roosevelt* and declared war on a cookie factory, more disastrous than when their pie fight had clogged the ship's protonic engines with strawberry, pineapple, and cheesecake filling, along with graham cracker crumbs, whipped creme, and rhubarb. Of course, such nonsense could not impede the performance of such mighty machines, but it did play havoc with Admiral Morey's white-glove-and-I'm-not-kidding inspection.

It was, in his opinion, worse than anything they had ever done before and most likely would do any time soon. Because, quite simply, for once his insane-as-a-flock-of-dice-addled-cephalopods crew had not done anything. He had no one upon whom he might cast the blame for this one. For once, the captain of the *Roosevelt* was as stuck as stuck could be, with no options in sight.

"So," he said, weakly, looking for a third highball while turning to the others in the room, those others besides himself responsible for getting the most important treaty in the history of Earth signed, "who's got any really bright ideas?"

The thundering lack of enthusiastic response did not surprise him greatly.

"Tell me again," asked Noodles, not at all certain about the wisdom involved in what he and Rocky were attempting, "why is it we're stealing a shuttle craft and heading for the surface?"

"Look, little buddy," answered the gunnery officer while he gave Quartermaster Harris the high-sign that they were ready to launch. "The captain is tied up in knots about his meetin' with these beachballs down below—right? Now, it seems gettin' these mugs on board with the Confederation is a big deal and so, I was thinkin', if we could crack whatever the big problem is, we could kinda make up for some of the little improprieties we've . . . well, you know . . ."

"Getting ourselves court-marshalled would probably add some small ray of happiness to the captain's otherwise present dismal outlook."

"You machinist, you're always so gloomy."

"That's only the machinists who run around with Italians."

"Look," replied Rocky, as he eased the shuttle out the side bay doors while Technician Second Class Thorner kept the perimeter radar jumbled so they might avoid detection, "we're a couple of clever guys. We figure out how to smooth things so the Confederation beats the League and all the other bozos to signin' up this bunch, and we'll be spendin' the rest of our days sittin' around swimmin' pools."

"With cleaning equipment," responded a particularly glum Noodles under his breath. He did not bother to argue further, though. Once Rocky had made his mind up on something, it was rare the machinist was ever able to talk him out of it. The reasons why he went along with said schemes were many and varied.

First, he liked Rocky and did not want to see him end up in more trouble than he could handle. Second, he was fairly certain the gunner had saved his life during one of their many drunken escapades, and so he felt a certain amount of obligation on that front as well. He also had to admit Rocky had a point. The *Roosevelt* on the whole would be in for tough times if Edilson decided to take a pass on joining the Confederation of Planets. Lastly, however, he went along with his pal's crazy plans usually because it just always turned out to be more fun doing things his way.

Machinists are a dull lot, he thought, keeping the notion as quiet within his noggin as possible. He would never admit to such a thing, of course. If questioned on the verve and vigor of his profession, he would point to the many fine activities he and the rest of the ship's tool jockeys enjoyed, from their shipwide Call of Cthulhu LARPs and their free-style origami fold-offs, to the week out of every year they lived for, their Sexy-Robot-Building Competition. Privately, he feared Intelligence Officer DiVico's assessment, "I've seen lead foil that was snappier than the average machinist," might sadly be true.

Regardless, it was but a matter of minutes after take-off that the pair of gobs found themselves loose in the capital city of the planet Edilson. After walking about more or less aimlessly for a half an hour, confident from their observation of various street signs and cafe notices that Edilson to Pan-Galactic to Earth Basic 9.8 translation was more or less working fine enough, Rocky approached a passing rubbery watermelon of an Edilsoni and asked;

"So, what's the story around here, chief?"

Bending back and forth so that all the eyes ringing its head could scrutinize the individual addressing it, the random citizen decided it had no idea what this bizarre new species wanted and, doing its best to make a motion with its shoulderless body that would translate to an alien as a confused shrug, it went about its business. The gunner gave his buddy a look meant to convey his mixture of confusion and annoyance, then tried again with the next native to pass by. The results were the same.

After that, both sailors attempted to communicate with the locals, trying this or that different idiom, working to keep their questions as simple as possible in case their problem was merely some translation difficulty. Nothing helped. Eventually, having been working on questioning a large flow of Edilsoni moving toward a stadium of sorts, they found themselves having been moved along with the flow to where they were indoors, awaiting some sort of performance. Frustrated, but hoping whatever was about to be presented on the field before them would give them some sort of clue, they managed to purchase a container of what seemed to be fried, bacon-flavored grass, and two milky fruit drinks which came in a kind of squeeze-bag affair. As they settled in, an announcer came out onto a small side stage and sang an introduction.

Since it seemed that all that he was introducing was the formal presentation from some alien world or the other to the Edilson government, the need for a tune-filled introduction struck the two humans as odd. When it turned out the aliens making the presentation were Danierians, Rocky and Noodles both began to titter with amusement. Bulbous, dour, and as exciting as a panda in fishnet stockings, the boys chuckled over how utterly awful the following would have to be.

"Danierians are gonna try and get these guys' attention," scoffed Rocky. "Now this, I'm glad I'm here ta see."

The chief gunnery officer's joy was short-lived. As he and Noodles finished off the last of their Crunchy Goodness snack pack, a troop of some four hundred Danierian warriors, outfitted in full battle gear, marched onto the field from three triangularly situated entrances. Flags unfurled, horns blaring, drums setting down an impressively unshakable cadence, the troopers met in the center of the parade ground, shouting out in their lumbering cadence as they began to file into formation;

> "Denieria, it is our home,
> That roasting world, so far away,
> Denieria, its red sky and foam,
> It's the best, on *any* day."

Looking first at each other, Rocky and Noodles then began to scan the crowd around them. Unlike their attempts to communicate with the Edilsoni on the streets, the Danierians were getting through to the natives. Indeed, as their simple forward marches began to intertwine, the crowd began tapping their tentacles to the martial rhythm.

> "We're here to tell you about our world,
> How splendid it is, to live in peace,
> With Danierian banners, everywhere unfurled,
> And all strife and despair made to cease."

"Noodles," asked Rocky, "is this as bad as I'm thinkin' it is?" When the machinist nodded in agreement, his partner answered, "Yeah, I was afraid of that."

> "The galaxy is filled with lies,
> Other races present intentions, but disguise
> Their true meaning,
> There's no gleaning,
> What, oh what, is an innocent race to do?"

Rocky shuddered, thinking he had a good idea what was about to be suggested.

> "Face front! And join
> The United Coalition
> Of Danierian Worlds.
>
> Be a member of the winning team,
> It's a lone and vulnerable planet's
> *Dream come true!*

As the marching and singing continued, Noodles was struck by how the Edilsoni were responding to the ever-more-intricate step-pattern the warriors below were developing. With increasingly complicated side turn, with each spin of their weapons and the tossing of banners from one team to another, the native inhabitants gave out with more and louder appreciative whistling noises. And then, the warriors offered up their next-to-final chorus;

> "Others offer chaos,
> We bring rules,
> Those who turn down order,
> We slaughter as fools!"

Eliciting cheers from every corner of the arena. As the Danierian Dress Guard broke into an even tighter, and it must be said rather snappy (well, snappy for Danierians), close order drill, chanting "Go Danieria" on every left step, the Edilsoni began singing to one another and performing a variety of three-legged jigs which left the two sailors both astounded and, it had to be admitted, a touch frightened.

> "Submit to our will,
> It's for your own good,
> Don't wonder if we kill,
> Just do what you should."

"Little buddy," whispered Rocky, "I'm thinkin' we'd better get back to the *Roosevelt*. The captain's gonna wanta know about this."

"He's not going to want to know it," answered Noodles, reaching for his bag o'juice, "but he needs to."

And with that, the swabbies returned to their borrowed shuttle craft, even as the Edilsoni picked up the admittedly catchy chorus of "Submit, Submit, just do it," sending its singular message wafting out over their capital city in all directions.

"So," asked Rocky quietly, "just how much trouble are we in, captain?"

"Vespucci," sighed Valance, heavily, "you only did what you did for ship and homeworld, and you did good, so let's just say you two have a bit of credit in reserve against your next knuckleheaded shenanigan—all right?"

"Sweet deal, sir."

At that point the *Roosevelt*'s commanding officer moved into as high a gear as his hangover would permit. With confirmation of the true nature of Edilsoni communication in hand, as well as intelligence on how effective had been the Danierians singing and marching negotiation, he dismissed the two gobs while ordering a channel opened to Earth High Command at once. Quickly outlining his overwhelmingly insurmountable problem, his desperate honesty was rewarded with the worst type of military logic.

Since his was the only ship in the area, the mission was still his. And, since he was the ranking officer, he and his diplomatic staff would simply have to dance and sing their way into the hearts of the planetary government and win the day. In the meantime, while Valance and his command staff were reduced to trying to form a not-completely-painful-to-listen-to barbershop quartet, Rocky and Noodles headed for the galley to wash down their planetside snacks with something a little more substantial than milk juice.

"Listen," said Noodles, after finishing his fourth tall and frosty mug of something-more-substantial, "you know, I wonder what the captain's going to do."

"Not our concern," answered his pal. "Hey, we're heroes for once. Little tiny minor heroes, sure. But, considerin' the esteem we're usually held in around here, I'll take it."

The machinist nodded, non-commitally. Rocky was right. The two of them had pushed their luck within the bounds of Navy regs to an extreme not seen since a drunken Admiral Chester William Nimitz had attempted to steer an aircraft carrier up the Venetian canals in search of a combination pizza parlor/chianti distributor/bordello he had been assured by Enrico Curuso was "really primo." Still, it was not in the machinist's internal make-up to simply allow nature to take its course. Running his finger around the inside of his mug to get the last delightful bits of foam, he licked up the delicious residue, then said;

"So, you think the captain can handle things?"

"Well, sure," answered Rocky automatically. Draining his own mug, he added with an equal lack of thought, "the captain's aces. Ain't he got us outta every mess we ever got ourselves into? He don't ever need any help—he's always got the answer."

"Not to be contrary, Rock, but . . . if the captain didn't ever need any help, then he wouldn't need a crew."

It was not so much Noodles' words, but the tone with which he delivered them that caught the gunnery officer's attention. Squinting hard, as if that might instantly negate the effects of his own eight tall portions of more-substantial, Rocky finally answered;

"You mean, you think the captain maybe can't handle singin' these guys into the Confederation?"

"Do you remember his trying to teach Christmas carols to those kids back on Embri?" The gunner shuddered at the memory, his fingers unconsciously reaching up to his ears to see if they were bleeding.

"So," asked Rocky, fairly certain he knew the answer he would receive, "you're sayin' that ah . . . you want us to steal a shuttle on the same day we already stole one shuttle, and then use said shuttle to head back down to the planet so we can interfere with the most important mission the *Roosevelt* was ever given?"

"Yeah—you want'a?"

"Hey," answered the gunner, grinning from ear to ear, "does the Buddha drink Mint Juleps?"

"Isn't that usually my line?"

"Ahhhh, tell it to the board of inquiry."

"Oh yeah," laughed Noodles. "Good thinking."

And, with no other pints of more-substantial in sight, the two swabbies got down to planning their course of action.

In all honesty, Captain Valance would never have believed it was possible for four people to sweat so intently. Indeed, the puddle growing around his feet, as well as those of the *Roosevelt*'s intelligence officer, her diplomatic attaché, and the ship's doctor, was spreading with such vigor, it left the Edilsoni to wonder if the human contingent might not actually be melting. To be fair, the makeshift quartet had tried their darnest, calling upon the spirit of a thousand long-sung sea chanteys to aid them in their hour of desperation.

Sadly, though, King Neptune had not seen fit to shower them with any such bounty. In fact, it had to be admitted that their feeble attempts to harmonize had failed so miserably that the Edilsoni's visceral reaction to their singing was the only thing that kept the aliens from noticing how utterly terrible the humans' lyrics were. Finally, when the four paused for a breath at the same moment, although it was obvious they had only covered a third of their points, the Edilsoni prime minister practically fell over his podium as he leaped forward to interrupt, asking if that concluded the Earth Confederation's presentation. Valance was just about to throw in the proverbial towel, considering losing the planet and his commission favorable to provoking interstellar warfare, when suddenly a shout was heard from the back of the amphitheater.

> "If you kind and noble Edilsoni will permit,
> I'd like to step up, while you sit . . . ,"

As Valance stared in disbelief, he saw Machinist First Mate Li Qui Kon actually doing a handy little two-step, making his way in between the central two rows of spectators down toward the staging area where he and his fellow officers had been dying by inches.

> "And discuss with you the ramifications,
> Of inter-galactic political integrations."

Reaching the captain and his officers, Rocky urged them to vacate the stage, telling them in an exaggerated stage whisper;
"Don't worry, sir. I think he knows what he's doin'."
"But Vespucci," answered Valance, "singing and dancing . . . a machinist?"
"With all due respect, a *Chinese* machinist, sir."

> "There are species descended from fish and bugs,
> Others that crawled up from oozing slugs,
> Some came from birds and some from rats,
> Insects, clams, giraffes and bats,"

"Chinese moms, sir," added Rocky. "How'd he say it? They expect their kids to . . . well, they have to be a credit to their family."

> "And they're all fine, in their own way,
> But they're kind of singular, I must say,
> Bred for a certain uni . . . form . . . ity,
> They lack that one human odd . . . i . . . ty."

"Mrs. Kon, you see . . ."

> "The thing that makes us the ones to choose,
> That quality that guarantees you never lose,
> It's our single greatest facility . . .
> Our hard-won, irritating . . .
>
> "Un . . . pre . . . dic . . . ta . . . bility!"

"She wanted an entertainer in the family."
And then, at a hand signal from Noodles, waiting in a lurkercraft hidden in the clouds, Technician Second Class Thorner began their free-air music broadcast, as well as sending down a blinding purple spotlight, illuminating the machinist in an iridescent glow as he warbled—

> "Oh, everything's better with monkeys,

We're the best bet in the show,
I'm certain you're getting a lot of offers,
But trust me, simian's the way to go."

While Noodles spun around, setting himself up for the next stanza, Rocky caught the captain's ear once more, telling him;
"Five years of tap and jazz dance, six of voice training, and apparently eight years of piano which, from what he says, were a really serious mistake."

"Yes everything's better with monkeys,
They're curious, funny, and true,
They'll stand by your side, go along for a ride,
And they'll make sure you get what you're due."

As Noodles went into a complicated dance routine, one that seemed to Rocky he had seen in a revival of "My Fair Lady," the two of them had been lured into by promises of a different type of entertainment, the gunnery officer and his captain began to notice that the crowd was responding favorably to the performance. Indeed, those who had been previously fleeing from the caterwauling of Valance and his officers actually seemed to be returning to their seats. While the captain dangerously tempted Fate by allowing his hopes to rise from actual imprisonment to a simple court-martial, Rocky sent the signal to Mac Michaels up above with Thorner to both turn up the music and begin the fountain of lights display. As the crowd began to "aaaaahhhhhhhhh" in synchronized harmony, Noodles went into his big finish.

"Yes, we earthlings, we make mistakes,
We've got our bad eggs, who will always disgrace,
We spill our own blood, and we're not always smart,
But the one thing I can assure you is . . .
The human race has . . . got . . . heart!"

And then, in that instant, even as the entire ship's company of the *Roosevelt* Machinist's Saturday Evening LARP Society surrounded the stage, decked in full costume from their upcoming Bambi versus Godzilla extravaganza, accompanied by all the final entries in the Sexiest Robot of All Time competition, all around the stadium Edilsoni began to jump up from their seats. Unable to restrain themselves, the rotund aliens began humming and dancing, slapping tentacles, spinning on their mouths, and in short throwing themselves with total abandon into the fierce joy of Noodle's song.

"We're not perfect,
We don't claim to be,
Hell what do you expect?
Twenty thousand years ago,
We were all still monkeys!

"But you can trust me, you can trust that fact,
'Cause even after all this time,

> You throw crap at us,
> And I guarantee . . .
> We'll throw it right back!"

The captain, of course, could only be overjoyed by the obvious shift in the average Edilsonian attitude toward humanity. But Rocky was set to wondering. He had seen the response the natives had shown the Danierians. They had gotten into the rhythm of things, had seemed ready to sign on to the program, so to speak. But, the reaction to Noodle's presentation was overwhelming. The aliens were actually dropping down onto the stadium grounds and rushing the stage, eager to join the machinists' newly forming macarana formation.

> "But we'll stand at your side,
> We'll be there at the end,
> We make lousy dictators,
> But we make really good friends.

> "Yes, everything's better with monkeys,
> The bad ones mixed in with the good,
> So, show a little trust, but keep your eye on us,
> And everything—
> I'm saying just *everything*—
> Will work out, as it . . . sshhhoooouuuullllddddd!"

And in that moment, as Noodles dropped to one knee and delivered the greatest display of jazz hands since Bob Fosse starred in "The Al Jolson Story," the long unfathomed secret of the Edilsoni came to light. Although the race *could* communicate through speech, they were *actually* a telepathic species, one bound by a hive mentality. As the native population cheered, not just there in the capital city's stadium, but across every continent, in every corner of the planet, their human guests' minds were suddenly filled with billions of voices, all of them sharing in the wonder that was the unquestionable uniqueness of the human race.

"Do you get it, Vespucci," shouted the captain, straining to be heard over the multitudinous ringing within his mind, "the Edilsoni have rejected every offer that's come their way because no one else has ever opened up completely to them!"

"Jiminy," answered Rocky, still a little befuddled over exactly what had happened, being distracted as he was by coordinating the start of the *Roosevelt* fireworks display, "I didn't think his song was that good."

"It's not the song," cried Valance, tears streaming down his face as an utterly alien race's reflected understanding of the true nobility of the human spirit washed through his mind, "it's not the song."

What happened over the next few days became somewhat of a blur in the intergalactic news items out of the Kebb Quadrant, the official reports sent from the *Roosevelt* back to the Confederation, and to be honest, in the minds of most of the ship's crew. That last, however, had more to do with the planet-wide party spontaneously thrown by every individual on Edilson than with any deficiency in the human ability to comprehend the situation.

Distrustful of aliens who masked their true intent, the Edilsoni had turned down every offer of alliance over the two hundred years since first contact. Understanding better than any others the upcoming importance of their world, they had kept communications open with all, dangling the hope of eventual alliance with one world, or league, or whatever, to keep any one of them from invading.

"Four hundred of your years," their prime minister eventually sang to Valance, "is not a great deal of time, galactically speaking, but it did give us some room in which to maneuver."

They had responded as well as they had to the Danierians because, vicious and cruel as that race might be, at least they were honest about it. Their warriors had held nothing back emotionally on the field, and for once someone had shown the Edilsoni true intent. Luckily, as the prime minister was happy to admit, someone else had come along and done the same who had something better to show.

The surprise hit of the negotiations, or whatever one would call the drunken insanity that had transpired on Edilson, had been the trio of Thorner, Harris, and Michaels, who had taken to the stage in their dress kilts to not only sing the Scottish ballad, the Blue Ribbon song, but to show off the fact that the Edilsoni were not the only sentient beings around who walked on three legs. Valance had been mortified at first, but the riotous response of the natives to the spontaneous gesture had been so positive the captain had been given no choice other than to return to attempting to drink the prime minister under the table.

In the end, the Confederation of Planets got the wished-for deal with Edilson. Valance was showered with praise from Earth Central, which he translated into as much shore leave and good favor as he possibly could for his crew. The next issue of the Monthly Newsletter of the Grand Gaggle of Confederation Machinists tripled in size and, once the ship's doctor had been able to synthesize enough Hangover-B-Gone, the crew of the *Roosevelt* had been able to finally remember how to break orbit and set a course that did not skew to a basanova beat.

Heroes all, loved and admired by an entire world, showered with gifts, the men and women of the *Roosevelt* set off for whatever the universe had in store for them next. The Edilsoni could tell the earthlings were reluctant to leave, and yet somehow eager to be on to whatever came next, and loved them all the more for it. But, beyond that display of all-too-human confusion of purpose, beyond everything they had heard and felt and learned of the gorilla-spawn who had won their hearts, there was one single moment that gave them greater insight than any other.

Being a collective species, having no actual experience with the idea of male or female, sons and daughters, or any of the other mammalian building blocks of individuality, nothing revealed more to the Edilsoni about their human visitors than when the prime minister met privately with Noodles. Asking the machinist what boon he might ask for his part in that which a united Edilson believed was the cementing of their security for the next four centuries, offering him anything the wealth and might of an entire planetary treasury might secure, the sailor asked if he might send a real-time message.

Yes, Noodles explained, he could send notes to Earth via the *Roosevelt*, but because of the distance they could take months, sometimes *years* to reach their intended destination. He did not want to send anything exceedingly long, he told them, just a few words. Understanding his request, touched to the core of what he had thought until meeting human beings was an emotionless heart beating within his breast, the prime minister not only agreed, but without the machinist's knowledge, he sent his own note as well.

Which is why, while the U.S.S. *Roosevelt* broke orbit and headed back out to their next destination in the stars, on the planet Earth, at 12/17 Seloon Street in one of the quieter corners of Canton, China, Mrs. Xiu Yue Kon received two messages. One that read;

"Thanks, Mom."

And a second that read;

"Yes, good Earthwoman, thank you, indeed."

Author Bios

Charles E. Gannon

RECIDIVISM

TO SPEC

Dr. Charles E. Gannon is a Distinguished Professor of English (St. Bonaventure U.) & Fulbright Senior Specialist (American Lit & Culture). He has had novellas in *Analog* and the *War World* series. His nonfiction book *Rumors of War and Infernal Machines* won the 2006 ALA Outstanding Text Award. He also worked as author and editor for GDW, and was a routine contributor to both the scientific/technical content and story-line in the award-winning games *Traveller*, and *2300 AD*. He has been awarded Fulbrights to England, Scotland, the Czech Republic, Slovakia, Netherlands, and worked eight years as scriptwriter/producer in NYC.

John C. Wright

THE LAST REPORT ON UNIT TWENTY-TWO

John C. Wright is a retired attorney, newspaperman, and newspaper editor, who was only once on the lam and forced to hide from the police who did not admire his newspaper. His works include a number of short stories in such publications as *Asimov's*, *Absolute Magnatude*, and several editions of *The Year's Best SF*. In addition he has eight novels to his credit published with TOR Books, including his first, *The Golden Age*, and the forthcoming *Titans of Chaos*. He presently works (successfully), as a writer in Virginia, where he lives in fairy-tale-like happiness with his wife, the authoress L. Jagi Lamplighter, and their three children: Orville, Wilbur, and Just Wright.

James Daniel Ross

THE NATURE OF MERCY

A native of Cincinnati, Ohio, James has been an actor, computer tech support operator, historic infotainment tour guide, armed self-defense retailer, automotive petrol attendant, youth entertainment stock replacement specialist, mass-market Italian chef, low-priority courier, monthly printed media retailer, automotive industry miscellaneous task facilitator, and ditch digger. *The Radiation Angels: The Chimerium Gambit* is his first novel. Most people are begging him to go back to ditch digging.

Jonathan Maberry

CLEAN SWEEPS

Jonathan Maberry is the multiple Bram Stoker Award-winning author of novels (*Patient Zero, Ghost Road Blues,* etc.), nonfiction books (*Zombie CSU, The Cryptopedia,* etc.), comics (*PUNISHER: Naked Kill* and *WOLVERINE: Ghosts*), and over 1100 magazine articles. Jonathan is the co-creator (with Laura Schrock) of *On The Slab,* an entertainment news show for ABC Disney/Stage 9, to be released on the Internet in 2009. Jonathan is a Contributing Editor for *The Big Thrill* (the newsletter of the International Thriller Writers), and is a member of SFWA, MWA, and HWA. Visit his website at www.jonathanmaberry.com or on Facebook and My-Space.

James Chambers

WAR MOVIES

James Chambers "writes stories that are paced fast enough to friction burn a reader's eyeballs," says Horror Reader.com. His tales of horror, fantasy, and science fiction have been published in *Bad-Ass Faeries, Breach the Hull, Crypto-Critters (Volume 1 and 2), Dark Furies, The Dead Walk, The Dead Walk Again, Hardboiled Cthulhu, Lin Carter's Anton Zarnak Supernatural Detective, No Longer Dreams, Sick: An Anthology of Illness, Weird Trails,* and *Warfear* as well as the magazines *Bare Bone, Cthulhu Sex,* and *Allen K's Inhuman.* His short story collection, with illustrator Jason Whitley, *The Midnight Hour: Saint Lawn Hill and Other Tales,* was published in 2005. His website is www.jameschambersonline.com.

Patrick Thomas

THE BATTLE FOR KNOB LICK

Patrick Thomas is the author of 80+ short stories and fifteen books including the popular fantasy humor series *Murphy's Lore.* The eighth book, *Empty Graves: Tales of Zombies,* was recently released from Padwolf Publishing. His tentatively titled *The Mystic Investigators of Patrick Thomas* and *Fairy With A Gun* (a Terrorbelle collection) will be out in 2009. Patrick co-edited *Hear Them Roar* and the upcoming *New Blood* vampire anthology. Patrick has novellas in *Go Not Gently* and *Flesh and*

Iron from the Two Backed Books imprint of Raw Dog Screaming. Patrick writes the syndicated satirical advice column *Dear Cthulhu*. Drop by his website at www.patthomas.net.

Andy Remic

JUNKED

Andy Remic is a hard-hitting kick-ass military science fiction author with five novels in print. In his spare time he enjoys mountain climbing, sword fighting and hacking computer systems. He can kill a man with a single blow of his chainsaw, but prefers photographing woodland wildlife and biomod engineering. He is sometimes accused of nihilism.

Danielle Ackley-McPhail

FIRST LINE

Award-winning author Danielle Ackley-McPhail has worked both sides of the publishing industry for nearly fifteen years. Her works include the urban fantasies, *Yesterday's Dreams*, its sequel, *Tomorrow's Memories*, the upcoming novella, *The Halfling's Court*, the anthologies, *Bad-Ass Faeries, Bad-Ass Faeries 2: Just Plain Bad*, and *No Longer Dreams*, all of which she co-edited, and contributions to numerous anthologies and collections, including *Breach the Hull*, *Space Pirates*, and the upcoming science fiction anthologies *New Blood* and *Barbarians at the Jumpgate*. She is a member of The Garden State Horror Writers, the electronic publishing organization EPIC, and Broad Universe, an organization promoting the works of women authors. To learn more about her work, visit www.sidhenadaire.com.

Jeffrey Lyman

GUNNERY SERGEANT

Jeffrey Lyman is a 2004 graduate of the Odyssey Fantasy Writing Workshop. Since then he has been published in various anthologies, including *No Longer Dreams* by Lite Circle Press, *Sails and Sorcery* by Fantasist Enterprises, and *Breach the Hull* by Marietta Publishing. He was involved in editing both *Bad Ass Fairies I* and *II*. He is currently finishing up a novel about some pretty rotten fairies. By day, he works as a mechanical engineer near New York City. Visit www.jdlyman.com.

Jack Campbell
GRENDEL

John G. Hemry, writing as Jack Campbell, is the author of the best-selling Lost Fleet series. Under his own name, he's also the author of the 'JAG in space' series, the latest of which is *Against All Enemies*. His short fiction has appeared in places as varied as the latest *Chicks in Chainmail* anthology (*Turn the Other Chick*), and *Analog* magazine (which published his Nebula Award-nominated story *Small Moments in Time*). John's nonfiction has appeared in *Analog* and *Artemis* magazines as well as BenBella books on *Charmed, Star Wars,* and *Superman*. John is a retired US Navy officer who lives in Maryland with his wife (the incomparable S), and three great kids.

Mike McPhail
CLING PEACHES

Mike McPhail is a member of Military Writers Society of America (MWSA), and the winner of the 2007 Dream Realm Award for Best Anthology (and finalist for Best Cover Art), as editor and cover artist for the military science fiction anthology *Breach the Hull* (book I in the *Defending the Future* series), as well as *By Other Means,* book III, planned for 2011. He is also the creator of the Alliance Archives (All'Arc) series and its related Martial Role-Playing Game (MRPG); a manual-based, military science fiction that realistically portrays the consequences of warfare. To learn more of his work, visit www.mcp-concepts.com.

Bud Sparhawk
GLASS BOX

Bud Sparhawk began writing science fiction stories in 1975 and, after two sales, stopped writing for thirteen years. Since again taking up the pen, his stories and articles have appeared frequently in *Analog, Asimov's,* and other SF magazines as well as anthologies. Bud has been a three-time finalist in the Nebula's Novella category in 1998, 2002, and 2006. More information may be found at http://sff.net/people/bud_sparhawk.

Tony Ruggiero

LOOKING FOR A GOOD TIME

Tony Ruggiero has been publishing fiction since 1998. His published novels include *Team of Darkness, Alien Deception, Alien Revelation*, and *Aliens and Satanic Creatures Wanted: Humans Need Not Apply*. Tony is also a contributing author to *The Fantasy Writers' Companion* from Dragon Moon Press. Other collaborative work includes *The Writers for Relief* anthology and *No Longer Dreams* anthology. Tony retired from the United States Navy in 2001 after twenty-three years of service. He and his family currently reside in Suffolk, Virginia. While continuing to write, Tony teaches at Old Dominion University, Saint Leo University, and Tidewater Community College in Norfolk, VA.

C.J. Henderson

EVERYTHING'S BETTER
WITH MONKEYS

CJ Henderson is the creator of the *Teddy London* supernatural detective series, author of such diverse yet fabulously interesting titles as *The Field Guide to Monsters, Babys First Mythos, The Encyclopedia of Science Fiction Movies* and some fifty other books and novels. He has had hundreds of short stories published along with hundreds of comics and thousands of non-fiction pieces. The first novel in his latest series, *Brooklyn Knights*, will be coming out from TOR later this year. For more check out his website, www.cjhenderson.com. If you send him a pie, he will remember you in his prayers.

David Sherman

SURRENDER OR DIE

With thirty novels and only one previously published short story to his credit, you could say that David Sherman writes long-form fiction. He is the author of eight out-of-print novels of US Marines in Vietnam (he was one); military SF series *Starfist* and its spinoff, *Starfist: Force Recon* (both with Dan Cragg); a Star Wars novel, *Jedi Trial* (also with Dan Cragg); and fantasy series *DemonTech*. "Surrender or Die" was written as the prolog of the fourth book in the DemonTech series, but, *alas*, that never happened. He invites readers to visit his website: www.novelier.com.

Bonus Content

Turn the page for:

David Sherman's *Surrender or Die*

*Special Announcements
about upcoming Releases*

*Information on the First Annual MilSciFi.com's
Reader's Choice Award*

USO Endorsement

The World of DemonTech

Onslaught (January 2002)
Rally Point (Febuary 2003)
Gulf Run (December 2003)

DemonTech is a series of military science fantasy novels where demons have been tamed and utilized in ways that mirror technology as we know it, particularly of a military nature. These demons may be visible or invisible and specific abilities they possess allow them to assume the function of many conventional tools with superior results, though they do require specially trained personnel to manage them.

Three novels have been published in this series. Unfortunately, while the first three novels remain in print, the publisher has declined to produce the fourth book. The story that follows was to be the prologue to that novel.

SURRENDER OR DIE

A DemonTech Adventure

David Sherman

INIONS FLUTTERED FROM CROSSPIECES AT THE TOPS OF TALL STAFFS THAT marched toward Handor's Bay. Long columns of soldiers tramped behind those pinions, or rode on dust cloud-enshrouded horses. The horsemen followed pinions of solid color; red, white, green, black, orange, and more. The footmen's pinions were checked or slashed or barred, all in multichrome. At the distant rear of the columns the supply wagons trundled, food-animals herded, camp followers trudged. Bugles, thin at the distance, sounded along the columns.

Duke Harrand Handor, Gate Master to The Easterlies, stood atop the highest tower of the keep that guarded the landward approaches to the harbor and its city. North, he saw ten columns of soldiers marching south. From the south, six columns of footmen and five of horse marched north. In the west the forest partly blocked his view, but he was sure of eight columns of foot and as many horse.

"There are too many," he said, dryly to General Lord Hendred Hexikles.

General Lord Hendred Hexikles knew better than Duke Handor how many Jokapkul closed on Handor's Bay—enough of his scouts had evaded capture to report the torrential numbers of Jokapcul flooding toward The Easterlies main seaport. He merely grunted.

"L-Lord," stammered Lord Mayor Hohten Hombor, the civil administrator of Handor's Bay, "th-there are enough sh-ships in port to eva-evacuate the most important p-people. And m-many of the rest of the c-citizens," he hastily added, when General Lord Hexikles glowered at him.

Duke Harrand Handor ignored the mayor, he looked at Baron Hirham Hibfroth.

Master of Lands, Baron Hirham Hibfroth said, solemnly, "The grains, vegetables, and fruits have all been harvested and brought into the city, even those not yet ripened. Many are siloed on the ships in port." He flashed his eyes at the mayor. "The herds are within. The Jokapcul will find naught to feed their hordes."

Lord Mayor Hohten Hombor paled. If the ships were serving as silos, how could they evacuate people? How could he escape?

That night, the cook fires of the Jokapcul army seemed to sprinkle the land as densely as stars did the sky. Fires were occasionally occluded as more columns tramped or rode into the camp. The noises of the soldiers and their animals washed over the city like the sound of the sea that lapped against its eastern side.

The ground mist burned off slowly in the morning. As the mist thinned, it revealed rank upon rank of Jokapcul soldiers facing the city, until they appeared as fields of spring wheat nearing harvest.

Duke Harrand Handor and his chief councilors again stood watching atop the tallest tower. The silence that surrounded the city was unnerving; not even birds cried where that army stood.

Behind the middle of the semicircle of soldiers stood a stark pavilion, its only decoration overlapping canvas roofs that mimicked a fir tree in form. A speck rose from low on the pavilion and spiraled upward. When it gained altitude higher than the height of the keep tower, it ceased spiraling and arrowed at the quintet. In moments they could discern its shape. The thing was vaguely like a gnarly human in form and flapped leathery, bat-like wings. The creature's eyes glowed red.

"It's an imbaluris." Scholar Hubart Hu'sk's voice cracked, and he had to repeat himself.

Duke Handor looked a question at him.

"A demon used as a messenger," came the explanation.

The hideous demon, the size of a large owl and armed with talons bigger than an eagle's, landed heavily on a crenellation and barely kept from falling off before it steadied into a squatting perch.

"*Oo zurr'ndr!*" the imbaluris screeched.

Duke Handor choked off a swallow before it made his throat bob. "Never!" he snarled at the demon.

"*Oo zurr'ndr!*" the imbaluris repeated. It swept an arm back at the Jokapcul army. "*Zjogabkul doo ztrong. Oo zurr'ndr or oo dzie!*"

Unsure of his voice in the face of the demon, Duke Handor shook his head.

"*Komm bak, one arr. Oo zurr'ndr then. Or oo dzie!*" The demon stuttered its feet around until it faced away from the Duke and his advisors, then launched itself into the air. It didn't spiral upward this time, simply flapped its way straight back to the pavilion. A chill wind eddied around the tower top.

General Lord Hendred Hexikles looked at the duke for instructions.

Duke Handor swallowed and found his voice. "The Jokapcul call coward all who surrender. They kill cowards. We do not surrender."

Lord Mayor Hohten Hombor looked fearfully at the duke. "The ships . . ." he croaked.

The others ignored him.

"How long can we hold?" Baron Hibfroth asked.

General Hexikles scanned the surrounding legions. He shrugged. "Weeks. Perhaps a few months. No more."

"Perhaps until reinforcements arrive?" Baron Hibfroth asked. "There are reports an army approaches to do battle with the Jokapcul."

General Hexikles slowly turned his gaze toward Baron Hibfroth.

"I have heard of this army," he said. "It has no general. It has no training as an army. It is a ragtag of deserters, escapees, bandits, and refugees. Put no hope in that army, Baron, it cannot help."

"I have heard it has bested Jokapcul forces many times," Hibfroth insisted.

Hexikles shrugged again. "Isolated units. Foraging parties unprepared for combat. Raiding parties flush with victory and not expecting opposition. It has not faced an army. If it faces this one," he looked outward again, "it will be crushed."

In the distance, they watched as lackeys set up a stage in front of the pavilion and mounted two thrones on it. When the thrones were ready, two men mounted the stage and sat, one a half beat before the other. They were too far away for the duke and his men to make out any details of their appearance or dress. The speck that was the imbaluris lighted between the thrones.

"Lackland?" Duke Handor asked.

"Likely," replied Scholar Hu'sk.

Lackland, self-named The Dark Prince, renegade fourth son of Good King Honritu of Matilda, was reputed to be the commander-in-chief of the Jokapcul armies that ravened across the continent of Nunimar. General Lord Hexikles doubted that. Whichever of the two thrones Lackland occupied, the man in the other throne had to be the kamazai who was in fact the commander-in-chief. Had Duke Handor known what General Hexikles thought, he would have agreed.

The imbaluris returned at the appointed time. *"Oo zurr'ndr!"* it screeched.

Almost too fast for the eye to follow, Hexikles drew his broad sword and swung it down onto the imbaluris' leg.

The demon shrieked and flopped onto its side. It struggled to turn about and flung itself from the tower and flapped away.

"Kill the messenger?" Duke Handor asked dryly.

General Hexikles shrugged. "It'll live." The razor-sharp blade hadn't been able to cut through the demon's hide, but the weight of the blow had broken the bone under the skin.

The Duke nodded. "They have our reply."

Moments after the imbaluris reached the pavilion, a whole flock of the demons took off and scattered to front line units. Men from each front line legion broke ranks and trotted closer to the keep's outer ramparts. They carried odd looking tubes. They stopped nearly two hundred paces from the outer ramparts and knelt with the tubes balanced on their shoulders, pointed at the stout walls. *Pthupping* noises came from the tubes, followed by puffs of rock dust and chips from the wall faces as the demon spitters began to slowly pulverize them.

General Hexikles called down the tower well for a messenger. The messenger raced up the ladder, accepted the general's orders, and sped down to where the next level of commanders waited for orders. Those commanders then sent orders to their sub-commanders on the ramparts. Longbowmen stood tall and drew arrows to their cheeks. The range was too great for accuracy, but enough arrows were fired that the Jokapcul firing the demon spitters began to fall. They were quickly replaced.

The battle was begun.

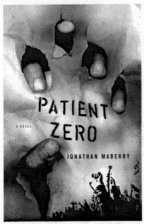

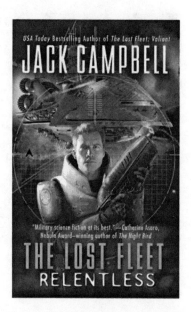

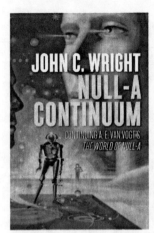
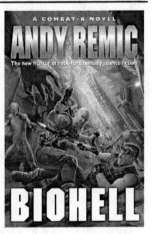

Now Announcing
The First Annual

MILSCIFI.COM™
Reader's Choice Awards

Interested in participating? It's easy...
Read *Breach the Hull* and/or *So It Begins*
and let us know which story was your favorite!

Prizes
The author of the story with the most votes
will receive a commemorative trophy.

Five randomly selected respondents will
win a selection of five patches based on
the artwork from *Breach the Hull*.

Rules and Regulations
One vote per person and address.
Duplicate or repeat votes will be disqualified.
Those directly involved with either publication and
their families are barred from entry.

To vote by email send your name, address, the author's name,
and the title of the story to RCA@milscifi.com
To vote by conventional mail write the above information
on a 3 x 5 card and mail to:

**MilSciFi.com Reader's Choice Award
PO Box 493
Stratford, NJ 08084**

Finally, There's Something We Can All Agree On.

It's something we've all said many times. And it does seem to be one of the few things that Americans unanimously agree on. But it takes more than agreeing with each other. It takes the USO. For more than 60 years, the USO has been the bridge back home for the men and women of our armed forces around the world. The USO receives no government funding and relies entirely on the generosity of the American people. We all want to support our troops. This is how it's done.

Until Every One Comes Home.